Air Boss

By
Rich Jessup

Acknowledgement

Many of these are true stories drawn from my father, Dr. Vince Jessup, and his group of special friends, whom I was fortunate to know from an early age. I used these stories for inspiration to write these adventures. I owe these men my sincere thanks for instilling in me their sense of humor and exemplary character. I appreciate them allowing me to be a junior partner in their men's club.

I will always treasure our hunting weekends at the Parks Ranch and ski trips to Mammoth Mountain. My thanks go out to my family ancestors, who gave me the right genetics, and to my parents, who stressed honor, character, and personality with me. I must admit that I used some dramatic license with a few dates for story continuity.

Forward

I thoroughly enjoyed reading this book. These stories took me back to many memories of my own. Looking back on my flying career, several of the characters were similar to old friends of mine. With a few name changes, I can picture myself in many of these stories with my old buddies. I like the main character, Jack Warner, because he did what it took to get the job done; "regulations be damned." I feel that results are what matter in life and certainly in all the branches of the armed services. I say, "To hell with the bureaucratic types with a stick up their ass who get in my way."

I served in World War II as a flight instructor at Luke Field in Arizona. I trained bomber pilots for their dangerous jobs overseas. If one of my pilots had been shot down, I'd want to know that a guy like Black Jack Warner was coming to save their ass and probably their life.

I appreciate that the author did his research and got the airplane models correct for the time periods with accurate specifications. He must have listened in at a few pilot briefings, because he got the pilot lingo right too.

If you want to get lost for a few evenings, give *Air Boss* a read. Sit down and prepare to laugh and cry while you picture Black Jack Warner getting the job done.

Edward Delong, Jr.

Lieutenant, USAF, Retired

CONTENTS

Introduction

While he was stationed in Vietnam during the war years, 'Black Jack' Warner rescued 21 pilots who had been shot down over North Vietnam. After returning home, he started one of the largest air cargo companies in the world and managed to stay out of jail while doing so.

"Growing up in Alaska taught me to love the untamed land and its wild lifestyle. My parents instilled self-reliance in me that I used to survive the Vietnam War and then build a company from the ground up. I couldn't have done this without the love and partnership of my wife, Gail. She deserves at least 51% of the credit.

"I never meant to, but I became famous for rescuing downed pilots in North Vietnam. After the number of rescues reached 21, my friend, Captain Chuck Reed, named me 'Black Jack.' It almost makes me regret that I saved his sorry butt so many years ago."
-Ret. Colonel Jack Warner

May you have kindness in your heart, warmth in your igloo, a plump woman in your furs, seal meat in your larder, oil in your lamp, and peace in your heart. - Eskimo Inuit proverb

"Help Me, Mr. Wizard"

Jack Warner awoke with a start. Where the hell was he? It was cold, dark, and loud. He needed a few seconds for his eyes to get used to the low light so he could focus and look around. Reality came galloping back to him. He was on an Air Force 707 troop transport plane bound for Saigon.

"Enlisting in the Air Force and volunteering to go to Vietnam might not have been the smartest thing I've ever done," thought Jack. "Oh, Mr. Wizard, please get me out of here."

When he was a kid, Jack used to love watching Tooter the Turtle cartoons. Tooter was a young, green turtle who would always ask for a wish to be granted from Mr. Wizard the Lizard, who wore a wizard's hat, robe, and pince-nez glasses. Mr. Wizard had the magical ability to change Tooter's life, sending him somewhere back in time.

Tooter's trips always became a catastrophe, and then he would yell out for Mr. Wizard's help, "Mr. Wizard, get me outtaaa... heereere."

Mr. Wizard always rescued him with the incantation "Twizzle, Twazzle, Twoozle, Twome; time for this one to come home." Afterward, Mr. Wizard always gave Tooter the same advice: "Be just what you is, not what you is not. Folks that do this are the happiest lot."

Jack wanted to go home, but Mr. Wizard didn't answer.

Alaskan Express

Jack's father, Ben Warner, was stationed in Anchorage, Alaska during WWII. The U.S. Army trained him to be a pilot, specializing in flying olive green bush planes. Ben hauled cargo to the troops stationed in the far North who were preparing for a possible Japanese invasion. He also delivered supplies to the construction crews working on the famed Alcan Highway.

With all this construction and thousands of troops stationed in Alaska, the Army had its own fleet of cargo planes. There were no roads or trains, and ocean shipping was slow. The most popular cargo aircraft during WWII was the Douglas C-47, also known as the DC-3. Pilots nicknamed it the "Gooney Bird," since it was such a short and stocky flying machine. It could hold three tons of cargo or troops and fly more than 1,500 miles, so it played a big part on all fronts of the war all around the world.

In addition to small bush planes, Ben also flew the larger C-47s north from Anchorage and south to Seattle to pick up freight. Flying a slow plane on long, monotonous flights gave Ben many hours to think. His copilot on most of these cargo flights was Kenny Beall from Yakima, Washington. They passed the time trading jokes and stories and became close friends. They lied about the women they had met and each embellished their own romantic escapades that always led to sweating up the sheets.

Ben told Kenny about growing up in Ketchum, Idaho. Every summer, Ben enjoyed fly fishing for steelhead trout in the famous Snake River. Kenny couldn't help but notice that with every fish story, the trout got heavier and longer. Kenny countered by telling Ben stories of picking giant Red Lion peaches at the Bartlett Orchards in Yakima when he was out of high school for the summer. Peach pickers worked hard in the hot sun and got paid for each crate that they filled with the heavy fruit. Ben noticed that the number of crates Kenny picked each day kept climbing as the stories went on. He asked Kenny, "What did all the other pickers do all day, since you seemed to be doing all the work yourself?" There seemed to be an unspoken competition to see who the bigger liar was.

When the C-47s flew north to Anchorage, they were loaded with men and cargo, but almost every plane was empty on the return trip to Seattle. The only passengers going south were a few GIs on leave. Ben Warner recognized this opportunity and dreamed about ways to take advantage of it.

Ben wondered, "What does Alaska have lots of that they want in the lower 48?" He answered his own question: fish and crab. Salmon and halibut seasons are in the late summer, but the crab season is during the winter, which isn't good for flying. Ben researched buying wholesale lots of salmon and halibut. He found Katie's Seafood, a seafood wholesaler at the docks in Anchorage that agreed to have pallets of iced fresh fish ready for transport. Ben planned to load the pallets on an empty C-47 and fly down to Seattle, where he knew the vendors at the Pike Place Fish Market could use whatever he could supply. With free air transportation, Ben could undercut every other fish supplier.

But that was only half of the equation. What could he get in Seattle and bring home that soldiers would want? He discussed his plan with Kenny, who came up with the obvious answer: "Women and booze!"

Ben shot back, "That's a great plan, but I think the Army would frown upon us flying in planeloads of girls for the soldiers. I'm sure the fellas would love it, but maybe we should concentrate on the booze."

For the rest of the flight, they expanded their plan to include liquor, chocolate, and fresh fruit. Kenny's reasoning was "Soldiers are getting paid every month, but there's hardly anything to buy. Booze is hard to find and damn expensive if you do. Everybody loves chocolate. They'd kill for some fresh fruit or anything with fresh fruit in it."

Kenny proposed another idea to Ben. "Yakima has an annual peach festival in two weeks. Why don't we go down there and see what we can buy that has peaches in it? Maybe we can check out some candy stores and find a wholesale liquor dealer."

The men did just that. They found Martino's Bakery, a Seattle landmark for more than 25 years. Martino's was famous for its addictive little teacakes with maple icing drizzled on top. Nobody could stop at just one. People just wolfed them down. Husbands would stop and buy two boxes, one to eat on the way home and the second to give to their wife. Martino's also made fresh peach pies when the peaches were in season. Ben and Kenny also found they could order cases of scotch from Porcell's Wholesale Liquor Supply.

A few weeks later, an Army C-47 left Anchorage loaded with 4,000 pounds of iced salmon and halibut, bound for Seattle. On the return trip, Ben and Kenny had 500 fresh peach pies and 50 dozen teacakes in Martino's signature pink boxes, 200 one-pound boxes of Grandma Garland's Homemade Milk Chocolates, and 25 cases of Johnny Walker Red Label Scotch going north.

There was a separate pallet with 25 pies, five more cases of Red Label, and 10 pounds of chocolate destined for the Army flight dispatcher at the Anchorage Air Base. As a thank you, the boys stopped off for five dozen Krunchy Kreme donuts. There was a Krunchy Kreme store near the Seattle Airport that always seemed to have the red neon "Enjoy Hot Donuts" sign turned on. They knew that the dispatcher loved 'em. On an impulse, Kenny ordered 10 more dozen for the barracks' soldiers. "Hey, it couldn't hurt, eh?" Of course, there was some shrinkage in the final number of donuts. Ben and Kenny ate almost an entire box during the long flight home. The next pilots who flew that plane couldn't figure out why the controls were all sticky.

Ben and Kenny were able to get away with these private cargo flights 11 times before the dispatcher got transferred. The new dispatcher was a rigid, by-the-book, stick-up-his-ass individual. But, by that time, they'd each managed to bank a small fortune for a rainy day. Ben knew it would go towards a bush plane of his own after the war. Kenny was thinking the same thing.

ML

Ben flew more flights out of Anchorage than any other Army Air Corps pilot. When he had a water landing scheduled during fishing season, he would always throw in his fishing rod and tackle box for a little angling before returning home. Alaska and Canada have a reputation for world-class salmon and halibut fishing.

During the 22 months that he had been stationed in Alaska, Ben ate a lot of meals at Tuma's Café. The food was way better than Army chow, but mainly it was because of Mary Lou, the waitress. Her regulars called her ML. There have always been 10 men for every woman in Alaska, so girls were in short supply. There's an old Alaskan saying that goes, "When any woman leaves Alaska, she's not a '10' anymore."

Soldiers liked to sit at the counter because ML would greet them with a smile, no matter how long her day was. Plus, she looked just as good walking away as she did coming toward them. Ben finally got the nerve to talk to her, past ordering his food. "ML, how would you like to go flying with me? I have to deliver a load of groceries up to Beaver Lake. We'd be back in a few hours."

"Can I bring my fishing pole?" she asked. That did it. Not only did ML have a nice smile and a twinkle in her eye, but she liked to fish! Ben knew she was the gal for him. Between the two of them that afternoon, they brought home a huge load of coho salmon. All through the next week, Tuma's had salmon steaks, salmon filets, salmon patties, and, finally, salmon coquettes on the menu.

ML was pouring him a cup of coffee one morning. "Ben Warner, do you know what I like about you?"

He answered, "The fact that I'm devilishly handsome like Cary Grant and cuddly like Spencer Tracy?"

"Keep dreaming, fly boy. Have you had your eyes tested lately? Actually, I like your smile, plus the fact that you're about the only man who didn't make a pest of himself trying to make time with me." After a few more fishing trips, they were married, and Jackson Benjamin Warner showed up 11 months later.

Home Sweet Home

Even to this day, Alaska has very few roads or trains, considering the size of the state. In many areas, almost everything comes by boat or bush plane. In winter, more choices may include snowmobiles, sled dogs, and snowshoes. Other options are to make it yourself or do without. Most Alaskans take the last two options. There are hardly any junkyards in Alaska. Anything leftover is usually made into something else that's needed.

After they got married, Ben and ML wanted to settle down near the little town of Homer, Alaska, on the Kenai Peninsula. ML asked every customer if they knew of anything for sale. One day, Musher Phillips, one of her regulars, polished off a bowl of caribou stew and asked, "Are you and your husband still looking for a place to live?"

"We sure are; do you know of something?"

"Do you know Hammy Parks, that trapper over by the mouth of the Cook Inlet? I rent my little cabin from him. I hear he has cancer and the doc just gave him six months to live. He lives in a nice, roomy cabin that he built on 50 acres that fronts on the Inlet. It's mostly flat, so Ben could put in an airstrip for his plane. You guys ought to fly over there and talk to him."

"Gee, thanks, Musher. We will."

"Look for the big red X on his roof. He painted that on to make it easy to find him. Of course, it doesn't work too well in the winter," laughed Musher.

Ben and ML parked little Jack with one of the off-duty waitresses and flew down to see Hammy. They found the log cabin and saw the big X. Ben circled over the property several times to get a bird's eye view of the surrounding countryside. The nearest town was Homer, about 35 miles away on the other side of the peninsula. Ben landed on the blue water and tied up to the old, gray, wooden dock below the cabin.

Many years before, Hammy had built a split-log cabin with two bedrooms, a kitchen, and a living room with a spare room he used as a workshop. There was no bathroom, just a privy out back. He built a 10-foot-tall tower with a tank on top to bring gravity-fed running water into the cabin. A few hundred feet away, a spring supplied crystal-clear water that was cold and refreshing. He told them, "You can buy a generator if you want electricity." Hammy gave them the nickel tour, pointing out the property boundaries and the freshwater spring. A Briggs & Stratton engine ran a pump that kept the water tank fed. "It also comes with three little cabins up at the north end. I rent those out in the summertime to hunters and fishermen. There's one larger cabin that I rent out year-round to Musher for $50 a month. He stays in it when he's not up in Anchorage."

"What are you gonna do when you sell?" asked ML.

"Well, the doc says that I only have a short time, so I figure I'll move up to Anchorage so I can be near him and the hospital."

Ben said, "We're sorry to hear about your health problems. Let me talk to my wife outside for a minute."

The Warners walked outside, where ML whispered, "Well, Honey, I don't think I need to ask you what you think. Here's a Kleenex. I can see you drooling from here."

"You're right. You like it too, don't ya, Babe?"

ML recommended, "Let's go inside and talk price."

Hammy and the Warners dickered back and forth until Ben finally stated, "Hammy, we've combined all of our savings. That was our best offer. We just don't have any more money."

Hammy sat down and thought for a minute while he scribbled some numbers on a yellow pad of paper. "Tell you what I'll do. I like you folks, and I don't have any family. If you can come up two thousand on your price, but instead of you paying all cash, just put half down and I'll carry the other half in a note at 4% interest. The monthly payments will help my cash flow while I'm living in Anchorage. The note can expire upon my death.

"Ben, you've got a bush plane. In addition to the price for the property, you throw in a free plane ride whenever I need to go somewhere. The doctor is only giving me about six months, so that shouldn't cost you too much."

Ben looked at ML, who was smiling and nodding her head. Ben stuck out his hand and said, "You've got a deal. Let's find a lawyer in Anchorage to draw up the papers."

Normally this would be the end of a nice, family dinner-table story, but the doctors were wrong. Hammy Parks didn't die in six months or even 46 months. The son-of-a-bitch lived to the ripe old age of 82. But, Ben kept his word and made his monthly payments on time until he paid off the loan. He also flew Hammy whenever he needed to go somewhere. It cost him much more than he planned, but he and ML lived in the cabin for 42 years, where they raised their son, Jack. It was a perfect property for their little family.

After solar panels were invented, Ben Warner read an article in *Popular Mechanics* that showed how you could build your own electrical system from a mail-order kit. Ben couldn't order it fast enough, and soon, ML had lights, hot water, and a refrigerator. As the famous saying goes, "Happy wife, happy life." Those words were true then, now, and tomorrow.

School Days

Since the Warners lived so far from town, home schooling for young Jack was a necessity. Ben and ML took turns with Jack's lessons and reading. ML sent for a mail-order homeschool course and handled most of the daytime lessons while Ben was flying his bush plane. Every evening, Jack would sit on his father's lap and read articles from old *Time* magazines and the *Wall Street Journal.* Ben had a friend in Anchorage who saved past issues for him to read when he had time. Jack seemed to enjoy this father-son time together and developed into quite a good reader, far better than other children his age.

Ben would take the time to explain the meanings of the big words and help with the pronunciation. Both ML and Ben felt that becoming a proficient reader would be a life-long asset to Jack and instill confidence to handle whatever field he went into. This proved to be quite true throughout Jack's life.

Who Shot the TV?

The day after Jack celebrated his 10th birthday, he was playing by himself with his little green Army men. Ben had flown a neighbor over to Homer for a shopping trip and ML was out collecting tree bark and other natural supplies for her crafting hobbies. Jack got bored and decided to look at his father's guns. He pulled out a Winchester Model 70 30.06 rifle and started imagining what it must be like to shoot a bull elk or a charging grizzly bear. Ben promised him that he would soon be old enough to go on his first hunting trip.

Ben exposed Jack to guns at an early age but had always stressed gun safety. Ben *always* stated, "Never, ever keep a loaded gun in the house." All of Ben's guns were kept in a locked cabinet, but the key was on the top of the high cabinet. Jack saw his dad put it there lots of times.

On this day, Jack pulled a chair over to the gun cabinet to stand on so he could reach the key. A minute later, he had the rifle lying across his lap while he sat on the sofa. Young Warner started fooling around with the gun, looking through the scope at the television screen and flipping the safety lever back and forth. He never gave danger a thought, since Ben *never* had a loaded gun in the house. Until today, Jack soon found out.

Ben had recently bought ML a Zenith black and white television as a 10th wedding anniversary gift. With an antenna on the roof, they got three stations that had programming from early morning until midnight when they all signed off. *The Farm Report* started the TV day and *Sermonette* ended it. It was their very first TV and ML was thrilled. They especially enjoyed *I Love Lucy* and Milton Berle.

Jack played with the rifle for a little while and was soon ready to put it away. He didn't want his dad to know, so he wanted to leave it the way that he found it. As he was playing with the safety lever, he noticed that when it was in one direction, a bright orange spot showed, but it didn't on the other. Jack forgot if the orange dot meant 'safety' or 'ready to fire.' He knew a quick way to find out. With the orange dot showing, Jack would just pull the trigger. If he heard a click, it would tell him that the safety was off in that position.

When Jack pulled the trigger, he heard a lot more than a click. The Winchester fired and the recoil almost made it jump clear off of Jack's lap. "Oh, my God," young Jack uttered, completely dazed. The cabin was full of smoke and dust. It took a minute for Jack to recover himself. He pulled the gun's slide bolt back, only to find an empty brass shell in the chamber, plus three more live rounds in the magazine. Ben had forgotten to unload the rifle after his last hunting trip.

Jack quickly put the gun away and locked the cabinet. He started sweeping and dusting as fast as he could before his parents got home. Every kid thinks he can easily fool his parents, like they were never young once themselves.

ML heard the shot while she was walking back to the cabin. It wasn't very loud, so she wasn't sure where it came from. When she entered the cabin, Jack was cleaning like a madman. He had a dust cloth in one hand and a broom in the other. "What are you doing, Honey?"

"I just thought I'd surprise you by doing a little cleaning, Mom."

It only took a few seconds for ML to guess the true story. "That's so nice of you, dear. Can you tell me why I smell gun smoke?"

"That must be the cleaner. Mr. Clean sure smells awful," Jack answered.

"I think Mr. Clean smells more like pine than gun smoke. Jack, maybe you can explain our TV screen." Jack turned and was shocked to see that the bullet had gone right through the middle of the glass screen. He knew he was caught and saw no way out. Jack made a full confession to his mother.

"Honey, I'm so happy you weren't hurt, but I think I'll let your dad handle this when he gets home." Jack was depressed for the rest of the day while waiting for Ben to get home. Jack feared a spanking or maybe his father's belt across his butt. He thought a little preparation might help, so he stuffed several paperback books down the rear of his blue jeans.

Ben learned of Jack's afternoon catastrophe when he returned from his trip to Homer. Ben sat down to think for a few minutes before he addressed the situation with young Jack.

Ben was especially troubled because he was partially at fault for leaving a loaded gun in the house, against his often-repeated orders. "Jack, what if you shot your mother, or me, or one of your friends? You know that you can never call a bullet back. Can you imagine your lifelong heartache if you had killed someone? How could you live with yourself if you had shot your mother?"

This was a more effective technique in dealing with Jack's reckless behavior than yelling or a spanking could have ever been. All Jack could think about was the scene of his friend shot dead, or worse, his mother. Tears poured down his face to be soaked up by ML's flannel shirt while she held him. Jack never played with a gun again and always double-checked to make sure every gun around him was unloaded.

Bartending

Jack liked Kenny Beall a lot. He was his favorite of all his dad's friends. When Jack was in the 5th grade, Kenny made him an offer. "Hey, buddy, how'd you like to be my partner today?"

"Sure, I'd love it." Jack buzzed around like a wooden top in one of those antique table games.

"After lunch, I'll teach you a new trade," stated Kenny.

"What's that?" asked Jack.

"I'm gonna teach you how to tend bar. Bartending is an honorable profession. You can do it anywhere, anytime, even in your old age. First, I'll teach you how to make an old fashioned, my favorite cocktail." Soon, Jack became the only 5th grader in Alaska who could make a perfect old fashioned.

After a successful day of bird hunting, the men were sitting out in the field, cleaning the birds. Kenny was telling dirty jokes, quoting off-color poetry from memory, and speaking famous quotations. Jack thought he made up some of the famous quotes. Kenny's favorite was "Every feather in the field is one less in the house." After that, Kenny stated, "I think we need another batch of old fashioneds."

Young Jack Warner sprang up and volunteered, "I'll go make 'em." Ben and the other men looked at Jack with a puzzled look in their eyes. Kenny didn't say a word as Jack ran back to the cabin. Jack remembered Kenny's directions to make the old fashioneds. He took a tall Mason jar and filled it with crushed ice. Then, he muddled the sugar with a little spring water, added several dashes of Angostura bitters, crushed some citrus rind, and topped it off with a several jiggers of whiskey and some cherries.

ML heard Jack working in the kitchen and walked over to investigate. "What *are* you doing with that whiskey?"

"I'm making old fashioneds for Pop and the guys. Uncle Kenny taught me how to make them."

"That's a fine job skill for a child, teaching my son the art of social lubrication. I think I need to have a little talk with your *Uncle* Kenny. He may not be your uncle much longer. I may change him from an uncle to an aunt."

When he returned with the big jar of old fashioneds, every man took a swig. "These are great! Who made 'em?" Ben asked Jack. "Did your mom make these?"

"No, Pop. She was busy at her craft table. I made 'em."

"Yeah, right. So who really made them?"

"I did, honest."

Kenny couldn't hold it in any longer and started laughing at Ben. "Warner, you should see the look on your face. I taught your kid how to bartend. I figured it might be the only way for anybody to get a decent drink around here." All the men joined in the hilarity and no one laughed harder than Ben. Jack just sat there, beaming from his accomplishment.

First in Flight

As Jack got older, Ben taught him to fish and hunt while enjoying the wild side of Alaska. Ben developed a business flying sportsmen to the best hunting and fishing locations in his bush plane. ML was a great cook and prepared all the food for these trips. She also ran the business, took reservations, kept the books, and paid the bills. Young Jack helped his father work on the plane and gradually became a good airplane mechanic. He had a good head for details, a critical quality for airplane repairs.

On the morning of Jack's 12th birthday, ML made him a special birthday breakfast of buttermilk waffles, elk sausage, and hash browns, with homemade hot chocolate to wash it all down. Ben announced that he and Jack were going flying that morning. "Sure, Pop, where are we going?"

"We're just going," uttered Ben, rather mysteriously.

Ben had Jack do the pre-flight check on the aircraft while he watched. Jack remembered to check the engine, wiring, fluids, all the flaps and the rudder, tires, wing, and prop. "Son, don't forget to check for bird nests and rodent damage. I don't know why they like to chew on wiring, hoses, and cables, but they sure do."

"Everything looks good to me, Pop."

"I agree, boy. Get in." Ben walked over to the right-hand side of the plane and got in.

"Hey, Pop, why are you in that seat?"

"Because that's where the copilot sits," said Ben, grinning.

"Huh?" It took Jack a moment to figure out that he had been promoted to pilot.

Ben reviewed the engine start and warm-up procedures with Jack. He covered the flap settings for takeoff. Jack tested the rudder pedals, flaps, and brakes. As soon as the oil warmed up, Ben said, "Well, whatcha waiting fer, boy? Let's git a-going," in his best hillbilly accent.

Jack taxied down the dirt strip and built up enough speed to take off. He pulled back on the steering yoke and away they went, leaving the earth behind and climbing for the white, puffy clouds.

As time went by, Jack Warner learned how to land on dirt airstrips, snowy glaciers, and finally on water. Being an Alaskan bush pilot was dangerous, but he loved it. "I can't believe you get paid for this," he always said. Little did Ben and Jack realize how valuable these elementary lessons would be in the years to come.

Big Nuggets Are Best

One rainy day, Ben was looking through their bills and bank statements. He had all their papers spread out on the kitchen table. "You know, Babe, Musher is only paying us $50 a month for rent. That seems pretty low. How about we raise his rent to $75?"

"Sounds fair to me. I vote that you're the one to tell him," she said with a grin. "How about telling him tomorrow? I think we need to give him a month's notice."

The next morning was cold and overcast with gray clouds. Ben walked up to the north end of the property to see Musher. There was black smoke wisping out of the chimney, so Ben figured he was home. Ben yelled out a loud "Hello" as he approached the cabin. In Alaska, you don't want to surprise a man. It's more polite, not to mention safer, to give him a heads-up from afar. Most Alaskans have a gun handy and know how to use it. Musher opened the door and invited him inside for a cup of coffee. "So, what's new, Ben? How's ML? They still miss her up at Tuma's."

Ben took the chair offered to him and watched Musher serve coffee. All of his furniture was made from old, wooden freight pallets. Musher had made the table, two chairs, his bed, and storage shelving from this free source of wood. Musher grabbed two blue spatterware metal cups and poured hot coffee from the pot that was sitting on the cast-iron wood stove. Ben was happy to see a box of dish soap flakes sitting by the dry sink. It was a reassuring sign as he lifted the coffee cup to his lips.

"I'm afraid that I'm here to talk a little business. You're only paying $50 a month rent, which is under what we feel is fair for this cabin. Most cabins like this rent for $100 or more to year-round tenants. So, we're going to raise your rent to $75 a month. That's still cheaper than other cabins."

"That's too bad, but I don't think so," countered Musher.

"What do you mean, you don't think so?" inquired Ben.

"I've got a lifetime lease from Hammy Parks for $50 a month."

"*What?*" yelped Ben.

"Yeah, I've got it here somewhere. Let me see if I can find it." After a few minutes of searching through several cardboard boxes that had papers overflowing on all four sides, Musher announced, "Ta-dah! Found it." He handed it to Ben, who hurriedly read through the half-page, handwritten agreement. The paper was wrinkled and had a coffee cup ring on it.

"This thing looks like the Magna Carta," Ben declared.

"That may be, but it's a legal agreement. Hammy and I both signed it over 15 years ago. He got caught up here during a blizzard and had to stay over for a few days. All we had to occupy the time were three bottles of scotch and a deck of cards. I beat him at a marathon run of Gin Rummy games, so he had to pay up. This is how he paid me."

"I don't believe this. I just don't believe this. ML is going to go ape. Do you mind if I show this to her? I'll make a copy next time I go up to Anchorage."

"Sure, just don't lose it. Hammy has a copy of it, too."

As Ben predicted, ML read the agreement and plopped down hard on a kitchen chair. "Babe, can we do anything about this?"

"No," answered Ben. "We have to live with it. Musher has to be in his late 60s, so who knows how long we're saddled with him."

The answer to that question turned out to be two years. When Jack was in seventh grade, Musher died peaceably in his sleep. Ben and ML had to radio for the sheriff to come down from Anchorage to take a report and make the arrangements.

Musher had no family that anybody knew of. Nobody even knew that his real name was Norman. The sheriff told Ben and ML that they could keep whatever was in the cabin. ML glanced at the homemade furniture and other simple possessions and sarcastically uttered, "Gee, thanks, Sheriff. We can sell all of this and take a trip around the world."

While ML and Jack were clearing out the cabin, Jack noticed a loose floorboard. He pried it up only to find a small metal box sitting underneath. He showed it to ML, and they sat down at the table to open it. On top was a bunch of handwritten letters tied with a faded, purple satin ribbon. The newest postmark was over 25 years old. There was a bundle of black and white pictures of various people. "Judging from their clothes, I'd say they're from the 1940s. Probably family," guessed ML.

There were trinkets from the World's Fair, an old Seattle library card, and some old brass keys. Looking around, she said, "I don't see anything worth locking up."

"Here, Mom," Jack said. "This feels like a rock." Jack handed her a black sock with what felt like a rock inside. She picked up the toe of the sock and let the "rock" drop out.

What fell onto the table with a clunk was the biggest nugget of gold either of them had ever seen. "Holy Moly! Mom, look at that chunk of gold. Do you think it's real?"

"Honey, I don't think Musher saved it because it's fake. Let's go show your father."

ML let Jack carry it home to show his father. Jack made a big presentation of showing it to his father. He uncovered it by whipping off a towel with a magician's flourish. "Shazaam!" After the oohing and aahing stopped, Jack asked, "So, Pop, what should I do with it?"

"I'll have to talk to your mother, but I think *we* ought to start off by taking it to the assay office in Anchorage to see if it's real. If so, they can weigh it to find out its value. I'm guessing the phrase 'college fund' is somewhere in its future."

ML agreed. "Your dad's right. It'll be a nice addition to the college fund we started for you after you were born. But I think we could give you $50 to spend any way you want."

Ben agreed. "I can live with that. How about you, King Midas?"

On their next trip to Anchorage, the first stop was the Alaska State Assay Office. The office clerk was all smiles when Jack showed him the nugget. "Let's put it on the scale, shall we?" He kept talking while he trued the scale. "Nuggets aren't usually pure gold. You can only get a true weight if you melt it down and weigh just pure gold. You never know how much rock and dirt is inside of a big nugget like this.

"Good news, it's 121.7 troy ounces. Today's price of gold is just over $35 an ounce, and depending on the purity of the nugget, it should be worth about $4,000. That's about two new cars in your hand, young man. How about them apples, Charlie Brown?"

ML interrupted, "His father and I prefer to think of it as his college education."

"Oh, Mom," complained Jack. "Hey, Pop, have you seen the pictures of next year's Chevy pickups? How about if we buy one of those and put the rest in the bank?"

"Ordinarily, I might agree with you, son, but in case you haven't noticed, the nearest dirt road to us is 35 miles away in Homer. The closest paved road is here in Anchorage, almost 400 miles away. Unless you want to just sit in it out in front of our cabin or drive it up and down the airstrip, I'm afraid it won't get much use. Even if you want to sit in the back with a girl someday, I believe the nearest one of those is 15 miles away."

"There's a smelter around the corner on 4th Avenue." The clerk sang out, "Good luck."

"How about if we go to the smelter, then the bank, and after that, I'll treat us to cheeseburgers and ice cream?" offered Ben. There were cheers all around.

Kaboom

Ben loved to take young Jack hunting for elk, caribou, moose, and bear. They also enjoyed bird hunting for ducks, geese, grouse, and ptarmigans. Before each hunting season, Ben saved money by reloading his empty brass rifle shells and red cardboard shotgun shells.

Reloading shotgun shells was easy. Jack learned the process when he was about 10 years old. The hand-operated reloader was a simple affair that sat on a table. Its handle stuck up in the air, connected to a horizontal, moveable bar of small punches and presses that were the size of your little finger and would fit inside of an empty shotgun shell. They would all move together vertically to accomplish their individual tasks. The hunter would simply move the empty shotgun shell to a different station to complete each step of the process.

Ben was a good teacher. "Okay, Jack, the first step is to punch out the used primer from the brass base of the shell. Then, place a new primer on the next station and pull down the handle to press it into the base. The third step is to put in a measure of gunpowder, followed by a cardboard wadding disc. This compresses the powder down against the primer. A measure of lead shot goes in next, then you crimp the top shut. That finishes it."

Ben continued the lesson. "There are different-sized rotating measurers for gunpowder and lead shot for each gauge. A larger 12-gauge shell takes more powder and shot than a smaller 16-gauge or a 20-gauge shell. Different-sized birds take different-sized lead shot. Geese and ducks need size 4 or 6 shot while ptarmigan, quail, and doves take smaller, 7½ shot.

"When we switch shell sizes, we'll change the powder and shot rotating measure cups so that the right amount goes into the shells. Let's get to work."

Each shell took about a minute to finish. They liked to do the reloading while watching football. It was a great father-son memory that Ben and Jack would always treasure. ML would make a hot lunch with toasted grilled cheese sandwiches, Fritos, and Hires root beer for her little hunters.

Early one morning, Ben and Jack were hunting for grouse and ptarmigan with Kenny Beall, Ben's old Army buddy who was also a bush pilot. ML saw them off. "I'm looking forward to making some meat pies with the birds. When you clean the birds, don't forget to save me the big feathers. I want to make some feather hair clips." ML loved to use the feathers to make women's accessories, which she'd then trade with storekeepers in town.

Alaskans love to barter. A fisherman would catch extra salmon, which he would trade for gasoline or groceries. A hunter might trade meat for eggs from a neighbor's chickens. Alaskan women's baked goods were especially prized. A fresh-baked homemade pie could almost be worth its weight in gold. That idea might not be too far off the mark given the right hungry gold miner and the distance to town. It was surprising how little real cash it took to survive in Alaska.

For that day's hunt, Ben was using his favorite gun: a Browning 20-Gauge Over & Under Superposed Lightning, a double-barreled shotgun.

"Hey, Pop, okay if I use the Model 21?" asked Jack. This double-barreled, 16-gauge Winchester Model 21 was a classic gun from the 1940s. It was housed in a dark red leather breakdown case with a Kelly green felt interior. It had an extra set of full-choke barrels that kept the shot pellets concentrated so the load would reach higher into the sky for ducks and geese. These guns only held two shells at a time, one in each barrel. Kenny was down a ways with a 12-gauge Winchester automatic that held five shells. Ben thought it was more sporting to only have two shells in the gun at a time.

Later in the morning, Ben jumped a covey of grouse, picked one, and fired his gun. KABOOM! It was way louder than a normal gun discharge. Jack looked over and saw his father drop the gun and clutch his right ear and face. "DAD!" He ran over to find him bleeding from some small wounds. Young Jack looked down at the gun and saw that the shell chamber had blown up. A big chunk of the blue steel barrel was missing and the top metal sight rail was curled up toward the front tip of the barrel.

Jack didn't know what happened, but he helped his father back to the house. Kenny grabbed all the guns and the bag of dead birds and followed them. ML saw the hunting party coming up the path to the front door. She put down her feather crafting that she was doing and went outside.

"What're you guys doing back so early? You want more of my biscuits..." ML saw her husband's bloody red hand over the right side of his face. "My God, what happened to you?" Ben told her the story while she cleaned his wounds and bandaged him.

After he had time to rest, Ben joined Jack and Kenny outside to examine the damaged gun. Browning shotguns were some of the best in the world, and Ben didn't think there was a problem with the gun. He wanted to check out the reloaded ammunition. Ben's gun was a 20-gauge and Jack's was a 16.

"Hey, Jack, when we were reloading shells last month, did you remember to change the gunpowder measure dies when we switched from loading 16s to 20s? If a 16-gauge load of gunpowder got put into a 20-gauge shell, that might explain the 20-gauge shotgun blowing up from too much powder."

"Gee, Dad. I don't remember. You and I were both reloading 20s and 16s. We did about a dozen boxes all together. We were watching the Redskins-49'ers game. I was so wrapped up in the game, and I just don't remember."

Both Ben and Kenny glanced at Jack with suspicion. It was an easy mistake to make, but since Ben and Jack both worked the reloader, who could be sure who was responsible? Besides, the mistake might have occurred a long time ago, maybe even before last year's hunting season. There was just no way to tell. Ben admitted, "I don't remember either. It could've been me."

Kenny made Ben an offer. "You know, I have the same model Browning shotgun as yours. I brought it with me today as a backup gun. If you'd like to borrow it, you're welcome to it. I'll even give you a couple of boxes of Winchester factory shells to use. But, please, please, just make sure you clean all those goddamn hand-loaded shells out of your hunting jacket."

It was a very generous offer. Most hunters don't lend out their guns. And they certainly never lend out nice ones like a Browning.

How could Ben refuse? He went through every pocket of his tan, canvas field-hunting coat and cleaned out all the shells he could find.

The men cleaned the birds and enjoyed a delicious lunch of BLT sandwiches and potato salad that ML had made. TV reception was spotty this far north, so today they listened to the football game on the radio. Afterwards, they left for the afternoon hunt.

Jack did well, bagging two grouse and four ptarmigans. Kenny got four grouse. Ben wasn't doing so well until he came through some brush and saw a large covey of snowy white ptarmigans feeding on some wild barley. He pulled up Kenny's gun, sighting a nice big male, and pulled the trigger.

KABOOM! again

"Oh, fuck!"

It was the same as before. Ben's bandaged face was bleeding all over again. The gun was lying in the dirt with destroyed barrels. Two shells were still in the chamber: a dark red, unfired Winchester factory shell and a bright green, spent, reloaded shell. Wisps of acrid gray gun smoke were still wafting out of the chamber.

"Son-of-a-bitch!" echoed from Kenny's mouth. "You blew up my fuckin' gun! I DO

NOT BELIEVE IT! I thought you cleaned out those goddamned reloads outta your jacket?"

'Thoroughly pissed' was a gross understatement to describe Kenny's mood.

Ben was speechless and in pain. He had, indeed, cleaned out his hunting jacket, but those canvas field jackets have so many inside and outside pockets, it was easy to miss something.

"Time to call it a day," Jack said, stating the obvious. "I think you guys need a drink. The old fashioneds are on me." But nobody laughed or felt like drinking.

Ben had been lucky a second time. The outside wood picnic table was now littered with the debris of two Browning shotguns. He said, "You know, I feel like I witnessed two Rolls-Royce cars get in a head-on collision."

Kenny took his birds and left without saying much. It was obviously an accident, and you don't throw away a 20-year friendship that easily. But he still didn't feel like talking. He was happy to fly home alone.

After Ben recovered for a few days, he wrote to the Browning Arms Company about what had happened. He took pictures of both guns and his injuries. Of course, it wasn't Browning's fault, but he wanted to tell them about it anyway. As soon as he got his pictures back in the mail, he mailed the letter and pictures to Browning.

A week later, the Warner letter with the pictures made it onto the desk of Browning's CEO, Jim McElderry. He was amazed at such an accident. He felt sad for Ben Warner and depressed that two of his company's beautiful guns were destroyed.

McElderry called in his secretary to take a letter. He sent Warner a condolence letter over the loss of his Superposed Lightning and the second gun belonging to his friend. He mentioned that he hoped Ben's injuries were healing quickly. He offered to sell Warner two new guns at factory cost.

When Ben received the letter from Browning, he was surprised. "Wow! How can I say no to this deal?" He knew he had to replace Kenny's gun and decided to take advantage of Browning's generosity to replace his own gun as well. He had always planned on Jack inheriting that Browning, and now he could make that possible. Of course, it put a dent in his bank balance, but a few extra bush charters would help that.

Afognak Island

Top Augur was a local hunting guide who lived in Homer, a short plane ride away from the Warners. For 22 years, he had been taking hunters from the "outside" (the lower 48 states) on successful hunting trips for big game. He was one of Ben's best charter customers. The de Havilland Beaver was the perfect bush plane for these hunting trips. Ben would drop off Top and his hunters for a few days. While they were hunting, the group would stay in one of Top's log cabins that he kept for his hunters to use.

Top's wood cabins had only one room, containing two sets of bunk beds, a wood stove, and a kitchen table for food preparation. There was an odd assortment of food staples left by previous hunters. An old dining table and wooden crate stools completed the furnishings. There was a lantern, plus an axe for chopping wood. Before the start of each hunting season, Top would stock the half-dozen cabins with five-gallon cans of lantern fuel, plus a case of toilet paper. Rustic would be a generous term to describe the accommodations.

The rule in Alaska was that anybody was welcome to use the cabin, but you had to leave a pile of chopped firewood and kindling stacked in the wood stove for the next guy. Most hunters left behind some dry or canned foods to replace what they had eaten. One time, Top found a half-full bottle of Johnny Walker Red Label Scotch Whiskey.

This collection of cabins had saved more than one sportsman lost in the wild with a snowstorm in full force. It was way better than camping out, especially during the horrible mosquito season in late summer. Top had found many thank-you notes over the years from people who had enjoyed his Alaskan hospitality.

At the end of a week, Ben would pick up Top's hunting party, take them back to Homer, and land on the dirt strip outside of town. Landing on dirt, water, or snow is known as an off-airport landing. That was about the only type of landing that Ben knew. He rarely landed on a paved asphalt runway. Anchorage was the nearest airport that had one.

One day, Top radioed Ben and Jack and made them an offer. "How'd you like to take a few days off and go elk hunting? You've helped me so many times with my hunters over the years, I'd like to say thanks. We can stay in my cabin on Afognak Island."

They jumped at the offer. How often do you get a chance to go on a free hunting trip with a professional guide? Jack and Ben loaded the guns, camping equipment, and supplies in the plane and took off for Afognak Island, about a 30-minute flight south of the Warner's home on Kachemak Bay. The weather was clear and the flight was smooth as silk.

The men woke up before dawn the next morning, and everybody was hungry. They enjoyed coffee and ML's homemade buttermilk biscuits, stuffed with bacon and homemade red raspberry jam. Licking his fingers clean, Jack asked, "Top, what's the plan this morning?"

"I think we ought to start up the canyon where your father and I saw several elk beds flattened down in the tall grass. A good hunter can sometimes walk up on the elk while they're still lying down. The elk's antlers will stick up above the grass and twitch back and forth while the bull elk wiggles his ears to swat away flies."

Top took the bottom of the canyon and Ben and Jack each took a high side. Top hoped to jump a bull and have him move in the direction of the Warners so they could get a shot. His plan was a good one and, within an hour, Top spotted a large bull elk with a nice rack of antlers. The elk slowly moved off through the aspen trees and started to climb up the hill below Jack.

Jack loved to hunt in the morning sun. He could smell the fresh sage that rubbed on his boots and pants. Jack was hiking along the slope, trying to keep one eye on the rocky path and watch for elk with the other. He noticed movement out in front him and got his gun ready, clicking off the safety as he raised his gun. Jack used a Winchester Model

70, 30.06 rifle with a Leupold scope. It was a great gun, passed down to him from his father. From behind a tree, out walked the big elk that Top had seen down below. Jack could see his rack of antlers. There must have been at least 12 points, certainly legal to shoot. He sighted the crosshairs of his scope on the bull, just behind the shoulder, where the heart is located.

Jack squeezed off a shot and the big elk dropped like a rock. But just as Jack fired, his downhill boot slipped on the loose rocks and he went down as well. His weight threw him backward, twisting his knee, causing intense pain. It was a good thing he killed the elk in one shot, because he wouldn't have been able to walk had he needed to chase after it for a second one.

Top and Ben both heard the shot and headed in Jack's direction. Top arrived first and saw Jack wincing in pain. "Let's get you up and plant your butt on this stump while I hike over to check on your elk." The elk was dead, so Top dragged the head of the animal downhill and slit its throat so the blood would drain out and help preserve the quality of the meat.

Ben was examining Jack's ankle when Top returned. "I think it might be broken. Top, let's get busy dressing that elk. It's going to take some time to skin and quarter him. Shuttling the meat down to the plane will be a job. We can pack up everything at the cabin and get ready to go."

"Hey, what about me?" whined Jack.

"What a crybaby! One little broken leg a hundred miles from the nearest hospital and you'd think it was serious. Your mother and I can always have more children, but nice bull elks don't come along very often," said Ben with a big grin on his face.

Top was smiling too, enjoying their father-son smack talk. Jack was nervously laughing but managed to retort with, "You know, Pop, if you let me croak up on this mountain, Mom is gonna be really pissed off at you. She's not going to be in the baby-making mood for a long, long time. Also, you've got quite an investment in me. Do you really want to start all over again? You might get some skeezix, dweeby kid; not a good lookin', cool son like me."

Ben agreed, "Okay, Jack, you sold me. I guess we better get you down the hill so you can see a doctor at the clinic." All three guys laughed like hell while they had a drink of water and planned their next move. Jack was sure that he couldn't walk on it without some serious help.

Top said, "Come over here, Ben. Let me show you the nice 12-point bull that your son got. He's about 60 yards away, by those aspens."

Returning to Jack, Top came up with a plan. "Well, boys, we're in for a busy after-noon. The good news is, the plane is only a half mile away, and it's all downhill. Here's my idea: we make an Eskimo travois. It's an A-frame that we lash together out of five small tree trunks. I have an axe, a hatchet, and some leather laces back at camp. Ben, take your gun with you in case you run into a bear. Bring back the axe, hatchet, and the laces. Also, grab those plastic tarps and rope to wrap the meat in. I'll skin the elk and start quartering him so we can move it down in manageable-sized pieces. Jack, when Ben returns, have him chop down five trees, about 10 feet tall. You take the hatchet and clean off all the smaller branches. You can do that work sitting down."

Top started butchering the elk. He would leave the guts in the field and take back everything else. Top's Inuit Eskimo wife, Nani, could make things from the leg bones, hooves, and antlers. It would be dark in several hours, and they didn't want to be stuck on top of the mountain overnight.

Using his hunting knife and camp saw, Top removed the head and legs. After skin-ning the animal, he opened the stomach cavity and carefully cleaned out the intestines and bladder without puncturing them. The heart, liver, and kidneys went into a plastic bag to keep them clean. He folded up the skin with the wet sides folded against each other, so that the fur was on the outside and easy to carry. Some lucky wolves or varmints would smell the powerful scent of the guts and have a feast that night.

After a couple of hours' work, Top went to check on Ben's progress with the travois. He had cut the trees and Jack had cleaned off the five trunks. They had the basic frame laid out and partly lashed together. Top helped them finish it and Ben got onboard to test it. After laying out the elk skin for padding, Jack held on while Top and Ben took the wood handles and started down the hill to the cabin.

If they'd only had Jack to move, they would have just put their arms around him to take his weight while he walked between them, using his one good leg. But they also had 600 pounds of elk meat to get down the hill. A front quarter of a bull elk is not only heavy, but it's awkward as hell to get a good grip on. The travois was just the ticket.

After Jack was delivered to camp, Ben and Top went back for the elk. The beauty of a travois hauler is that half of the weight still sits on the ground. You just pick up the long-handled ends and drag the rear pole tips along. They moved all four quarters of the meat and head with antlers in only five more trips.

Loading the de Havilland Beaver bush plane with the elk, guns, and equipment, plus the three men, put the load just under the factory specs. Ben took off and headed for Homer, where the nearest medical clinic was located. He radioed ahead for their van to meet him at the airstrip and transport Jack to the clinic.

While they were flying, Jack spoke out, "Top, I want to thank you for the hunting trip and also for your help getting me down the mountain." Ben chimed in with his praises as well.

Top appreciated their thanks and answered, "Jack, I'm happy to do it. On most hunting trips, you expect to carry out the meat, but when you go hunting with the Warners, you have to carry out the hunter as well!" They all laughed and spent the rest of the flight talking trash back and forth as men love to do.

The clinic X-rays showed Jack's ankle only had a hairline fracture. Jack would have to wear a cast for three weeks and then an ankle brace for two weeks. The doctor said since Jack was still young and his bones were still growing, he would heal easily. Ben playfully accused Jack of falling down on purpose to avoid carrying out the elk. His mother added her own thoughts. "Are you sure you didn't do it just to get out of your chores and loaf around the cabin?

'O Solo Mio

When Jack was seven years old, he used to love to ride his red Murray Cruiser bicycle up and down the dirt airstrip and through the woods in between the aspen trees. Ben had attached training wheels to help him. Jack hated them and always considered those for babies, not for big boys like him. The training wheels stuck out and would catch on rocks and branches along the trail.

The Harley family lived a few miles away with a boy about Jack's age. Brian Harley liked to do all the same things that Jack did. They hunted and fished together, built forts in the woods, made tree houses in the big Sitka spruce trees and started a Boys' Club that didn't allow girls. Of course, that was easy, since the nearest girl was miles away. Ben would go pick up Brian and his bike in his 17-foot Searunner skiff so the boys could play together. Sometimes Brian would stay overnight with Jack out in their tree house.

During one of Brian's visits, he made fun of Jack's training wheels. Brian's father had taken his off months ago, making Brian feel like a big boy. That was the last straw. The next morning, Jack unbolted his training wheels and threw them as far as he could out into Kachemak Bay. He got on his bike and steadied himself with one foot on a stump before taking off. With only a few wobbles, Jack pedaled all the way down the airstrip and back, whooping and hollering loud enough to scare any bears away. ML and Ben came running out to see what was going on. Smiles crept over their faces when they saw Jack racing toward them with no help from anyone or anything.

Years later, on his 14th birthday, Jack felt that he was ready to solo in his dad's bush plane. He untied the aircraft from its moorings and completed the pre-flight procedure. The only thing he didn't do was to tell his parents about his plan.

Jack got in and started the engine. After letting it idle and warm up, he kicked out the yellow wheel chock blocks and jumped in just as the plane was starting to roll forward. The plane picked up speed as he taxied down the dirt airstrip. Once he reached take-off speed, he pulled back on the yoke and the Beaver reached for the sky with the young pilot at the controls. "Bitchin'!" screamed Jack.

Ben heard the bush plane engine start and just thought Jack was working on the plane. Once he heard the motor rev up and saw the aircraft move, he sprinted out the door of the cabin in his blue flannel pajamas and his red wool Muk Luk slippers. ML was right behind him, still carrying the spatula she had been using to stir the eggs. They reached the end of the path to the airstrip just as Jack left the ground. They stood there speechless with their mouths open, holding onto each other.

"Son-of-a-bitch," murmured Ben. Although, deep down, he was thinking, "That's *my* boy."

ML was thinking, "I'm going to kill that boy, if he makes it back alive." "Well, he's your son," she said, digging her elbow into Ben's ribs.

Jack flew the FAA-required distance and flight pattern as outlined in the Official Rule Book. The only minor problem was that he was several years too young and couldn't fulfill any of the bureaucratic requirements for a license. Jack headed back home and started his approach. He had to buzz the field to chase a moose off of the airstrip. Running into a 1,500-pound moose would have spoiled an otherwise picture-perfect solo flight. It wouldn't have done the plane any good, either. He circled around and made a textbook landing, then taxied back to where his parents were patiently waiting for him.

ML threw her arms around him and kissed him on both cheeks. Ben, however, maintained the stern scowl on his face, then screamed at him, "What the hell were you thinking, boy?" He couldn't keep it up for long, and broke into smiles and reached out to hug Jack, too.

All of that was against every FAA rule. Many Alaskans, who live their lives hundreds of miles away from most big cities, don't feel that government rules apply to them. There was only one FAA official in Anchorage who had to cover thousands of square miles of sparsely populated territory. There were hundreds of isolated air strips with bush plane pilots scattered all over Alaska. Those pilots were pretty much on their own and lived their life that way.

Where's MacGyver?

Alaskan tourists love to go flight-seeing. While flying over the ocean bays, they can spot giant gray whales in the sapphire blue water. Traveling over lush green meadows lets them see bears and moose. Some of the most exciting trips are visits to the giant white glaciers. Huge chunks of white ice split off the end of the glacier and fall into the bright blue ocean. This *calving* creates a little tidal wave that can swamp small boats, kayaks, and canoes if they are too close. Falling into 35-degree water will give you hypothermia quickly and lead to your death if you don't get warmed up in a big damn hurry.

Bush pilots install skis over the wheels to make it possible to land on snow. Every ski landing has a degree of danger to it. The pilot can never tell where there might be an ice ridge or a crevasse hiding under the top layer of snow. A strong ice ridge can catch the ski tips, flip the aircraft over, and injure or kill everybody. If the radio breaks, survivors will have to wait for their plane to be missed and a search party to find them. A doctor might be days away or not available at all.

An incoming storm could finish off any survivors before help might arrive. Since glaciers are usually above the tree line, there's no wood for a fire. Every bush plane carries a survival box in the plane's tail with space blankets, food, and water to last several days.

The Warner's bush plane was a de Havilland Beaver made in Canada in 1951. It's known as a STOL aircraft, for "short takeoff and landing." Quite a few of them are still in business today. It's quite common for bush planes to be older than the pilots who fly them. Ben called it the 'half-ton truck' of the skies. The Beaver could carry six passengers, powered by its 450-horsepower radial engine. After the first snowfall, Ben and Jack installed skis on the bottom of the plane. They also had pontoons for water landings during the warmer months. Before landing, a good bush pilot makes several low passes over the landing area to check things out, whether it is on snow, dirt, or water. Floating logs or debris in the water can tear off the pontoons and really ruin your day.

One November day, Ben flew the de Havilland Beaver with 15-year-old Jack, plus two couples from Southern California. They were college students at USC, on vacation in the great white North. The weather was clear and 20 degrees, perfect for flying and landing on the slight upslope snowfield on the Tuxedni Glacier, located across the Cook Inlet. This glacier was a holdover from the Ice Age, three million years ago.

Ben planned a sightseeing trip for the students with a brief stopover on the way back at the ranger station at Twin Lakes. Ranger Todd Farcau needed some pipe to fix the broken water lines that fed fresh lake water down into his cabin. Bush pilots always need to keep track of passenger and cargo weights. Passengers always thought it strange that they had to step on a bathroom scale before they boarded the small aircraft. The load of pipe, parts, and the six occupants was just within the weight limit for the plane.

Ben and Jack approached the Tuxedni Glacier and came in low to check out the landing area. There was already a blue-and-white de Havilland Otter bush plane parked on the glacier. Ben and Jack recognized the plane as belonging to Kenny Beall. Ben could see that he was loading his passengers and would soon be taking off, clearing the way for him to land.

After circling for a few minutes, Ben's red-and-white Beaver came in for a landing on the pure white snow. Ben showed Jack every step so he could learn. The snowfield was a little rough, but had looked usable. Suddenly, the aircraft made a big jerk to the left and spun around into a snow drift on the side of the rough runway. There was a screeching sound of ripping metal as the plane stopped.

Jack automatically pulled out the fire extinguisher, but luckily there was no fire. He looked over toward his dad and saw blood trickling down his face. Ben had hit his head on the door frame. Jenny, one of the tour group members, sprang into action. She was a nursing student and went right to work. Jack gave her the medical kit and unfastened his dad's safety belt. Jack helped the rest of the passengers out of the injured aircraft. Jenny gave her diagnosis. "The cut needs a few stitches, but it isn't serious. I cleaned the wound and patched him up temporarily with some butterfly bandages that were in the first-aid kit."

The other students were shaken up but unhurt. Jack set up the small tent near the tail of the plane and gave them some water while he assessed the damage to the plane.

It looked like one of the ski tips had caught on an ice ridge under the snow. The ski wasn't broken, but the bracket that held it to the plane was. All he needed was a replacement bracket, and Jack could make the repair. But a new bracket was 500 miles away, plus they had no jack to lift the plane, and, to top it off, the radio was broken from the crash.

Jack took inventory of everything in the plane. He found a toolkit, flares, miscellaneous plane parts, a big roll of bailing wire, two rolls of duct tape, two tarps, a flashlight with extra batteries, food bars, elk jerky, water, tent, space blankets, toilet paper, and the pipes and fittings to be delivered to the park ranger.

He opened the tool box and drafted JC, one of the male students, to start unbolting the broken landing-gear bracket. He got the other students to spread out a tarp and lay out the pipes and fittings so Jack could see what he had to work with.

Ben was now nicely bandaged and sat on the edge of his seat and helped out by supervising. He started the girls on a water detail. Ben had them spread out the other dark blue tarp and cover it with a light layer of clean snow. They arranged a small fold in the tarp to collect melted snow. The sun would warm the snow on the dark tarp, melting it into water which the girls could collect into a plastic food container. Ben had no idea of how long they would be there, and people get dehydrated quickly in cold weather.

The collection of galvanized metal pipes was made up of one- and two-inch-diameter pieces about four feet long. Pipe usually comes in eight-foot lengths, but the plumbing supplier had cut them in half and threaded the new ends so they would fit better into Ben's plane. There was also a box of couplers and 90-degree elbows to connect the pipes. One thing Jack and Ben didn't have was a pipe wrench, so anything they made could only be hand-tightened with a pair of pliers.

Ben found a pencil and began sketching on the back cover of the map book. Jack soon understood what his dad had in mind. When JC removed the broken landing-gear bracket, Jack laid out some two-inch pipes with some one-inch reinforcing pieces. Some of the joints could be connected with the couplers and elbows, but others had no proper way to be connected. Ben said, "What I'd give for a welding torch right now."

Ben gave the colored smoke flares to the students and had them watch out for passing planes. "Don't light the flares unless I tell you to," he said. "A passing jetliner can't see them from 30,000 feet. What we need is for a low-flying bush plane to spot them."

Ben and Jack took out the wire cutters, the bailing wire, and the rolls of duct tape. Jack and JC got the ski into the original position with the pipes to be connected to the plane. Jack planned to connect this landing-gear-pipe invention to the original upper half of the broken bracket since it had the mounting bolts to connect with the plane's fuselage.

Jack first put on a layer of duct tape to hold things where he wanted them. He and JC started wrapping the bailing wire, overlapping the entire pipe and fitting areas. Over this wire wrap, he added another layer of duct tape to make the connection stronger. Four hands made the job go quickly.

They kept adding more wire and tape layers until they ran out of materials. Jack managed to build up eight layers of duct tape and bailing wire to connect the pipes. When they were done, it actually looked strong enough to really work.

Ben told the four students to pick up the edge of the plane's wing. All together, they had enough strength to raise half of the plane off of the snow while Jack slid in the jury-rigged landing gear. Jack and JC bolted the top half of the broken gear bracket to the plane's fuselage. The new landing gear was a little taller than the old one, making the plane tilt a little to one side, but it was better than staying overnight on the glacier. It was now late afternoon and surviving the night on the icy glacier would be cold and miserable.

Ben was able to start the engine and man the controls while everybody else spun the plane around and pushed it past the ice ridge that caused the accident. The runway was now downhill, which would help the plane build speed. Everybody jumped in and fastened their seatbelts. Ben taxied a few hundred feet with Jack hanging out the starboard door, watching the landing gear to see if it would handle the load. It appeared to be working just fine, so he gave his dad the thumbs up and closed his door.

Ben told Jack, "Why don't you take over? My head is throbbing."

"Okay, Pop." Jack accelerated and used every one of the Beaver's 450 horsepower to leave the snow just before the end of the snowfield. They climbed to 500 feet and headed home.

All they had to do now was to land on the jury-rigged ski assembly. ML heard them on approach. She had been getting worried about them, since they were several hours overdue. ML hadn't been able to reach them on the radio. She had been calling other bush pilots from her base radio, but no one had seen Ben and Jack until she reached Kenny, the pilot in the blue and white Otter. He updated her to their location on the glacier. He was about ready to take off to go check on them when she radioed him again to say they were in sight of their home runway.

ML looked at Ben's plane and noticed something looked different. The plane looked a little cockeyed. Of course, this was the homemade landing gear, but she couldn't know this. By the time she grabbed her binoculars, Jack was setting the Beaver down on the snow, making a goofy but safe landing. She ran over to the plane, quickly noticing her injured husband and the new landing gear.

After hugging them both, ML had about a thousand questions. She gave them both a bear hug, happy to have her guys home again, safe and sound. Everybody was happy to be home, no one more than the USC students, who took home a tale of adventure in Alaska to tell their family and friends.

Why Skycaps Hate Liver

When Jack was 15, four elk hunters from Pasadena, California chartered Ben's plane for a trip with Top Augur. Two of the hunters got an elk before having to return home to the lower 48. Old Alaskan sourdoughs call it *"down below."* The Warner's plane couldn't carry that much weight, so Jack had to make two trips. He still didn't have a pilot's license, but nobody ever asked him about it.

After Jack finally got the hunters and their elk meat to Anchorage, they called Woody Lee to come to the airport and pick up the giant quarters of elk meat. Woody was a butcher who would cut up your meat or fish, wrap it in white paper, freeze it solid, and then ship it by air freight. It was a handy service. How else could a hunter take home hundreds of pounds of meat without it spoiling?

While Woody was busy with the hunters, Jack unloaded their duffle bags and guns. In those days, there was no such thing as airport security. Hunters could carry their guns right onto the plane with them and stow them in the overhead compartments.

Once they got home to California, one of the hunters wrote to thank Jack and Ben for a successful hunt. He also told them the story of their arrival at LAX:

"When we landed in Los Angeles, a skycap loaded our bags onto a luggage cart and followed us. We were carrying our guns and a vinyl cooler, which was loaded with fresh elk liver. Unfortunately, the plastic bags inside were leaking and the blood leaked out through a crack in the cooler.

"As we walked through the L.A. airport, I guess we left a trail of blood behind us. The skycap noticed us carrying guns and then he saw the blood. As he was pushing a cart full of heavy duffel bags, I'm sure his imagination ran wild.

"I'll bet he was thinking, 'Oh, Lordy, what have I got myself into? What's inside of these bags?'

"Looking back on it, I'm sure the whole thing was pretty funny, but probably not to the airport janitor who had to mop up the floor."

License, Schmicense

While working alongside his father, Jack learned to perform the routine maintenance and many general repairs on the plane. Jack could also install the skis for snow, pontoons for water landings, and the big, cushy tires for landing on dirt airstrips and the rare paved runway.

When Jack was only 16, he was an illegal but accomplished bush pilot. After Jack soloed at 14, he started keeping his official pilot's log of every flight and hours flown. Jack's log was in a spiral-bound school notebook, not the official FAA edition that licensed pilots like his father filled out religiously.

One Friday in December, he and his father worked all day on the plane, finishing up just in time for dinner. Ben seemed tired, so Jack did most of the work. "Okay, Pop, all new control cables, tires and tubes, spark plugs, and fresh oil in the engine. The emergency supplies are all there with fresh water. I even gave it a bath inside and out. It's all ready for those caribou hunters." They would be arriving in a few days, so it was important to have the plane in top shape and ready to go.

That night, Jack and ML noticed that Ben was sitting in his recliner most of the evening. He didn't want any dinner and only had a few sips of water. ML was concerned that Ben's forehead was wet with perspiration, even though it was 15 degrees outside and 50 degrees inside the cabin.

When it was time to go to bed, Jack and ML had to help Ben out of the chair. He moaned when he leaned forward but said, "I'm okay, maybe I'm getting the flu. Just give me a hand getting to bed." When ML helped him get into his flannel pajamas, she accidently bumped against his stomach. He cried out in pain. She got him into bed and put a cold compress on his forehead and another on his red, inflamed stomach.

ML met Jack in the kitchen to talk things over. She grabbed the *Reader's Digest Home Medical Care* book that most Alaskans kept in their homes. Doctors were far away, so most of the time, you had to rely on yourself or your closest neighbor for medical care.

When she looked up "abdominal pain," she grew more worried. All of Ben's symptoms pointed to a swollen appendix. If it burst, the toxins inside would be released, ensuring eventual certain death of the patient. They had to get Ben to a hospital, but the nearest one was in Anchorage, about 380 miles away. With snow on the ground, Jack couldn't take off at night. Their flat airstrip was plowed but had no lights or markers. A pilot needed to be able to see ruts in the snow and avoid any debris in the way of the airplane's skis.

In December, the days were only five and a half hours long, so the Warners had a long wait for the sun to peek over the permafrost. While it was still dark, Jack fueled the plane, removed the rear seats, and laid out two sleeping bags and lots of blankets and pillows so Ben could lay down for the trip. He took a lantern and flashlight to give the runway a preliminary look-see while ML got Ben bundled up and ready to go. It took almost half an hour to get him to the plane and inside the rear fuselage. At the first glimmer of morning sun, Jack warmed up the plane and quickly ran up the airstrip to give it a final inspection. Jack jumped in and took to the sky. ML sat in the back next to Ben and comforted him as best she could in the loud, cold plane.

There's a famous saying about the weather in Alaska: "If you don't like the weather, wait an hour." When they took off, it was clear and cold. But after two hours, sinister black clouds were looming up ahead. If it was just an ordinary flight, Jack might have turned around and headed back. But there was no heading back today. Ben Warner's life depended on reaching the hospital in Anchorage. The plane was tossed about like a tennis shoe in a clothes dryer, but Jack managed to maintain control and keep his cool.

Jack saw ice building up on the leading edge of the wing. Luckily, they had recently modified the plane's wing, adding a heated de-icing strip to the front edge. Jack flipped the 'On' switch and took comfort when he saw the green indicator light come on.

An hour later, while watching the gauges, he noticed a drop in oil pressure. Jack didn't want to take the time to land because scouting a suitable, flat snowfield would take time that Ben Warner just didn't have. Jack yelled back to his mother to bring him several quarts of motor oil from the rear of the plane. She managed to bring them forward and put them in the passenger seat.

The de Havilland Beaver plane is unique in one important way that helped the Warner family that morning. With most planes, you would have to be on the ground and open the engine cowling cover to access the engine to add motor oil. This model de Havilland plane had an oil-filler spout that reached back into the cabin through the instrument dashboard, allowing you to add oil in mid-flight.

ML quickly opened two cans of oil and found a funnel from the tool kit. Jack opened the filler spout and held the funnel for his mother. A couple of quarts later, the oil-pressure gauge read back in the normal range.

Jack radioed the Anchorage Airport Control Tower and declared an emergency situation. He asked for an ambulance to be waiting for him upon landing. The plane made good time, making the trip in just over two hours. The skis on bush planes have openings in them that allow the plane's tires to peek through. This feature allows the pilot to land on snow or a hard surface. The plane has a hand-powered hydraulic pump in the cabin that retracts the skis enough for the tires to meet the tarmac.

Jack landed perfectly and taxied over to the ambulance and rescue personnel. They transferred Ben into the ambulance along with ML and sped away with red lights flashing and siren screeching through the early morning air.

The two airport controllers on duty watched all the commotion through the tower windows. "That was some piece of flying through that storm," they said. "He probably saved his dad's life." They commented to each other how Jack looked young for a pilot, but nobody thought to ask him if he had a license.

Ben made it through surgery just fine. ML and Jack told him the story of what it took to get him to Anchorage. He was proud of his family for doing what it took to save his life. While Ben recovered in the hospital, Jack and ML prepped the plane for the hunters arriving the following day. It was fortunate that the plane was already at the Anchorage airport. ML stayed behind with Ben at the hospital and Jack found a cushy recliner chair in the airport lounge.

This same good luck seemed to follow him throughout his life. At the end of the week-long hunting trip, Jack flew the hunters back to the airport, along with their caribou meat for Woody to cut and wrap. They gave Jack a nice tip for a job well done. ML checked Ben out of the hospital and the whole family returned home once again.

Hook, Line, & Senator

Warner Air Charter attracted fishermen from all over the world. They came from every state in the lower 48, plus other countries like Scotland, Ireland, England, France, and Italy. Once, two came all the way from Australia. Ben would deliver them to the summer camp that his family built 15 air minutes away on the coast of Kachemak Bay. There, they could catch halibut, steelhead, and salmon in the cold blue water. King salmon ran in early June. Sockeye salmon fishing started near the end of July. Pink salmon arrived in mid-July, and silver salmon fishing got busy in August. The nearby streams had prime fly fishing for the freshwater anglers.

Over the years, Ben and ML built eight rustic cabins by the bay for fisherman and hunters. They were generally booked solid a year in advance with a waiting list for cancellations. Each of them had a small kitchen with a black cast-iron wood stove and an equipment closet for tackle, waders, and hunting equipment. Kerosene-powered Coleman lanterns provided light at night. In later years, as technology improved, solar panels on the roof powered small refrigerators in each cabin. They added additional solar panels to provide hot water for showers and sinks. Three outhouses in the back served all eight cabins. A water well with a solar-powered pump supplied fresh water to each cabin. There was a little hot water for everybody if the sun was bright and if they used it sparingly.

Even though the cabins were primitive, many sportsmen rented them every year and paid in advance to guarantee their reservation. Many of their longtime customers would show their thanks by bringing a case of lemons or other fruit to their grateful innkeepers. Fresh peaches or a watermelon were rare things in Alaska in those days. Jack was 12 before he enjoyed his first banana.

Jack, now 16, would fly the fisherman in and out for a fabulous week of fishing. They would catch fresh king salmon and barbeque it with fresh lemons, dill, garlic, and olive oil over a campfire. Jack would fillet their catch and wrap it to travel home with them.

Two of their best customers were Senators Frank Molina and Glen Hope. They were accomplished fly fishermen who grew up fishing the lakes and streams of Idaho and Montana. They really enjoyed getting away from the hot and muggy Washington, D.C. summers and flying up to Alaska with their rods and tackle. Jack got to know both senators very well. He talked to them about his dream of going to college and then maybe joining the Air Force someday. You can't help but get to know people after spending hours with them fishing along the streams near Kachemak Bay.

On the morning of their next fishing trip, the senators got started at first light. Hope suggested working Dead Man Creek for salmon. "Last year, I had good luck fishing in a deep pool just below the road's end. The water is dark and deep with some buried logs that give the fish some cover."

Molina offered, "I'm going upstream past those little rapids." He was soon standing in the three-foot deep water, wearing his rubber wader overalls to keep out the cold water. The clear, chilly water was running about 38 degrees. Even with both men wearing waders, they would still get cold as time went on.

Senator Hope worked his rod like a pro, making the fly dance upon the water, hoping to catch the attention of a fat king salmon. As he took a step forward to get a better position, the rock he was standing on rolled forward down the side of the deep pool. The elderly senator went over backwards, completely submerging himself. Icy water poured down inside his bib-overall waders, quickly filling them up. As he struggled for a foothold, his movements only let in more water. He threw his rod toward shore and tried to tread water. He screamed for help, but the freezing water made it tough to be heard.

Molina was a hundred yards upstream with the rapids in between him and his friend. The roar of the rapids drowned out Glen Hope's feeble calls for help. With the water filling his overalls, treading water was getting tougher by the second. Senator Hope was now in serious trouble.

Jack Warner chose that moment to deliver lunch and some cold beer to the two senators. Tips were based upon good deeds like that, and he really liked these old guys. He saw their tackle boxes and camp stools, but there was no sign of the men. He left the food and had a choice to make – upstream or down? Luckily for all, Jack went downstream, rounding a curve in the river just in time to see a big floppy fisherman's hat floating in the water. A few steps later, he realized that it wasn't just a hat, but that there was a man under the hat trying to tread water. Jack kicked off his shoes and dove in the cold water like an Alaskan Tarzan. In just a few strokes, he reached Hope and pulled him back to the riverbank, probably saving the old man's life.

A few moments later, Frank Molina wandered up to the soggy twosome. He had walked back down to the tackle boxes, found the lunch basket, and wondered where everybody was. With Molina's help, Jack helped the cold and wet Senator Hope back to the camp stools. ML had packed hot tomato soup and sandwiches for that day's lunch. Hope said, "If it's okay with you, I'll pass on the cold beer and take the hot soup." The senators couldn't thank Jack Warner enough for his help.

A few months later, Jack turned 17. The family gathered with some close friends to celebrate with a tasty barbeque of salmon, halibut, and moose sausage. After a homemade triple-layer, chocolate-suicide birthday cake, singing, and presents, Ben Warner announced that there was one more gift.

Ben said that a special envelope had come a few days before and he and ML had hidden it from Jack. Inside were two Happy Birthday cards from some old friends:

Dear Jack,

Happy birthday to you on this special day. I can't tell you how much it means to me to still be here to write this card. Without you and your heroic actions, I wouldn't be. As I enjoy the rest of my life with friends and family, I have you to thank for saving my life last summer in the river. I'll never forget what you did for me.

Warmest regards,

Glen Hope
U.S. Senate

In the other birthday card was a second note:

Happy birthday, Jack!

At 17, you have your whole life to live out in front of you. I want to thank you for the many happy days I spent fishing in Alaska with my friend, Glen Hope. You and your family always made us feel at home and that is a very special thing. I also want to thank you for saving my friend's life. If he had gone down for the third time, who would I fish with? Of course, I'm just kidding. You're growing up into a fine man and we have your parents to thank for that.

As a birthday present from both of us, we have arranged for the vice president of the United States to nominate you for admission into the Air Force Academy at Colorado Springs, Colorado. You will receive a complete four-year college education, board, and room with all expenses paid. You will graduate as an officer of the United States Air Force. Our country will be the richer for your service.

Very truly yours,
Frank Molina
U.S. Senate

What a birthday present! How often does the rest of your life come inside of an envelope?

'Bout Time He Gets One

The day after he turned 17, Jack was one of the youngest pilots to ever apply for a license. He figured that passing the test should be easy since he had been flying since he was 12. No applicant had ever applied for a license with five years of flying experience before they even had a student license.

The FAA-registered instructor in Anchorage expected a rookie pilot when he first met Jack. But as he started to give Jack some basic instructions, it became clear that Jack was way ahead of the crowd. The only areas that Jack needed help with were basic aviation academics and formal weather planning. He picked that up quickly and took his classroom tests.

The final step was for Jack to take the required FAA flying test. Jack would have to fly this solo. After taking off, there was a series of prescribed flight patterns to make where he would be timed and monitored from start to finish. Ben was confident that his son would ace the test.

Ben's confidence was not misplaced. Jack received a perfect score from the FAA official. Jack also wanted a float plane pilot endorsement, so he had to takeoff, fly out five miles, and then return and land on the water out front of the FAA office. He had to do this procedure three times. Jack and Ben borrowed some pontoons from another pilot in Anchorage. They installed them on Ben's plane in a few hours, and Jack went for the FAA official to monitor the test.

Jack started his takeoffs. The first two takeoffs and landings went very well. Jack took off for the last time and flew out over the bay. Just after he made his 180-degree turn to come back, he spotted an overturned kayak in the water. There were two people clinging to it, waving for help. Warner knew that the water was near freezing, so there was no time to waste. He circled down to make his approach. As he lined up for his water landing, Jack noticed one person had disappeared. Jack hit the water and taxied over to the kayak just as one guy was reaching for his friend, who had sunk under the water.

Warner killed the engine and climbed out on the left pontoon. One of the kayakers blurted out, "Hey, Mister, thank God you saw us. My wife was going down to the bottom. Help me get her up, will ya?"

The woman was barely conscious. Luckily, she was light, and Jack could pick her up by himself while her husband climbed onto the rear of the pontoon. "Hey, buddy, open up that sliding door and we'll help your wife in." They got her inside so her husband could take care of her. "There's some blankets in that duffle bag," offered Jack.

Jack grabbed some rope and managed to catch the bow of the yellow plastic kayak. He pulled it up onto the pontoon and tied it fast, front and back. This was not uncommon, since bush planes carry things tied onto the undercarriage all the time.

Back at the dock, Ben and the FAA man were getting impatient, wondering what happened to Jack. "He's over the time limit. I'm going to have to fail him. Why don't we give him a call on the radio and see where he is?" asked the official. Just as they were opening the office door, Ben heard the familiar sound of his plane's engine.

As the plane got closer, coming in for a water landing, Ben said, "What the hell is that big yellow thing on my plane?" His question was answered in about 30 seconds. Ben and the FAA official were amazed when Jack tied up to the dock and two more people got out of the plane, covered with blankets.

Next, it was Ben and Jack's turn to be surprised when the young man that he rescued saw the FAA official and yelled out, "Dad! It's so good to see you. Rita and I were fishing out in the bay, and we capsized. This guy landed on the water and saved us. He even saved our kayak." Hugs were enjoyed all around.

After 10 minutes of storytelling and backslapping, Ben said to the FAA man, "Given the circumstances, do you think you can change my son's grade from a fail to a pass?"

Jack Warner passed with a perfect score and received his pilot's license with a float plane endorsement. Young Mr. Warner didn't know it at the time, but this was the first of many rescues that he would make in his flight career.

Air Force Academy

Even though he was nominated by the vice president of the United States, Jack still had to go through the application and qualification process to enter the Air Force Academy. But, no other applicant had the flying experience that Jack Warner brought to the table. When the day came for his oral interview before the School Evaluation Committee, they were more than a little skeptical about the flying experience listed on his application.

Colonel Regan Thompson, Dean of Admittance, had some questions about how an 18-year-old pilot managed to accrue more than 1,500 flying hours in four years of flying experience when he couldn't even get a license until he was 17.

Jack told them the story of learning to fly when he was only 12, soloing at 14, and having to wait to get his official pilot's license until his 17th birthday. He reached into his knapsack and pulled out his tattered spiral notebook. "Gentlemen, here is my pilot log book."

Colonel Thompson took it and leafed through the dog-eared pages and passed it to the other committee members to examine. Jack certainly stood out among the other candidates. Having two glowing reference letters from his old fishing buddies, Senator Hope and Senator Molina, didn't hurt either. After a quick huddle of the Evaluation Committee, Colonel Regan Thompson said, "Well, this is a first. When I was 14, all I had was a paper route and pimples. This kid was flying bush planes in Alaska! I think we better get him flying for the Air Force." Jack was quickly accepted into the Academy.

Jack was thrilled to hear the magic words, "Well, young man, your experience and connections got you in. Graduation will depend on your hard work and discipline."

Even though Jack had lots of flight experience, he had never studied aviation theory, flight dynamics, or taken any formal classes. He only had a few simple classes to get his pilot's license. There was a lot of math and meteorology to learn. His father really taught him to fly by the seat of his pants. If you wanted to know about the weather in Alaska, you looked out the window and listened to the radio. The Warners didn't have much TV reception until the later years. The first year of the AFA was a tough one for young Jack. He did well in the general education classes, and his roommates tutored him in many of his aviation classes until he got the hang of things.

When Jack was accepted at the AFA, he moved into a dorm room with three other cadets. It was a rather spartan existence: four to a room, two double bunk beds with four small closets, and four desks for studying. No TV or radio. Everything was GI, from the crisply ironed uniforms, polished brass buckles, and spit-shined leather boots to the beds made up so tightly that you could bounce a quarter off of them.

Jack's favorite roommate was Sonny Frazier from South Carolina. Sonny was one of the first black cadets admitted to the AFA. His father was Heavyweight Boxing Champion Joe Frazier.

Rumor had it that when Joe Frazier was invited to the White House to meet JFK, he was able to talk to the President for a few minutes. Kennedy was a huge boxing fan and reportedly won a $10,000 bet with Frank Sinatra on Joe Frazier's championship fight. Joe figured he would never have this chance again, so he asked JFK if he could arrange an interview for his son at the Air Force Academy. JFK was very gracious about it and agreed, with one condition. Kennedy said, "I'll get him in the front door, but whether he stays or not is up to him."

As AFA freshmen cadets, their class was charged with organizing all the food at the Annual Homecoming Alumni Picnic. They were told that the food better be special, no hot dogs, hamburgers or potato salad.

Jack Warner and his roommates volunteered to head up the effort. It turned out that his dorm room was a jackpot of party-planning possibilities. Jack wrote to his dad in Alaska and asked him to send him 50 pounds of salmon, 50 pounds of halibut, 50 pounds of caribou sausage, and 25 pounds of elk steaks. All the freshman cadets had donated to pay for the food. Jack wired money to Ben to cover the cost of what he had to buy. Ben sent it all back. He caught most of the fish himself and his hunting friends donated the rest. His pilot buddy, Kenny Beall, made the caribou sausage and smoked it himself.

Ben double-wrapped all the meat and seafood and loaded it into some big boxes. He labeled the boxes "Aircraft Parts." He was afraid that if the boxes said "Fresh Fish" or "Meat," part of the shipment might not make it. "Shrinkage" was a common problem along supply lines. He addressed the boxes to Jack's commanding officer, Colonel Ed Delong. Delong was a famous B-26 Marauder bomber pilot during WWII and now was the ranking officer at the AFA. He was on the Board of Directors that approved Jack Warner for entry into the AFA. Delong particularly enjoyed Jack's stories of his Alaskan adventures.

Jack asked Ben to fly the load to Elmendorf Air Force Base near Anchorage. From there, he would have it sent down to Colorado on the first Air Force cargo plane available. Evidently, someone on Delong's staff had alerted the Elmendorf Cargo Officer to look for the "Aircraft Parts," because they were loaded on the first flight out and arrived in Colorado eight hours later. Jack met the arriving plane and personally helped in transferring all the seafood and meat to the school kitchen's walk-in refrigerators. Every box arrived in perfect condition.

Sonny Frazier had his own gastronomic connections. Frazier grew up in South Carolina with his mother, two aunts, and a whole batch of uncles, brothers, sisters, and cousins. His mother, May Bell, ran the Just-Rite Soul Food Café with her two sisters. All the kids grew up working in the café, cooking, cleaning, and learning the basics of the food business.

Sonny wrote to his mother and placed an order "to go" and also included a money order. He asked for 10 gallons of shrimp gumbo, 25 pounds of her fried chicken, 25 pounds of hush puppies, and enough dirty rice and gravy to go with it. Sonny's Uncle Cletus delivered the whole thing to the Charleston Air Force Base, addressed to Colonel

Delong. He waited around while it was loaded onto a C-17 that was scheduled to stop in Colorado on the way to California. He figured that "shrinkage" could also happen in South Carolina.

The third roommate was Scott Morgan from nearby Denver. Scott's father was the catering director at the Denver Hilton. Morgan called his father and explained what he was doing for the Air Force Academy alumni. On the morning of the event, a Hilton delivery van arrived at the AFA, carrying a giant ice sculpture of the Air Force insignia, plus boxes of fresh flowers and real table linens to add a little class to the whole affair. All this was courtesy of the Denver Hilton as a "thank you for our Air Force personnel." Conrad Hilton had personally authorized the donation after the Hilton district manager heard about it and called him.

In addition, out of the van came a wedding cake that would serve 200 guests. A wedding had been cancelled at the last minute, so Mr. Morgan asked permission from the bride's family to donate the cake to the Air Force. They said, "Yes, take the cake and also give them the 200 New York strip steaks and all the hors d'oeuvres as well." Everything had already been paid for.

The fourth and final roommate was Frank Guerin from Key West, Florida. Frank's mother owned a bakery in Key West. Once she heard what her son was doing, she sent her delivery van up to MacDill Air Force Base with boxes of sweet potato pies, pecan pies, and key lime pies. She sent an additional six pies for the Air Force ground crew. She figured a little insurance wouldn't hurt the success of her shipment. The ground crew loved every bite. They even shared the pies with the pilots and air crew.

Let it be known that the 1966 Annual AFA Homecoming Day was the finest in the history of the school. The problem was that nobody wanted to leave the mess hall. There was hardly anyone at any of the school exhibits, the lectures, or the committee meetings, because everybody was still eating. The activities finally got started only after they ran out of food.

Colonel Delong's Staff Corporal found Cadets Warner, Frazier, Morgan, and Guerin. He ordered them to report to the colonel's office on the double. "Jesus, what's up?" they all thought. They all lined up at attention in the colonel's office as ordered.

"I understand that you four are responsible for today's menu, food delivery, and decorations," barked Colonel Delong.

"Yes, sir," answered all four in unison.

"I think that the fare served today has got to be the best chow ever served on any military base in the country. General Flynn is here today and wants to meet each of you and shake your hand. Flynn is from Atlanta, Georgia, and your lunch reminded him of home and family."

Each of the "Fabulous Food Foursome" did indeed meet the general. The school scheduled a dinner in the general's honor where the four cadets got to speak with him for a few minutes. During the dinner, Jack went up to the bar for a drink. The bartender was out in the kitchen on a cigarette break, so Jack figured what the hell, he'd help himself. He started to lay out all the ingredients for an old fashioned. Just as he was muddling the sugar, water, and bitters, General Flynn walked up.

"Can I get one of those?" asked Flynn.

"Sure, General. I guess the bartender is on a break or something. I figured, why wait around? I learned how to make old fashioneds when I was a kid in Alaska. An Air Force cadet is supposed to be resourceful, right?" answered Jack.

"I like your thinking, Warner. I've heard of generals having their own doctors. I wonder if I can have my own personal bartender." Both men laughed as Jack finished making the drinks.

"Here's how, General," toasted Jack.

"Hell, son, I know how. The question is when and how soon?" joked the general. The laughter continued.

Sonny, Scott, and Frank were over on the side of the room enjoying a beer, watching Jack and the general carry on. Sonny stated the obvious. "Look at that lucky mother f-er drinking with the general. After graduation, boys, I think we're all gonna be working for him."

Frank offered, "Maybe he'll make *us* some old fashioneds." The laughter continued.

They each received a commendation for their personnel file and each got a three-day pass at the next school break.

Demerits

The AFA had a demerit system for various infractions to the school rules, policies, and military decorum. Once a cadet had 10 demerits, he had to work an entire Saturday doing physical labor around the campus. This usually consisted of gardening, painting, washing vehicles, or general KP. The custodians could be very resourceful when it came time to dream up work for their temporary indentured servants.

Jack Warner and his roommates accumulated demerits for boyish pranks that most young men seem to enjoy. Scott Morgan earned his demerits by buying a large bag of crickets at a pet store where they sell them for reptile food. He thought it would be great fun to let them go inside the school offices, library, and the senior classrooms. The crickets chirped endlessly, driving everyone nuts except for Scott, Jack, Sonny, and Frank. They were delighted in the harmless mayhem Scott caused until the bugs eventually died off. It didn't take too much work to call the local pet stores and inquire about recent cricket sales. It would have been smarter if Morgan hadn't worn his uniform into the pet store.

Jack and Frank came up with some more technical trouble. They managed to sneak into the motor pool where Colonel Delong's staff car was parked. While Frank acted as lookout, Jack cross-wired the car's brake lights into the horn relay wiring. This way, every time the colonel's driver hit the brakes, the horn would honk incessantly, irritating everyone within earshot. But, while Jack was under the car, his wallet worked its way out of his rear pants pocket and got left behind. It's a good thing these boys weren't interested in the spy business. His partner, Frank Guerin, confessed immediately during the investigation.

Sonny Frazier took a more basic route to get into trouble. He went to the local art supply store and bought a few cans of spray adhesive. Early one morning, he hit all the faculty bathrooms, where he unrolled the rolls of toilet paper and glued it onto the roll as he rolled it back up. When he was done, all the TP was a solid mass of glued paper.

Unfortunately, Mr. Krabbe, the custodian, saw him coming out of the latrine and checked things out, noticing the TP handiwork.

At the next disciplinary hearing, the senior class officer stated the obvious punishment. "Well, boys, I see by the demerit list that this will put you all with more than 10 demerits. I'm sure that Mr. Krabbe, the custodian, will welcome four laborers this Saturday. Now you can all be together, working. Won't that be nice?"

There was a collective "Shit" from all the cadets at once.

On Saturday morning, the cadets reported to Arnold Krabbe's office for duty. Mr. Krabbe was about 64 and weighed about 350 lbs. He had salt-and-pepper hair and tattoos that peeked out below his shirt sleeves.

Krabbe always seemed to be buzzing around campus on his little Cushman electric cart. It was a faded industrial orange color with a flat cargo bed behind the seat. Nobody ever saw Krabbe walk anywhere, only driving his cart. As you watched him drive by, the view of the rear was somewhat comical. The whole cart leaned way over to the left, where Krabbe's seat was. His weight must have worn out the left-hand springs prematurely.

Krabbe welcomed his Saturday staff. "Hello, boys. I've been expecting you." Krabbe pulled out a to-do list that was so long, it reminded Jack of Santa Claus' gift list, cascading down toward the floor.

The cadets spent the day weeding, sanding, scraping, painting, and organizing storage buildings and dusty garages. Some of them got assigned to the kitchen, where they enjoyed peeling potatoes, polishing silver, and repairing broken tables and chairs.

There was an idea meeting between the foursome at their lunch break. They were trying to come up with something to mess with Krabbe's electric Cushman cart, but nothing came of it. They resolved to be much smarter with any future school shenanigans.

Pranks

The AFA cadets designed some fun pranks against their rival schools. For more than 50 years, the Air Force Academy had a major rivalry with nearby Colorado State University. Just about every year, there was a one-upmanship contest with pranks going back and forth. Even though both universities tried to keep their security tight, the pranksters always seemed to sneak through enemy lines.

During Jack's junior year, the CSU cheerleaders had created a detailed card display system for cheers. When they called out a number, the CSU fans in the stadium held up cards, which were black on one side and white on the other. By following the directions, they displayed an encouraging message for CSU players. Jack's roommates, Scott and Frank, snuck into the CSU cheerleaders' hotel rooms and replaced the instruction cards from the cheerleaders' pile with new and improved copies. There were 10 card stunts on the instruction cards. When #9 was announced, unsuspecting CSU fans held up their cards nice and high, displaying the unintended message "CSU SUCKS." Before the cheerleading squad could react, the main cheerleader announced #10, and the message, "Go Air Force," was displayed for the entire world to see.

Not to be outdone, CSU struck back in a big way. As the saying goes, "Revenge is sweet." The Air Force Academy was remodeling their student cafeteria. The kitchen was being upgraded, and all new tables and chairs were on order. There were also 12 booths due to be installed in the dining room. As part of the decor, 48 seat cushions and backs were to be upholstered in silver and blue, the AFA school colors.

A week before the grand opening, all the new furniture was delivered. School administrators and the AFA's Colonel Ed Delong were standing there, watching, and looking forward to finishing this long and expensive project.

The contractor's men unloaded the tables and chairs. When the booth seats were unloaded and carried into the cafeteria, the men took off the protective black plastic. The administrators and Colonel Delong all swallowed their collective gum. Instead of blue and silver booth seats, they were green and gold, the Colorado State University colors. "Get that goddamn decorator on the phone!" screamed Delong.

By the time Colonel Delong was back in his office, his secretary had Dylan Daniels, the project designer, on the phone. "Daniels, you moron. What happened to the booth seats in my cafeteria?"

"What's the matter, don't you like them? I think the new colors look cute," minced Daniels.

"What new fucking colors? I never changed any colors. Don't you realize those are the colors of Colorado State University?" barked Delong.

"But I got your change order six weeks ago telling me about the new green and gold colors."

"I never changed anything. Fax me over a copy of that change order."

A few minutes later, Delong's secretary brought him the faxed change order. "Mr. Daniels is on line one, sir," she said. Delong read the change order and punched line one.

"Daniels, you idiot. Read me the authorized signer's name on this change order."

"It's kind of hard to read, but it looks like Corporal M. Mouse," said Dylan.

"You get a change order signed by Mickey Mouse and you don't call about it? How long will it take to get new cushions in the blue and silver colors that we ordered?"

"Six weeks," he said meekly.

"Horseshit. Today is Friday the 10th. I want these 48 cushions ready next Friday morning. That gives you seven days. Then, I'm going to have two Air Force trucks with armed MPs at the upholstery shop address on this invoice next Friday at noon. They better be ready, or else you ain't getting paid. Comprende?"

"Yes, sir," trembled Daniels.

"Let me give you some career advice. Never fuck with a guy that can call in an air strike on your office."

Not only were the cushions ready as ordered, but Dylan Daniels personally escorted the delivery truck to the AFA cafeteria. Delong heard that Daniels had three different upholstery companies working 24/7 to get them done in time.

AFA Finals

At the Air Force Academy, each student must pass final written exams and then a series of oral exams. For the oral tests, there are no Scantron forms, no Blue Book essay questions or paperwork of any kind. Cadets must endure a question-and-answer session by a panel of five AFA professors. There is no time limit and most sessions last more than two hours. All five professors assign a number grade for the cadet's responses. Those grades are averaged into a final number between 60 and 100. A 75 is passing, an 80 is above average, and a 90+ is excellent.

Cadets have the chance to impress the panel by using their life experiences in addition to the knowledge they've acquired at the AFA. As the school put it, "Our graduates need to be able to make snap decisions at 30,000 feet flying at Mach 1. There's no time for books."

At Jack's panel review, first up was Norman Jutzi on flight dynamics. Second, Henry Tichenor handled aviation theory. Bernie Neupauer taught meteorology. Neal Poland lectured on aviation mechanics. Closing was Dr. Warren Walker, the head of the Aviation Medicine Department.

Each Professor asked an essay-type question. Based upon the cadet's answer, the professor marked the question completed and assigned a number grade.

Jutzi started with, "Gentlemen, I was a member of the evaluation panel when Cadet Warner applied to the AFA. I will ask him to repeat part of what he told us then and expand upon that. Warner, please tell the panel about your first solo flight experience."

Jack explained to the panel about his father giving him flying lessons starting when he was 12. "I learned to take off and land on dirt airstrips, snowfields using skis, and lakes using pontoons. On my 14th birthday, I felt that I was ready to solo. I completed my pre-flight check procedures and started the engine."

"Excuse me for interrupting, Cadet," Dr. Walker said. "Where was your father while this solo flight was going on?"

"He and my mother were inside our house. I did it all alone. I taxied down the dirt strip, reached take-off speed, and pulled back on the wheel and took off. Once I reached 1,500 feet, I flew the FAA-required distances and made the loops and turns as outlined in the FAA manual. I headed back home and started my landing approach. I had to buzz the field twice to chase a moose off of the airstrip so I could land."

After the professors stopped laughing, Neupauer spoke for the group. "You're giving us that old 'moose on the runway' excuse?" The examiners chuckled again. "I believe that's the first time we've heard of that one. Please continue, Warner."

"I was only 14 and didn't meet the FAA requirements for a license. My soloing was against the FAA rules but we Alaskans have a strong independent streak. We often have to improvise due to weather or wild animals. We have to learn to cope with breakdowns and the unexpected."

Tichenor asked, "What was your parents' reaction when you landed?"

"They were both very glad to see me back safe and sound. I think they both wanted to kill me, but they seemed proud of me. My mother turned to my dad and said, 'Well, he's your son.'"

Jutzi asked, "What flying did you do after that date?"

Jack replied, "I flew our bush plane four or five times a week. I picked up supplies, parts, and fuel. I picked up fishermen and hunters, then delivered them to their cabins or camps."

Jutzi was impressed and wrote down a score of 90. "No more questions from me."

Tichenor was next. "Mr. Warner, what can you tell me about your experience with aviation theory?"

Jack Warner expanded on learning to fly in his father's de Havilland Beaver bush plane. "When you land on dirt, snow, and water, each material calls for wheels, skis, or floats. Each type of takeoff and landing needs a completely different type of flying dynamics and experience." Jack continued, explaining the aerodynamics of skis and floats and how each affects the plane's flying abilities and characteristics.

Tichenor remarked, "Thank you. That will do." He wrote down a score of 89.

Bernie Neupauer said to Jack, "Tell me about your knowledge or experience with weather and aviation."

"Mr. Neupauer, we have a saying about the weather in Alaska: 'If you don't like the weather, wait an hour.' No truer words were ever spoken."

Jack discussed many of his experiences while flying in below-zero weather, dealing with icing problems and wind shear. Jack continued by telling the panel about the time he flew his father to the hospital 380 miles away for emergency appendicitis surgery. He had both of his parents on board and had to make it through black clouds, dealing with icing on the wing and enduring a wind storm. Jack explained the weather theories of each condition and how a pilot needed to deal with each item.

Mr. Neupauer said, "Very good, Cadet. That's fine. By the way, how old were you when this happened?"

"16, sir."

"So, this was before you had a license or had any formal aviation courses; an impressive accomplishment. Thank you." He wrote down a score of 88.

Neal Poland was the next to go. "Warner, what knowledge do you have regarding airplane design or construction?"

Jack thought for a moment and told the panel about working on the bush plane for years with his father. He could do any maintenance work and minor repairs. Next, he told the story of landing on the Tuxedni Glacier, redesigning and using plumbing pipes, wire, and duct tape to rebuild the broken landing gear, then successfully flying home with everyone on board.

"That's amazing, Warner, very resourceful. How old were you?" asked Poland.

"15, sir."

Poland smiled and gave him a 92.

Dr. Warren Walker was the go-to guy in aviation medicine. "Warner, what do you know about aviation medicine? I'm guessing your dad wasn't much help with that."

Jack started his answer with "You're right, sir. I learned all my knowledge in this area here at the AFA. Your classes were especially helpful, and my roommates formed a study group that reinforced your teaching." Jack wasn't above a little "brown-nosing," and he hoped that Dr. Walker's ego could use some stroking.

Jack Warner reviewed the Air Force's requirements for pilot health standards and readiness. Remembering his classes on high altitude's effect on the human body, he outlined the changes a pilot goes through as he flies higher and higher. He also explained the development of a G-suit, or "speed jeans" as some pilots call them.

Dr. Walker was happy and said so. He gave Warner an 88.

Warner made it through the AFA. His final oral exam scores averaged 89.4, but the administration liked his attitude and self-reliance. They rounded him up to a 90.

Most cadets come out as a second lieutenant, but due to Jack's personal achievements, accumulated flying hours, and test scores during his four years at AFA, he graduated two steps higher, coming out a captain. Next on the list was fighter pilot training.

Airport Kiss

To celebrate graduation, Jack invited his roommates to go fishing in Alaska. The king salmon were ready to start running. Most fishermen would agree that kings are just about the best salmon there are. Jack had all the tackle they needed. "Just pack your duffels, you guys, and let's go." So they took him up on his offer, and away they went.

Flying out of Denver, they had to change planes in Seattle. The four Air Force officers traveling in uniform were a handsome group of young men and attracted attention everywhere they went. The stewardesses also noticed these cute guys and hoped they would fly back on one of their flights. Walking through the Seattle airport, they had to take an escalator to reach their departure gate. Jack was first, followed by Frank, Scott, and Sonny. At the top of the escalator was a hot-looking blonde about 30 years old. Jack figured, "She must be waiting for somebody." Not one to shy away when opportunity knocks, the 22-year-old Air Force Captain decided to answer the door.

Stepping off the escalator, Jack took a few steps toward her and said, "Gee, Babe, you look *great!*" He gave her a big kiss and then kept on walking.

This poor woman didn't know what hit her. She turned around to see who the hell *that* was. When she turned back forward, she received the same treatment from Frank and then Scott, followed up by a similar dose from Sonny.

She was in complete shock. Talk about a hit-and-run accident! Her girlfriends will never believe her. Four gorgeous, handsome young men each gave her a nice kiss and a sweet compliment and didn't even stop to ask for her phone number.

"I've got to spend more time at the airport," she concluded.

Jets at Last

After graduating from the Air Force Academy, Jack was assigned to Randolph Air Force Base, near San Antonio, Texas, for basic fighter training. The first plane Warner learned to fly was a Cessna T-37 "Tweet" Trainer. To say it was a little different from his father's bush plane would be an understatement. Twin jet engines gave it more power than Jack had ever felt before. Jack was a good student and learned to fly the jet quickly. He turned out to be one of the best pilots in the class.

After acing his initial flying tests and passing classroom training, it was time for Warner to start flying fighter jets. He suited up one morning and went out to see his next ride, an MD F-4 Phantom. F-4 Phantom pilots refer to the plane as the "Double Ugly." She may be ugly, but they love the way she flies. He would be in the pilot's seat and Major Al Keppler, his flight instructor, would be in the rear copilot's seat. Keppler showed Jack how to do his preflight check walk-around.

While doing so, he started his "canned" new-pilot speech that he had given hundreds of times before. Jack thought he sounded just like Barney Fife from *The Andy Griffith Show*.

"The McDonnell Douglas F-4 Phantom is a tandem, two-seat, twin-engine, all-weather, long-range supersonic jet interceptor fighter-bomber originally developed for the United States Navy by the McDonnell Douglas Aircraft Corporation. It first entered military service in 1960 with the U.S. Navy. Proving highly adaptable, it was also adopted by the Marine Corps and the Air Force, and by the mid-1960s, it had become a major part of their respective air wings. The Phantom is a large fighter with a top speed of over Mach 2.2. It can carry over 18,000 pounds of weapons, including air-to-air missiles, air-to-ground missiles, and various types of bomb ordinance."

Their first flight together was anything *but* "canned." Keppler put the plane through its paces. He showed Jack the whole menu of acrobatic maneuvers. "These moves can save your life, plus $2.2 million for the U.S. taxpayer. It's bad enough when the Air Force has to inform your family that you're spam in a can. But, when we send them a $2 million invoice for the airplane because you're an idiot, they tend to get upset."

Keppler let that sit in for a minute until Jack finally smiled, getting the joke. "My dad would probably ask if the Air Force would take a check," he joked back.

As the fighter training proceeded, Warner was turning out to be one of the best pilots that Keppler had ever trained. Of course, he would never tell that to Jack. Warner mastered the controls, but more importantly, he had built-in flying instinct, which you can't teach to a pilot. It comes from within.

Jack did his best to translate his seat-of-the-pants bush flying experience into accepted Air Force practices and maneuvers. He thought about how to explain the difference in power to his father, but didn't think his words would cover it. Warner hoped to figure out a way to sneak his dad onto the base sometime and take him up in a Phantom for a ride. Keppler's final evaluation rated Jack Warner with 9.3 out of 10 points.

The rest of Jack Warner's fighter training went well. He graduated near the top of his class and figured he would be sent to Vietnam soon. His figuring was spot on.

Hazing

Air Force rookie pilots were subject to hazing by the senior airmen. Jack heard old stories about different hazing treatments given to rookies. He wanted to handle it like a man and do well in the fighter program. Your reputation follows you in the military.

Jack asked around but wasn't able to find out any details of what might happen to him. In the fighter pilot barracks, his bunkmate was Owen Stenzel. Jack liked Owen right away. His family owned a restaurant in nearby San Antonio called Pecos Bill's Okie BBQ. It had been in business for more than 75 years. Owen had invited Jack for dinner there sometime, and Jack was looking forward to it.

Jack thought a little preparedness for hazing might come in handy. Jack had five pairs of uniform pants counting his fatigues, service uniform, and dress uniform. Jack sewed two dimes into the bottom of a pocket in each pair of pants, figuring they might come in handy.

Handy, they did. In the middle of the night, a group of senior airmen stormed into Warner's dorm room, shouting at the rookies to get dressed and go outside into the night. All they could put on were fatigues and their boots. The seniors searched the rookies to make sure they had nothing else on them. Jack's hidden dimes weren't noticed. The rookies piled in the back of a "deuce and a half" truck with an olive green canvas bed cover.

The deuce and a half is a triple-axel, six-wheel drive, two-and-a-half-ton cargo truck. The M35 is the backbone of the U.S. armed services. It's been hauling their heavy cargo for over 80 years. Although it's rated to carry up to five tons of men and supplies, it's commonly loaded with twice that number. It does the job all around the world.

Jack and the other rookies were guarded, so they didn't know where they were being taken. After half an hour, Jack and Owen were dropped off in the middle of nowhere at 2:30 in the morning. The truck sped away to leave the remaining rookies elsewhere.

The point to this exercise was to see if the rookies were resourceful enough to make their way back to the base with no money and no help. Since Owen was a local boy, he had a good idea of where they were, about 10 miles outside of San Antonio and about 20 miles from Randolf. "Well, we have a long walk in front of us," said Owen.

"Maybe not," said Jack, tearing out the pocket threads and producing his shiny dimes.

"Beautiful!" exclaimed Owen. "If we can find a pay phone, I can call our restaurant. There are a few guys working all night. They clean the restaurant and start the meat smoking for tomorrow's customers."

Jack and Owen double-timed it down the dark road until they could see a Flying A gas station in the distance. The gas station was closed, but there was a phone booth. Owen called the restaurant. Smitty, the pitmaster, answered the phone. Smitty had worked at the restaurant for 42 years. He started working for Owen's grandfather and had watched Owen grow up. Owen worked there as a boy, washing dishes and busing tables. Smitty loved him because of his personality and the hard work ethic instilled by his parents.

Owen explained, "My buddy and I are stranded out here on Route 23 by Sheridan Road at the Flying A gas station. Could you please come and rescue us?"

"Can do," answered Smitty. "I just got all tomorrow's meat seasoned and put in 'da smoker. Yo' timing's perfect. Junior and Mikey is cleaning up, and they don't need me. I'll be 'dere in 15 minutes."

As promised, Smitty showed up at the Flying A to pick up the stranded soldiers. "So, Mr. Owen, what the hell are you doing out here in the middle of the fuckin' night wif no car or nuthin'? I thought you were in the Air Force learning to be a hotshot fighter pilot."

While they drove to the restaurant, Owen introduced Jack to Smitty and explained the trick being played on them. "Is you boys hungry?" asked Smitty.

Owen kidded him by saying, "Smitty, has anybody ever answered that question with a no?" Jack smiled in the dark back seat of Smitty's car. He couldn't wait.

Smitty heated up some pork spareribs and beef brisket. He laid out some platters and filled them with coleslaw, BBQ beans, garlic bread, and okra. That was followed by the ribs and brisket with a bowl of peppery BBQ sauce. He slid over some cold Lone Star beers to wash it all down with.

The young rookies ate as fast as they could. Owen forgot how much he missed great BBQ cooking. Compared to the Air Force mess cooking, it was manna from heaven. Jack was in a trance. He had never had real BBQ before. It was unbelievably good. "Smitty, do you have orders to go?"

"Sho'," said Smitty.

"Good, 'cuz I'm mailing a big box of this to my mom and dad in Alaska."

"You just give me their address, Mr. Jack, and I'll sho' get it to 'em."

Smitty took them back to the main gate of Randolph Air Force Base and dropped them off. The two rookie airmen arrived back in front of their barracks to the astonishment of the six senior airmen in charge of the hazing. It was only 5 a.m.! No rookie had ever made it back before breakfast. Plus, these guys were relaxed and in perfect shape, except for some BBQ-sauce stains on their shirts. When asked how they did it, both Owen and Jack answered, "We utilized proper Air Force training, sir. Permission to be excused, sir?" The senior airmen would never figure it out. The boys went back to bed. They were so full that they skipped breakfast and lunch. Jack and Owen didn't eat again till dinner that evening.

Riding Shotgun

Jack was enjoying a beer at the Randolph AFB Officer's Club one night when he overheard two guys talking about the MacDill Surplus Gun Sale coming up. MacDill Air Force Base is in Florida and was going to have a sale of used guns suitable for public use. Among the guns for sale were some Winchester shotguns that any hunter would love to own.

The MacDill Air Force Base is one of the largest bases in the United States and is home of the Air Force Exhibition Shotgun Team. They've competed in 14 Olympics and countless public exhibitions over the years.

The team uses 12-gauge Winchester Model 12 Shotguns. These are considered one of the best shotguns for shooting skeet. They're also great for hunting quail, doves, grouse, ducks, geese, and pheasants.

Every Air Force pilot needs to keep up his flight hours to maintain his pilot standing and flight pay qualification. Jack figured he would just check out a small trainer plane and head for MacDill to buy himself a shotgun and one for his dad.

Warner managed to wrangle a weekend pass and went to the BAAO (Base Aircraft Assignment Office) to see if he could check out a small Cessna Skymaster. The Air Force used them to ferry paperwork and small cargo like aircraft parts among the air bases. None were available, so he decided to climb up the aircraft ladder and asked if a Cessna T-37 Trainer was available. This was the same plane that he used during training. This jet-powered trainer had two seats and a small cargo hatch, large enough for some shotguns. Warner figured that his buddy, Owen Stenzel, would want to go and get a gun too, but, no luck, none available. Why not keep climbing the aeronautical ladder, as it were? Jack started looking at the flight dispatcher's clipboard to see what *was* available.

Next step up the ladder was a Grumman C-2 Greyhound Transport. They used them for moving personnel and supplies to carriers at sea. Two Allison turboprops have 4,800 horsepower, giving the plane a top speed of 345 knots. Their payload is 10,000 pounds and takes two pilots plus two crewmen. Jack was pretty sure this could handle a payload of four shotguns. But the four aircraft assigned to Randolph were on a transport shuttle assignment and were off-base.

It was back to the drawing board, or the dispatcher clipboard in this case. Major Rick Donnelly, the dispatcher, was starting to ask questions. Who was Warner and why did he need a plane for a weekend? Jack figured that he better level with him. Major Donnelly listened to the story of the shotgun sale with a straight poker face. He said nothing, but paused for a few moments before he picked up the phone and asked for Colonel Wolcott's office. "Oh, shit!" gulped Warner. He figured the MPs would show up and he'd be spending the weekend in the stockade.

Donnelly got Corporal McClusky, Colonel Wolcott's aide, on the phone. The first words out of his mouth were, "Does Colonel Wolcott still go duck hunting in Louisiana?" Warner started breathing again.

Two hours later, Owen Stenzel, Major Rick Donnelly, Colonel Oliver Wolcott, and his aide, Corporal McClusky, plus a crew of eight and two pilots plus Jack, took off in a McDonnell Douglas C-9 Skytrain Transport headed to MacDill Air Force Base in Florida for the surplus gun sale. A new Skytrain cost $35 million. The crew and fuel cost was $3,200 per hour. Everybody on board bought shotguns totaling $2,600. The colonel ordered the plane to stop off on the way home in Louisiana for a day of duck hunting at his ranch near Jefferson Parish, outside New Orleans. Warner figured that the shotguns really cost the U.S. Taxpayer about $45,000, and the ducks cost about $500 apiece.

Editor's Note: "Your tax dollars at work, eh?"

Saigon, Here I Come

After graduation from Randolph Air Force Base in Texas, Warner was sent to the Da Nang Air Base in South Vietnam. This was the Northernmost Air Base in SVN. Warner was known as a nugget, a first-tour aviator or rookie. Warner was part of the 421st Tactical Fighter Squadron and was assigned his own MD F-4 Phantom fighter jet. Jack's fighter group quickly developed a reputation for results. They only lost one plane on a sortie, and that was because of a mechanical failure.

Shortly after his arrival in Vietnam, Warner met the grizzled head of maintenance, Master Sergeant Lou Patroni. Patroni loved to lecture the flyboy pilots. "You guys know that my mechanics and I work all night to make sure that my planes are in top shape. These are my goddamn planes, and only 'cuz I'm such a generous S.O.B. do I let you borrow 'em for a few hours to go annoy those commie bastards. If you get 'em shot full of holes, I'll kick your ass all the way into next week."

During a mission, Warner found himself in a dogfight with an NVN pilot flying a Russian MiG who managed to get behind him. Jack had a favorite maneuver that his BBQ buddy, Owen, taught him. Warner would quickly dip down a few hundred feet to make sure the enemy pilot wasn't directly behind him. Then, he'd give the jet full flaps and put down the landing gear for a few seconds and then pull them back up again. This was like slamming on the brakes of a car. The enemy pilot wouldn't be expecting it and would shoot right by, thereby giving Jack the advantage, now being behind him. The F-4 Phantoms had an M61 Vulcan six-barreled, air-cooled, Gatling-style rotary 20 mm cannon that fired 100 rounds per second.

Jack would then give the enemy pilot a taste of the M61 at point-blank range and take him out. So many bullets fired together would almost cut the enemy plane in two. This worked well several times. Those pilots didn't survive to tell their buddies about Jack's little trick, and this helped him become a great fighter pilot.

During the Vietnam War, only two pilots achieved the title of Ace, after five aerial kills. One was a Navy pilot and the other was in the Air Force. That pilot's name was Jack Warner.

One rainy morning, Jack Warner was called down to Saigon to pick up some new planes and shuttle them up to Da Nang Air Base. While he was there, air control told him the delivery would be delayed due to weather. Jack had flown down with another pilot, Lieutenant John Wade from Baltimore, Maryland. Wade had been to Saigon several times and knew the city pretty well. Wade came up with an idea. "Hey, Warner, whaddaya think of picking up some seafood and taking it back with us to Da Nang? I bet old Patroni would like that. He might even be nice to us for a change."

"That's one of your better ideas, Lieutenant Wade. Let's go shopping." Wade and Warner grabbed a jeep and a driver to go into town. They didn't really need a driver, but he could guard the jeep and make sure all the parts were still on it when the boys came back. Too many times, servicemen returned to their parked jeeps only to find them stripped and up on wooden blocks, or just simply gone. Explaining this to the major at the motor pool wouldn't be pleasant. The paperwork would be even worse.

The WW boys returned to the Saigon base with 25 pounds of giant shrimp and 20 pounds of live lobsters. Fighter jets don't have compartments for luggage or cargo, so they had to improvise. They took a dummy bomb casing and opened it so they could shake out the sand inside. Then they stuffed all the lobsters and shrimp inside, along with some ice they got from the base kitchen, and attached it to a bomb mount on the wing of Jack's plane. It was either that or put all the seafood on their laps.

When they showed up in Da Nang with two new fighters and all that fresh seafood, the men greeted them like rock stars. Wade reached into his duffle bag and produced five cans of famous Old Bay Seafood Seasoning. "This is what we use back home. I knew this would come in handy someday," he said.

Patroni found some fresh dill growing behind the hangar building. Then, he liberated five pounds of real butter and a bag of fresh lemons from the general's mess. The mess sergeant and his staff enjoyed two bottles of Jack Daniel's that night in return.

VD

While Jack was overseas in SVN, he worked hard, followed orders, and risked his life on many fighter sorties over NVN. When the pilots got leave, they'd usually head into town to see what kind of trouble they could find. There were many places that offered it to them. Almost every corner had a bar with girls hanging out who would be friendly by the hour. There were also lots of electronics stores, cafés, a few golf courses, and some movie theaters. It was fun to watch an American movie with Vietnamese voice tracks. The soldiers loved watching *Beach Blanket Bingo* with Frankie Valle and Annette Funicello speaking Vietnamese.

One Saturday night, Jack and his friends hit a bar and worked out their right elbow for most of the night. Jack was hanging out with a bar girl who was getting friendlier by the hour. Warner didn't know that they got paid according to how much a soldier drank. This girl must have made a fortune that night, because Warner was getting completely hammered. Pretty soon, they were doing the horizontal mambo between the sheets. Jack's memory of the evening was hazy at best, and he couldn't remember how he made it back to the base.

Everything seemed okay for a few days, until Jack came down with the typical symptoms of VD and headed to sick bay. For years, every soldier was forced to watch those ancient Army training films. They had titles like *Women of Shame*, *Don't Be Foolish*, and *Nothing but Regret*. The medical symptoms still haven't changed since they made those old films.

When he arrived at sick bay, he saw the doctor, who examined the "old meatus," as he put it. The doctor referred him to a male nurse for treatment. When Jack got in line, there was a huge, black marine in front of him. This guy looked like a Rams linebacker. The nurse gave him a canned speech that he probably told to every soldier. "The whole penicillin dose is too much of a shock to the body to receive all at once. It will be given in two parts, half today and you will have to return for the second half tomorrow."

The big, black marine looked at this wimpy male nurse and said, "Listen, Pal, I got things to do and places to go. Just give me the whole fuckin' thing right now. I'm pretty damn sure I can handle it. I *am* a marine, in case you didn't notice."

"You're the boss," answered the nurse as he filled the syringe. He swabbed the soldier's butt with alcohol, inserted the needle, and down went the plunger. The soldier picked up his pants and zipped up. He put on his hat and took exactly two steps before he fell over forward like a falling redwood tree. He landed face-first, right on the hospital floor.

Jack was astounded. He heard the nurse talking to himself. "I warned him. It happens every time," said the nurse with a smile on his face. "*NEXT!*"

"Two shots are just fine with me, sir," said Jack as he gazed down at the unconscious marine on the floor.

MacGyver, At Last

Jack Warner got sick and tired of hearing about pilots shot down in North Vietnam beyond the reach of U.S. rescue helicopters. Most of the NVN prisoners of war were downed pilots. The most famous was Lieutenant Commander John McCain, who endured 5 ½ years of cruelty, far beyond what most people could ever imagine. He later became Senator John McCain and ran for president in 2008.

One rainy afternoon, Jack was enjoying a beer with Patroni and heard about another pilot shot down. He said, "What they need for long-distance SARs (search and rescues) is a rescue airplane built like the bush plane I flew in Alaska." He submitted his idea through the proper Air Force channels but got no response.

Patroni wasn't surprised. He dragged Jack out of the hangar one day to show him a small plane sitting behind the hangar, covered in dust. It was a Cessna T-41C Trainer. It was designed for short takeoffs and landings, so it would be perfect for Warner's purposes. He and Patroni got it running and made plans to customize it for some special duty.

While on leave in Tokyo, Warner was invited to play golf with some fellow pilots at Yokota Golf Course. The pilots were waiting for their tee time, which seemed to be taking forever. Just as they got to the head of the line, General Adam Hastings showed up with a colonel, a major, and a fat corporal. Clarence, the fat corporal with a puffy red face and glasses, was Hastings' wife's nephew. You can guess the rest of the story. The general's party jumped the line and cut in front of Warner's group. In addition to that, they played like crap. And slow crap, to boot. Warner's group had to wait at every hole for them to move on ahead. Normally, a faster group would respectfully ask to "play through" and go ahead. But who would do that to a general and a colonel?

Jack's caddy, Masaki, knew them well. "They come here all the time and they don't tip worth a damn," Masaki told Jack all about them. "General Hastings even has his own personal golf cart. Nobody else can use it."

Jack was studying the general's golf cart. He noticed the big, cushy tires, in particular. "Hey, Masaki, where do they keep the carts at night?"

"They plug them in to recharge in that lot behind the clubhouse. They're locked up behind that chained driveway."

"Masaki, my friend, how'd you like to make an easy $50 tonight?"

"If we're gonna fuck with General Hastings, I'll do it for 20."

Later that night, Warner and Masaki got some tools and stole the front and rear axle assemblies, including the wheels and tires, from General Hastings' golf cart and brought them back to Da Nang, where he and Patroni added them to some suspension parts he found bolted to an unattended Jeep. He and Patroni designed the whole thing so the Cessna Trainer could land in rough terrain like dirt fields or muddy roads.

Patroni heard about a Beechcraft back in Texas at Randolph Air Base that had been damaged in the tail and fuselage, but the engine was fine. He arranged for one of his mechanic buddies to pull the engine and ship it to him in Da Nang. They replaced the 210-horsepower engine with the Beechcraft turbo-charged engine that gave it extra power for even shorter takeoffs. This Cessna Trainer was like a hot rod in the sky. Patroni also rigged a sliding side door to allow for easy cargo loading and for men to jump in quickly.

Jack figured that he would do his own SARs, going and getting downed pilots. He didn't worry about orders. Jack just *had* to do something about his pilot friends ejecting from crippled fighter jets into NVN with no hope of rescue. Patroni asked him, "So how are you going to do these rescues?"

"I'm going to fly to the pilot's LKL (last known location) and circle a few times, looking for him. If I can find him, I'll see if there's a road or a field nearby to set down on. In a perfect world, he'll come running, and I'll take off and head back here."

"GFL, Jack-boy," said Lou.

"What's GFL?" asked Jack.

"Good Fucking Luck"

Lou had an idea to help hide the plane. Patroni painted the plane flat black to avoid detection. There were no Air Force insignias or numbers on it, either. This was great for avoiding the enemy, but Warner ran the risk that he might get shot by his own people — "friendly fire," they called it. Warner had an idea for putting little lights on the sides and bottom of the fuselage in the shape of a U.S. Air Force insignia. That way, he could turn them off when approaching enemy territory and back on when he was back over friendly skies. Patroni worked out a way to do it with perfect results.

Jack's buddy in the air base radio shack tipped him off about the next pilot that went down, 30 miles north of Da Nang. It was too far for a helo SAR. The Air Force Navigation Center assembled the necessary maps and gave him all the intel available to help him find the pilot.

He took off at 4:30 a.m., using only the moonlight, the plane's compass, and his maps for navigation. Warner was on the scene before 5 a.m., when the sun was barely peeking through the darkness, lighting the area. The downed pilot heard Jack's plane from his hiding place in some thick brush next to a dirt road. When Jack thought he was in the right place, he flashed the Air Force insignia lights on and off a few times. "I hope this guy sees them," wished Jack.

The pilot saw the plane but couldn't identify it. Was it an American plane? His heart sped up when he saw the insignia lights flash. The pilot blinked his flashlight on and off several times until he saw the plane's wings dip several times in answer to his signal. Jack only had a few moments to identify a place to land and take off again. This was insane. He could barely see any details of the dirt road. Any large rocks, tree branches, or other obstacles would cause the plane to crash and kill anybody on board.

Providence was smiling on Jack Warner that early dawn morning. He managed a bumpy landing and spun the plane around, getting in position for a takeoff. In just a few seconds, Warner and his grateful rescued pilot were heading home. He was surprised to later learn that the pilot he saved was the son of the United States Secretary of Defense, James Schlesinger.

Jack's in Trouble

A month after his son was rescued, James Schlesinger toured South Vietnam on a fact-finding mission. He told the president, "You can only read so many reports in Washington; I need to see things for myself and talk to the men in person." On his way home, he stopped in Da Nang to look up Jack Warner. For security reasons, he arrived unannounced. It was easier and safer that way.

Jack was relaxing in the pilot's lounge, laid out in a recliner chair with his nose buried in a *Mad Magazine* and drinking a Coke.

"Atten-hut!"

Jack launched himself out of the chair into attention. The soda and magazine went flying. He was flabbergasted to see the Secretary of Defense, James Schlesinger, standing in front of him, flanked by Colonel Devon Preston and Major Lawrence Howes.

Howes made the introductions. "Sir, this is Captain Warner. He's the pilot who stole a plane and then made an unauthorized flight into enemy airspace to rescue your son."

Schlesinger paused a minute and then finally spoke. "Son, do you know how many Air Force regulations you broke in doing such a dangerous maneuver?"

"No, sir. I just wanted to rescue the pilot. I didn't know he was your son, sir. I'm sorry if I broke some rules, sir."

"Well, I'm afraid you're going to face the consequences. Why don't we start off with me giving you membership in the Air Force's elite N.F.O.D. Club? That's 'No Fear of Death.' That's not all. Let's have dinner tonight at the Officer's Club. And, I'm afraid I can't let you fly for a while; let's say for one week."

"Why is that, sir?"

"Because you're going to be on leave in Tokyo. I'm punishing you with several grueling days of golf and massages from Japanese girls who will show you no mercy. It's all paid for, on me. Do you think you can handle that punishment, Captain?"

"Yes, sir!" exclaimed Jack with a toothpaste-commercial smile on his face.

The news media got wind of the story and published it across the country. It even made the news in Alaska, where Ben and ML heard about it. After that, even though he acted without any permission, he could do no wrong in the public's eye. The Air Force brass was powerless to discipline him. His successful results made everyone look good.

Patroni's maintenance crew kept Jack's rescue plane in top shape, fueled and ready to go at a moment's notice. Patroni scrounged parts anywhere he could find them. Patroni seemed to know the quartermasters in every branch of the service and kept them happy. He kept several cases of Johnny Walker Black and Jack Daniel's handy for thank-you gifts when somebody tipped him off to supplies he might need. If something was missing, chances were Patroni had it, knew about it, or had just traded it for something for one of his planes.

Patroni was busiest during a Bob Hope show or while air raid sirens were screaming and people were taking cover. Jack always thought it was odd how Patroni's 6x6 cargo truck always seemed to be speeding by during an air raid. And it was never hit by a bomb. Warner had a personal theory that Patroni slipped a bottle of Black Label to the air raid siren corporal whenever he needed to swipe something good. Patroni had a framed piece of art over his desk. Inside the frame was a ribbon with his motto in Latin: "Iacet in chaos occasionem" — "In chaos lies opportunity."

Take Two

Warner figured he got lucky with his first rescue. That pilot was hiding right next to a dirt road, large enough for him to land and take off. Jack figured the chances of that happening again were slim to none. And "Slim was out to lunch," as they used to say at the Air Force Academy.

Patroni and Jack Warner guessed that many pilots would be shot down in areas where there was no place to land, such as rice paddies or rough and rocky areas. Jack wished that rice paddies were longer and had more water so he could use pontoons like in Alaska.

Jack and Patroni put their heads together and filled up lots of scratch paper with plans of airplane modifications to make Jack's rescue ideas into reality. Jack finally had what he thought was a workable idea. "We install a winch in my rescue plane with a spool of nylon rope, plus a grappling hook so we can grab a pilot from the ground. Then, we take a 50-foot piece of nylon tubular webbing and make a long, Y-shaped loop on one end. The other end gets attached to a mountain climbing carabineer and a body harness for the downed pilot.

"The pilot would take the Y-shaped end and find some way to rig it so it would be at least 10 feet off the ground. Tree branches, fence posts, or wooden poles would all do the trick. This would leave the Y-shaped loop up in the air, with the pilot connected to the other end of the nylon webbing."

Patroni interrupted, "I haven't heard the rest of your idea, and already I'm glad I never learned to fly."

"I'll fly slowly; say 80 knots, just above the stall speed of the aircraft, about 25 feet above the ground. The winch hook will grab the Y end of the nylon cord and jerk the pilot up off the ground and into the air. The nylon rope and webbing will stretch and that will lessen the force against the pilot so it won't break him in two."

They decided to rig up a test flight for practice. At the far end of an unused runway, they rigged the nylon loop attached to some sandbags. Warner brought Patroni along on the test flight to guide the plane's winch hook and catch the loop. He worked the winch to crank in the 200 pounds of sandbags that were attached to it. "Hey, Boss. It works!"

"Let's give it a try for real. Patroni, how'd you like to volunteer to be the pilot on the rope?"

"With all due respect, sir, no fuckin' way. They don't pay me enough."

Jack couldn't find any volunteers for his scheme and decided he'd have to wait for a more motivated subject, like a real downed pilot that would be facing an NVN prison.

Jack tried to imagine the exact procedure of catching and retrieving a pilot. After spotting the pilot, he would have to fly over his location and Patroni would have to throw out the duffle bag containing the nylon webbing, the pilot's harness, a flashlight wrapped in lots of padding and directions to tell the pilot what to do. Of course, Jack would have to avoid hitting anything with a pilot dangling below the fast-moving airplane. As Patroni cranked the winch, the pilot would need to grab the wing strut and drag himself in through the sliding-door opening.

Nobody knew if it would work or not, but every pilot they talked to felt it was worth the gamble versus ending up in a North Vietnamese prison camp for who knows how long, facing certain torture and probable death.

It didn't take long before they had their chance to test Jack's theory. A corporal from the Army Intelligence Office tracked Jack down with news of another lost airman over the North Vietnam border. Warner found Patroni, and they went to work loading Jack's rescue plane and double-checking everything.

Bobbi & Clyde

Lieutenant Clyde Hemphill was the copilot in an F-4 Phantom fighter jet that lost a dogfight with an NVN MiG-21. The pilot didn't survive the encounter. Clyde knew that he was on his own. The shock of punching out of his jet and parachuting down into enemy territory was a scary ride indeed. He was able to finish his radio Mayday call with his map position coordinates before pulling the big red eject handle between his knees, firing the rockets and leaving the radio and his dying jet behind.

Hemphill couldn't believe the sudden blast of wind against his body. He'd undergone training for ejection, but like most pilots, had never experienced the real thing. The Martin-Baker rockets underneath propelled the seat frame pack up and out of the crippled jet. Ejecting pilots must endure severe g-forces of 12-14 g's. In some cases, this is enough to cause injuries to pilots' vertebrae. But it beats "dirt poisoning," as air crews like to joke.

The ejection rockets had a lifespan of only a few seconds, but it was enough to do their job. Hemphill saw the seat and frame fall away, and he was comforted to see the nylon parachute billow open to save his life.

As he was drifting down to earth, he thought of the plane's pilot, Chet Knox, whose call sign was "Goldy." Chet joked around the air base that his father owned Fort Knox, and all the gold belonged to him. Those jokes meant nothing to Clyde after his last memories of Knox were seeing his blood splashed all over the front cockpit of the F-4. A big chunk of his flight helmet was missing, leaving little doubt about his fatal condition.

Clyde hit the deck hard, smashing his ankle against some large rocks. He pulled the release pins for his chute harness and limped around, gathering the nylon cloud into a ball to be hidden from view. He expected Vietcong soldiers anytime. The word around the base was that NVN soldiers received a handsome bonus for each American they captured alive for interrogation. Plus, they got to keep the $100 and the Colt .45 automatic pistol carried by every American pilot.

Clyde hid the parachute, his helmet, and harness in some thick, green clumps of bamboo and buried it all the best that he could. He cut some small bamboo branches to finish the job. Stepping back and leaning on his one good leg, it looked like a pretty good job. He limped away from the hiding place as far as he could with his injury hampering his progress.

He made it a few hundred yards before collapsing from exhaustion. Clyde didn't want to go too far away from his reported position, in case the U.S. forces attempted a rescue. He hunkered down and waited, sipping sparingly on his single canteen of water.

Warner and Patroni left their air base before the sun had even peeked over the horizon. Jack had timed his flight so as to arrive at Hemphill's coordinates just as the first glimmers of light illuminated the area. The darkness also helped hide Warner's rescue plane from enemy eyes. He flew as low as he dared given the rough elevation numbers on the Air Force maps. As they closed in on the coordinates given by Hemphill before he bailed from the fatally injured jet, Patroni started to flick the Air Force insignia lights on and off.

Clyde Hemphill heard the plane and soon spotted the blinking Air Force insignia lights in the early-dawn darkness. He flashed his flashlight on and off several times until he spotted the pilot wagging his wings as an answer. Hemphill saw a black shape drop from the plane before it flew away. He limped over and found a black duffel bag sitting in the muddy water of a rice paddy. Dragging it behind him while limping back to his hiding spot took all the strength he could muster.

Clyde unpacked the equipment, found the flashlight, and started reading the directions. It was slow reading while he shielded the light from the flashlight so he wouldn't give away his position. He finished reading the instructions for a second time and paused to soak up the new knowledge. "Who the hell thought up this idea? This is INSANE."

After a few more minutes debating the merits of the pickup plan with himself, he came to the inevitable conclusion – "Why not?" He had heard rumors of barbaric treatment by the NVN prison staff. This pickup plan seemed to be his only hope.

Clyde Hemphill sorted out the straps and hardware parts. Using a small dead tree branch to lift the nylon, he strung up the pickup nylon tubular webbing between two small trees about 10 feet up in the air. Just about the time he clicked the carabiners into the webbing, he heard Jack Warner's plane returning.

Hemphill flashed his light on and off to guide Patroni's grappling hook into the suspended horizontal strap. Patroni missed him on the first pass and again on the second. He came even lower and slower, then hooked him on the third pass. He and Jack Warner felt the instant load on the plane's fuselage. As Jack struggled to gain some altitude, Patroni started to wind in the nylon rope and webbing. Everything was going fine but then – nothing, nada, zip, no strain the on line, no nothing. Patroni finished winding in the nylon only to see a shredded end of the nylon rope. Hemphill was gone. Warner turned the plane back to look for him, but by that time, enemy gun strafing was surrounding Warner and Patroni. Warner was a few hundred feet in the air when Hemphill was lost, so there was no chance he could have survived the fall.

Patroni looked at Warner with a stupefied look on his face. All they could do was return to base and debate what went wrong. Did the load on the rope cause it to fail? Did they hit something with the pilot dangling from the plane? They would never know for sure.

Jack Warner gave up on rescues for several weeks. He and Patroni examined what they had done and how they could have lost a man on their second rescue. Depression set in with Jack. His sense of humor was dimmed. His spark was gone until one day at mail call.

Jack received a letter from Bobbi Hemphill, Lieutenant Clyde Hemphill's widow. The main thrust of the message thanked him for attempting to rescue her husband. "I heard that you and another man risked your lives to try to rescue my Clyde. And neither of you knew Clyde or were even in the same flying group. I want to thank you for trying. We hear terrible things of the North Vietnamese prison camp torture. If Clyde could thank you himself, I know he would."

Warner showed the letter to Patroni and all the guys on his maintenance team. It made everyone feel a little better. They taped it up on the wall over the coffee machine. A week later, Patroni walked into Jack Warner's barracks with a very skinny soldier in an Air Force uniform. The man couldn't have weighed more than a hundred pounds. This guy looked like death warmed over. "Jack, I have somebody here who wants to meet you. This is Lieutenant Ray Stipe. I just picked him up from the base hospital. He's shipping out tomorrow to go home. You really need to hear his story before he leaves."

Jack offered Ray Stipe a chair and a cup of coffee. When Ray reached out to take the coffee cup, Jack noticed scars on both of his wrists. His arms seemed like toothpicks, swimming in the shirtsleeves of his uniform. Stipe's hands trembled while he slowly added sugar and cream to his coffee. His voice cracked as he started to speak.

"Lieutenant Warner, thank you for seeing me. Sergeant Patroni was kind enough to bring me over here after he heard about what I've been through."

Warner couldn't imagine what was about to be revealed by this skinny young airman.

"I apologize for my appearance. I was just rescued after escaping from a North Vietnamese prison camp. I spent the last 14 months in that hell hole. I was in solitary confinement the whole time. They tortured me several times a week."

Ray's voice broke and he couldn't talk. Warner gave him a sincere hug and Patroni urged him to continue. After a few minutes, Stipe started again telling his story.

"They connected battery jumper cables from a car battery and an ignition coil to my testicles. Every time I didn't answer their questions, they gave me a shock. I made up information to tell them, but it didn't always work. They would compare what I told them with what other U.S. soldiers told them. If it didn't line up, they would shock me anyway."

"I was hung by my wrists tied behind me. Both of my wrists broke from my weight hanging from them. Neither of them healed correctly, so I have only limited use of my arms and hands."

Ray Stipe continued with the horror stories that were all too real. Both Warner and Patroni listened with tears running down their faces. "After I was rescued, I was recuperating in the hospital. The guy in the next bed worked for Sergeant Patroni. He had fallen off a ladder and had a broken leg. We talked a lot about what I'd been through. He told me about fixing up Lieutenant Warner's plane for pilot rescues. I heard you rescued one pilot in your little plane but the next time you tried, that pilot didn't make it. He told me that you had stopped your rescues.

"Lieutenant Warner, I don't know the details of what went wrong, but I'm here today to beg you to not give up. Don't give up your rescues. I don't care if nine guys get killed and only one is saved. *Please, please, please* keep going. There's no way I can make you understand the fucking hell U.S. prisoners have to endure.

"I'm one of the lucky ones who get to go home to see my family. I wish you could see the mass grave that's growing larger up there in the jungle. They force us to toss our friend's bodies on the pile and cover them with dirt. Please do what you can to keep it from getting any bigger."

With that, Ray Stipe thanked Jack Warner and Lou Patroni for their time and left.

Stunned would be an understatement for their reaction. "I guess we need to go back to work, Boss," murmured Patroni.

Bungee Rescue

A week later, Jack was at an Air Force cargo hangar when the ground crew was loading pallets of equipment into a de Havilland C-7 Caribou cargo plane. Each pallet was topped with a pile of bungee cords and a bundle of parachutes. When the pilot needed to drop the equipment, the bundle of parachutes was thrown out of the rear cargo door. The wind would open the chutes and drag the heavy load out the door. The chutes were connected with thick bungee cords instead of ropes, which would have just snapped from the sudden load placed on them. The bungees evened out the stress from the instant parachute load.

Warner picked up some of the bungee cord and the idea light bulb came on. "Can I get some of this?" he asked Shorty, the ground crew chief.

Shorty turned to him and answered, "Sure, how much do you want?"

Jack said, "How about 150 feet and a box of those metal crimping bands you use to connect two ends together? Oh, and I'll need a pair of crimping pliers, too."

"10-4, sir," replied Shorty. "Would right now be too soon?"

Back in Patroni's hangar workshop, the men went to work examining the bungee cords.

The thick cargo bungees were made up of many strands of smaller bungees, similar to steel cables. If they used the whole thing, the light weight of one pilot wouldn't be enough to stretch the bungee and properly cushion the force upon the rescued pilot.

Warner and Patroni took the thick bungee cords and unbraided them to use just a few for a couple of hundred pounds of pilot weight.

They didn't have to wait long to put the new and improved rescue system to work.

Their first bungee-rescue attempt pilot was Lieutenant Tom McLaughlin from Glendale, California. His call sign was "Fireman," since that's what he did before joining the Air Force. While on air patrol, he mixed it up with a MiG-21 fighter and got into a dogfight. His jet lost hydraulics and went down. McLaughlin managed to radio his position before pulling the ejection seat handle and punching out of his damaged plane. He parachuted to safety and landed in a rice paddy, then buried his chute in the mud.

Tom looked all around and saw nothing but green rice paddies in every direction. There were a few small trees and bushes, but that was it, not much cover to hide in. He covered his flight suit in the wet mud to camouflage himself. "I look like the 'Mud Man of Da Nang,'" he laughed to himself. He hid in the bushes at the base of the trees and tried to stay out of sight while he prayed for rescue.

McLaughlin had his walkie-talkie and was listening but not transmitting. He was afraid of the Vietcong finding him if they got a fix on his position. Just as the sun was fading from the sky, he heard a voice from heaven.

"Fireman, Fireman, do you copy?" It was Jack Warner. McLaughlin managed to guide him with his flashlight until Patroni spotted him, which wasn't easy, since he was covered in mud. Warner made a low pass while Patroni dropped the duffle bag of equipment, which landed a hundred feet away from the downed pilot. Jack flew off so as not to attract any additional attention. The pilot needed time to read the directions and rig the nylon cord and harness. Jack stayed in the area, a few minutes away, ready to come in and pick up his package.

A North Vietnamese radio scanner truck heard the first exchange between the American pilots. They managed to triangulate the downed pilot's general location from the radio traffic. A squad of soldiers was quickly dispatched to investigate.

Tom McLaughlin followed the directions. He laid out the cord and found two trees about 15 feet apart. They weren't very tall, but they had some small branches 10 or 15 feet off the deck. After throwing the cord into the tree branches so it was at least 10 feet off the ground and stepping into the harness, he was ready. He radioed Warner and

Patroni to come and get him. That transmission was also picked up by the scanner truck, which fixed his exact position.

It was almost dark when McLaughlin saw Warner moving toward him, just skimming above the rice paddies. He heard truck motor noises from behind while he flashed his light at Warner. He turned around and saw two open trucks full of NVN soldiers speeding in his direction. They got within a hundred yards of him when he felt a huge jerk, and instantly he was airborne, going 80 mph.

McLaughlin was an experienced aircraft carrier pilot and was used to the steam-powered catapults that launched jet fighters into the air. On the opposite end of the spectrum were the steel arresting cables that caught the plane's tail hook when landing on the carrier. He had never felt such acceleration and deceleration on his body as when flying on and off a carrier at sea. But, he was securely belted into an ergonomically designed seat in a jet. His whole body was well supported to absorb the shock involved.

But this bungee rescue was very different – no seats and no belts. All he had was his muddy flight suit, wearing the body harness. He left his helmet behind so it wouldn't be an added load on his neck. On one hand, he was scared shitless, but on the other, it was the most exciting thing he had ever felt. "Disneyland would love this," he thought. "Talk about an E-ticket ride." McLaughlin rated this rescue a "pucker factor" of 10+.

He made it into the plane and kissed Patroni and Warner on the cheek for saving his life. Once back at the base, the pilot insisted on buying them both a steak and a beer. Warner asked McLaughlin what it felt like to be hooked like a bluefin tuna.

McLaughlin's eyes got wet with tears. All he could say was, "I'm gonna get to see my wife and my daughter again. Without you characters, that probably wouldn't happen. You gave me back my family. And for that, I thank you. I will be forever in your debt. If you ever want somebody shot down or blown up, give me a call." They all laughed.

Jack said, "I'll keep that in mind for the future. Ya never know." More laughter ensued.

It was simply amazing that a pilot survived the rescue despite minimal planning, zero product testing, and even less permission from the Air Force brass to conduct such a dangerous exercise. But who can argue with success? Tom McLaughlin was grateful to be alive.

Jack wrote a letter to Clyde Hemphill's widow, thanking her for her encouragement to keep going with his rescue attempts. He told her of the first successful rescue of Tom McLaughlin, who was so happy he could see his family again.

When Jack was flying rescue missions after that, he thought about McLaughlin and the other pilots. Jack started a collage of pictures showing the pilots he had rescued. They gave him motivation to keep going.

After Tom left Vietnam, he and Jack stayed in touch. Tom sent pictures of his wife and daughter, Emily, with a note: "You saved me for them, so I wanted to share them with you." All of it went up on the collage picture board.

Now Jack Needs Jack

Jack's unit received orders to escort a squadron of B-52s to drop their bomb payloads over Hanoi. Six planes called "playmates" from Jack's unit were scheduled to fly that day. Warner was flying with copilot Second Lieutenant Skeeter Jackson from Louisiana. It was no surprise that his pilot call sign was "Skeeter." Jack's call sign was "Alaska," because it reminded him of home. Warner and Skeeter suited up and went out on the tarmac to perform the pre-flight check of their F-4 Phantom.

After takeoff, the fighter group flew in formation to the rally point, where it met up with a squadron of B-52s. Jack admired the sleek, silver planes leaving their parallel white contrails against the blue sky with white, puffy clouds in the background. "Skeeter, I wish my dad was here to see this. He'd love it. This plane is a little zippier than the de Havilland Beaver bush plane that I grew up flying with him."

"I expect so, sir," answered Skeeter. "I bet your momma and daddy are pretty proud of you," he added.

The bombing run was right on target with the ordnance falling on the airport and shipping-yard targets near Hanoi. "Hey, Skeeter, I can't believe how those bombers can drop their bombs miles up in the air with such deadly accuracy. Remind me not to piss off those boys, will ya?"

"10-4, sir," replied Skeeter.

As they made their 180-degree turn to return to base, Jack saw the radar warning light flashing and the buzzer started screaming. "Somebody's tracking us! Let's get the hell outta here!"

The North Vietnamese Air Force flew Russian-made supersonic MiG-21s. They were a deadly threat to American flyers. The MiG-21 tactics became so effective that by late 1966, an operation was mounted specifically to deal with the MiG-21 threat. Led by Colonel Robin Olds on 2 January, 1967, "Operation Bolo" lured MiG-21s into the air, thinking they were intercepting an F-105 strike group, but instead finding a sky full of missile-armed F-4 Phantoms set for aerial combat. The result was a loss of almost half the inventory of MiG-21 interceptors, with zero U.S. losses or injuries. The NVAF stood down for rebuilding after this setback.

The radar tracking lock on Jack's fighter came from one of those menacing MiG-21s. Before he could take evasive action, the other pilot came up behind him, firing his GSh-23 cannon. The shell made a beeline right toward their fighter and blew off the horizontal tail section. Skeeter felt the explosion from the rear of the plane. Jack started to lose control.

"Hey, Alaska, I think we need to take the express elevator down before this plane blows up." Jack was thinking exactly the same thing. He and Skeeter tried to maintain some control using the wing's trim tabs, flaps, rudder, and ailerons, but it was hopeless.

Jack barked, "Mayday, Mayday, Mayday," along with his ID code and position into his plane's radio. "I hope that transmitted," thought Jack.

"Time to go, Boss!" screamed Skeeter.

"10-4, Skeeter. It's time for the nylon letdown. You go first, and I'm right behind you," replied Warner.

The "nylon letdown" is a pilot term for parachuting out of a plane. To eject from a fighter jet, the pilot reaches down between his knees and grabs a big, red "eject" handle and pulls with all his might. This action fires the exploding bolts for the clear Lexan canopy above their heads. It blows away and then two small rockets ignite, powering the pilot's seat module up and clear from the speeding jet. The seat and ejection framework fall away from the pilot, whose parachute is automatically deployed. Then, he takes what they call the "silk ride" all the way down to the deck or good, old terra firma. Unfortunately, in the early days, many pilots broke one or both legs ejecting from their aircraft. This could spell disaster or death for an unlucky pilot.

Besides the parachute, each pilot landed with a small supply pack containing a local map, flashlight, a compass, a knife, a 45-caliber automatic pistol, some food bars, $100 in American money, and two quarts of water. The money is to bribe locals to hide the pilot or help him back to U.S. forces.

As they ejected from the dying jet, Alaska and Skeeter entered some thick cloud cover. Since WWI, some enemy pilots strafed pilots in parachutes. Most pilots, on both sides, consider such behavior contemptible. Usually, there is a degree of respect toward your foe not to shoot an unarmed pilot drifting down under a parachute.

Alaska and Skeeter hit the ground without injury. It was raining, and the ground was muddy. They gathered their chutes and made a beeline for some nearby trees. Because they parachuted inside the clouds and landed in the rain, most North Vietnamese were inside and not looking up toward the sky. Jack and Skeeter buried their parachutes under some branches and put dirt and rocks on top to hide them. They made a little hidden shelter with more branches layered on top of them for camouflage. "Hell of a day, eh, Boss?" understated Skeeter.

"You got it. Well, I guess we're both members of the Martin-Baker Fan Club."

"What's that, sir?"

"Well, Skeeter, when you eject from a plane, you're a member of the Martin-Baker Fan Club. They manufacture our ejection seats. I heard that the company keeps an official list of the members."

"I look forward to the class reunions, sir," Skeeter said, laughing.

Their Mayday call was heard by the Da Nang Air Force Base. One of the corporals knew who "Alaska" was and jumped in a Jeep and found Patroni. He told him that Warner and his copilot were down over the North Vietnamese border. Patroni sat down to think while the Corporal unfolded a map and laid out the coordinates that Warner had radioed. Patroni was a great mechanic, but no pilot. Who could he get to rescue him?

He instantly thought of Tom McLaughlin, the first pilot Jack rescued with a bungee cord. He called the Air Force assignment desk in Saigon. They told him that Lieutenant McLaughlin was stationed at the Air Force base in Phu Cat, which was less than an hour away by chopper. Patroni called McLaughlin and told him the situation. Before Patroni could even ask him for help, McLaughlin blurted out, "Get your ass moving, Patroni. Get that flying deathtrap of Warner's fueled up and ready to go. I'll be there in 45 minutes. And take a shower, you smelly bastard, 'cuz you're going with me."

Patroni smiled as wide as a white picket fence. He started to light a cigar, but realized he didn't have time to smoke it. He scrambled his mechanics to get Jack's rescue plane ready for takeoff while he went and took a shower for McLaughlin's benefit. After all, he wanted to look good if he was going to save his best friend's life.

Patroni and McLaughlin soon took off into the inky black sky. It had been years since McLaughlin had flown such a small, propeller-driven aircraft, so his flying was a little erratic. Tom stayed just above the tree tops to avoid ground radar. Once they crossed the North Vietnamese border, beads of sweat appeared on both of their foreheads. In a few more minutes, they closed in on the coordinates given out by Jack just before he ejected.

Jack heard a familiar engine sound from the dark sky. "Quick, Skeeter, take your flashlight and run down that road about 200 yards and flash your light on and off, pointed up to the sky. I'll do the same up the other way. I think we're about to have visitors."

Patroni spotted the flashing lights and pointed them out to McLaughlin, who said, "Are you sure I can land this plane on that tiny dirt road? It's so short." McLaughlin didn't have the bush pilot experience that Warner did. McLaughlin managed to make a bumpy but successful landing, using every inch of suspension travel that Patroni had built into the landing gear. Skeeter sprinted toward the little plane as soon as it passed over his head. Jack got there about the same time. "Well, hellooo, stranger," he said to Tom McLaughlin, surprised as hell to see him again. "Jump in the back, Lieutenant. I'll fly us out of here."

Gunfire rang out of the darkness. Three mortars rained down near the plane. Skeeter yelled out, "Let's make like a shepherd and get the flock outta here!"

Tom couldn't believe that Jack got the plane off the ground in such a short distance. They headed southeast toward friendly territory. Skeeter told Tom how they were shot down and hid in the brush, hoping for a rescue. Patroni told Skeeter and Jack how he heard about it and thought of Tom McLaughlin to fly Jack's plane. Skeeter yelled out, "I'm glad you did, buddy! I'm buying the drinks when we get home."

Bungee Screw Up

Jack and Patroni were enjoying a lull in combat assignments, and Lou's mechanics had organized a softball team. They were working on the lineup for a game against the marine motor pool guys.

"Patroni, were you able to fix that broken spike on my baseball shoe?" Jack asked.

"Yeah, all done. I put your shoes back in your equipment bag. It's in your little plane, ready for game day tomorrow."

"Thanks, I owe ya."

"Hey, Patroni, look what I made," shouted Herman Homer, his chief mechanic. Herman had made a BBQ out of an old 55-gallon oil drum that he had cut in half. He'd also made an expanded metal grill to fit on top. "Let's break this bad boy in. Whaddya say? Where can we get our hands on some steaks?"

"That is an excellent idea, Herman my boy, worthy of immediate action," Patroni agreed.

The PA system barked, "Captain Warner, please report to the control tower."

Jack yelled as he ran, "Sounds like bad news! I don't think that BBQ is going to get hot today." Jack sprinted up the tower stairs, two at a time, to see what was up. Major Howes was waiting for him in the control tower.

"Warner, do you feel like taking that flying packing crate of yours to go get my pilot back?" Howes asked. "He radioed his position just before bailing out. We plotted it on the map, and it seems like he's in a farm area just South of Phu Dong. From what we know, it's a rice farming area. I don't know if you can land and take off from anywhere."

"If we can't land, we can use my bungee system," Jack replied. "It worked great the last time."

"Okay, Warner, give it a try. Do me a favor and don't screw this up. You know how I hate paperwork." Jack ran back to grab Patroni, who was busy screwing legs onto Herman's BBQ.

"You want to go for a ride and pick up Johnny Gleason? He got himself shot down about 20 miles over the NVN border. We might have to use the bungee cord. Is everything ready to go?"

"Gleason? You got it. That guy owes me 50 bucks. We *gotta* get him. The bungee system is all laid out in the duffle bag. Your plane's full of fuel. I guess lunch can wait."

Patroni turned and hollered at his mechanics, "Hey, you guys. Get the captain's rescue plane turned around so he can go make a pickup."

Jack flew low just over the treetops to avoid radar from both the U.S. and the NVN. Jack was flying with one hand while trying to read the map. Patroni checked the rescue duffle bag and had it ready to throw out.

"Make sure you throw down the rescue bag and not my baseball equipment bag!" yelled Jack.

"Real funny, buddy," answered Patroni. When Jack wasn't looking, he double-checked to make certain he really did have the right bag.

They approached the area where they expected to see Gleason. Major Howes was right; rice paddies, full of water, were everywhere. "No place to land. We gotta use the bungee," Jack barked.

Patroni spotted Gleason first. "Hey, Jack, there he is, flashing his signal mirror at us."

"Okay, Lou. I'll come in low, get ready to throw the bag." Jack came in low, like a crop duster, maybe 20 feet off the deck. Patroni gave the duffle a heave-ho, and they flew off so as not to pinpoint the pilot any more than they had already.

While they flew back to friendly territory, Gleason opened the duffle and followed the directions. He laid out the nylon cord and body harness. He found a tall pole that the rice farmers used to hold lanterns. It even had a branch making a yoke to hold one side of the nylon Y cord. Then, Gleason found a small tree nearby that he used to hold up the other side of the Y. He got into the body harness, hooked it to the tail end of the cord, and double-checked the connections. The time it took for the plane to return seemed like an eternity.

A while later, Jack yelled out, "I hope he's ready, 'cuz here I come!"

Patroni called to Jack, "There's the mirror signal. Let's go catch us a fish."

Jack flew close to the ground. The big hook trailed the small plane at just the right altitude. The wind blowing by made the hook face forward so that it could bite the nylon cord that was stretched out waiting for it. The bungee did its job, stretching and absorbing the shock of the pilot's sudden weight. This lessened the effect on his body. Jack Warner could feel the sudden load on the plane, meaning they had caught their fish. "I hope he survives this rescue," thought Jack.

Away they flew toward home, with Johnny Gleason hanging under the airplane doing 80 knots. That was the slowest Jack could fly without stalling.

"Okay, Lou, reel him in." The dangling pilot made the airplane unstable to fly and hard to control. Jack felt like he was flying drunk.

"10-4, Boss." Patroni slipped on his leather gloves and started cranking the winch. He had built it with the help of Herman Homer. A floor-mounted metal frame held the take-up spool, some simple transmission gears, and the cable guide arm that stuck out the door of the plane. The spool was big enough to hold 75 feet of steel cable and bungee cord with a safety hook on the end that would catch the pilot's nylon webbing cord and hold it.

The spool shaft was attached with Clevis pins. These spring pins could be pulled in order to remove the spool for maintenance. They could also be pulled to disconnect the spool and hanging cable, just in case of a life-threatening malfunction, to save the plane, pilot, and crew of one, usually Lou Patroni.

Patroni cranked as Jack flew back to the base. With only about 10 feet of cable plus the bungee cord left to go, the winch handle broke off. "Well, fuck me!" he yelled at the top of his voice.

"What's wrong?" Jack screamed. Patroni handed him the broken crank handle. "Oh, shit. This is no good."

"That's my boy," said Patroni nervously, "always understating the obvious."

"Can you fix it?" Jack bellowed.

"The handle broke right where it goes onto the crank shaft. I can't fix it up here in the plane. I need my machine shop."

Both men knew the hanging pilot was in deep shit. Jack couldn't land with the pilot hanging under the plane. The pilot would be ground up like hamburger meat by the time the plane stopped on the runway.

"Could we fly over the ocean near a Navy ship and cut him loose?" asked Patroni.

Jack answered, "Yeah, but we're going 80 mph. I think the fall would kill him."

"Okay, Jack, your turn. What's option number two?"

"There is no option number two. I think this guy's had it."

"Hold on," said Patroni. "I got an idea."

"I'm all ears, buddy. Whaddya got?"

"I got the Patroni Plan."

"So share. I can't wait to hear it."

"Here's the Patroni Plan:

Step one: This plane doesn't have autopilot, so you take this roll of duct tape and tape up the steering yoke to keep it flying pretty straight while you help me back here.

Step two: I grab the baseball bat from your equipment bag and jam it into the take-up spool spokes. You help me turn it, one half turn at a time. When we need to re-position the bat, I'll stick this hammer handle in the spokes to hold it until you move the bat into the new position. It'll take a little while, but it should work."

"I love the Patroni Plan, and I'm pretty damn sure that Gleason's gonna like the hell out of it just as soon as we haul his ass into this plane. Gimme that duct tape so I can set up the new Patroni autopilot system." Jack took the plane up to 1,000 feet so there was some margin of error for their passenger's benefit.

Patroni jammed in the baseball bat and got the hammer ready to go. Jack finished the taping job and helped Patroni move the bat. "You know, with the weight of the pilot, his boots, flight suit, cable, and bungee cord, we've got to be pulling in over 250 pounds."

"Probably so, Jack, but the long bat handle gives us some leverage, making it a little easier." Lou and Jack used the bat to rotate the spool a half turn, then one of them stuck in the hammer handle to hold their place while the other repositioned the bat for another half turn.

Poor Gleason was wondering what was going on. Even though it was a warm day, the sun was going down and the 80-mph breeze was making his wet flight suit freezing cold. "What's going on up there?" he thought. Of course, he couldn't do a damn thing about it. Finally, he noticed that the plane seemed to be getting closer. It took about 20 minutes to get the pilot up to the doorway of the plane, but it seemed like hours, especially to Gleason, whose ass was literally hanging out in the wind.

Jack had to take a few breaks to get the plane some altitude. The new duct-tape autopilot system wasn't exactly perfect. Patroni and Jack reached out and grabbed Gleason's body harness and yanked with all of their might. All three rolled over with Gleason on top of them, completely out of breath.

After a moment, Jack was able to utter the immortal words, "Lieutenant Gleason, I presume."

Patroni spoke up. "Jack, can you cut out the smart-ass remarks and go peek out the front window? Remember, there's nobody up there except a fucking roll of duct tape."

Master Sergeant Louis Vincenzo Patroni and Captain Jackson Benjamin Warner were awarded the Silver Star for that day's work. Captain Warner was now Major Warner for extreme bravery and initiative bringing credit to the Air Force. Master Sergeant Patroni was now Chief Master Sergeant Patroni.

In addition, a few weeks later, Johnny Gleason's mother sent them the biggest box of Tollhouse Chocolate Chip Cookies they had ever seen. They ate them until they were sick of chocolate. Lou and Jack shared them with everybody on the base for days.

Mrs. Warner, I Presume

One day, Charlie Gaugh, the Da Nang Control Tower chief, came running out to a plane that Lou Patroni was working on. Lou was talking to Jack while he was working. "Sir, a small transport was ferrying cargo and some new personnel for the base hospital. It got caught in a storm north of Da Nang and went down right near the North Vietnam border. Evidently, the air crew is dead, but a nurse and a medic survived the crash. She's been trying to work the radio and tell us where she is. The Army medic has a broken leg and is not much help. Our rescue helicopters are all out on runs to the west. They won't be available for a while. Can you go get them?" asked Gaugh.

"Sure," answered Warner. "Lou, can you fuel the plane and have your guys pull out the rear seat so we can put the medic with the broken leg back there? I'll go get maps and the intel."

Warner and his plane took off 20 minutes later on this double rescue. The first problem was he didn't know exactly where the plane crashed. The second was Jack didn't have any way to communicate with the nurse. She could talk on the plane's radio, but it was getting faint from a damaged battery, and Warner couldn't make out the conversation. The tower had a more powerful radio system and a quieter environment to listen to her faint broadcasts. They relayed the conversations to Warner in his plane, which complicated his progress.

Nurse Gail Richardson was trying to take care of the injured medic as best she could. Luckily, Steve Edminister, the medic, had his medical bag and a trunk of medical supplies with him. Between the two of them, Nurse Gail managed to set his leg with a splint and bandage it securely. She gave Steve a shot of morphine to ease his pain.

That kept him comfortable and sedated. The crashed plane was the only shelter available. She found a flashlight and a small saw in a tool box that was in the storage hatch. She took the saw and started cutting palm branches and brush to use for camouflaging the plane. She stacked the cut branches in a random pattern covering the wings, tail, and fuselage. Then, Gail added a second layer over the first to try to make it blend in with the hillside.

She must have done a good job, because a Vietcong patrol marched by about a hundred feet away and didn't notice them. She hunkered down next to the radio and prayed for help.

Her prayers must have been heard by someone, because Jack Warner was heading right toward her. Before the radio faded completely, she was able to describe some landmarks near the crash site. There was a dirt road, some rice paddies, and a temple with a two-story tower in the distance to the north.

The Air Base Control Tower staff guessed that the temple she described sounded like the one right above the DMZ. They gave Jack Warner directions and crossed their fingers.

Lady Luck was smiling on Jack Warner once again. Today was the Thay Pagoda Festival, a Buddhist holiday. The temple tower was lit up with hundreds of prayer candles. It was easy for Jack to spot from the air. The local villagers make an offering of food and drink for the departed and then buy a candle in memory of an ancestor and burn it in the temple tower. The music, fireworks, and loud drums made so much noise, it was almost impossible to hear Jack's plane.

Jack made a wide circle around the tower and headed back south. Gail heard an airplane engine and hoped it was a rescue party. She took a chance and flashed the light on and off several times. Warner noticed the blinking light and came in for a landing on the dirt road and prayed that it was Gail flashing the light. Gail limped up to the plane, holding Steve up with his arm around her shoulder and hobbling on one leg. With the engine idling, she helped Jack get the medic into the back of the plane and followed him inside. Warner jumped back into the pilot's seat.

Gail suddenly said, "Oh, wait, I forgot my purse." Jack looked over at her and was just about to start yelling when she started laughing, adding, "Just kidding. Let's blow this pop stand. Goose the throttle, flyboy."

Jack gave the engine full throttle and gained speed down the dark, dirt road. As soon as he could, he got airborne and climbed up into the dark sky. He glanced back at the nurse and thought, "Wow, this girl has some guts. She doesn't get rattled easily and can crack jokes in the middle of a rescue." Gail's heroic actions were attractive to Jack, proving that she wasn't some prom queen, afraid to get her hands dirty.

Jack Warner flew a few hundred feet above the ground and reached the Air Base without further incident. He turned on his Air Force insignia lights and radioed ahead so they wouldn't shoot him down. After landing, Steve and Gail couldn't thank him enough. Gail made him an offer of dinner and the best bottle of wine she could find. Jack took her up on her offer with no hesitation at all. Perhaps her auburn hair and sky blue eyes had something to do with it. It must have been a great wine, because it led to Champagne at their wedding after the war.

Fred-Ex

While in Vietnam, Warner met Fred Smith, a Marine FAC (forward air controller). They kept running into each other at the Officer's Club and were surprised at how many mutual friends they had. Smith loved hearing about Warner's latest fighter sorties and his heroic rescues. They coordinated their leaves together and became good friends.

As part of his work, Smith observed the military's logistical supply system firsthand. It was like a bank check clearinghouse. Boxes of parts, documents, and supplies were shipped to a central warehouse, where they were reloaded onto different planes or trucks to head out to their final destinations. Smith thought that the concept had possibilities for civilian life. He told Warner his idea for a civilian overnight courier service many times. Warner didn't give it much hope, thinking, "How many people need stuff that fast?"

After his years in the Marines were behind him, Smith enrolled at Yale. He wrote a term paper for a business class, outlining his idea for an overnight delivery business for documents and small packages. His paper said, "Consumers are hungry for mass-produced electronics, and their demand makes for logistical delivery problems. Necessary delivery speed can only be achieved by using air transport."

He continued, "The present air cargo system is stuck in a sea of red tape and is incapable of making fast deliveries. The air freight industry depends on cooperation between several different companies to get a shipment from origination to destination."

Smith's concept had one carrier responsible for pickup and delivery to a central sort facility. "They should run the sort facility; reload it onto another one of their planes to fly to the destination city, where the shipment would be loaded onto their truck for final delivery to the customer."

His Yale professor barely gave Smith a "C," since he didn't consider the idea feasible for the real world. "How many people need something overnight? Who would ever pay that much money for it? Not a chance," he thought.

Of course, this theory is the founding idea behind Federal Express. After receiving a large inheritance, Fred Smith founded Federal Express in the early 1970s. Smith went on to lead it to more than a billion dollars in sales, with worldwide service coverage.

The professor could not have been more wrong. Fred still has the term paper framed and hanging on the wall of his office. You can still read his "C" grade and the teacher's discouraging remarks in a red pencil.

In the early days, Federal Express marketed itself as "The freight company with 550-mph delivery trucks." However, the company began to experience financial difficulties, bleeding cash every month.

While waiting for a flight home from Chicago after being turned down for a capital infusion by General Dynamics, Smith impulsively hopped a flight to Las Vegas, where he gambled all his savings and won $27,000 playing blackjack. Those winnings enabled the cash-strapped company to meet the payroll the following Monday. The $27,000 carried them over until some other financing came through a week later.

Jack Warner admired Fred Smith for his can-do spirit and charge-ahead personality.

Adrian Cronauer

Every soldier, marine, or sailor near South Vietnam listened to the famous disc jockey, Corporal Adrian Cronauer. Patroni and Warner listened every chance they got. The mechanics always had the radio on while they were working on the planes. Everybody enjoyed Adrian's funny bits and rock music for two four-hour shows every day.

On his day off, Cronauer came to visit the Air Force personnel at the Da Nang Airfield, where Patroni and Warner were stationed. It really gave the men's morale a shot in the arm. Adrian had heard about Jack's rescues and stopped by to meet him. Adrian asked Jack if he could interview him sometime on his radio show. Jack was flattered when Adrian told him that he had never interviewed anybody in Vietnam, but Jack Warner was the first person that he thought was worth it.

They had a beer together and bullshitted about music. While they talked, Cronauer mentioned that he was having trouble getting rock 'n' roll records so far from home. Adrian said, "The Air Force will only get me music that your father hears on *Perry Como* or *Lawrence Welk*."

Jack told him, "Let me see what I can do." The next day, he mailed a check for $250 to Lieutenant Tom McLaughlin, now back home in Glendale, California. Jack thought that since Tom was his first bungee rescue, he might do Jack a favor. With the check was a letter asking Tom to get Adrian Cronauer some new records. Could he please buy every record he thought the soldiers would like and send them to Adrian?

As soon as Tom received Jack's letter, he jumped at the chance to do something for Jack and the guys back in Vietnam. Tom used to listen to Adrian Cronauer for hours every day. Tom drafted his wife to help. They took her station wagon to Zody's, a big discount store in Burbank. They grabbed a shopping cart and made a beeline for the music department. Tom and his wife started grabbing records from the Beach Boys,

Rolling Stones, Beatles, Diana Ross, all the Motown singers, the Animals, Hollies, Kinks, Hendrix, Cream, Elvis, Jan and Dean, the Rascals, the Turtles, Dylan, The Doors, and all the doo-wop artists. Then, they started on country and finished up with some jazz.

The Zody's store manager, wearing his skinny black tie, came over to politely ask why these people were buying so many 45s and LPs? "Can I help you find anything?" he asked. Tom told him his story about Vietnam, Jack rescuing him, and the favor he was doing for Adrian Cronauer and the soldiers.

The manager told him, "Well, I see you have your cart almost full of records. Why don't I get you another cart?"

Tom answered, "I think I only have enough money to pay for these."

The manager smiled and said, "We have a bunch of special records in the back that are markdowns, returns, or have water-damaged covers from a recent roof leak."

He came back with two more market baskets overflowing with records of all types. "Here ya go. I called our Zody's regional manager who said to give these to you, courtesy of Zody's." The manager met them at the register with some box boys to help load the car. Tom and his wife ended up with three more shopping carts loaded with hundreds of records.

Tom got 15 sturdy cardboard boxes, filled them, and addressed them to Cronauer in Saigon. Tom and his wife drove the records down to the Air Force base in El Segundo and turned the shipment over to the 61st Air Base wing operations officer, Colonel Dufresne. After Tom explained the destination for the boxes, the colonel promised that the boxes would be placed on the next C-9 Skytrain cargo plane headed for Saigon.

Adrian later wrote thank-you letters to Jack and Tom for their kindness. He also wanted to tell them what happened after the boxes arrived. Cronauer had just finished his afternoon show and was told that the station officer wanted to see him on the double. He figured, "Oh, God, more grief about the music that I play." He reported to the major's office but could barely get in the outer office because it was full of boxes. Cronauer should have brought an umbrella, because the shit storm hit him fast and furious.

"Cronauer! What the fuck are all these boxes clogging up my office? Why is your crap being delivered here from California of all places? I hate California! It's full of hippies and faggots. It's bad enough that I have to deal with you playing unauthorized rock music and screaming all the time on the radio, but now you fill up my office like it's your personal fuckin' warehouse! Get this shit out of here before the colonel sees it and chews my ass. You got 20 minutes, but that started 30 minutes ago. Do I make myself fairly clear?"

"*Yes*, sir! I don't know anything about these boxes, sir, but I'll make them disappear pronto, sir." Cronauer drafted a couple of the privates from the radio office to help him shuttle all the boxes into the storage room.

"Hey, Adrian, what's in all these boxes?" inquired Marko Swan, one of the privates.

"Hell if I know, Swan. Let's open them up and see." They found a knife and started opening all the boxes.

"Son-of-a-bitch, Corporal. There's hundreds of records: rock 'n' roll, oldies, country, jazz, everything," exclaimed Private Swan. "Hey, here's a note for you, Corporal."

Dear Adrian: This is a little gift from Capt. Jack Warner and me to say thank you for all the hours of entertainment you have given us. I thought you could put these records to good use. Please accept the love of the thousands of men and women in the field and on ships that enjoy you and your music every day. Keep up the good work.

Regards,
Lt. Tom McLaughlin

A couple of days later, Jack received a letter postmarked Glendale, CA. It was a short note from Tom. All it said was "Mission Accomplished, thanks again for saving my life." Also inside the envelope was his uncashed check for $250.

Jack's Last Rescue

Fred Smith worked long hours coordinating orders and deliveries of parts and supplies for the marines in Vietnam. His office window overlooked the runways used by the marine fighter planes. He longed for the chance to go on a mission. Fred was no pilot and certainly no hero. He just wanted to see what it was like.

Smith was friends with Lieutenant Chuck Reed, a fellow marine from Nine Mile Falls, Washington. Reed was better known by his pilot's call sign, "Husky." Chuck had 22 missions under his belt. Three more and he could rotate back to the States. Smith and Reed used to play poker at the Officer's Club with Air Force staffers and Army quartermasters.

During a poker game late one night, Reed had three queens, but Smith trumped him with three kings. The loss was going to leave Reed completely broke after he had lost his whole paycheck gambling. His wife was going to kill him. Smith made him an offer. "Take me up on your next mission and you can keep the whole pot."

Reed thought for a nanosecond and blurted out, "Deal!"

Reed's next flight was a bombing run to Khe Sanh. He switched his usual jet for a Douglas Skyhawk A-4 Trainer fighter jet that had a second seat in it for Smith. Fred Smith suited up in a pilot's flight suit and borrowed a helmet. He felt like Superman. As they took off, the g-forces pushed him back into the seat so hard, he could hardly raise his arms out in front of him. He didn't know how pilots could work the controls during such demanding, intense maneuvers.

The Skyhawk was capable of 600 knots and could outmaneuver most other planes in the sky at that time. One of the few things that had the potential to ruin Reed's day was a SAM (surface to air missile). And that's exactly what got him on that day over North Vietnam. The missile was actually a dud, in that it did not explode. But it did clip the tip of the Skyhawk's rear elevator trim tab. This put the plane into a soft dive but, with Chuck Reed's expert touch on the stick, he kept it from going out of control until it approached a few thousand feet above the ground, where they could safely pull their big, red ejection seat handles and punch out of the dying aircraft.

Reed and Smith were part of a large attack on Khe Sanh. The Air Force dropped tons of ordnance on NVN that day. With bombs dropping all around them, Reed wasn't looking forward to landing on NVN turf. The soldiers might shoot them, as they had done so many times in the past. These Americans probably would never see the inside of an NVN prison camp.

Prior to bailing out, Reed took time to radio a Mayday, giving the marine radio operator his map coordinates. Luckily, the plane kept gliding and crashed a few miles away from where Reed and Smith landed with their parachutes. NVN soldiers would search the crash site first. When they found no dead pilots, they would expand the search area until they eventually found the pilots, dead or alive.

Reed and Smith safely landed in a field and quickly rolled up their parachutes and made their way into the nearby jungle. They covered themselves with tree branches and dead leaves. North Vietnamese soldiers could walk right by and never see them. With their emergency food and water, the men could survive for a few days.

Back at the base, Jack Warner went into the hangar to get some coffee, but there wasn't any. After swearing about inconsiderate a-holes who drink your coffee and don't replace it, he walked over to the control tower to steal a pound from them. Jack walked in to hear the control staff talking about the latest pilot who was just shot down that morning. Warner pumped the staff members for all the info they had and took off running, looking for Patroni to warm up the rescue plane.

Patroni had just finished periodic maintenance on Warner's plane the day before. He also installed a new radio that could communicate with the pilots' walkie-talkies. Lieutenant Chuck Reed was glad he had put in fresh batteries that morning before his flight.

Warner packed some food, water, and supplies and took off. It was late in the day and would soon be dark. The moon was full that night and would give him just enough light to see the open field. Would there be ruts, rocks, stumps, logs, or a water-filled rice paddy? Who knows? He would just have to take his chances.

Warner flew low and slow in the darkening skies to the map coordinates given to him by the control tower crew. Nearing that spot, he got on his radio, barking out his call sign, "Alaska," and listening for Reed's pilot call sign, "Husky." Clearing the crest of a hill, Warner heard "Husky" loud and clear. Husky gave Alaska some quick directions on where to set down in a nearby field. Warner landed and rolled to a quick stop, the boys jumped aboard, and away they went. Warner's plane was on North Vietnam soil for just 82 seconds.

Rescuing Reed and Smith made his total number of pilot saves 21. Fred Smith and Chuck Reed bought him a ribeye steak to go with some 12-year-old Scotch that Reed had been saving for a special occasion. After dinner, Reed stood up and toasted Warner for his skill and bravery. He anointed him with the moniker "Black Jack Warner," reflecting the 21 pilots that he had saved. Revelry ensued, to say the least.

The Air Force brass heard about his latest rescue, and Warner was awarded the Air Force Cross for that little trip. He also made two friends for life with Fred Smith and Chuck Reed.

TTFN, Vietnam

Jack Warner won several other medals for his bravery during fighter sorties and pilot rescues from behind enemy lines. He was also awarded the Silver Star, the Medal of Honor, the Distinguished Flying Cross, the Bronze Star, and a Purple Heart. He was promoted to a full colonel by the war's end.

During the fall of Saigon in 1975, he "borrowed" a C-130 Hercules cargo plane and filled it with local Vietnamese citizens who had significantly assisted the Air Force during the war. The Air Force had taken some of the helpful South Vietnamese citizens but was going to leave the rest behind, but that meant that the Vietcong would have killed them and every member of their families.

Warner had some staff members start a list of South Vietnamese citizens that had helped the military over the years. This assistance came in the form of maps, road condition info, North Vietnam logistical info, language interpretation, utilities, train routes, and many other things. All this was tremendously important to the U.S. efforts.

This list of Vietnamese helpers was similar to a list of Jews in the World War II German concentration camps that were saved by Oscar Schindler. Warner's efforts certainly were not as dramatic as that, but he certainly saved hundreds of lives.

The exit scene from Saigon was complete chaos, shown in the famous newsreel footage. Vietnamese people were tossing their children into helicopters as they were taking off. Men and boys were clinging to the helicopter skids. Many fell to their deaths when they could no longer hold on.

Colonel Warner landed his C-130 Hercules cargo plane full of rescued South Vietnamese citizens in Hawaii. He was able to commandeer a bunch of Army tents and set up a tent city on some unused acreage at Hickham Field. Warner seemed to know everybody, from an aircraft line mechanic all way up the ladder to generals in Washington,

D.C. He was still in contact with his old friends, Senators Hope and Molina, now both retired.

When Colonel Jack Warner approached Lieutenant General Arnold Braswell for permission to set up this tent city, Braswell considered it for a minute and said, "Yes. People who helped us save American lives shouldn't be forgotten." Warner even worked with the U.S. Customs and Immigration Department to streamline the process for getting the refugees on the road to U.S. citizenship.

Within a short time, most of them got settled and started successful small businesses, such as fishing, fresh seafood stores, small restaurants, building maintenance, and farming. Pineapples, macadamia nuts, papayas, kiwi fruit, and exotic flowers all did well in the Hawaiian climate.

Pineapple Poker

Shortly after delivering his load of refugees from Vietnam at the end of the war, Jack retired from the Air Force. Warner stayed in Oahu for a few months, renting a small house near Hickham Field.

One Saturday night, he found himself in a high-stakes, no-limit poker game in the back of the Top Hat Bar. Most of his fellow players were local Air Force personnel, but there was a captain just in from California. Captain Tim Brockway had just been assigned to Hickham Air Force Base as a liaison to the general staff back in Washington, D.C.

Warner and Brockway had been playing for more than six hours but drinking for seven. All five players at the table had agreed to stop playing at three a.m., no matter who was winning or losing. Warner was enjoying his typical good luck, and Brockway was losing slowly. It was past their deadline, now almost four in the morning. There was more than 10 grand in the pot in the middle of the table. Brockway had a pair of black aces, a pair of black eights, plus a three, known as a "dead man's hand." This was the hand held by the famous gunfighter, Wild Bill Hickok, when he was shot in the back and killed in the days of the Wild West.

Warner had a straight – five through nine – a good hand, but certainly not a top hand in poker. Of course, he had no idea of what cards Brockway held. Half a bottle of Jack Daniel's wasn't helping Warner's concentration. Brockway preferred Johnny Walker Black. His bottle also seemed to have developed a hole in the bottom.

As a result of raises and calls around the table, everyone else had folded. It all came down to Warner, who said, "I'll raise you $15,000, Mr. Captain Tim Brockway." Warner was slurring his speech slightly at this point.

Brockway called. "Warner, I'm out of cash, but see if this will do." He reached into his jacket pocket and pulled out an envelope. He threw it on top of the towering pile of chips and cash. "What the hell is that?" asked Jack.

"It's a deed that I received from my uncle's attorney today in the mail. I just inherited 100 acres near Dallas, Texas. It's an abandoned airfield. My uncle was trying to sell it to the military, but they bought the bigger property next door instead. I figure that it's got to be easily worth 50 grand. If I lose, I'll sign it over to you, but you'll need to give me

$1,000 in pocket money. All my dough is on the table." Brockway crossed his arms, slumped back in his chair, and waited for an answer.

Even under the influence of so much liquor, Warner could see a million possibilities. He slowly counted to 10 and said, "Well, okay… I guess so. What the hell do I need with some old airfield in the middle of nowhere? I'm sure I'll regret this. Good enough, let's see those cards."

Two minutes later, Brockway had $1,000 in cash, and Warner owned a vacant Texas airfield outside of Dallas and right next door to McCann Air Force Base. Fortune had smiled on Jack Warner once again, the lucky son-of-a-bitch.

Marry Me?

Jack fell in love with Gail Richardson on the night they had dinner together after he rescued her. He had a rough-and-tumble upbringing, completely the opposite of hers. Gail's family was from the East Coast. She graduated from Wellesley, a famous girl's college, and went into nursing over the objections of her family. The Richardsons were hoping for her to marry a doctor, lawyer, or stockbroker from Wall Street. At dinner one evening, Gail told her parents, "I'm worried about all the U.S. soldiers being injured over in Vietnam. I want to help out. Today, I enlisted in the Army as a nurse. I've volunteered to go to Vietnam."

Mrs. Richardson dropped her sterling silver fork. It landed on the cherry wood dining room table and kept on going down to the oak floor with a clatter. Other than that, the room was silent, except for the ticking of the antique wall clock.

Both of her parents tried to talk her out of it, but it was no use. Gail was determined to go and save American lives. No matter how much parents love their children, it's pretty hard to argue with a motive like that.

Gail did, indeed, save American lives. She was assigned to the Army hospital in Da Nang. It was on the way to this post in Da Nang that she met Jack Warner literally by accident. She and Jack got together whenever their schedules allowed.

She also volunteered in a Vietnamese public medical clinic in her off hours. Gail worked her way up the nursing ladder into the operating room. Lieutenant Richardson came to be a top flight surgical nurse. The doctors liked working with her because of her professionalism and sense of humor. Nothing seemed to rattle her in the middle of a tough procedure. Gail seemed almost psychic in knowing what instrument the surgeon would need next. Nine times out of 10, it was in her hand, waiting for the doctor's request. This kind of working relationship shortened the time a patient was on the surgery table. The doctors were positive that her actions saved lives over the course of a year.

She was finally discharged as a major and was awarded the National Defense Service Medal for her nursing service.

Jack was honorably discharged before Gail was. Even though they were thousands of miles apart, they kept their relationship going with constant letters back and forth. Jack managed to write twice a week and Gail fit in three letters every week. Somehow, Jack got flowers delivered to her at the hospital on her birthday. She didn't know how he managed it from so far away, but she loved him for it.

By the time Gail was discharged, Jack was living in Oahu, Hawaii. She jumped on an Army transport bound for Hickham Field. Gail knew she had to stop off and see Jack before she flew the rest of the way home to the East Coast to see her family.

Jack met her at the airport with a fresh orchid lei to put around her neck. The next things to go around her were his arms in the longest bear hug and the most passionate kiss she could have ever hoped for. They loved each other and didn't want to break it off.

"I've got a great idea for something to do in Oahu, Babe," he told Gail. "What would you say to hanging out with a no-good, unemployed sky jockey like me for the rest of your life? Marry me, Babe; you know I love you. I can't imagine living my life without you," proposed Jack.

"How can I resist such an elegant proposal, Colonel Warner? Yes, yes, and, by the way, did you hear me? I said, 'Yes.'" Gail threw her arms around him again. "Thank you for making me the happiest girl in the world."

Jack managed to track down Lou Patroni, now at the Hickham Field Maintenance Hangar. He agreed to be his best man. Gail's best friend, Georgia, from her nursing unit was also in Hawaii. Georgia was thrilled to be Gail's maid of honor. Gail wore a long, white dress with orchids her hair. Jack borrowed a dark blue suit with a white dress shirt. They got married, barefoot in the sand at sunset under coconut palms overlooking the beautiful blue ocean bay. It was the stuff that postcards were made of.

After the wedding, Jack and Gail snuck off away from the others and he made Gail a promise: "I don't know where life is going to take us, but I promise it will be interesting. You won't be bored for a single minute." No truer words have ever been spoken.

Baby Noah Warner was born 10 months later. He looked just like Jack, including the dimple in his chin. Gail and Jack couldn't be happier. Lou sent a fighter jet pedal car for a baby gift. "I guess he'll have to grow into it," quipped Jack. Georgia sent a white Irish linen christening gown.

Nurse Gail

After leaving the Air Force, Jack took it easy for a while. He and Gail moved to Southern California. They rented a little house in Montrose, a nice, sleepy little town near three airports and five hospitals. Gail got a job at Glendale Memorial Hospital. She enjoyed being a surgical nurse assisting in the operating room. The hospital was ahead of its time, offering free child care for their employees. Noah could go to work with Gail in the morning. She could check in on him during the day and take him home at night. It was a great arrangement for employees and the hospital. It paid off for the hospital in terms of fewer employee sick days and tremendous job loyalty.

Gail enjoyed her work in the operating rooms. She was very popular with the doctors and the nurses. Most surgeons would request her for their operations. They needed to book her early or she would already be taken by another doctor.

The chief of surgery was Dr. Harrison Kurtz. Dr. Kurtz had been at Glendale Memorial for over 45 years. He started as a resident and worked his way up the surgical ladder. Harry Kurtz designed the surgery wing when the hospital was rebuilt years before. He was an institution there and Gail was his favorite assisting nurse.

Gail liked Dr. Kurtz and enjoyed working with him, but lately, he seemed a little fuzzy during some of the more difficult operations that were scheduled in the afternoon. The anesthesiologist would trade glances with her whenever Dr. Kurtz missed something.

On two occasions, he left the operating room after requesting that she close for him. This happens on TV shows all the time, but not so much in real life. Gail wondered if maybe he had a few drinks at lunch. Certainly, no nurse would ever make such an accusation without concrete proof.

Gail took it upon herself to follow Harry Kurtz at lunchtime several times and was relieved that he went nowhere near any alcohol at lunch. She resigned herself to just watching him carefully in the operating room and keeping her mouth shut. He started dropping instruments to the floor. Gail would just hand him another one and keep quiet. The other nurses started making comments, but she just told them Dr. Kurtz was just tired because it had been a long day.

One day, she was scheduled to assist Dr. Kurtz with a kidney transplant. Gail was in charge of prepping the operating room with the necessary equipment, drugs, instruments, and supplies before the doctor and patient entered.

The patient was brought in to have her right kidney removed and a kidney from her son implanted. Dr. Kurtz came marching in with the x-rays in hand. He put them up on the viewer near the table. He stood over the patient and surveyed the surgical cloth drapes surrounding the lower back. "Looks good, everybody. Let's get to work," announced Dr. Kurtz. While glancing at the x-rays, he started to use a purple medical marker to sketch out his incision lines, plus three x's for the laparoscopic incisions.

Gail watched quietly while Dr. Kurtz did his sketching and glanced repeatedly at the x-rays. Something seemed wrong, but she couldn't quite think what it could be. She looked at the x-rays, then the patient, and then the surgical work order. "Oh, my God, he's going to remove the wrong kidney." The work order called for the right kidney to be removed and the son's kidney implanted. But Dr. Kurtz was sketching over the left kidney. If something wasn't done, he would cut out the wrong kidney in about 30 seconds.

There was a surgical staff of five people in the surgical suite: Dr. Kurtz, Gail, the anesthesiologist, the blood machine technician, and the secondary RN for general duties. Gail didn't want to embarrass Dr. Kurtz in front of everybody. If she blurted out, "You fool, you're going to chop out the wrong kidney," it would destroy his reputation, plus the reputation of the hospital. Gail quickly grabbed a clipboard and scribbled on it with the purple marker, "*Wrong kidney! X-ray backwards.*"

"Dr. Kurtz, there are some last-minute medical conditions that I want to make sure you are aware of." Gail put the clipboard in his gloved hand where no one else could read it.

Harry read the note and glanced at Gail with terror in his eyes. "Thank you, Gail. Let me double-check the x-rays." Dr. Kurtz took down the x-rays and held them up to the big light over the table and pretended to be checking something. As he returned them to the viewer, he flipped them so they were now correct. No one but Gail spotted the switch.

"Okay, Gail, I'm ready to proceed now." No one else could get a clear view of the surgery site. Dr. Kurtz quickly made his main incision, plus the laparoscopic incisions for those instruments. Gail saw him relax under his mask and look at her with his kind eyes. The operation continued and turned out well.

Gail wheeled the patient into the post-op ward for a few hours of recovery before the family could see her. She found Dr. Kurtz in the doctor's lounge. They looked at each other like two old friends, even though they had only worked together for two years.

"Gail, thank you for saving my bacon in there. You may have saved the patient's life and the hospital and me from certain legal action." They sat down and Harry did some quick soul searching. "Gail, I've been here for almost 46 years. I'm 72 years old. I'm not sure what to do."

"Dr. Kurtz, I admire you greatly. You've built a top surgical staff and facility that will carry on long after you're gone. Forgive me for being blunt, but I think it's time for you to retire from performing surgeries. As the old saying goes, 'Don't stay too long at the fair.' Wouldn't it be better to retire while you are on top than to keep operating past your prime and retire in disgrace?"

Gail continued, "What if you keep operating and somebody dies on the table? I know you couldn't live with yourself."

"Gail, I don't have a daughter, but if I did, I would hope that she would be just as caring and direct as you. If anyone needs me, I'll be in my office, writing my retirement letter to the Hospital Board of Directors."

Jack's News Job

With Gail busy at the hospital, Jack looked for nearby pilot jobs. One Friday morning, he drove out to Whiteman Airport in the San Fernando Valley, north of Los Angeles. Whiteman was a small community airport, known as an uncontrolled airport, meaning no control tower. Pilots had to rely on visually spotting other aircraft in their flight

vicinity. Visual flight rules, or VFR, were the policy. The aviation business liked to shorten everything into initials. It was easier to transmit over the radio, among other things.

Jack heard that there were lots of private planes housed there. He stopped in to talk to Emmett Merritt, the airport manager. Walking into his office, Jack saw Emmett slouched back in his office chair with his scuffed brown shoes up on the desk and a cigarette butt hanging off his lower lip, like it was glued there. He was asleep with a copy of the horse racing form lying on his fat stomach.

Jack cleared his throat and knocked on the door frame, waking him up. "Mr. Merritt, I'm Jack Warner. I wondered if you could give me some information on the planes that are here. I'm looking for a job as a pilot. I thought..."

"Jack Warner? Excuse me for interrupting. Aren't you that famous pilot from Vietnam? I heard of you. Sit down and tell me what I can do for you," said Emmett while taking his feet off the desk and stubbing out the cigarette in the overflowing ashtray.

Emmett poured Jack a cup of coffee and told him about the aviation tenants at Whiteman. "Many companies keep their private jets here. TV and radio stations keep their traffic helicopters and planes here. The police department parks their helos here, and the fire department houses their fleet of water-dropping helos in that white hangar with the blue stripe on it."

Jack thanked Emmett for his time and went for a walk around the airport. He stopped in at the Channel 6 hangar. Gail Warner liked their nightly newscast the best. It probably didn't hurt that the weatherman was a handsome ex-NFL football star named Johnny Storm. "Why do all TV weathermen seem to have such cliché names?" Jack thought they all changed their names for TV work. Of course, on the flip side, Jack never minded watching Kelly Clark, the cute traffic girl.

Channel 6 had a Bell 206 Jet Ranger helicopter and a Cessna 182 airplane. They were both equipped with TV cameras and satellite feed equipment. The copter was flown by Chopper Dave, a local TV celebrity, known for his traffic reports and high-speed chase coverage. The Cessna was used for traffic reporting and filming major news events.

Almost every other pilot hated Chopper Dave with a passion. He would fly into prohibited air spaces. He would fly right in front of other stations' helicopters, ruining their camera shots. His narrated high-speed chases would go on endlessly, with Dave's irritating voice calling the action. The other pilots joked that he suffered from microphone disease and he probably slept with one under his pillow.

Other traffic pilots with military backgrounds used to gather at the bar near the airport for a few beers after the 11 o'clock news was over. "How do you think ABC would feel about us installing some machine guns on the Channel 7 copter and shooting Dave out of the sky?" asked one pilot.

"Probably about the same as NBC or CBS," said another. "As the Queen would say, 'We are not amused.'"

"But I think FOX might not have a problem with it. They live on the edge."

"Think of the video coverage of Dave going down in flames. It'll be on every video show all over the world." They all erupted in laughter and ordered another round.

In the summer, Chopper Dave had a habit of hovering low over houses in the Hollywood Hills, with his camera zoomed in on girls sunbathing topless by their pools. Kelly Clark, the Channel 6 traffic girl, had filed a sexual harassment complaint against Dave with the station management. Chopper Dave had learned where Kelly lived and repeatedly pulled his antics when she was out by the pool in her bikini, or half a bikini.

The Channel 6 management took no action until Kelly showed them some evidence. Kelly brought home a video camera from work and taped Dave in action. She even zoomed up to the helicopter so they could see him behind the windshield, hovering for several minutes until he spotted the camera. After watching Kelly's tape, management gave Dave two weeks off without pay and required him to apologize publicly to Kelly at a station staff meeting.

Dave was so pissed after he was booted off the air that he called other stations' news managers to see about working for them. Not one of Channel 6's competitors would even return Chopper Dave's call. That brought old Dave down to earth, as it were. Dave was under contract at a great salary. Saying goodbye to that money would hurt. He quietly accepted his punishment and made his apology to Kelly Clark.

Chopper Dave was in the hangar when Jack came in. Introductions were made. Dave was very impressed to meet Colonel Jack Warner. After all, who in the aviation community hadn't heard of Warner's experiences in the Air Force?

Jack asked Dave about any available pilot jobs. "We're looking for a pilot for that Cessna to shoot traffic and news footage. The guy to see is our aviation manager, Jerry Campbell. You'll find him in the office."

"Thanks, Dave. Nice to meet you."

"Would you like an autographed picture?" asked Chopper Dave. "I'd be happy to personalize it for you."

Jack smiled, said nothing, and quietly walked away. "What a putz," he said under his breath.

Emmett, the airport manager, had also told him that Channel 6 was looking for a pilot for their traffic plane. Jack found Jerry Campbell, the manager. "I'm Jack Warner. I hear you're looking for a pilot." Campbell and Warner talked for over an hour. It only took Jerry about two minutes after meeting Jack to know that he had found his new pilot. Campbell called the Channel 6 news manager to tell him about hiring Jack. As Jerry was talking, the manager was doodling on his desk blotter, "Colonel Jack Warner, Channel 6's eye in the sky."

On the way out of the airport, Jack stopped to thank Emmett for his help. Emmett asked Jack, "Have you had lunch? Let's walk across the street to The Bakery. They make great sandwiches. My treat."

The Bakery

Located just across from the Whiteman Airport gates was The Bakery. Nobody could remember the real name of the place. It was always just referred to as The Bakery. This famous greasy spoon had been in business for over 50 years. The little building was built in the 1920s totally from river rocks found on-site near the bottom of the Tujunga Canyon wash. Half of the building was a typical little bakery, and the other was a sandwich shop. There were a few tables and chairs outside on the patio. It was a very low-budget affair, owned by Rafael Velasco, his wife, and their three sons. Rafael and his wife did the baking, and the boys made and sold sandwiches.

The Bakery didn't seem to do much business, maybe because everything seemed to be the same color: white. Rafael's son, Raffi, helped his dad in the bakery. His job was to make the white frosting every week for the small bakery cakes and the occasional wedding cake.

When Raffi was a little boy, he liked to ride up and down on the giant Hobart mixer. Every bakery has at least one of these monstrous beasts. They stand about six feet high, with two massive jaws that gripped the sides of the huge, aluminum mixing kettle. The jaws were motorized to raise and lower the mixing kettle that could easily weigh over 175 pounds with a load of dough inside.

The frosting recipe was simple: a 100-pound sack of powdered sugar, a 50-pound box of shortening, some powdered Coffee Mate, a half bottle of vanilla, and a little almond extract. After the ingredients were dumped into the kettle, Raffi started the big mixer on "slow" speed until everything was well mixed. Then, he moved the speed selector up to "high." The huge beater attachment would slowly incorporate air into the frosting mixture. As Rafael Sr. liked to say, "Air is cheap. I like to put a lot in."

Little Raffi would let the Hobart churn away for about 30 minutes, leaving the kettle almost overflowing with a fluffy white cloud of sugary goodness. Then, he had to transfer the icing into plastic tubs for the cake decorator ladies to use during the week.

Even though all the Velasco boys had each made hundreds of batches of bakery frosting, none could resist walking by and sticking their finger in to grab a taste of sweet heaven. It was better if you didn't think of the recipe as you licked your finger.

The sandwich shop was more successful than the bakery. Behind the counter were two white kitchen stoves, each with a large, square roaster pan that covered all four burners. These pans were made out of aluminum but you'd never know it by looking at the outsides. They were blackened with residue baked on by five decades of use. The long line of dishwashers over the years had only cared about cleaning the inside of the pans, not the outside. This seems to be the practice in many restaurants.

Each roaster pan was full of sliced meat, cooked tender by hours in the oven each night. One was BBQ beef, and the other was peppery pastrami. On the counter was a big glass cabinet with long, white puffy sandwich rolls that Rafael Sr. baked fresh each morning. Customers didn't have many choices. The only other things to buy were chips and sodas. It doesn't get much simpler than that: four things on the menu.

The customers would request a single or double-dipped sandwich. Raffi would dip one or both parts of the roll in the meat drippings. If the customer asked for a submarino, he dunked the whole sandwich into the beefy goodness. The sandwiches were piled high with meat, overflowing over the sides.

The boys wrapped the sandwiches in white butcher paper, adding a drink and some chips, and then rang up the order. From late morning until mid-afternoon, there was a line of hungry customers snaking out the front door. The good thing was that the line moved quickly. A customer could order their sandwich and be out the door in only a minute or two.

Of course, it was an all-cash business. Every night, Rafael hid the cash in a dirty container labeled "Bacon Grease" and stuck it in the back of the freezer. Twice a week, Rafael's wife, Gracie, would walk out of the bakery with a pink box tied with white string. She would drive to the bank, making sure no one was following her. Gracie would deliver the box to the tellers at the Security Bank. But first, she took out the fat envelope of green currency to deposit, leaving behind a dozen fresh chocolate chip cookies for the bank staff.

Emmett walked Jack over to the bakery and ordered lunch for both of them. As usual, the left-hand side of the bakery was packed with throngs of people ordering lunch. The bakery side was empty. After lunch, Emmett introduced Jack Warner to Rafael and Gracie. Emmett explained who Jack was and told them about his new job.

"Well, Mr. Warner, we hope to see you in here as a regular customer," said Gracie.

"Only every day, I think. That sandwich was great. By the way, I'd like to buy a big box of your cookies. I hear great things about them." It was a funny thing. Even though Jack bought three dozen cookies, by the time the pink box made it home, there seemed to be some shrinkage in the cookie inventory. Both Gail and Noah remarked on the extra room in the box.

"Very mysterious," remarked Gail with a smirk.

Houston, We Have a Problem

Jack started flying the Channel 6 Cessna with Gina Oyama, a production assistant who rode on board to help him. Gina coordinated flying patterns over freeways or brush fires that warranted reporting. She wrote the traffic reports and displayed them on a portable teleprompter screen that sat next to Jack's seat. It didn't take long for Jack to learn the ropes of reporting and the Medusa-like L.A. freeway system. Jack got paid whether he flew or not, so on windy or stormy days, he got a paid day off.

Warner got to know all the pilots at Whiteman Airport. He liked the fire and police helo pilots the most. Most of them had military backgrounds, which led to long coffee sessions to see who the biggest liar was.

Chopper Dave behaved himself for a while but he was a born lech. He tried making time with Gina, who wouldn't have anything to do with him. After a few feeble attempts, she told Jack about it. "What a pig. The guy's twice my age and three times my weight. None of the women at the station can stand him."

Dave gave up on the topless girls by the pools, but he soon found a new aerial vice to explore. There was a high-rise condo building on Ventura Boulevard in Encino. The big draw of these units was a prestigious building with fabulous views. Most of the exterior walls were solid glass, including the master bedroom and bathroom. The showers were all glass overlooking the San Fernando Valley. Next to the shower was a double-wide jacuzzi tub with built-in pillows that faced a double-sided fireplace, opening up into the master bedroom.

One Saturday night, after finishing his traffic report for the late news, Dave was flying below the top of the building so he could check out the dark windows. One was all lit up, with quite a floor show of naked people. Two women and one man were getting busy on the floor of a bedroom. Chopper Dave circled the building several times and hovered for a minute or two, watching the goings-on. To keep the people from seeing him, Dave pulled out the circuit-breaker fuse that controlled the helicopter's running lights and put it in his pocket. This made the helo totally black except for his instrument lights. He enjoyed the show for several minutes before continuing his trip back to the airport.

About the same time, Jack Warner finished shooting dramatic coverage of a big brush fire in Topanga Canyon for the 11 o'clock news. His video footage showed an Army of flames marching up the canyon walls. Jack was looking forward to getting home, kicking off his shoes, and finishing the rest of the Strawberry Häagen Dazs that was waiting for him at home in the freezer. He had it stashed behind the frozen green peas so that Noah and Gail wouldn't find it before he got home.

He finally had the Whiteman Airport runway lights in sight. He adjusted the flaps and dropped down for landing. When he was about 50 feet off the deck, something flashed in front of his plane. There was a loud crunch and his plane went into a crazy lurching spin. Gina screamed. Warner yelled out, "What the hell was that?"

It took all of his skill to land the plane, so he didn't have time to wonder about what he had hit. The plane hit the runway at such a sharp angle that one wing tip hit the tarmac. The plane spun around, breaking off the right wheel, followed by the nose wheel. This let the front of the plane down so low that the propeller blades ground into the dirt next to the pavement. Jack finally slid to a stop. It wasn't so much a landing but more of a controlled crash. He yelled at Gina, "Get out fast, before it catches on fire!"

When they jumped out of the wrecked plane, Jack saw the Channel 6 helicopter coming down so hard that the helo skids broke off. It was hard to see with only the runway marker lights and the distant hangar flood lights illuminating the scene. The rear boom and tail rotor were missing on the copter. Chopper Dave crawled out of the wreckage and laid on the ground, trying to catch his breath.

Everybody was alive and basically all right, considering the deadly potential of a midair crash. Jack and Gina only had minor cuts and bruises. Dave's leg seemed to be broken. Jack got out the first-aid kit and a blanket he kept in the plane's storage compartment. He started some basic first aid while he sent Gina running for help. Warner covered Dave with a blanket and felt for his pulse, then took some gauze bandages and pushed down on two cuts on his forehead.

The L.A. Fire Department soon showed up with a pumper truck, a hook 'n' ladder, plus two ambulances. They called in two trailers with generators and floodlight towers that could be raised up to light the area. The paramedics gingerly put Dave on a raised gurney and put a splint on his leg. When the fire department notified the FAA of the crash, they asked for all parties to be kept at the accident scene if medically possible. 20 minutes later, the Channel 6 station manager showed up with a carload of office staff.

Ironically, every TV station in L.A. sent their news copter to cover the story. News vans soon stormed the airport gates, raising their antennas to relay the story back to their studios for the morning news. It was the lead story for almost every news program. Even CNN featured the story, complete with video coverage. The story also made the morning talk shows on NBC, CBS, and ABC. Those shows had time to dig up the history on Colonel Jack Warner to stretch out the story for a full show segment. One newspaper headline read, "War Ace Crashes into Company Helo." Jack was able to call Gail to let her know he was all right, before she saw it on the news. She called his parents in Alaska to alert them.

About an hour later, Max Helweg from the FAA showed up and started taking his report. Max interviewed Jack, Gina, and finally Chopper Dave. Jack and Gina told the FAA man what they could. Jack said, "I don't know where the helicopter came from. I never saw it until my landing lights picked it up just a few feet in front of my plane."

But Chopper Dave had plenty to say. "That son-of-a-bitch flew right into me, right into me like he never even saw me. I had the right of way. You better test him. I bet he's drunk, and her too! You oughta search their plane. There's probably a bottle or a bag of dope under their seat."

Max videotaped the entire scene and his interviews with all parties. Max searched both aircraft with a bright flashlight. Afterwards, he asked Jack and Dave for their pilot's licenses and Gina for her driver's license to complete his report.

Chopper Dave wasn't done yet. "Warner, I thought you were some hotshot pilot. Every student pilot knows to look where he's going. I'm gonna have your ass. First, I'm gonna get you fired. Then, I'm gonna have your pilot's license pulled. Next, I'm gonna find me the best Jew attorney I can and sue your ass from here into next week."

All Jack could counter with was, "I'm sorry, Dave. I just never saw you."

Max Helweg grabbed some paper bags and asked, "Dave, I know you're uncomfortable on that stretcher, but could you please empty everything in your pockets into this paper bag?"

Chopper Dave wondered why, but he did as he was told. Max made the same request of Jack and Gina. The fire department had set up a folding table under the floodlights. It was full of first-aid supplies, but there were a few feet left of open space.

Max asked the paramedics to wheel Chopper Dave over next to the table with Jack and Gina there too. With the video camera recording, Max dumped Jack's bag on the table. Jack's pile included a wallet, keys, gum, some beef jerky, change, and a small pen-knife. Gina's pile only had car keys, two pens, and some change. She said, "Most of my stuff is in my purse back in my car."

Last of all was Chopper Dave's bag. Max emptied it on the table. Out spilled car keys, half a pack of gum, some money, and a Trojan rubber. "Never hurts to be prepared, you know?" wisecracked Dave.

Last of all to tumble out was the missing circuit-breaker fuse from the Bell Jet Ranger's instrument panel. All Dave could think was, "Oh, fuck. I am *so* screwed." He was *so* right.

Max Helweg from the FAA had only one question: "Dave, can you please tell me why this fuse is in your pocket and not in the helicopter where it belongs?"

Dave was desperately trying to come up with a story, but failed. He thought about saying it had burned out and he was going to replace it back at the airport. But he knew the FAA would test it and reveal his lie.

Jack only had one thing to say: "Gee, Dave, I think it's *you* who's going to need a good attorney. I know one, but I don't think he's Jewish. Is that okay?"

The station decided to replace the news helicopter, but not the Cessna. The plane was a total loss, along with Jack's career at Channel 6. The news manager told Jack, "Give us a call if you get a helicopter rating. We'd love to have you back." The FAA ruled Chopper Dave totally at fault and pulled his license. Jack Warner got a clean report. Dave was immediately fired from Channel 6. He ended up flying tourists down in Acapulco. Gina requested a transfer to work in the news studio.

Jay Leno had a field day when he was guest-hosting on *The Tonight Show*, joking about the Channel 6 plane running into its own helicopter. He made a crack about two Channel 6 interns running out for Starbucks coffee and Winchell's donuts but crashing to each other in the parking lot. Jack decided that was enough television work for him and moved on.

Bumming a Ride

Jack started flying private charters for corporations and wealthy private plane owners. On his off days, he developed a foolproof method to bum an airplane ride whenever he needed to get somewhere. Anytime Jack wanted a free ride, he would go into the airport's private terminal. This is where pilots, owners, and passengers of private jets would gather for departures and arrivals. In those days, there was a courtesy lounge available where you could grab a sandwich or catch a nap in between flights or have a drink if you weren't flying any more that day.

Jack would go up to the dispatcher's counter where the departing flights were listed. Most of them were required to file a flight plan. They're public records, so Jack could see who owned the planes and where they were going. At most airports, Jack already knew the dispatcher. Warner would simply ask to be paged in a few minutes.

After his name was announced, he went up to the counter to thank the dispatcher and returned to his seat. "Colonel Jack Warner" was a famous name in aviation. Almost every time, one or two pilots would come over and introduce themselves and start chatting with him. It didn't take much effort for Jack to bum a ride with a private pilot who was flying where Jack wanted to go. The pilot would introduce Jack to the plane's owner and passengers as a war hero and minor celebrity. Jack had fun entertaining them with stories of his rescues and heroic deeds. They loved it. Most times, Jack Warner couldn't have bought an airline ticket if he wanted to.

Toddler Trauma

Jack received a call one day from Brian Lockwood, a new private pilot who had recently bought a Cessna 401. The 401 is a turbo-charged, twin-engine, propeller-driven airplane. It can cruise at 260 knots, up to an altitude of 26,000 feet. He was going to fly to Las Vegas for the weekend and wanted to hire Jack to be the primary pilot. Brian was still building his flight hours and felt more comfortable with an experienced pilot at the controls who could also serve as a private instructor. He told Jack to invite his wife along, since Jack would need to stay over in Vegas. "I'll pick up all of your expenses, except for gambling losses," he kidded.

Gail was delighted to go, since she didn't get to accompany Jack very often. She was able to park little Noah with their neighbors for the weekend.

Jack and Gail met Brian and Natalie Lockwood at the private terminal at the Burbank Airport, where introductions were made and the luggage loaded while Jack showed Brian how to pre-flight his airplane. Jack showed Brian extra items to check that weren't in the manual. These were things that only many years of experience would teach a pilot.

Jack sat in the pilot's seat, with Brian in the copilot's seat. Gail sat behind Jack, with Natalie behind her husband. Three-year-old Scotty Lockwood and his nanny sat in the third row.

With the luggage loaded and everybody belted in place, Jack went through the checklist with Brian to familiarize him with the startup procedures. Warner started the engines, one at a time, and let them warm up to operating temperature.

The flight went well, making good time through the calm, blue desert skies. As they approached Las Vegas, Jack started his descent down to McCarran Airport. He reduced his airspeed from 250 knots down to 180. The ladies chatted on about the shows they wanted to see and the colorful Cirque du Soleil costumes. The nanny read her *Cosmo* magazine for a while before falling asleep. Little Scotty slipped off his seat belt and went exploring around the interior of the plane, driving his little Hot Wheels car on every possible surface, making "vroom, vroom" sounds as he went.

On the Cessna 401, the two-piece cabin door is locked with a big, chrome D ring. To open the door, the ring is turned halfway, which releases the door locks. Nobody noticed when Scotty grabbed the D ring and hung from it, thereby rotating it to the open position. Now traveling at 2,500 feet and 180 knots, the top half of the door popped open. With Scotty still hanging onto the D ring and the sudden wind blast, he was quickly being sucked out of the plane. A moment before, Gail had released her seat belt so she could reach her purse on the floor near the door. She quickly lunged to grab Scotty by his one remaining ankle with her left hand and the arm of her seat with the right.

Hearing the door pop open and Gail's scream, Jack quickly rolled the Cessna to the right, letting gravity help Gail with her rescue. Natalie was the closest and helped get Scotty all the way back inside the plane. With some instruction from Jack, Gail was able to close the door and secure it shut.

Had the plane been equipped with heart monitors, the pilot and passengers would have registered off the charts. Nobody could believe what tragedy has just been averted.

Brian Lockwood jumped out of his seat to share hugs with Scotty and Natalie. The nanny slept through the whole thing. That was her last day on the payroll. The Lockwoods bought her a bus ticket back to California. They couldn't thank Gail enough. How can anyone really thank somebody for saving the life of their child?

Aspen Trip

Jack heard about a huge snowfall in Aspen, Colorado, and he sweet-talked Gail into giving him a "hall pass" to go skiing. Jack figured he would see if he could bum a ride on a jet at the private terminal at the Burbank Airport. He played his usual game and soon scored a ride on a Citation corporate jet flying to Aspen, leaving in an hour. While waiting in the lounge, Jack enjoyed talking to Captain Dan Wolfe, the pilot of the Citation. Wolfe was an ex-Navy pilot who flew fighters off of aircraft carriers during the Vietnam War. They had a blast trading stories of their exploits from days gone by.

Wolfe told him about a carrier takeoff where his engine failed just after the jet was launched off of the deck. He had only climbed to about 500 feet when the engine shut down. He couldn't restart it the first time, so Dan and his copilot, Bill Figge, punched out of the dead aircraft. Luckily, the ejection seat rockets pushed them up 250 feet to increase the parachute opening space. It was still below the altitude needed for a successful ejection and parachute landing on the water, but every foot helped. The two pilots hit the water hard, knocking them both unconscious.

Whenever an aircraft carrier is launching jets or landing them, there is a rescue helicopter hovering nearby, just in case. Lucky for Wolfe and Figge, they were close by. Two rescue swimmers jumped out of the helo and swam toward the pilots. The men were motionless in the water and certainly would have drowned if not for the efforts of the swimmers. The rescue swimmers unbuckled the parachutes and then swam around behind each pilot. They reached around to give each man a bear hug and squeezed repeatedly several times. This burped out the water in their throat and mouth, thereby opening the airway. After some coughing and choking, both men drew in fresh air.

By then, the rescue helo had lowered a sling to pull the men inside. The rescuers helped each pilot get in the copter and followed behind them. After a short rest and some drying out, the pilots were fine. When they got back to their bunks, there were some gifts waiting for them.

On Dan Wolfe's bunk, someone had placed a life vest and a yellow ducky. On Bill Figge's bunk, there were some little, yellow, inflatable arm floaties, along with a note from their fellow pilots: "Next time you take off, please wear these." The two pilots laughed. Men don't kid you unless they like you. It was all part of the camaraderie of men doing a difficult job in life-threatening conditions.

Jack enjoyed his free ride to Aspen. He skied all week, schussing through the deep powder. The owner of the Citation jet was Billy Robbins, a three-time Oscar-winning movie producer at Warner Brothers. He invited Jack to stay with him and his family at their beautiful house in Aspen. The whole family was thrilled when he accepted their offer. They wouldn't let him pay for anything during the whole week. Jack caught the admiration of the owner's 17-year-old daughter, who thought he was *way cute*! Even Mrs. Robbins, the producer's wife, had to remind herself, "I'm married, I'm married, damn it, I'm married." But Jack loved his wife and behaved himself, grateful for the producer's generosity.

The group flew home that Friday. On the return flight, Captain Wolfe invited Jack to act as copilot and sit up front, next to him. Jack jumped at the opportunity. These little jets were like rocket ships. They were very responsive, due to the high thrust and low weight ratio. Citations were like Ferraris with wings.

Captain Wolfe had the plane on autopilot, cruising at 33,000 feet, flying over the Rocky Mountains. The movie producer's 12-year-old son was standing behind him, getting a flying lesson. It reminded Jack of his days flying with his father in their bush plane. "Boy, has technology come a long way," thought Jack while he admired the vast instrument panel.

Dan Wolfe started wincing in pain and grabbing his left arm. He told the boy to please return to his seat. "What's up?" asked Warner.

"My chest feels like a 747 is parked on it. My left arm hurts like hell, and I can barely breathe," whispered Dan.

Jack quickly studied the GPS aeronautical map display to see their position. He grabbed Dan's charts out of his briefcase. After quickly completing some basic navigation, he figured that the closest suitable airport with a hospital nearby was in St. George, Utah.

Jack ordered Billy Robbins and his son to come into the flight deck. "You both have to help the captain. I think he is having a heart attack. I'm going to fly the plane to St. George, Utah where they have a hospital with a trauma center. I'll tell you what to do. Got it?"

The impromptu medical team nodded and pulled Captain Wolfe out of the pilot's seat and dragged him back to the leather sofa in the middle of the cabin. Robbins' wife and daughter helped him up on the sofa and started carrying out Jack's first-aid commands. Luckily, the plane had an oxygen tank with a mask on board. They put that on him and started the O2 flow.

Jack Warner moved over into the main pilot's seat and switched off the autopilot. "Everybody, fasten your seat belts." He put the jet into a steep, curving dive towards the new heading to St. George. He radioed Salt Lake Center to declare a medical emergency. They cleared traffic out of his way and patched him through to the St. George Airport, where he asked for a priority landing space and an ambulance to meet the plane. Jack also requested that the St. George Hospital Trauma Center be ready for a heart attack patient.

The St. George's controller arranged for the ambulance and then said to his partner in the control tower, "Priority Landing? Where does he think he is, New York City? I guess he doesn't know we haven't had a plane land here for the last two hours."

Jack quickly reached St. George and made a silky-smooth landing. The pilot was taken to the hospital, where he made a full recovery. Jack flew the Robbins family home to Burbank. Billy couldn't thank Jack enough. Once they got back to Burbank, he cornered

Jack in the terminal. "I'm going to send you a lifetime movie pass."

"Gee, thanks," said Jack. "I'll enjoy that. By the way, can you give me a lift to the taxi stand? I don't have a car here."

"Yes, you do. See that red Porsche 911 Turbo Carrera over there?"

"Yeah, why?" asked Jack, a little confused.

"Here, catch," said the producer, throwing him the keys. "It's yours. I really didn't think a movie pass would quite cover the tab," he said with a huge grin. "How can I ever thank you for saving my life and the lives of my entire family?" The Robbins family hugged him and the girls kissed him. "By the way, you have a paid poolside bungalow waiting for you at the Beverly Hills Hotel. Go grab your wife and stay as long as you like." Billy evidently had been busy on the plane's phone as they approached the Burbank Airport. There was also a black Lincoln Town Car waiting to take the producer's family home.

Jack drove home to surprise Gail. She peppered him with questions: "Whose car is that? Why are you driving it? Where did it come from? What do you mean, it's yours? What do you mean, get packed? Where are we going? Who do you know in Beverly Hills? What do you mean, a free bungalow? Why do we need a babysitter? Jackson Benjamin Warner, you better stop laughing and start answering my questions!"

Jack just couldn't stop laughing at her sputtering frustration.

Somebody in the Burbank Private Terminal must have heard the whole story and called the news people. By the time Jack drove his new Porsche home to surprise Gail and then zipped over to Beverly Hills, there were two TV news reporters waiting in front of the hotel to interview the hero who saved the famous producer and his family.

The story ran on the nightly news along with Jack's heroic war record outlined in great detail. Jack's parents, Ben and ML, were sitting in their living room, in Alaska, watching CNN, getting ready for bed, and Jack's face appeared on the TV! They could not have been more surprised or proud.

Here's Johnny!

One afternoon, Jack was deadheading a corporate jet back to Los Angeles. He had dropped off his executives at Jackson Hole, Wyoming to do some fly fishing. Jack was flying the empty jet back home and would return to pick them up in a week.

Warner stopped by the Jackson Hole Airport's private lounge to file his flight plan, fuel the aircraft, and hit the "toidy" before taking off. Walking through the lounge, who did he see but Johnny Carson and his wife, Joanna. They were having a spirited conversation with the airport counter man. Jack couldn't help but overhear their problem while he filled out his paperwork.

Evidently, the private jet that was supposed to pick them up and fly them back to California was grounded by bad weather in Chicago. Johnny was pleading, "But, I have a show to do!"

"I'm sorry about that, sir, but we can't control the weather," said the airport clerk, giving the Carsons that irritating, canned response that we've all heard, ad nauseam.

"Excuse me, Mr. Carson. My name's Jack Warner. I couldn't help but overhear your problem. If you need to get back to California, I'm leaving in a few minutes. I'd be happy to take you with me. My plane is empty. I'll be landing at LAX. A limo could meet you there."

For someone who talks for a living, Johnny Carson was momentarily speechless at this stroke of luck. It was actually his wife who took Jack up his offer. "Mr. Warner, I'm Joanna Carson. We'd love to take you up on your generous offer. I have a little dog, Oliver, with me. Is that okay? He's completely housebroken and is used to flying. He'll sleep all the way to California."

"Sure, Mrs. Carson, I love dogs."

Jack got the plane ready for flight. He helped Johnny carry their bags and stow them in the plane. After taking off, Mrs. Carson fell asleep in the rear of the plane with Oliver. Johnny came forward to the flight deck. "Captain Warner, would it be all right if I sat in this other seat?"

Who could say no to Johnny Carson? "Of course, Mr. Carson, but only if you call me Jack."

"Then please, lose the 'Mr. Carson.' I'm Johnny to my friends. Anybody who gives me a ride to L.A. is certainly a friend," he said with a smile and that familiar twinkle in his eye.

While Jack flew to Los Angeles, they spent the whole time talking. Jack told him stories about rescuing pilots in Vietnam and Johnny answered back with showbiz stories about everybody in Hollywood. Jack told him about growing up in Alaska, the Air Force Academy, and fighter training at Randolph AFB in Texas.

Johnny did some close-up magic tricks for Jack. He made a quarter come out of the altimeter gauge. "I think that's a first," said Jack. Johnny was a lifelong magician who could have easily made his living in that field if he had wanted to.

After they landed at LAX, the Carsons chatted with Jack before leaving. Johnny thanked Jack and said, "I was so impressed with your stories about building a rescue plane and saving the lives of those pilots in Vietnam. May I ask, were you awarded any medals?

"Normally I don't mention it, but since you asked, yes, I was honored to receive a couple."

"Do you have plans for tomorrow night?" Johnny finally asked.

"No, I don't have another flight for a couple of days," replied Jack.

"How about coming on *The Tonight Show* tomorrow night to tell the audience some of your rescue stories?"

"Ba, ba, ba, ba, ba," stammered Jack.

"Are you doing a Jackie Gleason impersonation?" quipped Johnny, laughing. "Just say yes."

Jack could only laugh and accept. Who turns down the chance to be on *The Tonight Show*? He called his parents and then told Gail the story too. Gail answered with, "I've got to go shopping for a new dress."

"Why do *you* need a new dress?" inquired Warner.

"Do you actually think you're going to NBC to be on *The Tonight Show* with Johnny Carson and I'm not going along?" Gail said this while pounding her finger into his chest, drill-sergeant style.

Prior to Jack Warner's appearance on *The Tonight Show*, Johnny's staff at Carson Productions did a little research through a contact at the Air Force. Warner had mentioned to Johnny that he was awarded "a couple of medals," which wasn't exactly true. Johnny was stunned at what his assistant had discovered.

Jack made his *Tonight Show* appearance right after Bob Newhart, who usually left after his guest segment was over. During the commercial, Johnny leaned over to tell Newhart to stick around. "You're gonna like my next guest."

As Johnny introduced Jack, he listed his many accomplishments. "Ladies and gentlemen, my crack staff did some research on our next guest. Colonel Jack Warner is not only an Air Force 'Ace' pilot, but he's the only member of the Air Force to ever be awarded all of the following: the Air Force Cross, the Silver Star, the Medal of Honor, the Distinguished Flying Cross, and the Bronze Star. There are 21 former pilots that are alive today with friends, family, and children who love them, all because of our next guest, retired Air Force Colonel 'Black Jack Warner.'"

As Jack came out from behind the rainbow curtain, the audience shot to its feet with a thunderous standing ovation. Warner received the longest standing ovation of any guest in the history of *The Tonight Show*. It was even longer than the famous Ed Ames' hatchet-throwing show segment. Jack found out later that Johnny cancelled a new co-median's debut, plus a big-breasted weather girl to allow Jack to stay on the show for two extra segments until the end of the show.

Johnny told the story of how he met Jack. Jack then told the audience about growing up in Alaska, his pilot rescues, and how he rescued his wife. He had a great time with Johnny, who invited him to please come back again.

When he left the studio that night, there were hundreds of audience members wait-ing outside the NBC gate to shake his hand and ask for his autograph and to please pose with them for a picture. Stan, the NBC limo driver, gave him a pen and said, "Go ahead, Colonel. Take all the time you need. I'll wait."

He called his parents and told them the story so they could watch their son on TV. Jack's phone didn't stop ringing for days. It seemed that everyone he had ever met called to congratulate him.

Anytime that Johnny needed to fly somewhere, he would always try to hire Jack. He always paid him double the usual rate. They grew to be close friends. Johnny even gave Jack tennis lessons. When Noah was older, Johnny would do magic tricks for him.

Several times when Johnny had a guest cancel on him at the last minute, he called Warner to see if could come on short notice. Jack had an endless supply of true adven-ture stories. After his appearance on *The Tonight Show*, Warner received dozens of invitations from talk shows, morning shows, game shows, and more. He politely turned them all down. He would only appear with Johnny. Jack didn't want to be a TV star, a movie star, or on magazine covers. Jack became one of the most popular guests in the history of *The Tonight Show*.

Pan Am Days

After Jack Warner retired from the Air Force and flew private jets for a while, he needed a steadier income, so he started flying for Pan Am. The stewardesses would always leak the identity of their famous pilot to the passengers. Any child traveling on board would be invited up to the cockpit to meet the captain, get a pair of wings pinned on, and have their picture taken with him. Quite a few ex-soldiers made sure to stop while exiting the plane to thank Colonel Warner for protecting them during the war. A few guys even knew some of the pilots that he'd rescued. As he got to know the flight crews, they started kidding him mercilessly about being demoted from a colonel in the Air Force to a captain at Pan Am.

The flight crew and stewardesses all liked flying with Jack Warner. He treated them like the professionals that they were. Miriam Garland, the chief stewardess, used to tell stories of other pilots. One pilot offered the female stewardesses what he called "lap time," where the women would sit on his lap in the cockpit.

One memorable day, the now-lowly Pan Am "Captain" Warner was flying from Los Angeles to London. Near the end of the long flight, they closed in on Heathrow Airport when a steady beeping caught the attention of copilot, Steve DePatie. "Sir, hydraulic pump failure on the main hydros," reported DePatie to Captain Warner.

"Kick in the auxiliary pump," ordered Warner.

"No response, sir," replied DePatie.

"Steve, check the circuit-breaker panel for a tripped breaker or a bad fuse."

He left his seat, grabbed a flashlight, and walked back behind the navigator to open the trap door in the floor. This accessed the lower mechanical crawlspace, where all the electrical lines, cables, and hydraulic lines were located. DePatie checked all the circuit breakers and fuses.

"All good down here, Captain," barked DePatie as he returned to his seat.

"Well, son, the official term for this is 'Oh, shit,'" said Warner with a nervous laugh. "Steve, ask the stewardesses to report to the flight deck. We need to huddle up."

All six stewardesses soon joined the navigator and copilot to hear Captain Warner's assessment of their situation. Warner started in. "Hello, girls; we have a hydraulic steering pump failure. The good news is the aircraft-control hydraulics still work, so we have brakes, flaps, rudder, and elevators. The bad news is we have no steering. When we first land, I can steer to some degree with the rudder and wing flaps. But, as we slow down, they won't have any effect anymore. When we took off in Los Angeles, the nose wheel was pointed straight. When we land at Heathrow, it should still be straight. I just can't control it if it isn't. Girls, prepare the passengers for crash positions after I explain things over the P.A. to break the news to them. That should make your job a little bit easier."

Warner radioed to the Heathrow Control Tower, declaring a mechanical emergency. They scrambled the airport's rescue fire trucks and cleared all air traffic, giving the Pan Am flight number-one priority to land. Jack got on the airplane's P.A. system, introduced himself, and told them in his most calm and reassuring voice the condition of the plane's steering system. He asked them to please follow the instructions from the stewardesses. "I think we're going to be just fine, folks. Now, please excuse me, I have to get back to work and land this plane."

After Captain Warner signed off from his address to the passengers, Miriam Garland explained the passenger crash positions. "When I give you the word, put your head down over your knees and cover the back of your head with your pillow. Just to let you know, you are in very good hands today. Captain Jack Warner is actually a retired Air Force colonel who flew fighter jets in Vietnam. He was awarded a chest full of medals for bravery and rescued 21 downed pilots. We're all very lucky that he's at the controls today."

As they made their final approach, Jack told Miriam to start the emergency procedures. A few moments later, everyone could feel the rear tires touch down with the familiar screeches. The nose of the jet floated down until the nose wheel also hit the tarmac. Using the rudder, flaps, and rear wheel brakes, Jack was able to keep the plane on the runway until the very end, when it veered to the starboard side. Only the rear starboard wheels left the pavement and rolled into the weeds and stopped.

The passengers erupted into cheers, whistles, and screams of delight. Jack was trying to talk over the P.A., but nobody could hear him. He had to postpone his congratulations and instead came out into the main cabin from the flight deck. The cheers had been dying down, but once Captain Warner appeared, the noise level got even louder than before. As Jack walked down the aisle, the men patted him on the back and shook his hands. The women tried to hug and kiss him if they were close enough.

After some sense of decorum had descended on the plane's interior, a little four-year-old girl walked up to Captain Jack. He knelt down to be face to face with her. "Thank you, sir, for saving our plane." She gave him a kiss on the cheek and the best hug she could with her little girl arms around his big shoulders. "This is for you." She handed him a picture of the plane in the blue sky that she had drawn with crayons.

That did it. Jack just lost it right there in front of 185 passengers. He couldn't keep his professional composure anymore. Tears of happiness ran down his face. He picked up the little girl and wouldn't put her down. Every passenger and crew member enjoyed this special moment.

After the airport ground crew towed the plane to the gate with a tug, they extended the jetway for the passengers. On most flights, passengers almost stampede to get off. But not today. Nobody would leave until they had a short audience with the famous captain. Everybody with a camera ran out of film. Some passengers wanted his autograph, but all they could find for paper were the white air sickness bags. "Well, now *that* is a first," whispered Miriam to her fellow stews.

A few months after the hydraulic-problem flight, Jack was flying to Paris. He was waiting to take off from JFK Airport in New York. After getting clearance from the tower, Jack pushed the throttles all the way forward. With the engines screaming and the thrust pushing the passengers and crew back in their seat cushions, the 800,000-pound plane accelerated from a standing start to the 180-mph takeoff speed in about 45 seconds.

As Warner lifted off, he saw some kind of dead animal on the far end of the runway. He radioed the control tower to let them know about it and decided to have fun with Jeff Kaplan, the air traffic controller on duty. Kaplan acknowledged the dead animal report and said he would inform the field maintenance department to haul it away.

Jack Warner said, "That's not necessary, we've already called the Pan Am caterers." Pan Am management heard about that conversation and was not at all amused.

Jack enjoyed his years flying for Pan Am. As he put it, "Flying is so much nicer when people aren't shooting at you."

SR-71

While in Vietnam, the last pilot Jack rescued was Lieutenant Chuck Reed, the marine pilot from Nine Mile Falls, Washington. Lieutenant Reed was now Colonel Reed, who was now a pilot in the SR-71 program. He had never forgotten that Warner had risked his life on that night so long ago to rescue him and Fred Smith.

The Lockheed SR-71 "Blackbird" was an advanced, long-range, Mach 3+, strategic reconnaissance aircraft. It was developed by Lockheed in Burbank, California by its top-secret Skunk Works Division. During reconnaissance missions, the SR-71 operated at super high speeds and extreme altitudes to allow it to outrace threats. If a surface-to-air missile launch was detected, the standard evasive action was simply to accelerate and outfly the missile.

Colonel Reed reached out to Jack Warner with an offer. After talking on the phone and catching up on old friends, Reed said, "I hear you're flying some pretty slow planes these days over at Pan Am."

Warner replied, "That's true. I miss the old days. A 747 just can't compare to an F-4 Phantom."

"Well, I think maybe I have something that can. How'd you like to be my copilot on an L.A.-to-Frankfurt run in an SR-71 Blackbird?"

After a few seconds, Jack responded with, "So, who do I have to sleep with? Is it a woman or man? For a ride in a Blackbird, I'm not necessarily ruling out men," he said, laughing.

The flight was scheduled in three weeks. He reported to Edwards Air Force Base the week before to be checked out by the flight surgeon. The hangar crew helped him with a pressure suit and helmet. Some pilots call it putting on your "speed slacks." The G-suit applies pressure to the legs to aid in preventing blackout during high-gravity-inducing maneuvering. Pilots refer to it as "high g's." All systems were checked and then checked again. When you're flying at 80,000 feet, it's hard to pull over and stop. Jack Warner walked around the long, sleek, inky black plane for two hours. "Did anybody call Batman and tell him that we found his plane?" joked Warner.

SR-71 pilots are intensely proud of the accomplishments of their Blackbirds. The SR-71 holds speed and altitude records that probably will never be broken. On flight day, Warner reported back to the Edwards Flight Center for a preflight briefing at five a.m. Reed was already there. "I like to kick the tires," joked Reed.

"When was your last flight?" inquired Warner.

"Last month, we flew from L.A. to Washington, D.C. in just over 64 minutes," answered Colonel Reed. "But that time was with a running start."

"You lying sack of shit!" blurted out Warner.

"No way, man," replied Reed. "'Fraid so; this bird can move. When you fly at more than 2,100 knots at 80,000 feet, time seems to fly right by. We didn't even finish the in-flight movie." Jack grinned at the remark.

Warner suited up and reported to the plane. It was surrounded by a special ground crew working to ready the grand aircraft for flight. Reed had to scream in his ear to be heard. "I'll give you the nickel tour. The two Pratt & Whitney engines need an external engine to get them started. Lockheed provides us with a 'start cart.' It contains two Buick V-8 engines to turn over the main engines, one at a time, until they fire. It's connected by a temporary vertical drive shaft. My idea was a rope-pull starter, like my lawnmower, but that idea was shot down." Reed started laughing even before he finished his funny comment. Warner was laughing too.

The pilots took their places in the cockpit. The Lexan canopy was lowered and locked into place. A crewman drove a mule tug to tow the SR-71 away from the gate area. The massive P & W engines had a flame kickback of over 50 feet, so the pilot had to be careful of what was behind the engines when they were started, like some unlucky ground crewmen, perhaps.

On one of the first flights, an Air Force general's driver had dropped off the general and then parked his Jeep a little too close to the rear of the plane. After they lit the engines, the Jeep looked like it rolled out of a campfire. It was rumored that the driver was transferred to Nome, Alaska to man a weather station.

Today, the start cart did its job and the engines roared to life. Reed taxied out to the runway while talking to the control tower. After getting final clearance, he pushed the throttle levers forward and Jack was thrown back into his seat. Colonel Warner had never felt such acceleration and handling from an airplane. After they reached altitude, Jack said to Reed, "You got any skis we can put on this bird? I'd like to stop at my dad's house in Alaska and show this to him."

"Are the salmon running?" asked Reed, laughing.

"We may have a problem with the airstrip. It's only 1,000 feet long."

Later, as the Blackbird was screaming over Canada, they picked up Chicago Center radio traffic. From 12 miles up in the air, Reed and Walker listened in on other aircraft radio transmissions as they entered Chicago airspace. Though Chicago Center didn't control the SR-71, they did monitor their movement across the control center scope. Jack heard a Cessna 180 ask for a readout of its groundspeed.

"120 knots," Chicago Center replied.

Moments later, a Twin Beechcraft asked the same question. "180 knots," Chicago Center answered.

Jack and Chuck weren't the only ones proud of their groundspeed that day, as a nearby

Air Force F-18 smugly transmitted, "Ah, Chicago Center, Dusty 52 requests a ground-speed readout."

There was a slight pause, then the response, "525 knots on the ground, Dusty."

After another silent pause, Jack was thinking how ripe a situation this was; he heard a click of a radio transmission coming from Chuck Reed.

"Chicago Center, this is Husky in Blackbird 71, you got a groundspeed readout for us?"

There was a longer than normal pause – "Husky, I show 1,742 knots."

No further inquiries were heard on that frequency. "Show off," quipped Jack into the intercom. Warner made Reed an offer: "I'll be happy to buy the first liter of German beer in Frankfurt."

"The first of many, I hope," replied Reed.

After Reed and Warner left Chicago behind, Reed announced that they were getting low on "go-go juice."

"Where do we land?" asked Jack.

Reed answered, "We don't go to the fuel. The fuel comes to us. A KC-33 747 tanker, that we call 'Texaco,' from the Air Force base in Bangor, Maine will rendezvous with us as we pass over. We'll slow down under Mach 1 to allow them to extend their high-speed fueling boom for us to connect with. It delivers 1,000 gallons per minute so it will take about 10 minutes. In pilot-speak, when you're low on go-go juice, Texaco hooks up with you and passes gas. The hard part is holding my credit card out the window at Mach 1 for the Texaco attendant."

Jack countered with, "Well, with all the gas this thing swallows, you must have an entire set of steak knives and all eight NFL glasses by now." Beneath their helmets, there were grins all around.

A few hours later, Reed and Warner were approaching Shanwick Flight Control Center in County Clare, Ireland. Colonel Reed radioed Shanwick. "Blackbird 71 requests clearance to FL 600 (60,000 feet)."

The incredulous controller, with some disdain in his voice, asked, "Exactly how do you plan to get up to 60,000 feet, if I might ask?"

Reed responded, "We don't plan to go *up* to it, we plan to go *down* to it."

Now the controller was paying attention and cleared them. "Yes, sir, 10-4, Blackbird 71. Yes, sir, that'll be fine, sir."

Jack was thinking, "I'd love to be a fly on the wall in that control tower."

Reed and Warner landed at Ramstein Air Force Base a few minutes later; less than four hours after they left California. "Now *that* was an E-ticket ride," said Jack to Chuck Reed.

Mothball Air Force

While flying for Pan Am, Jack got transferred to the Dallas/Fort Worth Airport. It was a major hub for flights for almost every airline in the U.S. Gail found a house outside of Dallas. She supervised the move, and the family settled into their new home.

Jack yearned for more than just flying around the world. He wanted to be in the aviation business. While flying from New York to Los Angeles one day, he was flying low due to some upper-air turbulence. He looked down to see hundreds of acres of parked airplanes in Arizona. The Air Force operated an aircraft storage facility outside of Scottsdale. There were hundreds and hundreds of aircraft stored there, known as the Mothball Air Force. In the years since WWII, planes and other military equipment of all kinds were brought there to be scrapped, cannibalized for parts, or sold outright to the highest bidder at auctions.

With the jet on autopilot, Warner had plenty of time to daydream during a long, boring flight. Watching that aluminum ocean of planes got him thinking. "There must be some opportunity sitting there for me."

He started on some self-analysis. "I've got my flying experience, military connections, and a certain amount of celebrity going for me, thanks to Johnny Carson. What could I do with all of that? What if I bought a bunch of used cargo planes and got Lou Patroni to get them into shape? I could start an air cargo business."

Jack owned an old air base outside of Dallas that he won in a poker game just after Vietnam. He had never even seen it. He loved the idea so much that he called his old friend, Patroni, and talked to him for hours about the idea. Patroni simply said, "Call me when you're ready to check out your airfield."

Married Life

Gail and Jack loved each other very much, but they had jobs that kept them separated a great deal of the time. Gail worked long hours at Dallas Memorial Hospital, and Jack was always flying, often spending nights in a faraway city. Gail always tried to make the most of the times that they were together. The couple designated Saturdays as "date night." Jack usually took Gail to dinner at Burger Continental, followed by a movie at the Alex Theater. One night over dinner, Gail asked Jack, "How come we don't see more movies?"

"'Cuz there's too much goddamned swearing." Jack could swear a blue streak with pilots or other men but almost never used foul language in front of women.

One night, as they were lying in bed, neither one could sleep. After tossing and turning for an hour, Gail started playing with Jack's hair, like young lovers do. It always made Jack smile, which was contagious to Gail. "Honey, could we rearrange our lives so that we can spend more time together? There's got to be something we could work on together. Between the hours I spend at the hospital and your crazy flying schedule, we never seem to see each other. That can't be good for any relationship. I love you and I miss seeing you every day and every night."

"Funny you should bring that up, Babe," murmured Jack. He told her about seeing all the surplus planes that were being scrapped or auctioned off and his ideas for an air-cargo business. He went on and on, detailing his dream. She was doing her own dreaming: What if they worked the business together? It would mean spending more time with Jack.

Gail said, "Honey, let's pull out some pads of paper and sketch out your ideas. Let's see if we can make this work."

"We? You mean you'll help me?" asked Jack.

"Why do you have a copilot seat in your plane? Every pilot needs some help. Let's do it together."

Even though it was the middle of the night, they both jumped out of bed and grabbed some legal pads and went to work. They cleared off the dining room table and moved all the chairs out of the way except for two. It was quite a sight; Jack in his boxer shorts and Gail in her oversized T-shirt. She was a natural organizer. Gail put headings on each page: Planes, Maintenance, Employees, Airfield, Warehouse Space, FAA Requirements, Sales, Marketing, Legal & Accounting, etc. She just kept going. Jack dictated and she wrote down notes along with her own ideas.

They took each main page and Gail wrote down more detailed points to work on. The business plan was taking shape. This had to be the strangest corporate meeting in history.

"What are we going to use for money, Honey?" asked Gail.

Jack answered, "I've got a pretty good nest egg I saved up since I went to Vietnam."

"I have an inheritance from my grandparents. I've never touched it. That ought to buy some used planes. How much is an old plane anyway, Jack?"

"Let's go shopping and see," Jack offered. So Gail scheduled a vacation from the hospital and Jack scheduled his vacation from Pan Am so they could do just that.

"I guess I'm in love with you, Jack Warner. Most women dream of a vacation to Europe or Hawaii, and here I am, going with you to see some goddamned airplane junkyard in the Arizona desert."

"I guess I must love you back, Babe. Most pilots would never want their wife to come on an airplane-buying trip, but I wouldn't dream of doing it without you."

So, a few days later, off they went, landing in Scottsdale. It was an odd sight, a couple holding hands, walking through an airplane junkyard with their son, Noah, riding his tricycle nearby. They quickly tired of walking in the hot Arizona sun, so Jack sweet-talked the Air Force staff into letting him use one of their golf carts. Gail had planned ahead and had brought an ice chest of waters and sodas. Jack tied the ice chest on the back of the cart where the golf clubs usually go.

The little aircraft exploratory team took off with Jack driving, Gail taking notes, and little Noah having a blast on this full-sized Hot Wheels car. They found hundreds of cargo planes, mountains of engines, landing gear assemblies, tires, and parts of all kinds. Of course, most of it was junk, but a great deal looked perfectly fine, with lots of life left in it.

In addition to the airplanes and associated parts, there was row after row of aviation equipment just sitting there. Jack was the proverbial kid in the candy store, pointing and explaining to Gail and Noah what everything was. Gail filled up her first yellow legal pad and two more, besides. Her pen ran out of ink and she had to fish through her purse for another.

Auction

At the Scottsdale Military Surplus Aircraft Storage Facility, planes scheduled to be sold were auctioned off in groups or lots. This cut down the workload for the Air Force staff who managed the facility. It took the same effort to sell 10 planes at once as it did for just one. Warner knew many of the staffers from his days in the Air Force. With a little help from his friends, Warner cherry-picked the best planes from the inventory and made up a dream lot of 12 planes for an upcoming auction.

Jack Warner called Lou Patroni and told him to hire some help and get his butt to Scottsdale. Somehow – due to a clerical error, I'm sure – this Lot #86 didn't make it onto the auction inventory sheet that was circulated to scrap and surplus aircraft buyers. Only buyers who actually attended that day's auction would see it as a last-minute add-on to the lot sale sheet.

Patroni got his hands on some blue wax crayons and scribbled "Engines N/G" and "Not Airworthy Scrap" on every plane's windshield in Lot #86. His mechanics disconnected all the control cables so the flaps dropped down. They let the air out of all the tires to make the planes look really depressing.

To make double sure of his success, the auction was scheduled for Monday, December 26th, the day after Christmas. Most buyers were home with their families. The attendance was light at best. Warner bought the whole lot for just a small percentage of scrap value. It was bordering on grand theft, but that didn't seem to worry Jack Warner. His conscience wrote it off as a government gratuity for rescuing so many pilots in Vietnam. On the whole, the U.S. Government actually made money on the deal. If you took the dollar value of all the pilots that Jack rescued in North Vietnam compared to the fair market value of everything Warner bought that day, the government came out a winner. Not to mention the personal value of the pilots' lives and their families' happiness. Jack Warner slept like a baby that night with a clear conscience.

The day after the sale, Patroni and his new team of mechanics descended on the scrap yard like locusts. They filled up the airplane tires, reconnected all the control cables, and gave each plane a thorough cleaning. They were able to drain fuel from other planes and fill up the Warner Air Force. They also got fuel from other planes on the field and stored it in some old fuel trucks. Patroni set up a makeshift repair facility in an empty hangar at the Scottsdale scrap yard. The mechanics borrowed an Air Force mule and towed each plane in and got the planes in working order. They weren't in good enough shape to pass FAA inspection, but they would fly the short distance to Texas. When they needed a part, the auction staff just said, "Leave us alone. Just go find what you need and take it. We need to make room."

The Patroni Platoon grabbed several forklifts and kept them busy all day accumulating everything they could find from Gail's lists. Since they had almost 500 acres of spare parts available for the taking, every plane came out in flying shape and ready for cargo use. With 12 empty cargo planes available, Patroni filled them up with extra engines and every part that they might possibly need in the future. When the time came for Warner's new air force to leave, the planes could barely get off the ground, since they carried a full load of fuel and were loaded to the maximum weight limit with extra airplane engines, fuel, tires, and spare parts.

Jack hired 11 more retired Air Force pilots and Patroni rented some semitrucks to haul what the planes couldn't carry. Jack flew the lead plane, followed in formation by his personal air force to the new Warner Airfield outside of Dallas. Warner's new field shared a border fence with McCann Air Force Base.

Lou Patroni hired every FAA-certified aviation mechanic that he could find. His team of mechanics put the whole fleet of planes in factory-fresh condition within 90 days. Even though most of the replacement parts were scavenged from other planes, they all functioned perfectly. It was rather convenient having the cargo company's airfield right next door to the McCann Air Force Base. You never know when you might want to borrow an electronic stabilizer control from your neighbor or a truckload of aviation fuel.

While Jack started planning the work needed for the base buildings, runway, lighting, and utilities, Patroni and his men started on the plane maintenance and spare parts organization. 12 cargo planes full of spare parts from Scottsdale took an enormous amount of work to label everything and put it where the mechanics could find it again.

Patroni cornered Jack one day. "Boss, we need about a million feet of that heavy-duty industrial shelving to store all of this equipment in some kind of order." The answer to that need came the next day.

Idaho

Jack received a call from his old poker pal, Tim Brockway, now a lieutenant colonel. Warner felt bad about Brockway losing the airfield to him during that infamous poker game years ago in Hawaii. Jack had tried to make up for it by forwarding information to the Air Force about airplane feedback from pilots and crewmen. This was inside information that upper-class officers generally wouldn't hear about. It didn't take committees, studies, or reports. It was the real intel, right from the men experiencing the problems.

There were several times over the years that Warner told Brockway about a problem with a fighter jet or an ordinance hiccup. Brockway would forward this info to the appropriate Air Force contractor liaisons so the manufacturer could be forced to correct the problems with no charge to the Air Force. Jack's intel had saved lives and millions of tax dollars. Brockway couldn't be happier, especially since he took credit for the ideas.

"I've got something you might be interested in, Jack," said Lieutenant Colonel Brockway. "The air base at Eagle Point, Idaho is closing." Brockway knew that Warner had just taken over his old dilapidated airfield next door to McCann Air Base. "I thought maybe you could use a few things from Eagle Point. It's all gonna be torn down anyway. The demo contractor will be there in two weeks. I'll get you an authorization letter giving you permission to scavenge anything on the base. You've got 14 days, no more. Remember, 14 isn't 15. Capiche?"

Warner called Patroni and told him to get four planes ready to fly to Idaho with 20 guys outfitted with jeeps, flatbed trailers, hoists, tools, ladders, lights, generators, fuel, food, and all the equipment needed to sustain them for two weeks. They were going shopping. The planes were like a flying Home Depot.

Upon landing, Warner had the men set up camp with tents, storage tents, and latrines. He and Patroni took a Jeep and went shopping. The Eagle Point Air Base was almost 300 acres. Warner considered it the world's largest garage sale and he had the golden ticket.

Warner was dictating so fast that Patroni couldn't write the shopping list items on his pad fast enough. Just about everything they needed for the field in Texas was right here for the taking. Runway lights, fuel tanks, fuel trucks, office equipment and furniture, spotlights, a complete kitchen full of appliances in good shape, motor pool equipment, airplane shop equipment, lots of airplane spare parts that Patroni could use, compressors, and lots more. Warner turned to Patroni and simply said, "We're gonna need a bigger boat."

The original four planes made repeat trips shuttling equipment back to Texas, plus Warner had four more planes come to help out. Lieutenant Colonel Brockway called to say the demo contractor was delayed on another job, so they had an extra week to scavenge. They had already been there for 12 days. The men were getting irritable and tired of the camp kitchen and there was nothing to do at night. Warner had a brainstorm. He drove off by himself and made the 12-mile trip into the town of Eagle Point. After stopping at the bank, he drove around town for the rest of the afternoon.

As the sun was almost setting, a caravan of vehicles followed Jack Warner back onto the Eagle Point Air Base to the temporary camp city they had constructed. There was a taco truck, a BBQ truck, a Good Humor Ice Cream truck, and a van from the Red Carpet Liquor Store full of beer, ice, and cases of Jack Daniel's, Bacardi, and Jose Cuervo tequila. Another van from Eagle Point Sporting Goods brought up the rear. Those guys emptied out footballs, basketball hoops, balls, baseball equipment, a ping-pong table, Frisbees, and two tables full of New Balance cross-trainer shoes in an assortment of sizes.

All of Warner's men went friggin' nuts! They grabbed him and hoisted him up on their shoulders and carried him around the field, all while singing, "He's a jolly good fellow." Then, they hugged him and patted him on the back for five minutes. Next, they set up the bar with all the booze.

About the time they all quieted down, the food trucks were ready to serve dinner. Patroni leaned over to Jack and said, "The ice cream's nice, but didn't they have any hookers in that town?"

"Eagle Point, Idaho is not exactly a hotbed of prostitution, Lou," replied Jack. They both laughed like hell and poured another drink.

Dallas

Patroni and his crew set up the Warner Dallas Airfield with all of the bounty from the Idaho scavenger hunt. Between Jack and Lou's efforts, the base was coming along nicely. One afternoon, Lou noticed some big chain-link gates in a scrap pile on the McCann base. He found the air base manager and offered to haul them away. The manager, Captain Berman, said, "Go ahead, take them. I can use the room." Berman quickly wrote out an authorization permit for Patroni.

It wasn't quite the deal that Berman thought it was going to be. Patroni cut a 25-foot hole in the fence between Warner's property and the air base. As he installed the gates in the fence, he made sure to use old bolts and hardware. The entire gate installation took place late on a moonless night. When the Air Force MPs stopped by to question the work, Patroni told them he had a work permit. He showed them his receipt signed by Captain Berman. Patroni held the paper for the MPs with his thumb over the word "Authorization." The MPs didn't realize that it was just a permission slip and not a work permit. They saw Captain Berman's signature and went on their way, leaving Patroni's men to finish the job just before sun up.

McCann Air Force Base was secure again, except for an extra set of gates that only Lou Patroni had the key to. Since it was made out of old galvanized chain-link fence, weathered by 25 years of Texas sun, it blended in with rest of the miles of perimeter fence. The fox had a gate to the henhouse and the only key for the lock.

That key came in real handy a few months later. Since McCann Air Base was out in the boonies, there was no connection to municipal sewer services. The base kitchen and latrines all drained their sewage and gray water into a system of septic tanks and a large leech field next to Warner's fence. Leech fields consist of a network of plastic drain pipes with little holes in them to allow the dirty water to trickle out into the earth.

Warner's air base had a similar but much smaller system, which was older than the McCann system next door. Unfortunately, on a Friday afternoon, it clogged up and failed. All of a sudden, Jack's airfield had no working sewer system for the bathrooms or the kitchen.

Patroni came in to troubleshoot the situation, and then he huddled up with Jack Warner. His report: "Well, the typical solution would be to dig trenches for a whole new leech field and install new septic tanks. Digging trenches, permits, ordering a truckload of drain pipe, and installing it plus new septic tanks ought to cost about 50 grand and take 2-3 weeks."

"Mr. Patroni, something tells me that you have an alternative solution," said Warner.

"As a matter of fact, I do," spouted Patroni with a wide grin. "Do you see what's right over there, on the other side of the fence? That's the leech field for McCann's sewer system. You know the government. They always build everything twice the size of what they need. Why don't we just tap into it? Tomorrow is Saturday. Hows about if tonight I get a bunch of guys start digging a trench from our leech field over to the government's leech field? While I'm doing that, I'll have my son, Dino, take a truck and get a load of drain pipe and some supplies. We can have the whole job done by Sunday night. It will probably be the first time that a taxpayer gives shit back to the government."

Jack Warner couldn't stop laughing. He peeled off a bunch of $100 bills and stuffed them in Patroni's hand. All he could say was, "I don't want to know anything. I just own the joint."

By Sunday night, the Warner sewage system drained quite nicely through the new pipe under the border fence and into the McCann Air Base leech field system. Jack Warner saved at least 50 grand and weeks of work. And it didn't cost the U.S. Government a dime to let Warner's waste water drain into their dirt.

Aire Cargo Is Born

One afternoon, Jack called Gail into his office, which consisted of a folding table and two folding chairs flanked by a few second-hand file cabinets. "Hey, Babe, what are we going to call this company?"

Gail had an idea. "Honey, I'll take a stack of 3x5 index cards. You tell me every word you can think of that has to do with air freight. Then, we'll lay them out in different combinations and see if there's a name that you like."

"That sounds too simple. You're gonna put some Madison Avenue ad man out of a job," he said with a big smile. "I suppose I have to pay the 89 cents for the package of index cards?"

"You got it, Rockefeller," laughed Gail.

Jack dictated and Gail wrote on the cards. When Jack's brain was empty, there was a big pile of cards on the rickety table. "Well, let's start moving 'em around into phrases," suggested Gail.

"This looks like some kind of kid's game," offered Jack.

The Warners pushed the cards around into different combinations. When something looked promising, Gail would pushpin the cards up on an old bulletin board that Patroni found in Idaho. After a few hours, they had narrowed down the suggestions to five different arrangements up on the board to consider. Patroni walked in to see where Jack had disappeared to.

"Whaddya think, Lou? These are some possible names for the company," said Jack.

Worldwide Cargo Warner Cargo Worldwide Express Freight Express Air Cargo

"Worldwide Cargo is too long and difficult to say. Warner Cargo is personal. A generic name sounds like a bigger company. Freight Express is no good. There's too much chance for confusion with Federal Express. You can expect a letter from their attorneys before the ink is dry on your plane. I like Air Cargo. It's short, sweet, and tells the customer what we do. It won't take too much room on the planes, trucks, or shirt pockets. It'll save you money in printing and painting. But, I have one idea: Change it to Aire Cargo, with an e on the end. It sounds more sophisticated, and no one else will have it."

"Son-of-a-bitch, Patroni. You're good. I think you're wasting your time turning wrenches. Maybe you should head up the marketing department. What do you think, Gail?"

"I think Lou likes to play with his planes too much. He'd go nuts sitting behind a desk wearing a tie. Plus, I won't let him smoke his cigars in the office."

Lou started laughing. "Jack, you rescued one smart broad that night back in Vietnam."

The laughter was infectious. "Okay, steaks are on the new company, Aire Cargo. Wash your hands, Lou, and let's go," offered Warner.

If there's one thing that they do right in Texas, it's beef. The ribeye steaks at Monty's were just perfect. They grilled them with those little crisscross grill marks on each side and topped them with Monty Butter: a mixture of sweet butter, fresh garlic, and real bleu cheese. It all seemed to melt in your mouth.

Of course, that gorgeous hunk of beef needed something else on the platter. Grilled fresh spinach in olive oil with fresh garlic, sliced razor thin, fresh creamed corn, and the lightest homemade garlic toast you've ever had filled the bill. The waiter would always remind you to pre-order their chocolate soufflé. Heaven in a bowl!

Patroni asked Jack, "Are there any more ideas you need help with? I'm available every day, morning, noon, or night." *Clink* went the wine glasses.

Jack got the warehouses figured out and Gail worked on the office, telephones, and marketing. She set Jack down for a whole day and picked his brain for names of people that he knew in the military or aviation business. One day turned into three. She filled up eight legal pads with names and all the contact info Jack could remember. Then, she did the same thing with Lou Patroni. He filled up four more pads. Gail was going to make a mailing list to announce their new business.

One of Jack's first jobs was to fly a bunch of computer equipment from the San Francisco Airport to Las Vegas for a company Jack had never heard of: Apple Computers. There was a new trade show for computers called COMDEX. He had never heard of that either, but figured that a job's a job. Gail had been hearing about these new small computers, so she tagged along too.

After delivering the computers, she and Jack checked out the show. While grabbing a cup of coffee, they heard people talking. The people being talked about were two young guys who were very impressive – Steve Jobs, who made the Apple computers Jack had delivered, and Bill Gates, who made something called "software" that made the computers work. There was such a big crowd around their show booths that the Warners could never get close enough to meet them. It didn't take long for Jack and Gail to realize that a computer was exactly what they needed for Aire Cargo.

She did some research and was going to buy an Apple III. But then a man explained that IBM had just come out with the IBM Personal Computer that did exactly the jobs Aire Cargo needed, plus it was quite a bit cheaper than the Apple. Since their startup money was almost gone, they bought the IBM. Aire Cargo was one of the first small companies to use a computer. Only a few years before, only big corporations used room-sized computers that needed several people to operate it.

Gail learned how to input all the contact information she got from Jack and Lou. She sent out an announcement that Aire Cargo was in business. Their slogan was "Aire Cargo Delivery – Affordable & On Time." Jack thought her efforts were commendable, but he needed more if he wanted to get his business off the ground, literally.

He personally called all of his military connections. Soon, he was hauling air freight for all the branches of the military. Even though they had cargo planes too, Jack was so efficient, he could do it faster and cheaper. The military brass could utilize their transportation budget money elsewhere, which made them very happy.

He tried to get the airmail and parcel post business from the U.S. Post Office, but his old friend, Fred Smith, had that business locked up in a long-term contract with FedEx. But Jack was able to work out a subcontractor deal to haul oversized items for FedEx. Jack had larger planes and equipment that could handle things that FedEx couldn't.

One of the pilots Jack rescued in Vietnam was now on the Board of Directors of the Xerox Corporation. He was able to get Jack an appointment with Cameron Carothers, the shipping director. Cameron was very impressed with Jack's presentation, but not totally convinced. He decided to test Aire Cargo's performance by shipping a pallet with a washing machine inside of a large Xerox box. They shipped the pallet with the "Xerox" machine across the United States several times. Each and every time, everything went perfectly, and they tested the washing machine after each trip. Cameron called Jack and told him of their test. He laughed at the originality and said, "Not a bad idea. How'd we do?"

"10 out of 10. Sign us up." Xerox turned out to be one of Jack's largest customers. Most Xerox copiers and office equipment were normally sent by truck, but parts and accessories were usually needed immediately, so they hired Aire Cargo to handle those shipments.

Moles

Jack still needed more cargo business to keep his business aloft, as it were. Advertising was too expensive, plus Warner didn't want to advertise to the general public, since they seldom used air freight. He came up with an original idea. He hired a dozen new employees with a confidential assignment. Each employee lived in a different big city in America. Jack called them moles. The mole's job was to stake out competitors' air freight loading docks and see who the customers were. If a private freight forwarder picked up a shipment, he had the mole follow the truck and see who the end customer was. Late at night, the mole put on some coveralls, grabbed a flashlight, and jumped in trash dumpsters to retrieve old shipping invoices or telephone message slips.

Jack paid them handsomely for every customer lead they came up with. He heard rumors of some enterprising moles slipping some cash to the air freight delivery drivers for a copy of their delivery manifest for that day. He was pretty sure that many delivery drivers had new color TVs, and some were driving new cars. Gail gathered all of the moles' info and entered it in the computer. She and Jack put it to good use.

The first dozen moles soon became 25. Jack spread them all across the U.S. in every major city. He also hired moles in major European cities. Next, he organized moles in the Mideast, India, Japan, Hong Kong, South Korea, and the Philippines.

Customers are often neglected by the businesses they patronize. Companies will spend thousands of advertising dollars to attract new customers, but their sales reps never seem to get off their asses and pick up the phone to call their existing customers. They start taking them for granted. A simple call to say, "Thank you for your past business. Is there anything we can do better for you? Have your business needs changed in ways that we can help you with?" doesn't cost anything, but most salespeople don't do it.

Air freight customers and their sales reps were no different. It didn't take much effort for Jack to take advantage of that neglect and ask a potential customer to give Aire Cargo a try. This worked especially well when Jack said, "Your first delivery is free!"

Today, efforts like these are known by the term "guerilla marketing," but in the 1980s, Jack Warner didn't have any money for advertising or marketing. He just wanted to do something different to break through into a new business.

Unions

A few years later, the Airline Workers Union wanted to organize Aire Cargo's employees. They called Jack to arrange a visit to Aire Cargo in Texas. They were surprised when he said, "Sure, come on over anytime."

When they arrived and introduced themselves to a crowd of employees, they started their canned speech about the benefits of being brothers together in the union and all the promises of what the union could do for them. The whole group of employees started jeering and yelling at them. The workers grabbed broomsticks, bricks, and 2x4s, and chased the union organizers off the property. The union boys jumped into their car and tore out of the parking lot, laying rubber around the corner, heading for the airport. Never in the history of union organizing had they ever been treated in such a manner. The two union guys turned to each other, still panting from their escape, and muttered, "What the fuck was that?"

Jack Warner just gazed down from his office window with tears streaming down his face. His employees loved him. Gail and Jack treated their employees with courtesy and respect. They were paid well for a job well done. In his later years, Jack Warner went into the hospital for some kidney surgery. There was a line of employees around the hospital parking lot who wanted to donate blood for him. Airmen from the Air Force base showed up too. The hospital had so much blood on hand that the donations supplied the entire central region of the Red Cross network. 14 employees offered him one of their kidneys if he needed one.

The union reps never came back to Aire Cargo again.

Black Market Shuttle

Lou Patroni had a wife and two kids, Gina and Dino. In the mid-1980s, Dino was going to school at UCLA, majoring in International Business Administration. While there, he met Amir Milani, a student from Iran. They were roommates in the UCLA dorm. Amir's father was the Director of Iranian Customs.

One Saturday afternoon, Dino took Amir shopping at Fedco in West L.A. Fedco was a forerunner to today's Costco, Target, and Walmart. They sold everything at a big discount. Amir was astounded by the variety of products and the quantities available. All you needed was money and a big car. The boys stocked up on everything from shampoo to batteries and bought all the latest record albums.

That night, over music and a few beers, they were sitting out on their dorm room balcony. Amir and Dino came up with an idea. While Dino was in high school, he worked almost every summer at Aire Cargo, loading and unloading cargo planes. Airplanes carried freight in metal cargo containers that have a curved side to fit snuggly into the plane's fuselage. The most common unit had a capacity of 181 cubic feet and a weight limit of 3,500 pounds.

Amir used to work at Tehran International Airport, where his father was in charge of the customs office. Like many airport employees, Amir's family had connections to dealers in Iran's lucrative black market.

Dino and Amir pooled their money and borrowed some more from Dino's father, Lou. They had a total of $7,500. It was enough to do some serious shopping at Fedco. They had to make several trips, since Amir had no car and Dino only had a beat-up Datsun pickup.

They slowly built a mountain of goods in their dorm room. Space was limited, so they stacked the boxes on the floor and put their beds on top of them. By the time they were done, there was barely any space to sleep between the mattresses and the ceiling. Long tunnels led through the boxes all over the apartment, to the kitchen, bathroom, closets, desks, and beds. The dorm room below developed cracks in their ceiling, which was starting to droop down from all the weight on the floor above.

The manager of the Fedco store couldn't understand the increase in sales of so many items. Shelves were being cleared off every night of Johnny Walker Black Label, Jack Daniel's, Marlboro cigarettes, Levi's jeans, Crest toothpaste, rock 'n' roll record albums, Nike tennis shoes, Tabasco sauce, Similac baby formula, Hershey's bars, cases of Coors and Budweiser, Bayer Aspirin, and Trojan rubbers.

Amir and Dino went shopping at the UCLA Student Store. They negotiated a great discount with the store manager for 500 blue UCLA T-shirts. Iranians called them "ook-la" shirts. It was a very prestigious garment to wear in Tehran. It meant your child went to school in the U.S.

The company was always hungry for cargo jobs. Dino negotiated an employee discount to ship the loaded container to Iran. The container was picked up at LAX in Los Angeles and flown to Tehran.

On the shipping manifest, Amir listed the contents as "ballast." Occasionally, companies would ship heavy loads which might throw off the place's balance. A container would be partially loaded with bags of sand in order to balance the plane's center of gravity. This would ensure the airworthiness of the aircraft. A few of these ballast containers would travel back and forth between airports. The boys' scheme evaded customs and airport taxes in the U.S. and Iranian Customs duties.

Once the plane landed in Tehran, Amir's Uncle Hamid supervised the unloading of the cargo. All of the containers, except one, were transported to the customs warehouse for inspection and clearance procedures. The "ballast" container was moved to the airport's utility yard, where it sat outside in a simple fenced yard. Later that night,

Hamid and his sons borrowed a truck, unloaded the container, and moved the goods into the family's warehouse nearby. From there, they would be sold into the black-market system at 10 times Amir and Dino's cost.

This first container soon became two, and then two became four, and so on. With the number of air cargo containers climbing, the "ballast" classification wouldn't hold up.

In the early days, Jack was flying some planes himself. He would radio Tehran that the plane was having some mechanical difficulty and needed assistance upon landing. The airport would send out a tug to tow the plane. The Tehran Air Controllers started joking about what crappy planes Aire Cargo had. "Those Aire Cargo jets are pieces of shit. Every time they land, their plane needs a tow to the maintenance hangar," they laughed.

After the plane was towed to the maintenance hangar, Dino and Amir's containers were removed. At LAX, their containers had been loaded last so they could easily come off first. The black-market goods were quickly unloaded, and the now-empty containers were returned to the plane.

Dino and Amir's little enterprise kept growing. They kept adding American-made goods to their inventory. They bought anything legal that the black-market customers wanted to buy. Within a year, they were chartering an entire Aire Cargo 747 Cargo Freighter to Tehran every month. They filled the whole plane all by themselves. It took some serious bribe money to have a 747 evade Iranian Customs, but they were making serious profits. Amir's father made it all work. Amir's Uncle Hamid had expanded to supply black-market activity all over the Mid-East in several countries. There were no U.S. laws about exporting American goods to foreign countries, as long as they weren't weapons, ammunition, or electronic technology items.

Amir and Dino's share of the sale proceeds were wired into two accounts in the Cayman Islands. Paying UCLA tuition was not going to be a problem. Amir and Dino were each making $100,000 every month. They were careful to declare their income and pay any U.S. income taxes that were due. Dino didn't want problems from the IRS, and Amir didn't want to threaten his immigration status. They soon left the UCLA dorm behind and each paid cash for a luxury condo in high-rise buildings on Wilshire Boulevard, near UCLA.

Jack got busy in Dallas, so another pilot took over the Iran charter flights. Aire Cargo was very pleased with the monthly charter to Iran. They were also making serious money with every trip.

The Aire Cargo pilots and crew developed their own little enterprise. U.S. laws limited exporting cash to $10,000 per trip. Every member of the flight crew carried $9,950 in U.S. currency on every trip. They would offer better exchange rates than were available to most Iranian citizens. All the airport personnel started exchanging their rial Iranian banknotes for U.S. currency. This surplus of Iranian rials would normally present a problem for an American. How would you explain it? It was too much cash to import through American Customs.

Amir and Dino analyzed the situation and came up with a new business: Iran has sand, oil, and seafood. Their share of the cargo sales proceeds, along with the crew's cash exchange profits, went into a seafood business. The new A&D Seafood Company took the rials and bought Iranian seafood. The empty Aire Cargo plane was now loaded with refrigerated cargo containers of frozen bluefin tuna, Iranian caviar, shrimp, tilapia, salmon, and eels. The plane made regular deliveries to the famous Tokyo Fish Market in Japan.

While the seafood was unloaded and the plane serviced, the crew made a trip to the Tokyo International Bank, where they exchanged Iranian rials and Japanese yen for U.S. dollars. Then, they had the dollars wired to their accounts in the Cayman Islands. Dino was making way more money than his father, Lou Patroni, and Dino was only a junior in college.

Like Grandfather, Like Father, Like Son

The summer that Noah turned 12, Gail kissed him and Jack goodbye and then watched them leave for a hunting trip to Alaska. They landed at Burbank Airport and went to the private terminal.

A few years after Jack had saved the movie producer, Billy Robbins, Billy bought a new Hawker 400XP jet. He hired Warner to fly it whenever Jack was available on the West Coast. Even though Jack was busy running Aire Cargo, he still loved to fly small corporate jets. They were so small and nimble, like a go-kart in the sky. Robbins had offered the Hawker to Jack countless times for personal use, but Warner had never taken him up on it until now.

"Hey, Pop, how come we're over here instead of at the Alaskan Airlines Terminal?"

"I thought maybe you'd like a little nicer ride for our trip to see your grandparents in Alaska."

"Cool" was the only response from young Master Warner.

Out on the tarmac, Jack quickly found the Hawker and opened the door. "Noah, please load the bags inside and then come back outside. I'll show you how to pre-flight this bird." Noah watched Jack's every move and listened to all his instructions.

When they were ready to go, Noah sat in the copilot's seat and took in all that he could see. "Wow, Pop. How do you ever remember what this stuff does?" He was like a little sponge. Noah was certainly his father's son. His questions were endless. Jack answered all of them, but after a while, was ready for a bit of quiet time.

Four hours later, they were setting down in Anchorage. "Too bad they don't make pontoons for Hawker jets, huh? We could land in the bay near Grandpa and Grandma's cabin."

"This would be the first $7 million bush plane. You'd really be stylin', pal."

"Now, that would indeed be a sight," thought Jack. It's a good thing nobody gave Jack that idea 20 years earlier. He probably would have tried it.

Both Ben and ML were delighted to see young Noah and Jack. It had been far too long between visits. It was hard to tell who was happier, Ben and ML or Noah when Jack told him the surprise. "Your grandparents would like you to stay up here for the whole summer. Grandpa will show you how to fish for salmon and halibut. Grandma will show you to clean and cook them like a real chef. And best of all, Grandpa Ben said he would teach you to fly. If you work hard and study, you could be qualified to solo by the end of the summer. What do you think of that?" asked Jack.

Noah threw his arms around his grandparents and gave each one a kiss on the cheek. "That's *great*! I'm so excited. Thank you, thank you, thank you. But, Pop, I'm only 12. Can I get a license?"

"Not for a few years yet, but you can be learning. Grandpa gave me lessons when I was 12. You can take official lessons from a certified instructor when you're ready."

Noah turned to his dad and hugged him too. "Bitchin'! Thank mom for me, will ya?"

Overnight Aire

While Jack Warner was getting Aire Cargo literally off the ground, his old Vietnam friend, Fred Smith, had been busy. Fred had inherited some money from his father in 1971. Fred Smith took his $4 million inheritance and founded Federal Express. In 1973, the company started offering service to 25 cities. It began with small packages and documents and a fleet of 14 used Falcon 20 jets.

Smith developed the FedEx business as a package shipment version of a bank check clearing house. One bank clearing house was located in the middle of the bank group and the bank representatives would go to the central location to exchange money and checks.

Warner noticed the success his old friend was enjoying with FedEx. Jack had built the Aire Cargo business up until it was one of the largest air freight companies in the U.S., so he decided to give Fred Smith a little competition. Jack had the planes and connections to copy FedEx, plus he had larger cargo planes to carry bigger packages and equipment that FedEx couldn't. In the 1990s, he added overnight delivery service for his customers.

Instead of discarding the famous Aire Cargo name and starting a new brand, he added an overnight division to Aire Cargo. The new division's name was Overnight Aire. Gail thought of it in about 10 minutes. "Short and sweet is always best, Babe. Like Aire Cargo, it won't take up much room or cost a lot to print signs and paint artwork on the planes."

Overnight Aire never got to be a big competitor for FedEx. It was really just an offshoot of Aire Cargo, mainly for the convenience of their existing customers. Each cargo plane would carry a few containers with overnight packages. It basically cost Jack just a little extra labor and fuel to supply this service. He already had the personnel, trucks, planes, and facilities to support the company.

Cabo Cargo

Jack Warner thought that a small cargo plane might be good for smaller, specialized cargo jobs. He decided to test his theory before spending the money buying such a plane. Warner leased a Citation Cargo King 1000. The twin-engine turbo prop plane could cruise at 225 knots up to a ceiling of 10,000 feet. This plane would hold a 3,200-pound payload. The rear of the plane had a drop-down cargo door that could be lowered to allow loads to be wheeled up and right into the plane. Jack thought that this aircraft was a perfect addition for his business.

Just after he took delivery of the Cargo King, he got a call for a small cargo job that would be perfect for his new plane. Miguel Ortiz wanted to take three pallets of Lone Star Beer down to Cabo San Lucas, Mexico for the Cinco de Mayo weekend and haul back some tourist goods to Dallas. Jack prepared a written quote for him that covered fuel, airport charges, overnight hotel expenses, and his time flying the round trip from Texas to Mexico. Ortiz agreed to the price and terms and paid cash for the entire round trip in advance. Jack Warner was surprised by the cash payment, but who's gonna argue about getting paid? He marked the invoice "paid in full" and prepared a bill of lading and the necessary customs forms for the cargo shipment.

Warner supervised the beer loading, making sure the three pallets were well secured by multiple nylon cinching straps. Air turbulence can make cargo airborne in a nanosecond. Ortiz insisted on riding along with his cargo. Jack reluctantly agreed and offered him one of the fold-down jump seats. They weren't very comfortable, especially for a three-hour flight, but what the hell – Jack warned Miguel and he agreed to it.

The flight was fine and the landing and cargo offload went perfectly normal. Jack supervised the refueling and performed a maintenance check to be ready to go in the morning. After a comfortable night at the Sheraton, Jack was rested and itching to take off after breakfast.

Ortiz showed up with a cargo van with three pallets inside for the return trip. Jack noticed that he came from the opposite side of the airport from the Mexican Customs yard. The pallets were loaded with some kind of soft goods all covered with tarps. Ortiz's two helpers loaded them into the plane with a forklift. Warner didn't see any customs forms, but he didn't mention it, thinking of the thousands of dollars in cash locked in his safe, back in Dallas. Gail had the money targeted for a stack of fuel bills.

Jack had to prepare a handwritten bill of lading for the return flight. He gave Ortiz some blank commercial customs entry forms to fill out during the flight.

Jack took off from Cabo and proceeded to Dallas. As they were entering U.S. airspace again, Jack received a radio transmission from the Dallas control tower. He was instructed to land in Dallas and then proceed to a secure hangar for a U.S. Customs inspection. "Roger that. Aire Cargo 32 out," answered Jack.

Ortiz heard the radio call and asked Jack where they were.

"We're about 15 minutes south of Austin."

"Perfect," Ortiz said. "We'll be getting out there."

"Austin?" asked Warner. "I'm not landing at Austin."

"Who said anything about landing?" Miguel got up and pulled the tarps off of the loads in the cargo bay. Two guys jumped up from their hidden places and proceeded to move three duffle bags to the rear of the plane near the cargo door. They opened up a fourth duffle bag and pulled out parachutes, helmets, goggles, and body harnesses.

Jack was stunned, but he noticed that both men were armed with pistols on their belts. Miguel Ortiz and his men put on their parachute equipment and hooked up some smaller chutes to the duffle bags. "Warner, thanks for a great ride. Here's a little bonus for you," Ortiz said, tossing him an envelope. "This should make up for the hassle with customs. Drop down the rear door, won't you?" Ortiz wasn't smiling anymore and neither were his two associates.

Warner did as he was told. The guys each took a duffle bag and jumped out the back of the plane. Jack was still in shock, but he closed the rear door and radioed the Dallas control tower to patch him through to the customs office. He explained what had just happened, but he had much more to explain once he landed on the ground at DFW.

When Jack taxied to the customs hangar, there were six armed customs officers waiting to greet him. They detained him in a secure interrogation room for two hours while they searched his plane, examined his paperwork, and verified his identity. Once the captain of the customs office did some research and realized just who Jack Warner was, he came inside to speak with him personally.

"Colonel Warner, it appears that you are an innocent victim of a drug smuggling operation. You had the proper paperwork and did all the correct things by informing us of the events as you traveled over Texas. We are currently searching for Mr. Ortiz, although I'm sure that isn't his real name. You are free to go and you may keep the charter fee." Gail was astounded at Jack's story of the trip, but she was delighted with the envelope of $10,000 bonus cash in addition to the prepaid charter fee.

Fuel Foolish

Most airlines have annual fuel contracts so they can budget accordingly and not be affected by daily movements in the price of jet fuel. Planes with turbo prop engines and jet planes use a fuel called "Jet A."

Jack Warner was always a gambler. In January 1990, he thought fuel prices would rise. Instead of negotiating a one-year contract with the fuel suppliers, he asked for a three-year contract, unheard of in the fuel business.

American Fuel Company went for the deal. They knew that Aire Cargo used a lot of fuel and they were growing every year. In addition, their planes were older and burned more fuel than a more modern fleet. Some of their short-hop planes were turboprop models.

American Fuel Company signed a three-year contract with Aire Cargo Inc. in February of 1990 guaranteeing Jet A fuel for a price of 53 cents per gallon for three years. Right after the contract was signed, prices dropped as low as 49 cents per gallon in June. Everybody thought Jack goofed. AFC was very happy and the CEO was considered a hero.

But fortune smiled on Jack Warner once again. Gas prices jumped up in the summer of 1990, and aviation fuel followed right along. Jet A fuel rose from 49 cents to $1.20 per gallon in October. That was tough on all the passenger and cargo airlines except for Aire Cargo. Warner was saving a fortune on his fuel and it almost put American Fuel into bankruptcy. Luckily, they were a subsidiary of British Petroleum, so they weren't going anywhere. BP was the largest petroleum producer in the world. Of course, Jack Warner knew this before he negotiated the contract with them. What good is a contract if the other side goes BK and has no assets? Who needs years of lawsuits and legal bills? Even if you win, you don't win.

Prices settled down later on, but Jack Warner still saved a fortune over the life of the contract. The CEO of American Fuel Company had his ass handed to him. He was soon out of a job and the company never signed a long-term contract again.

U.S. Government Contract

In the early 1990s, Warner heard about a U.S. Government contract in the works for cargo freight forwarding for domestic and international service. The U.S. Government sends documents back and forth from all over the world. The U.S. Military relies on reliable shipments of aircraft and vehicle parts to keep their machines and aircraft running. Government hospitals and veterans' medical centers also rely on mailing lab test samples and drug shipments on a continuing basis.

Warner's chief competitor for this new contract was his old friend, Fred Smith, and Federal Express. Warner would need to go into debt for additional planes to expand the business and get this government contract.

But there was an unknown factor at work that would sink the expansion hopes of both Aire Cargo and Federal Express. Senator Buford Simpson had represented the State of Texas for the last 29 years. Simpson was out to further his own agenda and build up his family's fortune. Simpson was on the Senate Ways and Means Committee that oversaw the contract bids and awarded winning contracts to the lowest bidder.

Senator Simpson had access to all of the bids submitted by the prospective shipping contractors. Simpson's brother-in-law was Howie Shermer, the owner of Acme Air Freight, a small Texas-based freight forwarder. He was able to send copies of competitors' bids to Howie so that he could undercut the best bid by a small percentage and secure the contract.

Acme wasn't capable of handling all of the government's, business but they planned on just being an intermediary. They would be subcontracting the actual shipping to Aire Cargo. AC would do all the work and Howie would make a percentage markup on each package. With thousands of packages every month, the markup would add up to a small fortune for Acme Air Freight for doing virtually nothing.

Jack Warner knew nothing of Howie's plan, but Howie's success would depend on Warner's agreement to be a subcontractor, doing all the shipping work.

Shermer met Jack at the Longhorn Bar & Grill in Dallas one evening to talk a little business. Shermer dropped the bomb that Acme was going to be awarded the government shipping contract. Jack inquired, "But how are you going to service it? You're way too small to handle that much business. It's going to take way more planes and people than you have."

"You're right, Jack. That's where you come in. Let's talk turkey."

"Better yet, let's have some Wild Turkey," laughed Jack, intrigued at what was coming around the corner and right at him.

Shermer offered Jack his proposal of Aire Cargo handling all the U.S. Government shipping business as a subcontractor of Acme Air Freight. Jack thought about it for a few minutes while Howie went to the bathroom. After all, it would add almost 40% to their business volume. On one hand, Warner was seriously pissed at losing the dishonest bidding war, but business is business, as they say. A 40% increase in his business was nothing to sneeze at. As Warner would say, "Millions is millions and more millions is more better."

Jack made Howie a counter offer:

1) Aire Cargo would pick up the government packages in an Aire Cargo truck, but with a magnetic Acme Air Freight sign on each door covering the Aire Cargo logo.

They would use Acme shipping labels that were exactly the same as Aire Cargo's except for the logo at the top. This way, they would go through all of Aire Cargo's scanning equipment. Aire Cargo's delivery people would wear an Acme hat over a plain uniform shirt. Once the driver got back in the truck, they would ditch the hat. They would reach out the door and pull off the magnetic sign and toss it on the passenger seat. A smart driver would park the truck so the Acme sign showed toward the loading dock. That way, they would only have to put on one magnetic sign.

2) Another condition of the deal was that Aire Cargo picked up all the packages and paid a 5% markup only on document envelopes and small packages. Aire Cargo and Overnight Aire kept the entire fee on anything larger than a shoe box.

Only a few people knew that the whole deal was really run by Aire Cargo. It wasn't very high tech, but most people don't pay too much attention to delivery trucks. Of course, none of this was disclosed to the U.S. Government. If they had known about it, the Acme bid would never have been considered.

After a few years of this questionable arrangement, the GAO (general accounting office) decided to audit the contract. It didn't take long to discover who was really picking up and delivering the packages as Acme Air Freight. The GAO sent out a deputy investigator, none other than retired Captain John Wade, Jack Warner's fellow pilot from Vietnam.

It only took Wade about half a day to uncover the entire seamy plot involving Senator Buford Simpson, Howie Shermer, and Acme Air Freight. In order to avoid prosecution, Senator Simpson quickly retired for "health reasons." Howie Shermer lost his U.S. Government Contractor status. He went bankrupt and sold what few planes he actually owned. He offered to sell the planes to Jack, but Warner turned him down. Shermer was never very interested in maintenance, and Warner loved his employees too much to ever put them in jeopardy.

Since Warner and Aire Cargo had been coerced into this arrangement by unfair and fraudulent efforts, bordering on extortion, they were held as innocent parties. Their original bid was resurrected and ratified into full force and effect. All of the personnel and equipment were re-branded back to Aire Cargo and Overnight Aire. All the Acme magnetic signs, forms, and hats went into the trash dumpster.

Jack's New Pilot

Jack and Gail slowly built up their staff of pilots, maintenance people, ground crew, cargo handlers, and package sorters over the years. It was time for another new pilot to be added to the staff. Jack put the word out that he had an opening for a pilot. Word spread throughout the aviation community. Jack Warner was known as a fair boss, and Aire Cargo was a good company to work for.

Eleanor buzzed Jack on the intercom. "You have a call on line two, a Tom McLaughlin from California."

"Whoopee!" yelled Jack. "Eleanor, I saved his life in Vietnam and then the son-of-a-bitch turned around and saved mine right back. Whaddya think of that?"

"Well, Boss, there are some days I'd like to punch him right in the nose," joked Eleanor.

Jack punched the button on the telephone. "Tom, how the hell are ya? Long time, no hear."

"Good to hear your voice too, Jack. Rumor has it that you've got an opening for a sky jockey."

"That rumor's true. Know anybody who can fly worth damn?" asked Jack.

"Could be. My license and educational requirements are all up to date. We're moving to Texas to be closer to my wife's family. Why don't we meet and discuss it?"

"10-4, buddy. I'm looking forward to it," responded Warner.

"Great, I'll be in town next Saturday. It's a date."

Within a week, Tom McLaughlin was flying cargo planes for Aire Cargo and his wife was packing up the house in Glendale, California. Gail helped them find a new house outside of Dallas.

New Toys

The original surplus planes that Warner and Patroni bought (stole, finagled, purloined, etc.) from the U.S. Government were getting old. Even with regular maintenance and replacement engines and parts, everything mechanical has a life span. Airframes develop metal fatigue, resulting in hairline cracks that will grow larger over time.

In addition, the jet engines from the 60s and 70s burned a lot of fuel compared to the more efficient modern engines. Every old plane was costing the company thousands of dollars every month in additional fuel cost.

Aire Cargo always needed new planes. It was as simple as that. No company would have enough cash to buy that many new aircraft at once. It would cost hundreds of millions of dollars to replace them all. So Lou Patroni and Jack Warner were always on the hunt for replacements for their fleet.

Aire Cargo had a variety of cargo planes, but the work horses of the fleet were 727 Freighters. Warner would scour used aircraft dealers for deals on 727s. Occasionally, an airline would go bankrupt or upgrade their fleet and put their planes on the market. Leased airplanes would be sold at the end of the lease period. Warner also would buy used jets that were repossessed by a bank. Patroni had a network of informants who would steer him in the direction of an available plane.

Patroni would replace the oldest planes first as he found newer ones. He would wholesale the old ones to smaller cargo companies in the U.S., but more likely to companies in foreign countries. It's a sorry fact that many foreign countries have fewer regulations in regards to airplane maintenance. Patroni was always careful to disclose in writing all pertinent facts about the aircraft for sale and include the log books and maintenance records on each one. The buyer had to sign a receipt for the documentation as well as all the aircraft transfer papers and the bill of sale.

Trans World Cargo, a competitor of Aire Cargo, had a 727 cargo plane that had lost its brakes and ran off the runway pavement into the soft shoulder at an airport in Cleveland. Pulling the plane out damaged the nose gear and both sides of the main landing gear. The plane sat there, almost at ground level, like a turtle with no legs. Cleveland Airport was leveling fines of $10,000 per day for blocking a runway. What to do? The plane couldn't be towed. It didn't seem to make financial sense to execute a very expensive recovery of an old jet and then buy new landing gear to be installed. The insurance company had declared the damaged plane a total loss and had paid TWC for the depreciated value of the plane. The insurance company planned to hire a contractor to cut it up into manageable-sized sections and sell it for scrap.

Jack Warner heard about it and called Patroni, who just happened to have a complete used landing gear package in stock from the Scottsdale auction days. Jack and Lou flew to Cleveland to examine the wreckage. He met with the company's insurance representative, company controller, and TWC's chief of maintenance. Jack agreed that the plane should be scrapped. "I'll tell you what I'll do. It will probably cost you 50 grand to cut it up and remove it. There's also the fuel tanks and hydraulics to deal with as hazardous waste. That's another chunk of dough."

"I didn't even think of that," muttered the TWC maintenance chief.

"By the time you're done, you're talking over 70 grand to get it outta here. Add on the airport per diem penalties and your staff's labor. Now you're well over 100 grand, easy. You'll get about a quarter of that back in scrap value, so we're talking at least $75,000 out of your pocket. Pay me $50,000 and the title to the plane and I'll have it moved within three days."

The insurance company controller stepped away to huddle up with the chief of maintenance. After a minute, they returned to stick out their hands. "You got a deal."

So that is how Jack Warner got a free 727 cargo plane and $50,000 in cash. Patroni and some mechanics flew to Cleveland with air lift bags, a fork lift and new landing gear. They replaced the landing gear and towed it to an airport maintenance hangar. Then Patroni had the jet re-certified by the FAA. The next day, Jack flew the plane out. The $50,000 paid most of the repair costs.

Somebody on the Cleveland Airport staff told Jack that the owner of Trans World Cargo heard about it and blew a gasket. He couldn't fire his people fast enough.

One Last Rescue

The U.S. Embassy operations in Bagdad, Iraq were moved inside the Belgian Embassy in 1984. The U.S. Embassy building itself was abandoned.

After Iraqi forces invaded neighboring Kuwait in 1990, the U.N. Security Council imposed economic sanctions on Iraq, providing for a full trade embargo, excluding medical supplies, food, and other items of humanitarian necessity. In November of 1990, the U.N. authorized military action against Iraqi forces occupying Kuwait and demanded a complete withdrawal by January 15, 1991.

U.S. Embassy employees were ordered to pack up their offices and their personals. They were scheduled to leave the next morning on the first commercial flight out. Most of the employees made it to the airport and checked in for their flights. Iraqi Republican Guard soldiers jeered at them, but they didn't interfere with the staffers clearing customs and getting on an Air France plane bound for Paris.

Five key male employees stayed behind to shred documents and destroy embassy electronics. They were scheduled to take a later flight that afternoon to Paris and rendezvous with the rest of the embassy staff for an overnight flight to New York.

The five staffers were loading their luggage in the Belgian Embassy van to leave for the Bagdad Airport. The embassy chargé d'affaires came running out to stop them. "Messieurs, we just heard that Saddam Hussein has closed the airport for all passenger flights leaving the country. You better come back inside while we figure out what to do."

When Saddam Hussein failed to comply with the demand to vacate Kuwait on January 15th, the Persian Gulf War, Operation Desert Storm, began on January 17th, 1991. Approximately 100,000 Iraqi soldiers and thousands of civilians were killed.

By March 1991, Saddam Hussein managed to suppress rebellions with massive force to maintain power. Hussein's Iraqi Republican Guard terrorized ordinary citizens. Tens of thousands of people were killed. Nearly two million Iraqis fled for their lives. In the aftermath, the Allies established the Iraqi no-fly zones.

Back in Dallas at the Aire Cargo offices, Jack Warner returned from lunch one day to see Eleanor, his secretary, all flustered. "What's up, Eleanor?"

"There are some men waiting for you in your office. They won't say who they are or why they want to see you. I think they're kind of scary," whimpered Eleanor.

"Do they have flowers and balloons? Maybe I won the Publisher's Clearing House Sweepstakes?" quipped Jack, smiling.

"Quit clowning around. They look serious."

"Well, then I guess I better quit talking to you and see what they want." Jack walked into his office and introduced himself. "Gentlemen, how can I help you?" Although, down deep inside, Jack was hoping they weren't from the IRS, the FAA, or something like that.

"Mr. Warner, I am Brian Goodman and this is Regis Tate. We are with the U.S. Government. We heard about your rescue missions while you were in Vietnam. There's a situation that we think you can help with. Would you mind closing your office door?"

Goodman explained about the five stranded embassy employees stuck in the Belgian Embassy basement. "They've been living there for months. We think Saddam Hussein will never let them leave the country."

"They'll eventually become hostages or worse," added Tate.

"What would you like me to do?" asked Jack.

Goodman elaborated, "Tate and I are with the CIA." After both men showed their CIA IDs to Jack, he continued. "We'd like to hire you to haul a load of dry food stores to Iraq. After unloading your cargo, the five embassy staffers will get onboard your plane and then you fly them to the closest U.S. Air Force Base, which is in Turkey."

"It sounds dangerous," he said, smiling. "I'll do it. Let me get some details."

The men pulled out maps showing Iraqi airspace, the airport details, and a 3D view of the local terrain. They also had the latest weather maps, along with the forecast for the next seven days.

"Here are summaries with pictures of each of the five embassy staffers," offered Tate. "Four of them are married. Three have children. They are all volunteers."

Jack was reminiscing. "Boy, this really takes me back to my days rescuing pilots in Vietnam. How am I going to get into Iraq, land, and then take off with your people?"

Goodman and Tate arranged to get a load of U.N. foodstuffs as the reason for Jack's trip into Iraq. This would include several pallets of wheat, corn, rice, powdered milk, and sugar. There would be some general medicines and school supplies as well. The load could pass an Iraqi Customs inspection if necessary. This load would also be permitted under the terms of the U.N. embargo. Because Aire Cargo's plane would contain U.N. dry food stores, it was granted special permission to enter Iraqi airspace and land at Bagdad International Airport.

"The cover story for this mission is that you are just delivering food and medicine for the U.N. Please keep your return cargo info 100% confidential. Any questions?" asked Goodman.

"I will have to tell a few of my key people, but I have known them for years and trust them completely."

Goodman and Tate reviewed the details of the dry food pickup in New York. Warner said he would organize some onboard supplies for the Fearsome Five, as he now called them.

Goodman and Tate sent a coded message to the Belgian Embassy in New York. They asked for it to be included in the Belgian diplomatic pouch going to Bagdad and given to the five Americans.

The message outlined the details of the upcoming rescue flight, scheduled to arrive early Monday morning and leave a few hours later. Monday was always the busiest day at the airport. Goodman and Tate figured that the soldiers and airport staff would be the most distracted. Allowing time for Iraqi Customs clearance and the cargo to be unloaded, the five passengers were expected to be at the Iraqi Customs warehouse by 9 a.m. This would allow an hour for the embassy driver to arrange for his diplomatic pouch clearance.

The Belgian Embassy's chargé d'affaires coordinated the plan to help the five men get out of Iraq. "Iraqi police are watching the International Airport, especially the passenger flights. But they only have a skeleton crew in the cargo warehouse bays."

"Our embassy driver, Julien, delivers boxes of documents to the Bagdad Airport twice a week, so he is well known. These are considered part of the diplomatic pouch. We will hide the five of you inside the boxes as part of the diplomatic pouch. It is exempt from inspection."

In Bagdad, Julien planned the details with the five staffers. "I will cut up some cardboard boxes and build what looks like a top layer of a pallet of boxes. You can hide in the space underneath. I will stack real boxes around the pallet so if they want to inspect one, they can. Anything within arms' reach will be a real file box. The guards are lazy. They're not going to unpack anything."

The chargé d'affaires continued, "I'm afraid you will have to leave all of your luggage and personal things behind. There is only room for you to take a purse or a small knapsack. We will ship your things to the U.S. as soon as we can."

Jack got Lou Patroni and Tom McLaughlin down to the maintenance hangar. He outlined the CIA's plan to rescue the five Americans. "We need to make a hiding place for them inside the plane. It should have food, water, and sleeping bags. And go buy one of those portable camping toilets and TP. Who knows when we'll get a bathroom stop?"

Lou suggested, "How about some empty refrigerator boxes? One can be for the food and supplies and two or three for sleeping bags."

"Tom, would you be my copilot?" asked Jack.

"Sure, Boss."

Lou asked, "Jack, aren't you gonna need a stewardess, a navigator, an engineer, or something?"

"Lou, are trying to say that you'd like to go?"

"So you figured that out, huh?" answered Lou, grinning.

"Well let's forget the stewardess. I don't want to see you in a mini skirt and high heels. And as for a navigator, you can't even fold up a map. I guess we better make you the flight engineer."

After prepping the plane and filing a flight plan, the trio of rescuers took off to pick up the dry food stores before winging their way across the Atlantic.

In Iraq, Julien started cutting and taping boxes. All five staffers joined in to help him.

They took a pallet as a base and bolted on the legs of a folding table. The top of the false boxes covered the top of the table. They added cardboard box sides to the table legs on all four sides, with a small access door for the embassy guys to crawl inside. Julien said, "I think two pallets will leave enough room for the people inside each false pile of boxes. The two largest guys go in one pallet and the three smallest in the other." After the staffers got in, Julien added some real boxes on top, just in case. He whispered to the staffers, "Here we go, you should only have to be in there for about 20 minutes. I cut in some flaps close to your faces for air, just in case."

A few hours earlier, the Aire Cargo flight had landed, cleared Iranian Customs, and unloaded. Jack taxied over to a gate by the warehouse. He waited along with Tom and Lou.

Julien, the Belgian driver, delivered the load of file boxes to the Iraqi Customs warehouse at the airport. As they drove in, a Customs officer asked for the shipping manifest. Julien gave it to him, along with the Belgian Embassy's diplomatic pouch inspection exception form. After giving the documents a brief scan, the officer waved the driver over to the airline cargo loading area.

Julien parked the van at the far end of the warehouse, next to an empty airplane cargo container. He opened the aluminum container and first started loading the real file boxes inside. Checking around to make sure the coast was clear, he opened the pallet's hidden cardboard doors and helped the five men out and into the container. Just as he was securing the door, two of the airport ground crew showed up. Julien told them in his broken Arabic that he had already loaded the container and gave them copies of the shipping manifest and the Belgian Embassy's diplomatic pouch inspection exception form. He tipped them 50,000 dinar each and thanked them for their assistance.

Julien sat in his van and watched the ground crew drive the elevator cargo delivery truck out to the Aire Cargo plane, which was waiting. The truck's bed had a scissor lift to raise the container up to the cargo door. Lou and Tom took over from there, sliding it into the hold of the plane.

After closing the cargo door, Lou opened the aluminum cargo container and had the Fearsome Five scurry to the front of the plane's cargo bay so they could get inside the larger cardboard appliance boxes that Jack brought with sleeping bags, shaving kits, clean clothes, food, drinks, books, and magazines inside. The guys were surprised and delighted that in the big food box were two dozen Krunchy Kreme donuts. Even though they were now day-old from New York, the donuts tasted pretty damn good to the Americans. They were literally a taste of home.

Jack and Tom received clearance from the Iraqi Control Tower and taxied out to the runway. Jack pushed the throttles forward and the jet picked up speed. At 140 knots, Jack rotated the yoke back and the plane left the ground.

The next stop was the U.S. Air Force Base in Incirlik, Turkey. After showering and resting overnight, they took off for home. A week later, Aire Cargo received a personal, handwritten thank-you note from President George H.W. Bush. "Very cool," thought Jack. Jack also received a shoebox full of thank-you notes from the Fearsome Five's family members.

Pandas East, Rolls-Royce West

Eleanor, Jack's secretary, buzzed him on the intercom just as she was leaving for the day. "Jack, the head of the San Diego Zoo is on line two."

"What on earth could he be calling me for?" Jack thought. "Hello, this is Jack Warner, how can I help you?"

"This is Roy Hinkley from the San Diego Zoo. We need to transport two young pandas to the London Zoo sometime in the few weeks. Is that something you can handle?"

The word "no" wasn't in Jack Warner's vocabulary. He had never turned down a flight in Alaska (except for weather), an assignment at the Air Force Academy, a fighter task in Vietnam or a pilot rescue when one came up. Warner would always find a way. He might have to break a few rules or push the legal envelope a little, but that's how things get done.

"Mr. Hinkley, we can do it. Let me get some details from you..." Hinkley gave Jack all the info he needed to plan the trip and arrange for the aircraft involved. Two zoo keepers would travel with the pandas for animal care and monitoring. The pandas would be in two large plastic cages, mounted on pallets for ease of loading. There would be a third pallet for food, water, and supplies. "Let me get on it. I'll get back to you."

A few days after the San Diego Zoo called, Jack received a long-distance phone call from London. "Mr. Warner? Please hold for Sir Chiles." Jack knew this wasn't going to be a boring call.

"Mr. Warner? This is Sir William Chiles. I'm the Chairman of the Rolls-Royce Motor Company. I'd like to discuss some business with you. Would it be possible for you to meet me at the New York City Rolls-Royce dealership on Monday morning?"

Jack was used to hauling air freight in packing crates. He couldn't wait to hear what Sir Chiles had in mind. Rolls-Royce airplane engines were world famous. Maybe they needed some parts or engines transported?

When Gail heard who he was meeting, she mentioned, "Hey, Babe, my Buick is getting a little old, I could use a new car... hint-hint." Jack laughed nervously.

Gail decided Jack needed some wardrobe help. She wanted him to look like he had at least ridden in a Rolls-Royce when he met Sir Chiles. After she took him shopping at a fine men's shop, he looked the part. Dragging Jack shopping for clothes was torture for him. Gail loved it, but Jack was like a little kid shopping with his mother. Jack kept grabbing jeans and tennis shoes, but Gail insisted on nicer things. "It's about time you looked nice for a change," she murmured. When Monday came around, she drove him to the airport and kissed him goodbye. He felt like a little boy going to his first day at school.

When Jack entered the Rolls-Royce dealership in Manhattan, he wore a blue blazer with a white linen handkerchief in the pocket, a blue oxford cloth button-down shirt and some khaki wool slacks. In addition, he was sporting argyle socks and some new Cole Haan loafers with tassels. Gail had done her magic well. The last words out of her mouth into his ear were "I love you, Babe. *Now* you look like you drive a Rolls."

After the introductions were made and tea served, Warner settled down into a burgundy leather sofa in the walnut-paneled office. There were thick oriental carpets on the floor and a huge tapestry hanging on the wall. Jack felt like he was sitting in the Queen's palace.

"Mr. Warner, I hear your air freight company can move anything you can fit into an airplane. Is that about right?" inquired Sir William Chiles.

"Yes, yes, sir," stuttered Jack, feeling a little intimidated. He decided to take some initiative. "Please call me Jack. Otherwise, I'll think you're talking to my father."

Sir Chiles laughed and said, "Good enough, Jack. Let me get to the point."

Jack thought to himself, "He didn't ask me to call him Bill. I guess he's used to the help calling him Sir Chiles." He figured that he would save that little comment for Gail when he got home. He was sure she would pump him for every detail of this mystery trip.

Sir Chiles began. "In 1907, Rolls Royce manufactured their iconic automobile, the 'Silver Ghost,' which has gone on to become the most famous and valuable car in the world. The Silver Ghost was the most important car that Charles Rolls and Henry Royce ever built in the history of Rolls-Royce Motorcars. She proved the bulletproof quality and reliability of their cars by running in numerous rallies and road tours. This automobile completed a Scottish reliability trial, driving from London to Glasgow 27 times, totaling more than 14,000 miles with nary a problem. The Silver Ghost proved that cars could not only be quiet, powerful, and smooth, but also reliable.

"The Silver Ghost got its name because it was largely unpainted, revealing its polished aluminum body, and was 'quiet as a ghost,' an often-noted sentiment by passersby, who were amazed by how silent the car was.

"After completing those history-making trials, the car was purchased by a Rolls Royce employee, who drove the car an additional 500,000 miles before returning the car to the factory for minor servicing. Unfortunately, he died while the car was in the shop, but his family decided to donate the car to the Rolls-Royce Motorcar company."

All Jack Warner could come up with was "Wow! What a story! How can I be of help?"

Sir Chiles continued, "The Rolls-Royce Company has completely restored this iconic motor car from bonnet to boot. We have entered it in the Pebble Beach Concours de

Elegance Automobile Show this coming summer in California. Prince Charles and Lady Diana will attend the show to help promote British tourism, business, and industry. The car is in London and the show is in California. This is where you can help us. Would you be able to safely transport this automobile both ways and assure us of its absolute safety?"

"I'd be honored, Sir Chiles. My company can do the job. I'll even sit in the back seat the whole way just to keep an eye on it," offered Warner.

Sir Chiles smiled at this bit of American humor. "I'm not sure that will be necessary, but I would appreciate your personal attention throughout the process. I will have Charles MacGregor, my transportation director, call you to work out the details."

Jack returned home to a big hug from Gail. "So, where's my new Rolls? I'd look good in a baby blue Corniche convertible."

Jack countered with, "So it's true, you did marry me for my money."

She laughed and joked back, "Yeah, I did. I just haven't been able to find any. When I do, I'm going shopping."

Jack got Patroni involved with the Rolls-Royce project. The car was almost 13 feet long and weighed almost three tons. "We gotta treat this with kid gloves. It's worth more than our plane."

Lou had an idea. "First thing we do is buy a bunch of those blue quilted furniture pads. There's a lady in town that owns an upholstery shop. Let's get her to sew them into one giant, big-ass car cover. Mr. MacGregor sent me the car's measurements. Let's connect a bunch of pallets together and then I'll install some cargo caster wheels on the bottom. That way the car will be all wrapped up for safety and we can push it around on the pallets. It will be totally insulated from possible damage."

"I hope," added Jack, laughing nervously.

Mr. MacGregor liked Lou's plan to cover the car with the quilted pads and strap it down on several pallets all bolted together. Warner's job was figuring how the hell he was going to get a priceless, classic car from England to California and back without damaging it. He also had to make a profit on the deal. The only planes he owned with an open tail and a loading ramp were 747s. The car would take up so much room in the back of that plane that it would cost a fortune in lost cargo sales. What he needed was a smaller version of that style cargo plane.

Jack was alone one afternoon, having lunch by himself in his office. He was eating a cheeseburger at his desk and was feeling bored. "I gotta get a TV in here one of these days," he thought. "What's there to read around here?" There was a stack of magazines on his side table. He grabbed a copy of *Aviation Week*.

On the cover was a new plane that the Air Force was considering buying, the C-23 Sherpa Utility Transport. It was a short, wide-bodied multi-use aircraft with a wide, flat ramp in the tail. It could carry 10,000 pounds of cargo, as well as fuel and two crew members. It was a good plane if you weren't in a hurry. It had two Pratt & Whitney turboprops with 1,200 hp each. With a full load, it could cruise at 255 knots, with a range of 770 miles.

Jack forgot about his cheeseburger. He thought to himself, "A nonstop flight from London to California isn't going to work. How can I make this happen?" He got out the aircraft charts covering the U.S. and across the Atlantic to England. Jack was spreading them out on a table when Gail walked in, so Jack shared his idea with her.

"The only way to make this work is a series of short hops of less than 750 miles, to 'get across the pond,' as the Brits say. London to Iceland, then to Greenland, then to Gander, Newfoundland. From there, we could fly to Maine and easily make our way to California."

"I like it, Babe. I only see one tiny insignificant problem, almost not even worth mentioning," she said with a smirk on her face.

"Could that be the simple fact in that I don't own a C-23 Sherpa or know anybody that does?"

"Yes, that would be it, Einstein."

"I figured I'd just borrow one," said Jack.

"Why didn't I think of that? Borrow from whom, Jack, if I might be so bold as to inquire?"

"I haven't quite worked that out. I'll get back to you."

Jack grabbed the magazine and read the article again, taking notes as he did so. Jack grabbed the phone and called his old poker-playing buddy, Lieutenant Colonel Tim Brockway. Besides losing his airfield to Jack in poker, Brockway had told Jack about the Idaho air base garage sale. Jack had tried to repay him whenever he could. "Brockway's gonna love me calling him for a favor," he thought to himself.

He tracked Brockway down and asked about the Air Force's new plane, the C-23 Sherpa. "Well, we haven't made up our mind on that yet. We have a prototype model at Edwards Air Force Base in California. We are about to start our testing and evaluation procedures. It ought to take six months. Then, we can take our recommendations to the committee so they can make a qualified final decision."

"What's the Air Force budget for this testing and evaluation?" asked Jack.

"About half a million, once you count staff time, pilots, ground crew, maintenance, and fuel," said Brockway.

"Tim, I've got a proposition for you. How'd you like to save half a million bucks and six months of your life?"

"How'zat?" asked Brockway.

"Give me the plane. I'll fly a load of cargo to England. Then, I'll pick up some cargo in London and fly it back to California. I'll even fly a third trip back to London. Those three international flights with a few dozen stops en route should be enough of a test for your committee members. I'll write a report and even present it to your evaluation committee in person."

Brockway could see himself showing up at the evaluation committee meeting with the famous Colonel Jack Warner in tow. He'd tell everyone that it was his idea. "I saved the government a fortune and I got us the best test pilot anybody could imagine. And, I got him to make a personal appearance and testify, all for free. They'll throw me a goddamn parade!"

"Well..." Brockway silently counted to three, and then to six, "...okay... As a special favor to you, I guess I can pull some strings and make that happen. You've got a deal. But you're gonna owe me, Warner." Brockway thought, "I might as well try to get all I can out of this deal."

"Will you buy the fuel?" asked Jack.

"Since you're saving us half a million bucks, I guess I can do that."

And, that is how Jack Warner got a free cargo plane, with free fuel, to fly his pandas to London, pick up a priceless show car, fly it back to California, and then return it back to London again with the Rolls on board. And it all went off without a hitch.

The San Diego Zoo and the London Zoo were delighted with the panda delivery. They arrived fat and sassy. Both local and national news teams covered their trip. Jack was interviewed multiple times while he stood in front of his plane's logo with the pandas in the foreground. Jack made sure that he and his transport team all had on Aire Cargo shirts with a big logo on them. You can't buy that kind of advertising.

Jack made sure to get a business card from all of the news crews. He told them that, in a few days, he was transporting the famous Rolls-Royce Silver Ghost automobile to California. Every newscaster was distracted, picturing their face in front of a beautiful, classic show car on the evening news. When Jack was leaving London with the Silver Ghost, he invited the press to watch it being loaded with the Rolls-Royce crew. 47 news crews showed up from 14 countries. He was interviewed about the Rolls, the pandas and about his former exploits rescuing pilots. He was invited to appear on three different English chat shows.

The Pebble Beach people were happy. Rolls-Royce was happy. Prince Charles and Diana loved the trip. The Air Force got their plane tested for free. Short Brothers, the airplane manufacturer in Belfast, Ireland was ecstatic. The U.S. Military bought almost a hundred C-23s. Jack left the Sherpa plane in Belfast and flew home with his crew on a commercial flight, first class.

But nobody was happier than Jack Warner when he cashed the check from Rolls-Royce. When he got home, Gail had a stack of messages with jobs waiting for him. He ripped the San Diego Zoo's check in half and mailed it back to them. He enclosed it in a note that read, "Consider this a donation to the zoo from the Warner family."

After all that, Aire Cargo's phones were ringing off the hook.

Noah's Bad Decision

While all of this great business was going on, Noah had enrolled at USC in Los Angeles. He was majoring in Business Administration with plans to work at Aire Cargo. Jack and Gail figured that if they had been successful without any formal business training, think how far Noah could progress with a top-rated college business degree in his pocket.

Noah enjoyed school and pledged at the Sigma Alpha Epsilon fraternity. Everybody liked Noah and he was accepted without hesitation by all the SAE brothers. Noah did well in his classes and made several good friends at the SAE house.

At the spring dance, Noah met a tall, willowy blonde named Terri Fox. He asked her out and they started dating all through his junior year. Noah was quite smitten with her and felt like he was falling in love. That winter, Noah invited Terri to go skiing at Mammoth Mountain, located North of L.A. in California's High Sierras. They had a great time skiing and planned on leaving Sunday afternoon for the long drive south back to school.

Noah quit skiing early that day and went back to their room. As Noah was packing his clothes in the hotel room, the phone rang. Terri told him that she met some girlfriends from school and wanted to stay a few days more. She would ride back with them on Wednesday. Noah was disappointed at not being able to say goodbye in person, but what man can ever figure out women?

Wednesday night rolled around and Noah called Terri's dorm room to see if she was back yet. Her roommate hadn't heard from her. Noah called the motel in Mammoth to see if she was still there, but they said she had checked out last Sunday night after Noah had left. "What the hell is going on?" thought Noah. He started calling her friends but couldn't reach anybody who had talked with her recently.

Thursday, he stayed home from class and kept calling Terri's friends. He hung up the phone when there was a knock on his door. "Hey, Warner, a letter just came for ya."

Noah recognized the handwriting as Terri's. He ripped open the letter and started reading. "Dear Noah, this is the hardest letter I've ever had to write..." Terri continued by telling him that she had met a ski patrolman at Mammoth and was going to quit school and move in with him. Noah Warner sat down hard and tears came to his eyes. He started to throw everything off his desk, getting madder by the second. His room-mate stopped him before he trashed his entire room. "Buddy, relax. You've got to forget her. Let's go out for a drink. I know a great club in Pasadena. Let's go out."

They managed to round up a few more guys and made the quick trip up the Pasadena Freeway to the One West nightclub. The club's address was 1 West California Boulevard, hence the name. Noah's first drink turned into four, which turned into eight. By the time the group decided to leave, Noah was totally hammered. The boys all went out the front door, where their designated driver volunteered to go get the car while everybody else waited there.

Noah sat on a bench with his college pals and noticed a limousine parked right there in front of them. It belonged to the owner of the nightclub. Lamont, the chauffeur, was a big, tall black guy with a shaved head and a gold loop earring in one ear. He also played bouncer from time to time. Lamont didn't take shit from nobody and was a loyal employee to his boss. The car's engine was idling with the driver's door open. Lamont was busy helping his boss and his girlfriend out of the car.

At that moment, Noah made the worst decision of his young life. Clouded by depression and a lot of alcohol, Noah thought it would be funny if he drove the limousine around the parking lot. He jumped in and put the car in drive and started to go on his little joy ride. Lamont sprang toward the open door and grabbed Noah's arm and jerked him out of the car. Unfortunately for all concerned, the limo kept going with nobody behind the wheel.

Even more unfortunate was the fact that directly across California Boulevard was the Pasadena Lighting Store. The whole front of the store was all glass display windows. The black stretch Lincoln limousine proceeded to cross the street and plow right through the front of the store. It finally stopped with just the tail lights poking out over the sidewalk.

Lamont and Noah were sitting on the asphalt parking lot. Everybody within 500 feet just stared at the catastrophe. The only lucky thing was that the car was not going very fast and nobody got hurt.

The phone rang back in Dallas at five in the morning. Gail reached for the phone, saying, "This can't be good news." She answered with, "Hello."

"Mom, I'm in trouble. I'm in jail. I need to talk to Pop."

"Who is it?" asked Jack, barely awake.

"*Your* son is in jail."

The charges were serious: drunken driving, car theft, malicious mischief, and destruction of private property. Jack flew to L.A. as fast as he could and hired the best criminal attorney he could find. Carroll Anderson was the top criminal attorney in Los Angeles. He played golf with several Superior Court judges and the district attorney. He made sure to support their wives' favorite charities. Carroll figured that it was good for business.

After Carroll worked on Noah's case over the weekend, he met with Jack and Noah at the Pasadena jail. Jack left Noah in jail to teach him a lesson. Noah was learning his lesson damn fast. Carroll was able to quickly get Noah transferred to administrative segregation, away from the general population of hardcore gang members and serious criminals. "Well, Noah, here's the deal. I made some progress with the district attorney. I explained your situation about receiving a Dear John letter, the fact that you have no

record, you're a college student at USC, and an SAE fraternity member. The D.A. graduated from USC Law School, so I made sure to mention it. I did some research and found
out that he is also an SAE fraternity member. All this can't hurt."

Since the limo driver yanked you out of the car, they agreed to drop the malicious
mischief charge. You didn't drive the car anywhere, so they dropped the drunk driving
charge. I talked to the owner of the lighting store and the nightclub. Jack, it's going to
cost you some dough, but here's their proposition for you: You pay for all the damage to
the lighting store and his loss of business for the time the store was closed for repairs.
You buy the owner of One West a new Lincoln stretch limo. His chauffeur gets his salary
for the time he was out of work, plus a new custom tailored suit from Nordstrom's.

"Noah, the judge will agree to reduce all of the charges to reckless driving and sen-
tence you to time served, three years' probation, and a $5,000 fine. You also have to
complete drunk driving traffic school and surrender your driver's license for six months.
You will have an arrest record for reckless driving, which is only a misdemeanor traffic
matter, not a felony."

Carroll continued, "Noah, no matter the reason, you did a very stupid thing that
could have landed you in prison and ruined your life. You also might have killed somebody. If this is all agreeable to your family, you'll be released from jail today and can go
back to school. I'm sure you can make up your missed schoolwork, but I wouldn't volunteer the reason for your absence."

Jack agreed and hugged Noah for a long time with tears in his eyes. "Your mom is
gonna kill you, boy. By the way, you're grounded for life. And you're going to be washing
my airplanes until you turn 65.

Better News for Noah

After the nightclub-limo disaster night, Noah needed to find a job to pay back his father all the money he cost him. He managed to get a job at the Los Angeles Airport, or LAX, as it's better known. A friend got him an interview with the airport manager of National Car Rental. They were open 24/7, so the work shifts could be arranged around his school schedule at USC. Plus, on quiet nights, he could do his homework while he waited for customers.

In those days, the rental car lots were located in the middle of the airport roundabout next to the short-term passenger parking lot. Noah was a popular guy at work and soon got to know employees at other rental car companies and airport personnel. In the first floor of the famous LAX Theme Building was an employee cafeteria with a nice selection of tasty dishes at reasonable employee prices.

One guy that Noah ate with on a regular basis was Lionel Washington. Lionel worked at the short-term parking lot right next to the National rental lot. Part of his duties included monitoring cars parked in the lot. Parking lot personnel take roll of every car each night that it's parked in the parking structure. This prevents some salesman from leaving his car for a week or two and then jumping on the parking entrance sensor pad to trigger a fresh ticket. Smart-ass people are always trying to claim that they were only there for 15 minutes when their car was actually there for days on end.

During dinner one night, Lionel shared a story about a yellow Cordoba with Noah. "This piece of shit has been on our lot for over 30 days," muttered Lionel. "I'm supposed to call the airport tow service and the airport police to have it impounded."

"Such a fine example of American automotive craftsmanship, all that Corinthian leather," laughed Noah. "Maybe you should call Ricardo Montalban," he continued.

Lionel wondered out loud, "Do you suppose there's anything inside worth a damn?"

Noah answered, "Oh sure… people always leave gold and diamonds inside a crappy car at the airport for a month at a time." Both guys laughed as they finished their cheeseburgers and fries.

"Hey, why don't we look before we call the cops?" whispered Lionel. "Do you guys still have that key-making gun?"

All the rental companies had a car-key-making gun for cars with lost keys. The rental office manager just looked up the VIN # in the manufacturer's key specification book then dialed in the die cutters on the gun, put in a new key blank, and click, click, "boom," you have keys to the car.

Noah answered, "Yeah, I can get it anytime. We could go after work. It'll be 4 a.m. and nobody will be around. Let's do it."

Noah met Lionel in the parking structure with the key gun and the spec book. Within three minutes, they had keys and were inside.

"Shit, nothing in here, just a bunch of Slurpee cups and trash. Let's check the trunk," suggested Noah.

They opened the cavernous trunk and both yelled, "Bingo!" at the same time. There were two monster-sized black leather suitcases laying side by side in the trunk. Noah looked around the parking lot carefully before uttering, "Holy Shit, those are expensive bags. Real leather."

Lionel stated the obvious: "Let's look inside. We can split whatever we find."

They unzipped the bags and just about had simultaneous heart attacks. Stacks and stacks of green $50 and $100 bills filled both suitcases. Each bundle had paper wrap strips with the San Francisco Federal Reserve Bank logo on them, followed by the number $10,000.

"Motherfucker! Mother*fucker*! screamed Lionel under his breath. What do we do?"

They closed the bags and the trunk and found a nearby bench to sit on while they discussed their options.

"First of all, there's no way that's honest money. It's got to be stolen, maybe drug money or something like that," suggested Noah. He continued, "If we call the police, we'll get in trouble for breaking into the car, lose our jobs, and probably both go to jail."

"That leaves us three options: Take the money, take part of the money, or run away and do nothing."

Lionel suggested they grab one bag, stuff it with most of the money, and then wipe the car down to clean off their fingerprints. "And then, I'll just call the cops and tow company like I'm supposed to. Let's leave $50,000 in cash. The cops will find it and they'll be heroes. If anybody turns up looking for the money, they won't know who took it. It'll look like the tow truck guys or the cops took it. Nobody will know about us."

So that's what they did. Noah and Lionel each took home $375,000 in cash. They each got a safety deposit box and made an agreement to only spend the cash on groceries, small electronics, and restaurants, and donate most of it to charity. Lionel sent a large anonymous cash donation to his mother's church. He also sent a six-figure donation to the South Central YWCA Battered Women's Shelter. It took a while to convert the cash because of the banking cash deposit IRS disclosure laws. They had to take less than

$10,000 at a time to get money orders or cashier's checks without filling out IRS forms. Noah sent a nice donation to the American Cancer Society. They both sent large donations to the Los Angeles Zoo, the local chapter of the Boy Scouts, the Girl Scouts, the YMCA, and the Boys Clubs of America. The most fun they had was going all over town, putting $100 bills in the Salvation Army's little red kettles manned by Santa Claus volunteers ringing those damn bells.

With the rest of his money, Noah slowly paid off his father in full for all his expenses incurred by his night of drinking. Noah never drank again.

Diamonds

Eleanor, Jack's long time secretary, scheduled a Monday morning meeting with Mr. Smith, a potential customer. As Jack was reviewing his schedule, he asked her, "So, who is Mr. Smith?"

Eleanor replied, "He wouldn't state his business. He wants to discuss a very important delivery with you. He's flying in from overseas just to talk to you."

"Sounds very mysterious. I hope it's legal – or pretty legal," kidded Jack to Eleanor.

At 10 a.m., Eleanor announced Mr. Smith and showed him into Jack's office. A tall, white-haired man in an elegant dark pinstriped suit walked in.

"Please let me introduce myself. My name is actually Christiaan de Klerk. Please forgive the theatrics with my identity. I own the Orapa diamond mine in Botswana, Africa. We are one of the largest producers of top-quality diamonds in the world. Last year, we unearthed the largest rough diamond in our history. We took the stone to Tel Aviv, where it was cut into a world-class diamond that we christened 'The Star of Orapa.' The finished diamond is more than 82 carats.

"The Star of Orapa is currently in our vault in Botswana. The diamond must be picked up and delivered to New York City. A Wall Street investment group is purchasing the stone for a price in excess of $10 million USD. I cannot divulge the exact price. Normally we ship our diamonds by armed couriers on commercial flights, but I believe this calls for a different tack."

"You have my undivided attention, Mr. de Klerk," murmured Jack.

"Lovely, then I'll continue. When Harry Winston donated the famous Hope Diamond to the Smithsonian Institute in Washington, D.C., he wrapped it in a brown paper box and mailed it to them by registered U.S. Mail, parcel post. It arrived on time and in fine condition. If only that mailman knew what he was delivering, hmm?

"To guard against theft during the Hope Diamond's trip to Paris for the 1962 Louvre exhibition, mineralogist George Switzer had a different plan. He traveled to Paris with the diamond tucked inside a velvet pouch, sewn by his wife and pinned inside Switzer's pants pocket for the flight.

"For this trip, due to the current political unrest in Africa, we think shipping the diamond to New York would be more secure if we disguise it and use you to hand-deliver it to New York. Would you be willing to personally accept such a shipment on those terms? It goes without saying that 100% confidentiality is a must."

"Sounds like fun, Mr. de Klerk. I'll do it under the terms you outlined."

All of Aire Cargo's planes were too big and expensive to zip over to South Africa and back. Even if he swapped planes with a charter company, the fuel costs alone would be prohibitive. Instead, he simply bought a first-class commercial ticket through Europe with connecting flights to Botswana.

He rented a Range Rover at the airport and drove to the Orapa Mining offices, where he met with de Klerk. Jack was carrying an old coffee Thermos with him. Mr. de Klerk mentioned that they *did* have coffee, should he like some, but Jack said, "No thank you. I like a special blend." Jack enjoyed his tour of the mining operations. He was surprised that rough-cut diamonds look like broken bits of safety glass. He would never have recognized them as diamonds.

Warner and de Klerk met back in his office, where de Klerk opened his safe. He took out a black velvet box with the Orapa logo on top. De Klerk opened it and showed it to Jack.

"Wow! Now that's impressive."

De Klerk told Jack the stone's history and described the cutting process of the diamond. The miner who uncovered it received a promotion to mine manager and a new house for his family.

De Klerk put the diamond back into its box and handed it to Jack, who picked up his Thermos. He unscrewed the body of the Thermos to show de Klerk that it was empty inside. Jack took the black jewel box and wrapped it in some cotton batting. Then he put that into the plastic Thermos body. "I'm using a glass vacuum container from a smaller Thermos model. It's shorter and leaves a void that I will utilize." said Jack. He added the glass vacuum container and screwed the case back together. He showed it to de Klerk. "No one but you and I know what I'm carrying. When I go through the airports on my way to New York, I'll ask for a customs inspector supervisor. I will show them your travel authorization paperwork, the bill of lading, customs importation forms, and the necessary duty paperwork. The Thermos will be full of hot coffee, but I will dump it out and show everything to the customs inspector. Everything should work fine."

"Looks good, Mr. Warner. Let's sign some paperwork," offered de Klerk.

"Great. Before I leave, I have something to discuss with you. It has nothing to do with my trip. It is more of a personal nature." Jack spoke with Mr. de Klerk for a few more minutes. They shook hands and he escorted Jack to his car.

Jack had invited his wife to meet him in Paris. He just said he had gone to Europe to look at some airplanes. She flew in a few days early with some girlfriends for shopping, restaurants, and museums. She enjoyed flying with Jack as a passenger. It didn't happen often, but she could see him tense up just a little when he wasn't at the airplane controls. "Relax, Babe. I'm sure the Air France pilots have done this before."

Landing at JFK in New York City, they got separated going through customs. They had planned to meet outside by the baggage claim. Gail waited almost 20 minutes for Jack.

Gail noticed that Jack was now carrying a paper bag from McDonald's. "What the hell, Jack? Didn't you get enough to eat on the plane?"

"This is just case I get hungry," Jack explained.

Gail rolled her eyes. "Men!"

Christiaan de Klerk was waiting for Jack's arrival with the diamond investors at the Manhattan branch of Citibank. With zero fanfare and no audience, Jack and Gail got out of a yellow Checker taxi and strolled into the bank. "What are we doing here? Do you need some cash? We don't have a Citibank account," stated Gail.

"It's okay, let's just go in and meet a guy," whispered Jack to Gail.

The bank manager was waiting for them with two armed bank guards. After introducing himself, he escorted them downstairs into the vault area with the safe deposit boxes. The investors, their jewelry expert, and de Klerk were waiting in a secure conference room inside the vault. The manager asked the guards to wait outside the vault area. De Klerk made the necessary introductions and Jack introduced Gail.

Warner started off, "Gentlemen, I didn't tell my wife the reason for our trip to New York, but, Honey, I can tell you now." He set his McDonald's bag down on the table. "Well, let me get something out so you all can start breathing again." The bank manager *was* wondering why Mr. Warner brought his lunch with him into the bank.

Jack pulled a Big Mac box out of the bag and opened it to reveal a smaller, black velvet box inside. He handed it to Gail and said, "Open it, but remember it's not yours."

Gail opened the box and gasped at the sight of the stunning yellow diamond inside. Nobody spoke. She passed the box to Jack, who handed it to de Klerk. "I'll let you make the final delivery to your customers, Mr. de Klerk."

The buyer's jewelry expert set up a halogen desk light and a microscope and pulled out his loupe. He examined the diamond and verified its identity. Everyone was happy, but none more so than Jack Warner. Gail whispered to Jack, "Now, *that*'s what I call a real McDonald's Happy Meal."

After a few minutes, the diamond was photographed and locked up in a special secure box inside the vault. The investors left, and de Klerk asked the Warners to stay behind for a moment.

"Mr. Warner, I should like to thank you for the flawless execution of your pickup and delivery. With your permission, I have a small present for Mrs. Warner." De Klerk handed Gail a small black Orapa box. She grinned when she opened it. "These are some pink diamond stud earrings that I hope she likes. With them go my sincere thanks and appreciation."

Now it was Jack's turn to speak. "Honey, before we leave, there is one more detail. When I was in Botswana with Mr. de Klerk, I told him that this week was our 20th wedding anniversary. I asked him if he could find something special that I could buy for you while I was there."

From his suit pocket, de Klerk pulled out a small black velvet box, also with the Orapa logo on the top.

"What else could happen to me today?" thought Gail. With trembling hands, she opened the box to reveal a diamond cocktail ring. "Oh myyyyyyyy Gawd!" she exclaimed.

As she tried it on, de Klerk told her, "It's a three-carat, flawless diamond with perfect clarity. It's mounted in a rose gold setting. I hope you like it. We can have it sized for you while you are here in New York." Gail almost fainted. She profusely thanked de Klerk and gave him a big hug and kissed him on both cheeks.

She turned to show her ring to Jack and said, "So, big guy, where are you taking me next?" There's an old Chinese saying: "Happy wife equals a happy life." It was certainly true with the Warners. They were still madly in love after 20 years. When they arrived home in Dallas, there was a long, skinny package and a card waiting for Jack.

Jack opened the wrapping paper to reveal a custom-made, bamboo Tom Morgan fly rod and a Hardy Zane fishing reel. "Oh shit, Babe, do you know how special this rod 'n' reel setup is? They're the best in the world. My, God, how did you know about them? There's like a two-year waiting list for either one of these, if you can even still get a Morgan reel."

"I called your father and he checked around, then he gave me a little advice. When are we going fishing?"

"Gail, darling. I thought I loved you before, but 20 years has only made it better. As they say in the diamond commercials, I think I'll keep you."

Russian Air Show

In late 1995, the Russian Air Force hosted the annual International Air Show outside of Moscow. All the major aircraft manufacturers were invited to bring their latest models to show off to potential international buyers. The Russians specifically invited Boeing to bring its new 747 Cargo King. They offered to buy the plane at the end of the show. This plane had a flip-up nose and a drop-down cargo ramp in the tail. You could drive in a semitruck with double trailers in one end and out the other. Boeing jumped at the chance to show their new super cargo plane to the world. The aircraft was a big hit with the show attendees. Boeing thought they had the sample plane sold to the Russians and expected orders for more planes to come in. At the end of the successful show, Boeing executives approached the Russian Air Force leaders to finalize the purchase of the Cargo King.

This is when the Russians sprang their trap on Boeing. They claimed that their budgets had been cut and they only had a fraction of the money available for buying the plane. Of course, their plan all along had been to lure the plane over to Moscow, display it at the air show, and then offer a very low price for it, about 25% of list price; in this case, $15 million.

The Boeing executives collectively swallowed their gum. They had gambled millions on building the plane to display at the show with the assumption that it was sold to the Russians. And now their buyer was playing games. The executives could only see forced retirement in their future when the Boeing board of directors found out about this debacle.

Before that happened, Jack Warner heard about it. He was at the air show and had been admiring the plane. It was love at first sight. He had talked to the fleet salesman about the plane but was told it was sold, but he could have one built in 18 months for $60 million. "Too much money and too long to wait," thought Jack.

He was checking out of the Moscow Hilton when he heard some of the Lockheed brass talking about the sales disaster with the Cargo King plane. Jack Warner offered to buy them a drink and casually pumped them for more information. When Jack heard the whole story, he asked about the whereabouts of the Boeing sales director. He learned that the man happened to be staying upstairs in the very same hotel. Warner quickly left the group. He paused at an empty table to collect his thoughts and sketch a few notes on a cocktail napkin before heading upstairs.

The elevators were full of people checking out, with trolleys full of luggage, so Jack took the stairs two at a time to the fourth floor. He paused a few moments to catch his breath and knocked on the door. Bob Morris, Sales Director for Boeing Aircraft, answered the door in his bathrobe. They knew each other by reputation but had never actually met. After a quick introduction, Morris invited Warner in and offered him some coffee.

Jack told Morris, "I heard about the sales fiasco with the Cargo King. I feel so sorry that Boeing's going to be stuck with this special plane for some time to come."

Bob Morris was no dummy. He could see Warner's plan coming up Moscow Avenue. "What do you have in mind, Warner?"

Warner started laying the groundwork that he had practiced coming up the stairs. "Maybe I could take it off your hands and let you save face with your board of directors and the world's press. Think of the headlines in the *Wall Street Journal* and *Aviation Week* magazine, when they write an article about how Boeing was fleeced by the Russians. Every other country will try the same thing. You'll be the laughing stock among the aircraft manufacturers. It will cost you future sales and your company stock value will take a hit for millions. Your reputation and corporate credit rating will suffer in the eyes of the commercial banks that lend you money."

Sadly, Morris knew all this was very true.

"Why don't we help each other out? Tell you what I'm gonna do." Warner elaborated,

"I'll take delivery of the Cargo King today, and by tomorrow, I'll have $18 million wired to Boeing's bank in Seattle. I won't release the purchase price to anyone. My company is private, so there's no board of directors or public disclosure of financial information. Boeing can announce that the Cargo King was in such high demand that there were multiple offers to buy it. The Russians were simply outbid. The beauty of this is that it's all true. Just don't let Boeing advertise the final sales price versus the initial retail asking price."

There were a number of positive points that Morris could use to spin this story to his benefit. One, the plane would be sold to an American company for $3 million more than the Russians were offering. Two, the CEO of the company buying the plane was a popular war hero, charismatic, handsome, and looked good at a press conference. Three, Warner knew almost everybody in the armed services who bought airplanes. Having him for a friend would not be a bad thing. And four, Morris could act like it was all his idea, making American lemonade out of Russian lemons.

Morris said he would accept Warner's offer on one condition: Warner would do print advertising promotion work and appear at air shows endorsing Boeing planes for the next two years.

Jack Warner stuck out his hand and said, "You got a deal."

Jack Warner cancelled his first-class ticket home to Texas and instead flew home in a brand-new $60 million airplane that he just bought for $18 million. "A 70% discount is not a bad thing, eh, Jack boy?" thought Warner. Plus, the Boeing sales director was now his pal, especially after Jack invited him to go salmon fishing in Alaska.

Time to Sell

Aire Cargo could undercut almost every other shipper out there. They were a non-union company, the employees loved Jack Warner, and AC had great benefits. The workers earned top salaries and saved money by not having to pay union dues, so they were happy. Every year, they moved more packages and delivered more freight than the year before. Business was better every year, at least until the 1990s.

Email started in 1995, and its usage grew steadily. After 1998, the number of emails zoomed upwards like a Saturn rocket. As email became wildly popular, snail mail delivery was tanking. The U.S. Post Office was losing millions, closing facilities, and laying off employees. Overnight delivery of envelopes suffered as well. Jack Warner could see this trend coming and only increasing in the future, thereby hurting his Overnight Aire business. Email was immediate, free, and could be broadcast widely (i.e. spamming). Business documents, the mainstay of overnight packages, were beginning to be scanned and then emailed, again for free. Scanners that used to cost several thousand dollars were dropping in price every year and getting smaller. Gail even bought one for the AC office.

Noah liked flying but wasn't interested in the company. There seemed to be more competitors in the air freight business every year. Government regulations were multiplying like rabbits. It just wasn't fun anymore. Jack had run the company for almost 20 years, and this seemed like the ideal time to sell. He had received offers every year from competitors and Wall Street firms. He had even considered taking the company public, but then he would have to give up control to a board of directors and disclose private financial information. He liked having a free hand, running the company out of his back pocket, so to speak.

He contacted Red Arnold of United Business Brokers in New York City to see about selling Aire Cargo. Warner had been following Arnold's experiences in selling other companies. Two years ago, Red Arnold sold Catalina Shipping, a tristate area cargo shipping company, for an astounding price. Red had recently found a corporate buyer for Pet Shmet, a chain of 132 pet stores in the U.S. and Canada.

There was one deal that really convinced Warner to use Red Arnold. When the owner of the Wild Horse Ranch Brothel in Nevada was convicted of tax fraud and racketeering, the U.S. Government confiscated the brothel property and put a government receiver in charge of the business.

The IRS wanted to realize as much money as possible from the sale of the business. If it was closed, the asset's value would plummet, so the government kept it open until it could be sold. Warner loved it! He always knew the government liked screwing people, but now they were actually in the business of doing so. Jay Leno and David Letterman thought that their comedy dreams had come true. Their monologue jokes about the situation seemed endless. Chris Rock devoted over 15 minutes to the subject on one of his HBO specials.

Red Arnold arranged for the sale of the brothel to a competitor. The sale included the real estate, buildings, women, and PR, or 'blue sky,' as it was it was called in the business-sales trade. The government was out of the brothel business and got a record price for the seized asset. Jack Warner knew Red Arnold was the business broker for him.

Red flew to Dallas to meet Jack Warner and tour the company facilities. Warner showed off the planes, the airfield, and the package-sort facility. There was an inventory of all aircraft, delivery trucks, and miscellaneous vehicles, aircraft maintenance hangars, executive offices, and vehicle-maintenance garages. Warner gave him a huge package of business information, which included sales income figures, expenses, leases on planes and vehicles, employee records, retirement pension account info, plus tax returns for the last five years.

Aire Cargo had three things that most other shipping competitors didn't: no debt, cash in the bank, and a well-funded pension plan. This meant that a new buyer could finance part of the purchase by taking out new loans and letting the company service the purchase debt. The company could help pay for itself, thereby requiring less cash from a buyer.

Red Arnold solicited potential buyers in America, Europe, Canada, the Middle East, and the Far East. Within 30 days, two potential buyers submitted offers.

The first offer was from a company in Dubai that was supposedly owned by Prince Al-Admir of the Royal Family. His offer was respectable, but it was made up three parts: 1) 50% of the price in cash, 2) 25% in stock secured by his Dubai real-estate holdings, and 3) asking Warner to finance the last 25%.

Jack Warner didn't want to finance the sale, and he didn't want anything to do with Dubai real estate. Foreigners can't own real property in Dubai, which is why he was offered stock. Jack thought the Dubai deal was too flammable. Who knew what effect violent happenings in the Middle East could have on the value of the real estate securing his future?

The second offer was from China-Panda, a Chinese corporation in Sing Mai, near Hong Kong. They were offering all cash, an encouraging sign. They assured Warner that they wanted to buy Aire Cargo with the promise of no name change, no layoffs, no relocation, and no changes to the traditions of Aire Cargo that made it so successful.

China-Panda was offering $191 million in cash, plus a series of perks and benefits. Jack Warner would be on the payroll as operations consultant for two years at a salary of
$250,000 per year. He would be given access to a Beechcraft King Air for his personal use anytime he wanted it. His family would have full medical insurance benefits for life. "This sounds more like it," thought Jack and Gail.

At that time, email was not a widespread practice in China. The communist government kept a tight rein on all communications. While Jack Warner could see the value of his company declining, the Chinese weren't as familiar with email as the rest of the world. Super-fast telephone lines were not common in China. Therefore, China-Panda didn't consider email such a big threat to Overnight Aire and Aire Cargo as Jack did.

The only overnight-type service offered in China was by foreign companies only delivering into China, which actually took 3-5 days. China was tired of so much money being made on their business and then having it going out of the country to foreigners. As China was loosening the restrictions on their business practices, China-Panda predicted an avalanche in overnight envelopes and packages. They wanted to monopolize on that business.

The whole package sounded good for Warner and his employees. He and Gail accepted their offer. They were very happy, and Red Arnold was ecstatic.

Bonus Time

When Jack and Gail left the escrow company with the closing statement for selling Aire Cargo, neither of them was speaking too much. The sales proceeds were wired into their personal account in Texas. When their bank manager saw the size of the wire that came into the Warner bank account, she let out a low whistle.

Back in their car, Gail remarked, "I've always wanted to sleep with a millionaire," playfully digging her elbow into Jack's ribs.

"And I've always wanted a rich broad," answered Jack, smiling. "How about I buy you some lunch? We'll treat ourselves to some pecan pie a la mode?"

Over lunch, they did some talking and financial planning. Jack murmured, "You know, Babe, we didn't build this business alone. What would you say to sharing some of this money with a few key employees?"

"I was thinking the same thing. They say great minds think alike," said Gail.

Jack thought out loud. "How about a nice slice for Lou Patroni and a bonus for all the employees that have been with us since the beginning? We can give a smaller bonus for staff members that have been here for at least 10 years."

"I like it. How about an early Christmas bonus for the rest of the employees too?" asked Gail. "Instead of putting Lou's check into an envelope, how about we put it inside a new pickup truck?"

"You're pretty generous with my money, Gail."

"*Our* money, Flyboy," laughed Gail.

"Oh, yeah, thanks for reminding me," laughed Jack.

Two weeks later, Jack and Gail sent out an email to every employee asking them to please meet in the big maintenance hangar for lunch. There was a catered BBQ lunch and pecan pie with kegs of beer and sodas to wash it all down. Lou Patroni ate his lunch and was standing there waiting for them, checking his watch. "Goddamn, Warner. He calls me to meet him and then he's late. Where is that son-of-a-bitch?"

His curiosity was soon satisfied. Jack and Gail pulled up in a new, red Ford 4x4 pickup with some snazzy wheels and white pin striping. Hooked to the back of the truck was a new, top-of-the-line Bass Tracker bass boat with an 80-hp Mercruiser motor on the back.

"What a goddamn showoff. You got a new pickup truck? Shit-howdy! And a new fishing boat! My buddy sells his company and treats himself to a new goddamn pickup and a boat to boot!" screamed Patroni while he walked around the truck. He continued his expletive-filled tirade until he saw the Texas license plate on the truck: PATRONI.

The air went silent.

"Well, I guess that shut him up," joked Jack to Gail.

Patroni took a few steps back to get a better look, and then he could see the boat trailer license plate: LILPAT. All he could do was give Jack a hug, while tears streamed down his face. Dino and Gina came over for a hug from the old man, as well.

"The pickup and boat are a little overdue. Thank you for helping save my life that night back in Vietnam."

While tears streamed down the big man's face, Gail handed him an envelope. "This should pay for some new tackle, Honey. This is from Jack and me for all your years of friendship and your endless help getting this company started."

Lou was just a blubbering mess. His wife and kids were hugging him. Dino yelled out, "So, Dad, when are we going fishing in our new boat?"

"What's this 'our boat' shit, boy?

Later, when Lou could gather himself and it got quiet, his wife saw the envelope in his pocket. "What's this, Lou?"

"Gail gave it to me after Jack threw me the keys to the new truck."

Mrs. Patroni opened the envelope and saw a check inside for $1 million. "Jesus Christ," she said.

Jack and Gail had almost as much fun handing out bonuses to the other long-term employees.

Red's Toys

Red Arnold handled the entire Aire Cargo sales transaction to China-Panda. Of course, each side had their own attorneys, but Red brokered both sides of the deal. With part of his sales commission, Arnold bought a red 1998 Ferrari 355 F1 Spyder. To fill up the other side of his garage, Red attended the world-famous Las Vegas Motor Auction. He learned that they were going to sell James Dean's 1946 Indian Chief motorcycle. His mind was made up that he wanted that bike.

At the sale, Red happened to be standing right next to Jay Leno. Jay already had a famous car and bike collection, but he loved attending car auctions. The best thing about the Las Vegas sale was that he could perform at the casino at night and look for cars and motorcycles during the day.

Red looked over Jay's shoulder at his catalog. Jay had circled in red the same James Dean 1946 Indian Chief motorcycle that Red wanted to bid on. The bike was coming to the stage in just a few minutes. He quickly went and found a nearby busboy. "What's your name, pal?"

"Ernie, sir. What can I do for you?"

"How'd you like to make $100 for 30 seconds' work?"

"Is it illegal?" asked Ernie.

"Nope," answered Red. "When I give you the signal, I want you to accidently dump an entire tray of drinks on the guy next to me with the gray hair."

"Are you nuts? That's Jay Leno! I'll get fired. You better make it $500."

"Done," agreed Red as he pulled out five Ben Franklins from his silver money clip.

As they were rolling the bike on stage for the next auction, Red signaled Ernie to go into action. Ernie walked in front of Jay Leno and proceeded to dump a tray of six margaritas all over the front of the famous comedian. While the James Dean bike was garnering bids, Jay was totally distracted, covered by the frozen yellow mess. Red kept bidding with his yellow card while yelling at Ernie. Poor Jay didn't know what hit him. By the time Jay got toweled off, Red Arnold owned James Dean's 1946 Indian motorcycle.

Red Arnold knew how to make money, but he really knew how to spend it. Red's favorite saying was, "Whoever said that money can't buy happiness doesn't know where to shop!"

Fly Fishing in Alaska

After the sale closed escrow and the dust settled, Jack told Gail, "Honey, I think it's time for a long-overdue vacation."

"Why don't we make it a second honeymoon?" cooed Gail.

"Where do you want to go, Babe? I've got that Twin Beech sitting there, just waiting to be flown somewhere."

"Jack, you've told me about Alaska for all these years. We've only been there a few times. Why don't we go there and you can really show it to me? Bring your fly rod and reel that I bought you for our 20th wedding anniversary."

"That's an awesome idea. We can stop and see my folks while we're there."

"You can take me flying over Alaska. Those glaciers are so pretty. The mountain ranges are majestic, and the animals are spectacular."

"Sure, the king salmon will be running pretty soon. This will be perfect."

Jack and Gail made all the preparations for the trip. Jack had the Beechcraft King Air in tip-top shape and ready to go. He'd just had the avionics updated with the latest electronic navigation aids available. He also had a Weather Master 100 installed. It automatically downloaded the latest weather data from the satellites.

When they landed in Anchorage, Jack stopped off at Mountain View Sports, the oldest fly-fishing store in town. He asked for the most experienced salesman they had. Rocky came over and asked, "May I help you, sir?"

Seeing his name badge, Jack went to work. "Yeah, Rocky, my name is Jack and this is my wife, Gail. I need a fly-fishing setup for my dad. He's turning 75 next month, so this will be an early birthday present. I want a nine-foot, 10-weight, fast-taper fly rod. I like the Shakespeare Ugly Stick. I'll also need an assortment of new flies. Do you have any Fast Freddie or King Killer flies with a short shank 2/0 to 4/0 hook? I also want an Abel Super 6N fly-fishing reel, along with a couple of spools of floating fly line."

"I take it you've fly fished before," said Rocky, grinning.

"Once or twice. And, while we're at it, let's look at a tackle box, a new vest, and a pair of waders. I'm sure all of my dad's stuff is worn out."

Gail chimed in with, "Let's get the same setup for your mom. She likes to fish just as much as your dad does. Rocky, my husband's gonna make you the salesman of the month," assured Gail.

"With anybody else in the store, that would be really special, but I happen to own the store," laughed Rocky. "But I'll buy myself a cigar with your compliments."

Ben Warner had retired from flying, so Jack rented a float plane at the Anchorage Airport. Bush charter companies don't usually rent their planes out, but the Warner name was still famous in Alaska. Jack called on an old friend, Todd Rust. Rust's Flying Service was started in 1963 by Henry Rust, Todd's father. Jack explained that he and Gail were in town to see his parents and show Gail around.

Todd said, "You're in luck. One of my pilots is down in the lower 48 visiting his family. His plane is free. Why don't you take that one for a few days? It's a real nice de Havilland Beaver with lots of room for you, your parents, and all of your stuff."

"Sounds great! My dad has the same model. What'll I owe you for it?"

"Let's see... Jack, your pop tells me you have an air cargo business. Do you ever haul anything up here to Anchorage?"

"Yeah, every once in a while."

"I got an offer for you. I'll let you use the Beaver while you're in town. When you go back down south, I need a favor. There's a de Havilland Otter in Montana that I bought, but I need to get it up here. It was involved in a fender bender at the airport and needs some work. I got a good deal on it. Are any of your cargo planes big enough to hold it, if the wing was removed?"

"Sure, I can handle that, no problem," offered Jack.

"Great, you give me a discount on the freight charge and I'll have the wing off by the time you get there."

Jack gave Todd a low quote: "You have the plane, wing, and the parts ready to load, drain the fuel tank, and I'll haul it up here for you. You throw in this rental and gas. Later you take me, my dad, and my son halibut fishing and we'll call it a deal. How'zat?"

Todd Rust couldn't put out his hand fast enough.

Now, all Jack Warner had to do was to convince China-Panda to give Todd a huge discount on the cargo flight. Sometimes Jack forgot that he didn't own the company anymore.

Jack & Noah's AK Trip

After Jack and Gail returned from Alaska, Jack arranged to deliver Rust's damaged plane from Montana, as promised. He had finagled his old Aire Cargo friends to divert a partially full Cargo Freighter to Montana and then up to Alaska. The Chinese company executives were 8,000 miles away near Hong Kong. Jack Warner figured that what they didn't know couldn't hurt him.

Jack flew his Twin Beechcraft King Air, escorting the cargo plane all the way to Alaska. Noah came along as copilot. "Hey, Noah, what do you think of going halibut fishing with your old man? We can probably talk your grandparents into going with us."

"Great, Pop, sounds good to me. I haven't seen Grandpa and Grandma in way too long."

They packed the fishing tackle and outdoor gear. Noah had a pickup truck, so Jack let Noah drive to the China-Panda Aire Cargo facility where the plane was kept. "What are we flying today?" Noah asked.

"That Twin Beech that they let me use. I don't think you've ever been in a Twin Beech. A Beechcraft King Air is just about the nicest propeller-driven plane in the sky. With its twin turboprop engines, it really cooks, cruises at 250 knots with a range of 1,500 miles. Since it has a pressurized cabin, we can fly over most weather up to 30,000 feet."

"Awesome, Pop. Can I do some of the flying?"

"Sure. I'll get you used to everything and then you can take over while I snooze my way to Alaska. It's the oooooonnnnnly way to fly," kidded Jack.

When they rolled up on the plane, Noah said, "Damn, it looks fast just sitting on the tarmac. I love the nose of the plane, with those two big engines on the sides."

After all the equipment was loaded, Jack and Noah did their pre-flight check together, got in, and buttoned it up. Jack took the pilot's seat and Noah slipped into the copilot's. "You know, Pop, this reminds me of that Hawker we flew up to Alaska. I thought this bird had everything, but I don't see a cup holder."

"Funny man," murmured Jack. "The instruments don't work so well when you spill your Big Gulp all over them."

After getting clearance from the tower, they took off and made good time toward Alaska. The boys stopped in Spokane, Washington for fuel, some lunch, and a bathroom break.

Jack talked Noah through his takeoff from the Spokane Airport. He did okay, but he would still need more flight time. "Pop, was Grandpa a good flying teacher?"

"Yeah, he was very patient. And just like you, I thought I knew it all right away."

"What do you mean?" quizzed Noah.

Soft Mud Takeoff

"Well, one morning, I got the plane ready for flying. It had been raining all night, but the sun came up to a clear, blue-sky day. I was planning to fly over to Homer to pick up some airplane parts that had come in. Grandpa had second thoughts about my trip. He told me, 'You better check out the airstrip, boy. All that rain might have turned it into a swamp.'

"I went, 'Yeah, yeah, yeah,' you know, like you talk to me when I try to tell you something, Noah? But, I *did* walk down the dirt airstrip as Grandpa suggested. Unfortunately, I only went about halfway. There was a bear out in the meadow next to the airstrip, and I got distracted watching him. I always carried a Smith & Wesson Python .44 caliber pistol just for this reason. If a bear charges you, you can't say, 'Just a second, Mr. Bear. I'll be right back. I have to go get my gun.' The .44 is damn handy to have, just in case.

"But that day, this bear stayed out in the meadow, molesting a raspberry thicket, and paid no attention to me. I was about a hundred yards away.

"After walking only half of the airstrip and watching the bear, I went back to the plane. I did my last-minute check of the plane and started the engine. After it warmed up, I pushed the throttle forward and started taxiing down the dirt strip. I gave it full throttle, and the plane picked up speed. Normally, the plane would need to be traveling about 45-50 knots to lift off in about 550 feet of space, but I couldn't get it going faster than 40. The airstrip was only a thousand feet long, and I was quickly running out of real estate.

"As Grandpa had warned me, the all-night rain *had* softened the dirt strip, especially at the far end where I needed my speed the most. Like an idiot, I foolishly passed the point of no return. I either had to lift off or run off the end of the runway into the weeds.

"Well, this occurred to me a little too late, so I cut the throttle and hit the brakes. The plane rolled into the weeds and had almost stopped by the time it hit the barbed-wire fence. The fence stopped the plane, but the momentum threw the plane over onto its propeller, where it stayed like a toy plane stuck in the sand at the beach. Worst of all, I had to unbelt myself and climb out the airplane's door and shimmy down to the ground, where I fell right on my ass in the wet mud.

"Just about that time, your grandparents came running up. Your grandpa could tell by the engine noise that the plane didn't take off. He flew through the cabin's screen door and ran down the path to the airstrip. Your grandma started behind him, but I guess her mother's love propelled her into first place in the race to find me and see if I was all right.

"After seeing that I was unhurt and sitting in the mud, they couldn't help but start laughing. 'Maybe you'll listen to your old man someday, eh, boy?' your grandpa blurted out, wearing this big Cheshire-cat smile. You know that look that he gets?

"To pay for the damage, I had to wax and polish the entire plane and clean and shampoo the interior. To fix the propeller, I had to pull it and then sweet-talk Grandpa's friend, Kenny Beall, to fly it to Anchorage for repairs and have the blade straightened. During the several hours we had to wait, I had to detail Beall's bush plane. Grandpa and Kenny were pretty happy when it was all over, but I was damn tired. I never made the mistake of not listening to your Grandpa again, at least not when it came to flying."

As they approached Anchorage, Jack let Noah land the plane. Jack had his left hand down low on the on the wheel, so Noah wouldn't notice it. He also had his feet on the control rudder pedals with a feather-light touch, just in case. But Jack's help wasn't needed. Noah had the Warner instinct for flying. When they were getting off the plane, Jack quipped, "Escaped death, once again, eh, boy?"

"Real funny, Pop."

Todd Rush flew them down to Ben and ML's cabin. Todd thanked Jack again for hauling his broken bush plane up from Montana. "We've got it all taken apart. I'm just waiting for parts to come from Canada. I'll be back to pick you up on Sunday morning, unless I hear any different."

The Warner family had a great reunion. ML was so happy to see Jack and Noah. She grilled fresh salmon with garlic sauce while listening to the boys tell all the old stories, plus some new ones from Texas. Jack was always traveling, and she and Ben lived vicariously through him.

The next morning, ML woke Noah early so they could go pick raspberries for breakfast. Noah shared a life dream with her. "You know, Grandma, someday I want to move up here. I'm going to talk to Pop about it. Maybe I could work for Todd Rust in Anchorage or buy a bush plane of my own."

ML made buttermilk biscuits, caribou sausage, and scrambled eggs from her own chickens. After breakfast, everybody took off after salmon and halibut. Ben and Jack enjoyed fishing together again after so many years apart. They taught Noah the finer points of lure placement and line casting. Ben caught several good-sized halibut to help fill his freezer. Jack caught his limit, but Noah only caught one; but it was a whopper, probably 50 pounds. Ben said, "Let's clean these fish and freeze them. That way you boys can take them home with you. You can pick up some dry ice in Anchorage at Woody's Meat Market."

Todd Rust picked up Jack and Noah as scheduled on Sunday and flew them back to Anchorage. While they were flying, Todd asked Jack, "Does this plane look familiar?"

It suddenly dawned on him. "Duh! It's my dad's plane. I learned how to fly in it when I was 12. How did you get it?"

"When Ben stopped flying some years back, I tried to buy it from him. You know de Havilland Beavers are hard to find, especially a nice plane like this one."

"Gee, Todd, I didn't know he sold it to you," said Jack.

"He didn't. Ben wouldn't sell it. I'm leasing it from him. I think he has future plans for it, but he never would tell me what they were."

Todd explained further. "My dad has been running Ben's fish cabin businesses for him. It's a good retirement business for my dad, and we split the money 50/50 with Ben and ML."

On the way back to the lower 48, Noah had a chance for a long talk with Jack. "Hey, Pop, what do you think of the idea of me moving up to Alaska? I'd like to get more bush flying experience and get my license. Maybe I could work for Todd Rust? I'd be close by if Grandpa or Grandma needed me. How old are they now, late 70s?"

"Your mother and I would sure miss you. But all little birds have to leave the nest sometime. Why don't you give it some thought and planning for a few days? You can talk to your mother about it. She's a smart cookie. You know she helped me organize Aire Cargo in its early days. Then, you can call your grandparents and see what they have to say about it."

Ben and ML were overjoyed. Ben was looking forward to teaching Noah everything he knew about bush plane flying. He would get his Beaver back from Todd Rust and give it to Noah when he moved up north. ML had a heart-to-heart talk with Ben. "Honey, why don't we leave this property to Noah? Jack doesn't need it, and he could certainly stay anytime he came up. The plane, charter business, fishing cabins, and the property would make a nice start for Noah's life. Plus, he likes doing all those things."

"Let's do it. We can call the estate attorney in Anchorage to draw up a trust and update our will."

Firefighting

Jack planned to let Noah fly the plane all the way back to Texas. When they were passing over Colorado, Noah gave Jack a poke in the ribs to wake him up. "Hey, Pop, I feel a little vibration from the left side of the plane. Do you feel it?"

It took Jack a few seconds to wake up and absorb what Noah was talking about. "You're right. I do feel a little something. Why don't we set this bird down and check it out?
Where are we, boy?"

"The closest airport is Peterson Air Base in Colorado Springs. It's just a few minutes away. I read about it in the Pilot's Guide Book. They use it for those firefighting airplanes that drop water and fire retardant. I think they train pilots from all over the country there."

"Gee, Noah, you're like my own, private tour guide," kidded Jack. "How about if I get on the radio and see if we can get clearance to land?"

Jack radioed the Peterson tower and declared a mechanical condition. He asked for landing clearance and instructions. "10-4, Beech, Runway B right. Do you need assistance?" asked the tower.

"No, we'll just taxi over to your maintenance hangar and ask a mechanic to check us out."

The boys landed the Twin Beech and talked to the aviation mechanic on duty. He said, "Why don't you guys go have a cup of coffee and give me a few minutes? I'll see what I can find."

He found the problem right away. A bad circuit breaker wasn't letting the left propeller feather correctly. He fixed it in just a few minutes before they got back.

Jack and Noah walked around the airstrip, looking at the water-dropping airplanes. Some were from the Vietnam era, and others were even older, from the Korean War years. They were all wheeled planes that had to land on airstrips.

"Noah, check these bad boys out. These bright yellow planes are Canadair Bombardier 415 Super Scoopers. I read an article about these planes. Because the bottom of the fuselage is shaped like a boat, they're amphibious. The wheels can also be lowered for airport landings. They have four water scoops so the pilot can skim over a calm lake or river and fill up the 1,620-gallon tank and then climb up again. It can even mix in a chemical fire suppressant if needed. One of these planes can do the work of five or six standard water-dropping planes. The 415s were developed to deliver big loads of water in quick response to fires. They build them at the Bombardier Aerospace facility near North Bay, Ontario in Canada."

"Wow, Pop, what a cool bush plane that would make, huh?"

Bert Ethan, the fire dispatcher, was walking by and stopped to eavesdrop on Jack talking to Noah. "You want a job as our tour guide?"

Jack introduced himself and Noah. Afterwards, Bert said, "Jack Warner, the owner of Aire Cargo – that Jack Warner? The Jack Warner that rescued all of those downed American pilots in Vietnam? *That* Jack Warner?"

"Guilty as charged," answered Jack. Noah was beaming. He was proud of his father and didn't get to witness his father being recognized in public very often.

"Well, I'll be damned," exclaimed Bert. They made small talk for a few minutes, telling Bert why they had landed at his airport.

The loud shriek of a claxon horn broke the quiet morning air. "Aahooga, Aahooga, Aahooga," it went over and over.

The Warners watched as the fire crews scrambled and the water bombers warmed up and took off. Jack noticed that the Super Scoopers were just sitting there all by themselves. He walked over to Bert, the dispatcher, and asked him about it.

"Hey, Bert, I know you're busy, but how come you're not using the 415s?"

"We're leasing those from Canada, but their pilots haven't arrived yet. They're all fueled and ready to go, but we don't have anybody to fly them. None of our pilots are qualified to land or take off on water. Also, they haven't been trained in skimming the lakes to fill them with water. It's too bad, 'cuz we really could use them today."

Jack made him an offer: "How'd you like a volunteer? I can do it. I grew up flying bush planes in Alaska. I've landed on dirt, snow, and water hundreds of times. I still have my water-landing license certification. If you can give me a navigator to guide me and an engineer who knows how to work the water mechanicals, I'm your man. My son, Noah, will help anywhere you can use him."

Noah jumped in. "Sure, I'd be glad to help out."

"Jack, are you sure you can fly one of those?" asked Bert.

"Bert, I've flown just about everything, including a de Havilland Beaver, an F-4 Phantom fighter, 707s, 727s, 747s, Citation X jets, Hawkers, a C-23 Sherpa, and that Twin Beech you see over there. I left the Air Force as a full colonel. They even gave me a couple of medals. I'm your man. Let's do it."

"Let me see if I can find a navigator and a flight engineer. Be right back."

Jack got in the pilot seat and studied the instrument panel while Bert rounded up the crewmen. Noah was standing behind him and stated, "I only see three seats, so I guess I'm not going. Good luck, Pop. I'll stay here and see if there's any way I can help out until you get back."

Bert got the crew on board and made the introductions. "Jack Warner, this is George Yates, your navigator, and that sketchy-looking guy is your flight engineer, Juan Carlos. George knows the mountains where the fire is burning. He'll walk you through what to do while you're flying. Kind of a 'learn as you go' program. Juan will operate the water drops and mix the fire retardant."

Juan explained his duties: "I have a padded horizontal bed with a small windshield on the bottom of the plane. I can lie down and watch the fire locations. I have a trigger control that I use to open the water drop hatches or I can open the fill scoops while we skim over the water. I'm like a WWII bomber pilot, except I'm dropping water for a good reason, instead of bombs for a bad one."

Jack started the plane, warmed up the engines, taxied, and took off. George announced, "We going toward Lopez Lake. You'll like this lake because it's got an easy approach and a clear take-off path between the hills. Some lakes are tough to access with too many mountains."

With George's help, Jack came in low and skimmed the smooth water while Juan opened the scoops to fill the water tank. "Okay, we're full. Head for heaven," instructed Juan over the intercom.

"Boy, that was fast," said Jack.

"Yeah, it only takes 10 seconds to fill up. Amazing, huh?" answered Juan.

"Follow a heading of 140 degrees, altitude of 1,500 feet. The fire boss wants this H2O on the right side of Long Canyon," commanded George. "This is part of the famous Huasna Ranch. I used to hunt quail here every fall with my dad and his buddies. I know it well. There are some high-tension power lines at the top of this canyon. Watch for the big towers. They're about 250 feet tall."

Jack spotted the fire crew on the ground and saw the brush and trees ablaze just above them. "You ready on the trigger, Juan?" asked Jack. "How high off the deck do you want me, Cisco?"

"Si, Pancho. Can you dive down to about 200 feet and pull up just as we approach the fire crew? You'll see them in their yellow jackets and helmets."

"Can do." Jack followed orders and Juan dropped the water perfectly on a big chunk of forest fire, knocking it down in a cloud of white steam.

"Awww, Cisco... Awww, Pancho. Good job, boys!" screamed George into the intercom. "You guys think you're the only ones who used to watch *The Cisco Kid* on TV?"

Everybody laughed as Jack pulled up and headed back for Lopez Lake for another drink of water. "Where to next, Coach?" asked Jack.

George was in radio contact with the fire boss on the ground. "The boss wants five or six more drops just like that one. But with these, Juan, mix in some sugar, okay?" George meant for Juan to add red fire retardant into the water tank. The retardant colored the water red and made it thicker so it would stick to the trees and bushes, helping them resist burning.

As Jack headed back up Long Canyon, setting up for his next drop, George gave him a warning: "Don't forget the power lines. And, Juan, try not to hit the fire crew with the Kool Aid." George explained to Jack, "Last summer, Juan dropped his load right on top of the crew. They got that red sticky shit all over them. Boy, were they pissed!"

"Yeah, but at least, they didn't burn up," laughed Juan.

"But they got back at me and Juan later. When we got back to our cabin, everything was coated in water with that red retardant shit. All of our clothes, boots, helmets, turnout gear, everything. Juan and I had to wear pink socks and underwear for the rest of the summer."

"You can't imagine the joking we had to take from all the guys, and the women too. The girls accused us of stealing their pink panties and wearing 'em," added Juan.

Jack laughed as he started his dive run. He nailed the spot. "Right on the money, baby," bragged Jack.

"Hey, Jack, where did you learn to fly? We saw you fly in aboard that Twin Beech King Air and all of a sudden you're a fire pilot. What gives?" asked Juan.

While they flew back to reload with water, Jack told them about his life in Alaska and Vietnam.

"Wow, no wonder you know how to skim the lake so well and make dive runs," said George. "What are you doing now?"

Jack simply said, "I used to be a pilot for an air freight company called Aire Cargo." He skipped the part about being the former owner.

Juan yelled out, "Did you have to wear those little brown shorts?"

"No, Juan. That's UPS. We just wore khaki pants and green polo shirts."

George said, "That's a big company. Maybe I could get a job there someday? Do you know anybody in the head office?"

"One or two," said Jack. "Call me when you're ready and I'll put in a good word for you."

George received a radio call from the fire boss. After listening to him, he yelled at Jack, "We've got an eight-man fire crew in trouble over in Portuguese Flats. They're working a fire line, but the wind just shifted and they've got fire all around them. We can fill up at Hansen Dam. It's on the way. We gotta hurry or they're gonna be toast."

Jack followed George's directions to the lake behind Hansen Dam. As he skimmed the surface, Juan filled up the tank with water. "Jack, look out for power lines up ahead, 150 feet off the water. Watch for the orange plastic warning balls. They should be easy to spot. Jack, give me a heading of 190 north by northwest. By the way, how're we doing on go-go juice?"

"This bird is low on gas, only about 200 pounds left. Hey, George, how far away are those boys?"

"About 10 miles. We're not going to have enough fuel to water 'em down and make it back to base. We should turn around and re-fuel."

Right then, the radio came alive with a message from the control tower. "Scooper1, status report, please."

Jack updated Bert with their rescue mission situation.

"What's your fuel status?"

Jack told them, "200 pounds."

"Negative on the Portuguese Flats trip, return to base for fuel."

"George, if we go back to base, who's gonna help those boys in the Flats?"

"Nobody. We're it." George shrugged.

"Well, fuck that shit, we're gonna go save their asses."

"Scooper1 to Base, I misread the fuel gauge. It reads 500 pounds."

"This is Base, Scooper1. Either you're getting world-record mileage or you are so full of shit, your eyes are brown. Return to base, now."

"Hey, Jack, aren't you going to turn back?" asked Juan.

"Those eight boys on the fire crew are your friends, right? I'm betting they've got wives and kids. Well, boys, this is what we're in business for. When I told you about me being a fighter pilot in Vietnam, I left out the part where I rescued 21 pilots that were shot down over North Vietnam. This will be a piece of cake, 'cuz nobody's shooting at us."

"You mean other than Bert in the control tower?" quipped George. "I'm up for it, how about you, Juan?"

"Go get 'em, Pancho. It's the Cisco Kid to the rescue. Whoooya!"

George guided Jack up to Portuguese Flats. He circled while Juan and George spotted the fire crew hunkered down under their silver space blankets. Fire crews have little tents they can crawl into, made out of fire-resistant space blanket material. The fire fighters call them "baked potatoes." This is the bastion of last resort. If it's burn up or get in the tents, they'll use the tents to save their lives.

The silver tents were easy to see. Jack set up his run, diving steeply toward the men.

"You're clear, Jack, no power lines or anything. Go for it!" yelled George.

"Okay, Cisco, it's up to you, mi amigo. George, I'm gonna need your help to pull out of this dive."

Juan pulled the trigger right at the bottom of Jack's steep dive. Almost seven tons of water showered the area. It knocked the hell out of the men and one woman in their little tents, but they loved every gallon of it. Instead of being in the middle of a big campfire, they were now laying in a wet, swampy mess. "Wow, I never thought I'd love mud so much!" the female firefighter yelled out.

Jack and George pulled back with all of their might. "Didn't I see this in some Spencer Tracy movie?" screamed George. Jack was straining too much to smile. And, like Spencer Tracey, they managed to pull the plane up toward blue sky.

"Hey, Jack, when we land, will you help me pull the pine needles out of the wheels?"

"Base this is Scooper1, returning to base," said George.

"I hope," thought Jack.

"Base here. Good luck, Scooper1."

"How far back to the base, George?"

"About 25 miles, Captain."

"Any airstrips between us and the air base?"

"Negative."

"Any lakes or rivers?"

"Negative."

"Golf courses, fields, freeways, straight roads? Someone's big back yard?" kidded Jack.

"Negative on all that."

"That's *not* the answer I was looking for," answered Jack. "Why don't you boys keep your eyes peeled for anything blue, larger than a cattle watering trough?"

"Your fuel gauge reads 25 pounds. The engines are going to quit in about 90 seconds, sir," said George.

"Yeah, I can read."

Just then, Juan screamed, "Look down at five o'clock! It's a small lake, a pond or something. Captain, can you put it down there?"

Jack saw it and said, "No problemo, Cisco."

George told Jack, "Sir, do you notice that hill at the far end of the pond?"

"You mean that really big, solid-looking hill?" asked Jack.

"That would be the one. It looks very hard, like it's made out of rock or something." kidded George. "Juan and I would *really* appreciate it if you didn't overshoot the water."

"Yeah, my family would too."

With all his years of experience as a bush pilot and a fighter pilot, Jack was able to touch down on the water just past a little sandy beach. Luckily, a plane landing on water stops almost immediately, much faster than on land. George and Juan weren't ready for that, but Jack knew it would. Jack's bush plane experience landing on water proved to be a lifesaver that day.

"Jack, I was reading the airplane manual under "specifications," and according to the book, that landing was friggin' impossible," kidded Juan.

"That's why they pay me the big money," said Jack with a big-ass grin on his face. "So, George, where are we?"

"About a mile north of Nipomo by Mount Tom."

Jack radioed Bert in the tower to tell him where they were. "Think you could helo us in some fuel, pretty please?"

"You son-of-a-bitch, if you worked for me, I'd fire your ass. But, since you're a volunteer, and all eight of those guys you just saved happened to be really close friends of mine, I guess I'm going let it go. Is some 12-year-old scotch okay with you?"

"And I was just going to ask for a raise in pay," Jack kidded back.

Bert sent a helicopter with 75 gallons of fuel on board. The helo set down, and, surprise, Noah opened the door and jumped out to start unloading the shiny five-gallon fuel cans.

"Fill it up with high-test, check the oil, wash the windshield, and air up the tires, will you, boy?" Jack joked to his son.

"Yes, sir, will this be cash or credit?" asked Noah.

"In the TV commercials, the gas attendants all wear little bow ties with a snappy white hat. What happened to yours?" continued Jack.

"I had to take off the uniform to load all this fuel so I could save your ass, sir. Come back and see us again," joked Noah. He had inherited Jack's sense of humor along with his love of flying.

After they emptied all 15 cans, Noah loaded the empties back on the helo and they all took off for the air base.

With 75 gallons of fuel on board, Jack started his takeoff. It was a good thing the plane's water tanks were empty and the gas tanks almost empty too. If they were full, he never would have gotten up. He needed every inch of the little lake for enough airspeed to leave the water behind and head for the blue skies.

"Jack, I don't want to be critical, but I think if you check our wheels when we land, there's gonna be sand in the wheel well from that takeoff," wisecracked Juan.

A few minutes later, Warner safely landed the Super Scooper back at the air base.

Bert Ethan came running out of the tower to thank Jack. George and Juan were both talking at once, telling Bert what a great pilot Jack was. Noah's helo landed a few minutes later. He came over to give his dad a hug too. Jack glanced at Noah and he could swear there was a tear in his eye.

Sharing the Wealth

When Jack and Noah returned from their trip to Alaska, Gail prepared a special dinner for the three of them. Jack's favorite foods were roast leg of lamb with fresh rosemary, new red potatoes, and asparagus, followed by vanilla ice cream with fresh strawberries. After dinner, Noah went to his room to surf the net while Jack and Gail relaxed by the fire. Jack sat there quietly for several minutes before he spoke to Gail. "Thanks for a great dinner. It was wonderful.

"You know, Babe, with the sale of the company, we've got more money than we can ever spend. Same with Noah. I've been thinking of a quote that Jack Lemmon recently said to Jay Leno on *The Tonight Show*."

"What's that, Honey?" asked Gail.

"He said that 'as a successful actor, you need to send the elevator back down for the next guy.' Of course, he meant to help a younger, struggling actor, but I'm thinking of the younger bush pilots in Alaska."

"That's a pretty cute saying. What do you have in mind?" asked Gail.

"I was thinking of researching how many bush planes have bank loans on them and finding out which banks are holding the paper. We could get in touch with them and pay off the notes confidentially. We can handle the whole thing through an attorney with an escrow company. Neither the banks nor the pilots will know who we are."

"I think that's a great idea! I bet having to make loan payments every month for a pilot's family is a tough nut to crack, especially when business is so uncertain. Let's do it, Jack. How would we get started?"

"Let's get Noah involved. He's always on that internet searching for god-knows-what. I've heard about something called Google. Maybe that will help him."

They approached Noah with their idea, and he loved it immediately. "Let me get to work and see what I can find out." Noah did indeed start searching on Google. He found out that airplane ownership information in Alaska is a public record. He was able to edit the list for owners with lienholders on the title. It was similar to a car pink slip. Lenders are listed at the bottom of the slip. Then, he searched by make and model of the airplanes to leave him with only bush planes that had loans on them, owned by Alaskan pilots or companies.

Jack, Gail, and Noah decided to do a little research on the plane owners before they just paid off their loans anonymously. First, Noah called the bush plane company to see what kind of reception he got. He acted like an interested customer who wanted to book a flight in the near future. Most of the time, the office staff was very nice and helpful in answering his questions. Usually, the pilot's wife ran the business, as ML and Ben did for so many years. Noah chatted with the women, making notes as he did so.

He put stars on the list by the particularly nice ones for further investigation.

Noah was surprised when he received some rather rude remarks from one pilot. "Well, there you go, off of the list," he'd say as he put a red line through that name. The rude pilot would never know how much his negative attitude cost him.

Noah flew around the state meeting the potentially lucky pilots. He hired them for a sightseeing trip and took notes of their professionalism, manners, and their answers to his questions.

After a few weeks, Noah had compiled a list of 23 pilots that met his criteria. He found a great business attorney in Anchorage who knew of a local escrow company that could contact the airplane lenders for payoff figures and procedures. The banks didn't know who was paying them. They all just assumed it was the plane's owner.

One by one, each of the 23 bush plane owners received notices by registered mail that their loans had been paid in full. Each time, they contacted the escrow company, confused by the letter. The escrow company could only tell them that an anonymous benefactor had paid off their loan. Escrow had no idea who it was. Funds were just wired into their trust account with payoff instructions.

Jack, Gail, and Noah were delighted by the progress. Several times they traveled to the bush plane offices on the day that the registered letters were scheduled to arrive. They just acted like a typical family who wanted to hire a bush plane for a sightseeing tour. It was like being a "fly on the wall." Or better, because they could see and hear for themselves how appreciated the loan payoffs were. On several occasions, the pilot's family was talking about how their child could now go to college or could now afford medical school. One time, a pilot's family was ready to lose their cabin in foreclosure. Noah heard about it, he told his parents, and they paid that loan off too.

Other than their attorney, nobody ever knew who the mysterious Alaskan benefactor was. Several stories were in the newspaper and on the TV news. It caused a number of copycat charitable acts throughout the Northwest and Canada. The Warners never planned on that but were delighted with the results.

Panda Air Cargo

China-Panda may have told the Warners that they planned on no changes, but as everyone knows, plans change. Buyers are generally liars in this area. It can be as simple as house buyers telling a little-old-lady seller that they just love her house and will never change a thing. The next thing the old lady knows, her house is quickly torn down and a new mini-mansion is then built on the site.

The same phenomenon happens in large business sales. A corporate buyer assures the seller that they will continue the existing business as-is and keep all the faithful long-term employees, only to have a corporate garage sale right after the sale closes. Plus, many of the employees lose their jobs and are sent packing.

Within six months of the Aire Cargo sale to China-Panda, they re-named the company "Panda Air Cargo." In addition, living and working in Texas apparently was not to their liking. China-Panda broke ground on an office complex near their headquarters in Sing Mai, outside of Hong Kong. They wanted to base their corporate and sales departments close to home. Most of the U.S. employees were going to be given two choices: move to China and learn to speak Chinese or be laid off.

Another change coming soon was the airplane maintenance work was going to be outsourced and performed by outside contractors. Most of Patroni's old workforce was going to be laid off. One of the few departments to be untouched was the Dallas airfield and sort facility due to its physical location value.

Jack never anticipated this turn of events. But he couldn't do a damn thing about it. He often said, "Selling my company to China-Panda was the biggest mistake I ever made. I'll regret it to my dying day."

Dino Gets Busy

After China-Panda moved such a big slice of the company operation to China, the old Aire Cargo staff was decimated. Only the pilots and package-sorting personnel were left in Dallas. Most of the upper management was gone, and the airplane maintenance staff was just a shell of the former number. They farmed out all the heavy work to the Midwest Air Maintenance facility in Tulsa, Oklahoma. The remaining mechanics were just there for light work on the planes. The dispatch and tracking departments were still there, but not for long. The whole spirit of the company that Jack and Gail had worked so hard to create was quickly evaporating.

Dino Patroni and his college partner, Amir, had retired from their exporting business supplying the Middle Eastern black markets. It was getting a little scary being in business there with all of the unrest going on. Amir's father had been fired from his position in Iranian Customs. Other family members had been imprisoned without charges. Trying to do business in Iran was a dangerous business indeed.

Dino went to work at Panda Air Cargo as a dispatcher. With his computer science education from UCLA, he designed a plane tracking and maintenance software program. It kept track of every plane's location, a manifest of all packages and cargo on board, the air crew labor costs, and maintenance and expense records. It also calculated the net profit on every flight.

Dino also designed an automatic information backup procedure for the main company computer system. This backed up all the customer records, business, and airplane-related records every 24 hours. In a nutshell, this was the entire company on a computer disk. Dino included a hidden instruction in the backup procedure so that the same data would be transferred daily to his computer at home, just in case. He didn't trust the Chinese PAC executives. So many of the old Aire Cargo crew were gone, he wanted the information for a rainy day.

When Dino designed the backup procedure, he also buried a sub-routine instruction for an automatic hard drive reformat procedure in the startup commands. If "Dino Patroni" was ever dropped from an "active" designation on the employee's payroll roster, all the company's computer hard drives would start "reformatting," or erasing themselves. Only Dino would have a current backup disk drive with all of the previous data on it. That might come in handy if he ever needed to renegotiate his severance package.

What Pension Fund?

Besides airplanes, real estate, and the package and cargo business, Panda Air Cargo had one other asset: the Aire Cargo employee pension fund. PAC borrowed against it to pay for the new headquarters in China and to buy new planes. In China, there were no restrictions against such borrowing like there are in the U.S.

When the downturn in business occurred that Jack Warner had predicted, PAC started bleeding cash like a stuck pig. PAC used up most of their cash reserves. The son of the Panda Air Cargo CEO embezzled millions of dollars from the employee pension fund. Between the nonperforming loans secured by the pension fund and the embezzlement, this wiped out most of the pension fund, leaving the retired Aire Cargo employees with almost zero income.

Lou Patroni was affected by this almost immediately. His retirement check would barely cover his food and utilities. He had other investment money, but nobody wants to lose their hard-earned pension check. When he complained to the Dallas office, he was told that the pension management department had been transferred to China. All of the U.S. pension staff had been let go. Lou started his inquiries with the pension department in Sing Mai but only met a series of delays in getting an answer to the reason for his decimated retirement check.

Lou Patroni's daughter, Gina, worked for Panda Air Cargo as a plane handler. She was married to Mark Liu, who was a firstborn generation of Chinese immigrants to the U.S. He spoke perfect English and Chinese, and he was pretty fair with two other dialects, Mandarin and Yue. Mark worked in the IT department in the Dallas office. He and Dino shared the work on many computer-related projects and got to be close friends.

Mark was sent to Sing Mai for two weeks in order to train the local staff in the company computer system. Mark discussed his pet theory with Dino: that he was probably training his replacement staff. "Yeah, I agree, and mine too," agreed Dino. "I think our days here are numbered."

While on his trip to China, Mark stumbled across a series of high-level corporate communications outlining the entire history of the pension fund downfall. The downturn in the company savings and the pension fund had been kept from the employees. What management had been quoting was untrue. Hardly any money was left. Mark printed hard copies of all these emails for his personal files to go home. He hid them in the middle of some computer instruction manuals, in case his belongings were ever searched.

Mark didn't know if his company emails might be monitored or if company phones were tapped, so he waited until he got home to tell Gina and Lou about the pension money problems. He showed them copies of all the emails from the PAC brass. They went out for drinks and invited Jack, Gail, and Dino to join them. Mark reviewed everything for the newcomers. They huddled up and commiserated over the pension fund status.

Jack offered a glimmer of hope. "Tomorrow is Saturday. Let's meet at Brand Park tomorrow morning at 9 a.m. Bring some drinks and munchies, because I think we'll be there for a while. I have an idea that will help you out of this mess. But I'm going to need everybody's help." They all agreed to meet in the morning as planned.

Midwest Air Maintenance

Every private or commercial aircraft owner must maintain their planes in an FAA-approved manner and on schedule by licensed aircraft mechanics in an authorized maintenance facility. Some large airlines perform this work in-house. Most aircraft owners outsource the work to specialized shops, depending on the model of the plane. A few large airlines' maintenance facilities not only maintain their own planes but work on competitors' planes as well. This additional work can become another profit center for the company.

Planes come in for their periodic work to satisfy the FAA requirements for minor and major services. With the major service jobs, the plane is literally ripped apart. The entire interior of the plane is removed. The metal frame is x-rayed for cracks to be repaired. Passenger seats are reworked and repaired where necessary. Engines are completely inspected and repaired or replaced where necessary. Electronics and avionics are updated to the latest technology available. Fuel tanks are cleaned and resealed. All hoses and rubber fittings are replaced. The landing gear is rebuilt and new tires are installed. The entire plane is gone over and updated wherever possible. The aircraft enters the facility in a used condition but exits the hangar bay as a virtually new plane.

One of the largest commercial maintenance facilities in the U.S. is Midwest Air Maintenance in Tulsa, Oklahoma. The owner is Tad Hankey, a B-26 bomber pilot from WWII. Tad also flew F-105 Thunderchief bombers in Vietnam before becoming an instructor. He was a little long in the tooth for a pilot, but the Air Force couldn't pass up his boatload of experience. When Tad was flying his last mission, he was shot down with a SAM (surface to air missile). After he survived the silk ride down, Jack rescued him. Tad was the seventh of Jack's 21 saved pilots.

His production manager was his son, Mike Hankey. Mike flew Bell Huey helicopters in Vietnam. They were the only father-son team of pilots that anybody knew of. Mike would fly a combat mission with his right hand on the stick controlling the helicopter. With his left, he held a Kodak movie camera out the window, filming the action. His home movies showed the Gatling gun tracer bullets in a steady stream toward the target. "In between each of the tracers that you see are seven more bullets that you can't. After a while, we'd have to let the machine gun barrels cool off or they would get distorted." It was amazing film footage for its day.

The Hankeys had been dealing with Jack Warner, Lou Patroni, and the rest of the crew at Aire Cargo since they opened for business. So far, they had only done two planes for the new company, Panda Air Cargo, but they already didn't like the new staff.

After the first meeting with Mark and Dino, Jack called Mike Hankey to see how it was going with PAC. Mike had nothing good to say about them. "They're a bunch of morons with no aviation experience. I spend more time explaining why something needs to be replaced than the mechanic does doing the job. We've lost money on both jobs we did for them."

"Plus, they take forever to pay. We have to hound them to pay every invoice. They play all kinds of games, like 'forgetting the sign the check,' so that delays payment a couple more weeks while the check gets sent back to China."

Jack answered with, "Well, I have some business to discuss with you and your father. I'm flying in to Tulsa. Let's have lunch."

Planning in the Park

Everybody arrived early for the morning meeting. With their retirement income on the line, they needed Jack now more than ever. Everyone was looking forward to hearing Jack's big plan for their financial future.

Jack and Gail were there with their son, Noah. Lou, his son Dino, and his daughter Gina were there with her husband, Mark Liu. Jack started off, "Gina, what are the next planes due to go in for a major service at Midwest Air Maintenance?"

"I'll have to double-check, but I think it's a 1982 Boeing 747 Freighter and a 1984 Boeing 727 Cargo Master. They're both going in next week."

"Great. After those planes are totally gone through by Midwest, they should be worth about $35 million. If we can make those two planes disappear afterwards, we can sell them and put the money in a trust account that will earn interest for pension income for the original Aire Cargo employees."

Gina raised her hand. "Boss, I have one little question. Could you add a few details to this master plan of yours? Specifically, can you review the part about the planes disappearing and then us selling them?"

"Details, details, don't bother me with details," chanted Jack with a grin on his face. "I'll lay it out for you."

"I don't think Gina is the only curious person, Boss," added Lou.

Jack started in, "Here's my little plan. There's an old child's game called 'Button, Button, Who's Got the Button?' Kids stand in a circle and a button gets hidden in one kid's hand. Then, everybody tries to guess who has the button.

"Here's phase one: Right now, Gina and Dino keep track of all plane movements and their status, right? This includes flights, downtime, and maintenance, among other things. Gina, as dispatcher, arranges for the 727 and 747 cargo planes to be transferred to Midwest Maintenance for a major service, including a full safety check, electronics upgrade, and the entire air frame x-rayed. When they're repainted, the colors on the work order will be PAC's standard paint scheme. But actually we'll choose a new generic color scheme. The planes will be a basic white with some simple blue stripes on the sides.

"While the planes are there, Tad and Mike Hankey will help us by switching the identity of the planes. They'll change the FAA serial numbers at each location on the fuselage airframe. The big ID numbers on the fuselage will be switched to different ones. We'll buy two salvaged planes and use their tail numbers on these two planes. More details on that later.

"Midwest will give us some new FAA transponders that Patroni can install later, completing the new identification. The best part of all is that $10 million worth of work will be done at Panda Air Cargo's expense.

"The first problem that needs to be solved is getting Midwest's bill paid by Panda before the planes disappear. Mark, you will need to hack into the PAC accounting records and prioritize the final Midwest bill so it can be paid right away. Otherwise, it will take months for PAC to get around to paying it in their usual slowpoke manner.

"Gina, you and Dino show the two rebuilt planes back in the Panda Air Cargo inventory. The planes will be finished but will actually be elsewhere, in our possession. Just don't assign the planes to any flights for the time being. Since the Panda execs are 8,000 miles away in China, what are they gonna know?"

"Interesting so far. What's next, Coach?" asked Dino.

Jack continued, "Phase two. Now that the planes are rebuilt, we'll need an airport to hide them at. My old roommate from the Air Force Academy, Sonny Frazier, now runs an aircraft scrap boneyard in the desert outside of Mojave, California. It has a long paved airstrip.

"I'll fly one plane and Tom McLaughlin will fly the other. We'll fly the planes to Tucson, Arizona, where we'll fill up and charge the fuel to Panda. I'm too well known to show up at the PAC airfield, so Gail is going to fix me up a disguise. I'll sign the FPO (fuel purchase order) with a fake name. No one at Tucson knows me, and I'll still have on my disguise. It's a pretty small airport, so they won't have any sneaky-peeky cameras.

"While the planes are being fueled, Lou will disconnect the FAA transponders. This way, the trail will show that Panda's two planes flew to Tucson, fueled, and then disappeared.

Tom and I will leave the next morning at first light and fly them at minimum altitude to avoid radar detection to Mojave, California. With the transponders turned off, we'll be flying them under VFR (visual flight rules), so we won't file a flight plan with the FAA. If someone ever traces the planes, the trail will end in Arizona. Any investigator will assume the planes were flown south to Mexico or Central America.

"Finally, Tom and I will take a bus back to Dallas. That way, there won't be any record connecting Dallas to Mojave."

"Why don't you guys just fly back commercial?" asked Gina.

Tom McLaughlin answered her. "Because our names would be on the airline's passenger manifest. Bus companies don't keep passenger records. They don't even ask your name if you pay cash for your ticket."

Jack kept talking. "Eventually, the next quarterly audit will show the missing planes. We need a way to make the planes disappear without getting anybody in trouble. Eventually, we sell the two planes and use the money for employee pensions.

"Well, that's my plan. Whaddya think?" asked Jack.

First there was silence, and then nervous laughter from the little group of conspirators.

Finally Dino spoke. "You want us to steal $35 million worth of airplanes and then sell them? That's your idea? I respect you as an old friend of my Dad's and my former boss, but that's fuckin' nuts! You should be locked up."

Lou added a comment. "Dino, part of that idea is mine."

"Then you should be locked up too. Maybe the Laughing Academy has double cells with padded walls? You guys can be crazy together."

After discussing the plan and rehashing it over and over, they actually voted to go ahead. If the plan for rebuilding and relocating the planes to California actually worked perfectly, it would then be time for phase three, selling the planes.

D-Day

Gina arranged for the 727 and the 747 to be delivered to Midwest Air Maintenance in Oklahoma. Tad and Mike Hankey were ready and waiting for them. The Panda Air Cargo work orders and purchase orders were complete and signed by the company controller. They were accompanied by a $2,500,000 cashier's check for a deposit on the
$10 million work estimate.

Midwest had arranged for two progress payments of $2.5 million every 15 days as the work progressed along the contract timeline. The final $2.5 million, plus any cost overruns, was due within 10 days of completion. Jack's phase two would start after this final payment was received by Midwest.

Phase one went off without a hitch. The final work came in just over the $10 million budget. Two landing-gear assemblies had to be replaced and some cracks were discovered in eight areas of the air frames of the two jets. Those parts had to be removed and replaced. The total bill to renovate both planes came to $10,762,496.49. That was a perfectly acceptable number in the world of aviation repair.

Midwest Maintenance sent the final invoice for $3,262,496.49 by Panda's overnight delivery to PAC in China. They delivered the planes back to Panda Air Cargo in Dallas. The planes landed late at night. The PAC airfield manager signed the delivery receipt for the company. Nobody noticed the new tail numbers or the new paint colors on the fuselage in the dark Texas night. The Hankeys instructed their pilots to park them in the back of the field behind other aircraft, if possible.

Tom McLaughlin, who still worked for PAC, arranged for both planes to be fueled and checked over. Tom arrived at the Dallas airfield at 5 a.m. He had just started his preflight procedure when a man wearing a hoodie approached him. The man had dark glasses on with a beard and moustache. "Hi, Tom. How's it going?"

The guy sounded familiar, but it took Tom a few seconds to realize it was Jack Warner. "Shit, man. Gail did a good job. I'd never have recognized you. You look like the Unabomber." Both pilots finished their pre-flights and boarded their planes. Noah joined his father in the 747 as copilot. He wasn't FAA qualified, but he could follow any instructions given to him by the old man.

Lou Patroni got on board the 727 with Tom. He didn't know how to fly, but he could read off the checklists and look out the window for clearances, etc. Lou had to disconnect the transponders when they got to Tucson.

Everything went like clockwork: landing in Tucson, refueling, and flying to Mojave and meeting Sonny Frazier. Jack and Tom landed both planes on Sonny's airstrip. Sonny drove up in a pickup truck with an extension ladder to access the 747. Jack and Noah opened the door and looked down the 17 feet to the ground. Sonny struggled to get the ladder set up. "Is that what you crazy rednecks in the desert call a 'jetway'?" screamed Jack.

"Shut the hell up and get your ass down here. We need to move this redneck jetway over to the other plane." As Jack and Noah climbed down, hugs and introductions were exchanged all around. They jumped in the pickup and went over to the 727 to help Sonny with the ladder so Tom and Lou could get down and join them.

Once the whole group had deplaned, Sonny loaded them in his truck and drove to his office, which was an old mobile home trailer. Lou spoke up. "You know, Jack, I'm not looking forward to riding in a friggin' bus for two whole days to get back to Dallas."

"Me either, Lou, but I couldn't think of any other way without leaving a fingerprint, so to speak. I couldn't have Gail come and pick us up, either. She needs to have an alibi in Dallas."

"I think you boys are in for a nice surprise," Sonny blurted out as they rounded the corner of his hangar. Sitting there was a beautiful Cessna Citation jet. Next to it was a lawn chair with a red striped umbrella mounted on the back. Sitting in the shade in the lawn chair was a guy drinking a big glass of ice tea and munching on a bag of peanuts.

"What the hell?" murmured Jack.

It wasn't until a few moments later when they got out of the truck and the unknown guy removed his dark glasses that Jack Warner recognized him. "Oh, my God, it's Dan Wolfe!" Jack ran over and the two guys exchanged real hugs, not dopey "man hugs" with the back pats going on.

"Noah, Lou, Tom, Sonny, this is Dan Wolfe, an old pilot friend of mine. Before I started Aire Cargo, Dan gave me a ride from Aspen to L.A., but he had the poor manners to have a heart attack at 30,000 feet. I took pity on the poor S.O.B., so I dumped him off at the nearest hospital."

"Yeah, that's all true, Warner, but you left out the part where you flew off in my fucking plane."

"But I came back to pick you up in Utah when the hospital kicked you out." The men's insulting smack talk continued. Noah loved it. This is how young men learn to deal with other men. Books don't teach it and women can't understand it.

"So what the hell are you doing here?" asked Jack.

"Your wife, Gail, called me and said you could use a lift back to Dallas."

"Gee, Dan, all the guys were really looking forward to a 48-hour bus ride, but I guess we could cancel it and go with you. I mean, since you're here and everything," the smack continued.

After they had a quick beer with Sonny, everybody else climbed into the Citation.

The decor was unbelievable, baby-soft, camel-colored leather captain's seats, walnut wood trim everywhere, thick carpeting, mood lighting throughout, and a galley with deli sandwiches, fresh summer fruit, and salads waiting for the guys.

"Hey, Wolfe, you call this flying? I wouldn't let my dog fly in such squalor."

Wolfe answered back, "I'm sorry if you're displeased. I'll let you off at the next corner. At 33,000 feet, it might be a little breezy when you open the door."

Noah asked, "Hey, Pop, how much does a jet like this cost?"

"Decked out like this, about 10 million bucks."

Low whistles were heard throughout the cabin.

Uncle Milty

One unknown fly in the ointment with Jack's plan was the company auditor, Milton Cohen. About the time that Jack was executing phase two of his plan, Milton was doing his quarterly inventory audit on PAC equipment and expenses. He noticed a discrepancy in the maintenance records with two planes, a 747 and a 727. As he investigated further, he was puzzled. "Why were those two planes that were just rebuilt for over $10 million not actively carrying any cargo shipments? It's like they're just parked at the airfield. Very queer indeed," he thought.

In the beginning, he thought it must be a dispatcher error, but then he got more involved. Milton called Dino in the dispatcher's office for a quick meeting. "Dino, why are these two planes just sitting and not working for the company? According to the records, they just got completely rebuilt at Midwest. Are there problems with the two aircraft that keep them from flying? Having two expensive planes sitting there day after day is costing us a fortune."

Dino answered Milton, "That can't be right. Let me look into it. I'll get back to you tomorrow." Dino remembered some advice he had heard from an attorney years before: "If you don't have an answer, delay, delay, delay."

Several days went by, and on Friday, Milton still hadn't heard a word from Dino. Milton drove around the airfield and tried to find the missing airplanes with no luck. "Where are these planes? They were simply missing. This doesn't make any sense. Something strange is going on," thought Milton.

He came into the office the next morning with the intention of meeting with Young Fu, the Panda Air Cargo Vice President of Operations. He wanted to share his concerns and see if he knew anything about it. As Milton arrived at work, there was a note taped on his office door to please see the Mr. Fu, first thing.

"Great, perfect timing," thought Milton. As he entered Fu's office, Milton started, "Mr. Fu, I wanted to talk to you. There's someth…"

Young Fu interrupted Milton. "Please let me go first. Milton. We have valued your work highly since we purchased this business. However, we are making a change in staffing. My nephew, Hamilton, will be doing your auditing job from now on. He will work three weeks per month in China and the fourth week here in Dallas. If you'd like to stay on, perhaps you can train him for a week or two?"

Milton held in his feelings and decided to hope for the best. He answered, "Is there a different position you'd like me to fill? Some other job I can do? I've worked here for 15 years, years of many late nights and often weekends away from my family."

Fu responded, "No, there are no positions open here at this time. We will keep you in mind if something comes up. My secretary has an envelope with your severance check." offered Fu. "By the way, Milton, you said you had something to talk to me about. What was that?"

One rare quality that Milton possessed was the ability to hold his tongue while he could collect his thoughts. "Oh, nothing really, I just wanted to ask you about my vacation dates."

Leaving Fu's office, Milton was furious. "What a prick! What a bunch of jerks. Train his nephew, that little four-eyed twerp! I'd rather park a 747 on his face," thought Milton.

Milton drove around for a while and cooled off. He started thinking about the missing planes again. Just for the hell of it, he drove over to Dino's house. Gina happened to be there too and answered the door. Gina and Dino were surprised to see Milton. "Gee, hi, Milton. How are ya?"

"I've had better days. They just fired me, after 15 years of loyal service. How about a drink? Dino, I think we need to have a little talk."

One drink became two and then three. Dino and Gina soon told Milton the whole story about the evaporated pension fund.

Milton was quite upset. "What am I going to use for retirement? My wife and I were counting on that money. We can't survive on social security alone."

Since he was now laid off and wouldn't receive much of a pension, Dino slowly let Milton in on the whole story of "Jack's new retirement plan."

"Well this has been quite a day. First, I uncover a multimillion-dollar equipment theft ring in my company. Then, my own company fires me without cause. Next, I find out that the pension fund I've been contributing to for 15 years and counting on has all but disappeared. And finally, my former co-workers are going to sell the stolen company equipment and start a pension fund for the fired workers of my former company. Forgive me, but I need a few moments to absorb and process all of this."

Gina said, "I should think so. Take all the time you need."

Milton sat quietly for about 30 seconds and then quietly spoke. "How can I help?"

Can You Sell Jets on Craigslist?

Pete Cristy was an airplane broker who represented Aire Cargo in many aircraft sales over the years. He was close friends with Jack and Gail. With the modernization of the FAA system, the old handwritten pilot's log books were now kept electronically. With a little computer help from Mark Liu, Jack and Lou worked up a new file and log book on each of the two planes. Mark merged the old maintenance work history with the new plane ID to make a complete accurate package that would command full value when it came time to sell. Aircraft without their log books sell for a greatly discounted price. The buyer doesn't know what they're getting and must assume the worst regarding maintenance. Dino was still showing the missing planes as part of PAC's fleet, so there would be no suspicion regarding the two available planes.

Chin Lee was the aircraft fleet manager at Panda Air Cargo. Lee had a weakness for 20-year-old scotch and blondes of the same age. Pete Cristy met him for cocktails in the bar at the Dallas Hilton.

"Chin, I appreciate you traveling so far to meet with me. I'm sure we can do business with an outcome that will benefit both of us." Just then, two beautiful, young, tall blondes in stiletto heels and short skirts, walked up to the booth where the men were sitting, enjoying their drinks.

The first girl greeted Pete, "Petey! How nice to run into you. This is my friend Tawny. She goes to school with me at SMU right here in Dallas."

Pete spoke his lines, just as they had rehearsed them. "Heather, how nice to see you again. With you two gorgeous girls out on the town, I'd call you Double Trouble. Are you still on the cheerleading squad?"

"Sure, Tawny is a cheerleader too. Maybe we can put on our little skirts and you can watch us practice sometime? We could use any advice you can offer."

Pete introduced Chin Lee to Heather and Tawny. Chin Lee never knew what hit him. Heather and Tawny weren't cheerleaders, they didn't go to SMU, and their names weren't even Heather and Tawny. "Ooh, he's cute, Tawny. There's something about Asian men that makes me crazy. They're so Oriental." They each gave Chin Lee a hug. The girls being so tall in high heels, Chin's face nestled right between their large breasts. He was in heaven!

In real life, they were better known at Diamond and Sultra. They were strippers at the Dallas Gentlemen's Club. Pete Cristy had hired them for $2,000 each to assume the cheerleader roles and to be ever so nice to Chin Lee. He assured them that Mr. Lee would also be generous when he heard that they were short on tuition money for next semester, especially if they weren't wearing any panties under their short skirts.

While they were both naked and in bed with Chin Lee, Heather and Tawny managed to talk him into "loaning" them $5,000 for tuition. He promised to call them when he was back in town. The telephone number the girls gave him was for the local Catholic church. He never saw them or his $5,000 again.

Pete met Chin Lee the next day for a late lunch. He figured Chin would need some time to sleep it off and recover from an evening with the girls. Pete called him and told him that he heard about some planes for sale. He told Chin that he met a Swiss attorney at an aircraft convention who had two cargo planes for sale. "I don't know the guy too well, but I'll introduce you two and let you take it from there," he said.

Pete had dealt with Chin Lee on several purchases and knew his negotiation strategy. As part of his negotiating strategy, he always claimed that the company had no cash available. Pete usually knew better, but he never saw any reason to disclose that info. Pete used to work at the DFW Airport and still kept in touch with everybody. As an airplane broker, contacts are everything. Knowledge is money and Pete liked money.

Pete invited Chin to join him for drinks so he could meet the seller of the two aircraft. Pete made it clear to Chin that he wasn't involved in the transaction and he was only introducing him to the seller's attorney, Mr. Henri Favre, of Zurich, Switzerland. Pete could never be associated with selling these two airplanes since they were technically stolen property.

After making the introductions and having a drink with Lee and Favre, Pete excused himself so the two men could talk price. After another cocktail, Favre stated that the asking price for the 727 and 747 aircraft was $40 million USD. Lee complained about the asking price and the financial strain it would put on his struggling airline.

Henri Favre asked him if PAC had anything to barter with. Chin reviewed a mental inventory and couldn't think of any unused aircraft. "Well, we do have two gates in the cargo terminal at the DFW Airport. We recently shifted some plane routes and are no longer using these ports."

Every air cargo company paid a stiff fee to buy a cargo port gate. In addition, they had to pay a monthly rent and a monthly maintenance fee. Under the terms of their contract with the airport, cargo airlines were not allowed to sublease an unused port gate to another carrier. So unused cargo gates just sat there but still accrued monthly fees. Therefore, they appeared on PAC's books as a liability.

When some other gates recently became available for sale, the asking prices were just over $1 million each. Christy knew that years ago, Jack Warner originally bought these gates for Aire Cargo for $100,000 apiece. So now PAC would be looking at a taxable gain of just under $2 million.

Favre suggested to Chin Lee that PAC use the two cargo gates as a down payment toward the purchase of the planes. Chin Lee seemed agreeable if the price was right.

There was one other PAC asset that might be available. With most of the maintenance subcontracted to Oklahoma and all of the office staff moved to China, a big parcel of land at the airport was sitting there unused. The 75-acre parcel was worth about $35 million. In addition, there was no loan on it. The property was free and clear.

Of course, Favre knew all of this information ahead of time. Henri Favre was not an attorney from Zurich. He was really Pierre Benton who lived in Quebec. He was an old drinking buddy of Pete Cristy's who owed him a big favor. Favre got into debt with the wrong people while on a casino trip to Atlantic City. Cristy paid off his gambling debt and hustled Benton out of town before he got hurt.

Henri Favre/Pierre Benton suggested that they contact Pete Cristy and hire him to draw up a barter-sales agreement for the planes' trade for the cargo gates and airport acreage. Chin Lee agreed to the deal. The men further agreed to each pay $25,000 as a reduced commission for Cristy to handle all the paperwork.

Pete drew up the documents for the barter property transfer. He made sure to insert a clause that he knew nothing of the transaction details and was only hired to handle the paperwork.

Pete structured an offer where Panda Air Cargo received the 727 and 747 planes in exchange for the two cargo gates at the DFW Airport plus the 75 acres of vacant airport land. The two cargo gates and the 75 acres of land could be appraised by a very friendly business appraiser that Pete knew, thereby lowering the capital gain income taxes owed by PAC. Chin liked it because no cash was required. PAC would trade property that they had no use for. It was a sweet deal for them. Of course, Panda Air Cargo didn't know they were buying their own planes back again.

For the former Aire Cargo employees, it was a beautiful deal. After they got screwed out of their pension fund, they basically swiped two expensive cargo planes. PAC had just paid $10 million to completely rehab them before the Aire Cargo employees scurried them away, hid them, and gave the planes a new identity.

The next step would be to sell the gates and the airport land.

Time to Sell the Buttons

Sonny fixed the purloined planes up with new ownership papers made out to FUBAR, LLC, a Cayman Island corporation. Sonny then transferred the title from FUBAR, LLC to the FUBAR Employee Trust. Then, Panda Air Cargo bought their own planes back by trading commercial real estate and airport cargo gates for them. The former Aire Cargo employees were the beneficiaries of the FUBAR trust.

Berlin Shipping Inc. was a German-owned international delivery company. Pete Cristy knew that Berlin Shipping was sitting on a mountain of cash and was looking for a U.S. airport facility with room for a sorting warehouse to expand its American operation. He could only dream of the sales commissions for this whole deal.

Pete Cristy then pulled off another miracle, selling the two cargo gates and the 75 acres at the airport to Berlin Shipping for $50 million in cash. At the close of escrow, the $50 million was wired to a Cayman Islands trust account in the name of the Fubar Employee Trust. Pete called Jack. "You're in business."

"How can we ever thank you?" asked Jack.

"Let's go fishing in Alaska. Do you know any spots?" asked Pete.

"Maybe," laughed Jack.

Garbage In – Garbage Out

A few months after that, Dino and Gina were given notice and left the company. Dino and Gina were the last of the old Aire Cargo employees hired by Jack Warner. With all the recent departures, nobody who was left at PAC seemed to know where anything was unless they could see it out of their window. As soon as Dino Patroni's employee status was changed from active to unemployed, his computer disk reformat procedure kicked in. Every computer in Texas and China started erasing their disk drives. When the procedure finished, all the computers sat there empty, like they had just come from the computer store.

The Chinese computer staff was mystified. When the disk drives got erased, so did Dino's secret program instructions. To put it politely, the company was screwed. Impolitely, it was SOL. Dino was the only person who had all the Panda Air Cargo business files. They were on his home computer, but could be restored to PAC in just a few minutes.

Young Fu and his nephew, Hamilton, called Dino to see if he could help. Hamilton had tried to repair the computer system, but there was nothing that could be done. The rest of the Chinese computer staff tried their best but also had no luck. Hamilton called his uncle, Young Fu, to see if he would be willing to call Dino. "Uncle, I know that Dino doesn't work for us anymore, but maybe we could hire him on a temporary basis. He's in Dallas and so are you. Could you please call him? I'm flying in tomorrow."

Dino was not surprised to hear from his old co-workers at Panda Air Cargo. After Hamilton related the events that led up to the computer disaster, he pleaded with Dino to help them.

"I'm willing to help you on three conditions:

"One: I want an indemnification letter addressed to all former Aire Cargo employees, every single one. It must state that you have investigated all matters that took place during and after their employment and PAC is satisfied with the results of that investigation and holds them harmless for all matters, known and unknown, past, present, and future.

"Two: I want $500,000 USD wired into a bank account that I manage. This money is to help retired employees that are hurting for money and ready to lose their houses in foreclosure. Panda employees in China stole their pension money. It's the least that the company can do.

"Three: I want a transfer of title from Panda Air Cargo to Jack and Gail Warner for that Beechcraft King Air that Jack Warner has been flying as part of his sale of the company. There should be a bill of sale for a $1 purchase price. Send me the keys to the plane and all transfer papers along with the indemnification letter.

"As soon as you deliver on all three of these conditions, I'll have your computer system restored that same afternoon. These terms are non-negotiable."

Young Fu and Hamilton looked at each other with their mouths wide open. Young turned to Dino and simply stated, "Let me make a call."

Three days later, at 10 o'clock in the morning, a security guard showed up at Dino's house outside of Dallas. He delivered an overnight document pouch from Panda Air Cargo Inc. Inside was the indemnification letter with the employee name addendum, just as Dino requested. There was also a package of title transfer papers for the Twin Beech and the keys to the plane. A few minutes later, Dino received an emailed receipt from his bank in the Cayman Islands for the $500,000.

Dino got on his computer and started the restoration procedure. 20 minutes later, all of the Panda Air Cargo computers sputtered to life with all the missing data restored. As an additional insurance policy, as part of the data restoration, Dino buried another data-delete sub-routine that he could trigger at will, just in case.

Dino called Hamilton at the PAC headquarters in China to make sure everything worked out all right. Hamilton was overjoyed. "I don't know how you did it, but everything is back the way it was. A million thanks for rescuing us."

"The best way to thank me is to let this be our last telephone call. It would be a shame if the computers got erased again, wouldn't it? Goodbye," said Dino in closing.

Hamilton just stared at the telephone receiver in his hand. He didn't know what happened and didn't much care. His job was safe and PAC was back in business. He reported as much to the PAC bosses.

Good News

Dino called Jack, Gail, Noah, Lou, Gina, Mark, and Milton and asked them to meet him at Baskin Robbins – 31 Flavors. They all asked why. "You'll love it; just meet me at 3 o'clock."

The whole team showed up as ordered. Dino took orders and bought everybody hot fudge sundaes. Gina broke the ice. "Okay, brother dear, what's with the mysterious phone call to meet you here?"

Dino opened a file of papers and started in. "It's not Christmas, but I have presents for everyone. First, Jack and Gail, here is a little something for you." He handed them a copy of the Panda Air Cargo indemnification letter with the name list attached. There were gasps all around. Everybody saw their name on the list. "This is our 'Get Out of Jail Free' card." Milton was really astounded.

Jack asked, "How the hell did you get them to give you *this*?"

"Quiet, Grasshopper. All will be revealed soon." Dino was having a great time at their expense.

"Now, here's a little frosting on the cake." Dino showed everybody the bank receipt for the $500,000 from Panda. "This is some additional money for the FUBAR Trust. This trust account will administer the retirement pension checks for all former Aire Cargo employees.

"And finally, here's one thing more." Dino handed Jack the keys to the Twin Beech that Jack loved flying so much. He handed Gail the title transfer paperwork.

"Dino, I'm astounded and I'm pretty sure Gail is too, 'cuz this is one of the few times since we've been married that she is speechless. I don't know how you did this and I've got a feeling that I don't want to know." Hugs went on for at least five minutes, all around. Everybody had tears in their eyes and a 31 Flavors napkin in their hand to act as a Kleenex.

FUBAR

The proceeds from the sale of the cargo gates and airport real estate went into the FUBAR trust account in the Cayman Islands. Lou Patroni, Dino Patroni, Mark Liu, Noah Warner, and Gail Warner were appointed trustees to administer the trust. Every qualified former Aire Cargo employee received all money due them retroactively plus ongoing monthly payments equal to what the proper pension fund should have disbursed if Panda Air Cargo hadn't screwed it up.

The Trustees also established the Jack & Gail Warner Scholarship Program. Any former Aire Cargo employee could apply for a college scholarship for themselves or for their kids. Single parents could get additional job training and necessary child care would be covered while they were in school if they maintained a "B" grade-point average.

Any families with an income earner on active duty in the military were entitled to a monthly allowance to make their military pay equal to their civilian earnings. The trustees figured that it's hard to make house payments on a military salary.

Injured Aire Cargo veterans also would receive an allowance to help them make ends meet. Anything that the military wouldn't provide in the way of physical therapy, the latest in handicapped equipment, or prosthetics was paid for. Programs for alcohol, drugs, or suicide prevention were also covered.

Members could get car loans at below market interest rates. Former employees were also signed up for health insurance coverage that covered dental and vision care.

After the success of the Warners' bush plane loan payoff plan, they decided to try it for former employee home loans. Gail applied the same procedures to any employee that had worked for Aire Cargo for more than 10 years. Gail did this work herself. She completed a short scenario for every employee to rate their situation. She didn't want to pay off loans on "dream homes" that were unwise from the get-go. If employees had made stupid decisions and overbought or overpaid, they weren't qualified to be part of the program. Gail and Jack wanted to pay off modest, comfortable homes for long-term, loyal employees to make their retirement years as headache free as possible.

Goodbye, Jack

The years went by and life went on. The Warners and the FUBAR trust enjoyed being philanthropists for deserving people. Each morning for years, Jack and Gail started their morning with a two-mile walk. Lately it had become a one-mile walk, and then Jack was down to a half mile. Some days he didn't go at all. "I just don't seem to have any steam," he said.

Gail urged him to go to the doctor, but he refused. "It's nothing. I'm just tired. It'll pass." Finally, he asked her to make him an appointment. After seeing his regular doctor, he was referred to Dr. Webster Shoenau, a cancer specialist, who ran a full series of tests including a CT scan and an MRI.

Later, Dr. Shoenau took a biopsy and had it tested, then he repeated the test procedures. Gail took Jack to Dr. Shoenau's office for the results. "Well, Doc, what's the story?" asked Jack, sitting on the sofa with his wife next to him.

Dr. Shoenau liked to give bad news quickly, like pulling off a Band-Aid. "Mr. Warner, first of all, no more flying. You're grounded."

"For how long?" asked Jack.

"Permanently, I'm afraid. The results from all the tests and scans point to one problem. You have pancreatic cancer. I repeated the biopsies and tests two separate times and used two different labs and received the same results. You need to get your affairs in order. I would give you about six weeks. I will refer you to a hospice nurse that will help you and your family. You should certainly get a second opinion. There are a number of other top cancer specialists in Texas. My nurse will give you a list of other board-certified doctors in the Dallas area."

All Gail and Jack could do was to wrap their arms around each other and say nothing for a long, long time.

The hospice nurse was great and helped Jack Warner die peacefully in his sleep, at home, seven weeks later. During the hospice, Gail only told his closest friends, who all wanted to come and say goodbye. Jack only saw a handful of them.

Every American-based Panda Air Cargo employee called in sick and turned out for Jack's funeral. The service was held at the Dallas-Fort Worth Airport. DFW was always the hub for Aire Cargo. The DFW Airport Authority gave the family an empty hangar to host the funeral service. Every current or former pilot, maintenance person, office worker, and employee of Aire Cargo was there. Lou Patroni, now retired, flew in all the way from Spokane, Washington to be there to honor his old friend. Lou's daughter, Gina, and her husband, Mark, Lou's son, Dino, and his black market partner, Amir, also came to remember Jack.

Jack's longtime buddy, Kenny Beall, was the first to arrive with his wife and grown kids. While he was still flying charters in Alaska, Kenny started buying small chunks of Northern Alaskan coastal property. After years of appreciation, he sold them to an oil exploration company, but he kept a share of the oil and mineral rights. He leased out some tracts of land for mining. First, copper ore was discovered, and later, tracts of gold were found while mining the copper. Years later, oil deposits came to light, making him quite wealthy.

This success enabled him to start a private jet company that sold fractional shares of planes to wealthy people and corporations. Ken-Jet was the first company to sell private jet ownership in this manner. Kenny's son piloted his Citation X jet to DFW for Jack's memorial service.

Local Panda Air Cargo management (all former Warner employees) arranged the memorial service without informing the Chinese PAC executives. It shut the entire United States' operation down for a whole business day, unheard of in the corporate world.

When the Chinese PAC brass heard about the shutdown, they went into orbit. It cost the company a fortune in lost sales and refunds for thousands of late shipments. Three of the senior managers in Dallas who authorized the shutdown were fired. But they were retiring anyway and didn't care. There wasn't any pension money from PAC, so what did they have to lose? Without Jack Warner, it just wasn't the same company.

Fred Smith of Fed Ex was there too, along with most of his corporate staff and every pilot that he could spare. It cost Smith financially to a lesser degree, but he never considered that a factor in honoring his friend who had saved his life.

There was a huge group of Air Force members, both active and retired. Reed, Brockway, and McLaughlin were all there. Jack's old AFA roommate, Sonny Frazier, came too. Owen Stenzel, his hazing partner who had the BBQ restaurant, came even though he hadn't seen Jack in years. Jack's fellow Vietnam pilot and GAO Investigator, John Wade, came with his wife. Every single one of the 21 pilots came to honor the man who saved their lives. Many of them flew thousands of miles to be there. One rescued pilot came all the way from Ireland to say thank you and goodbye.

During the week that Jack Warner died, it was hard to find flowers at florist shops anywhere in Texas or Oklahoma. The unexplained shortage was explained during the memorial service when a Midwest Air Maintenance 747 Freighter cargo plane flew over the DFW Airport. The plane's crew shoved four tons of flower petals out the back of the plane from a thousand feet up in the air as a tribute to Jack Warner. The Hankeys had diverted every flower they could find from refrigerated warehouses in Texas and Oklahoma. They had closed down their maintenance operation for a day and had all of their employees strip thousands of flower petals off of their stems. The petals floated down upon the thousands of mourners gathered at the airfield for Jack Warner's memorial service. It looked like somebody dropped the entire Pasadena Rose Parade from the blue Texas sky.

Patroni's Finest Hour

Gail and Noah Warner asked Lou to give the eulogy for Jack. Lou responded with, "I don't know anything about eulogies, but I'll try my best."

"How can I ask more than that, Honey? Just speak from your heart and you'll be wonderful," said Gail.

At the funeral, Lou stood at the microphone in front of hundreds of Jack's friends and colleagues.

"We are here today to honor our dear, dear friend. For one woman, he's your husband, and for one young man, he's your father. I think that many really great men don't think they ever did anything special. These special guys just think they did the best that they could and plodded along through life. They never expect to be remembered for anything after they leave this earth.

"For this great man that I had the pleasure of knowing for 42 years, he couldn't have been more wrong. Let's recap a few of the accomplishments of Colonel Jack Warner. Many of them are well known, but I bet some will be news to you. As we all know, Jack didn't advertise what he did to help so many people.

"When he was 16, his dad came down with life-threatening appendicitis. Jack got him in his father's bush plane and flew him 380 miles to Anchorage, Alaska. I should mention that Jack didn't even have a pilot's license.

"That same summer, Montana Senator Glen Hope fell into an icy river and was drowning. This same 16-year-old kid jumped in and saved the senator's life."

"Later, he became an Air Force fighter pilot. That's when I met him. He flew 25 combat missions and became an Ace among pilots. In his off hours, he rescued 21 pilots and one Army nurse. All 21 pilots traveled from great distances to be here with us today because of Jackson Benjamin Warner. By the way, he ended up marrying that nurse, and Gail is also here with us today. Their son, Noah, learned to fly when he was 12, the same as his dad.

"Once, he bummed a ride with a big-time Hollywood producer and his family of three. During the flight, the pilot had a heart attack. Jack directed the family in first-aid treatment for the man while jumping into the pilot's seat and headed for the closest hospital. That pilot was Captain Dan Wolfe, who survived and is also here with us today.

"At the end of the Vietnam War, the Army was going to abandon hundreds of South Vietnamese citizens who had risked their lives to help American forces. Jack commandeered an Air Force cargo plane and took 269 men, women, and children to Hawaii, where every single one of them became U.S. citizens. Dozens of them are here today with their children and grandchildren to pay homage to the man who saved them.

"You probably never heard about when Jack and I went to Iraq to smuggle out five Americans that were trapped in the country by that crazy S.O.B., Saddam Hussein. All five of them are also here with us today to honor Jack Warner.

"Jack helped America in so many ways. He is a brave example of what a great American is. He inspired others to be better human beings. Jack Warner would be the first to admit that he worked the system many times to his benefit. The United States of America wasn't built by men who followed the rules. But, the United States was the real beneficiary in the end. Yes, he pushed the ethical envelope, but he accomplished great things for us all.

"With his wife's help, Jack started a company, which ended with a charitable trust that gives job training, child care, veterans' health care, and preventive programs to those who need it. So far, the FUBAR trust has provided 62 college scholarships.

"The trust also provides retirement income for employees who were left high and dry by an embezzling son-of-a-bitch.

"If you could look up 'great men' in Webster's Dictionary, I think there would be a picture of Jack Warner."

Lou pulled out a bottle of Jack Daniel's from behind the podium. He poured a generous shot into a glass and raised it. "Here's to you, buddy! I'll miss the hell out of you." He swallowed the drink and walked over to Gail to give her and Noah big hugs.

There wasn't a dry eye in the house.

Normally, at memorial services, people make excuses to leave after the talking or lunch is over. On this day, most of the crowd stayed until midnight.

If Jack Warner could have, he would have said, "Thanks, Lord. It was one hell of a ride!"

ABOUT THE AUTHOR

Rich Jessup grew up in Southern California, the son of a veterinarian and grandson of one the largest dairymen in the State. He spent many week-ends over the years at the Parks Ranch enjoying hunting trips with his father and his friends. Their stories told around the dinner table were the basis of many chapters in *Air Boss*. It was our version of the Rat Pack.

He started working at age 12, putting new milk bottles into wooden milk cases. He worked at many different positions until eventually attending college at U.S.C.

Rich worked at a variety of jobs while attending school, including catering weddings and serving dinners for cast members of television shows at NBC. These experiences added more story fodder for *Air Boss*.

After working at National Car Rental, he started in real estate sales. His sales career expanded into property management and real estate loans. Dealing with a variety of customers opened up many additional story ideas for this book.

A good friend of Rich's worked at a Ferrari dealership and later for Rolls Royce. Those customer contact stories gave Rich ideas for several chapters as well.

Over the years, Rich enjoyed the different television shows about living in Alaska. He absorbed many details of life in the bush. All of the aircraft references throughout the book are accurate in every detail.

This myriad of Rich's life experiences, along with his family and friend, lends an air of authenticity to this collection of stories of Black Jack Warner. Probably 80% of the stories are based in fact with the remaining 20% fictional.

"I hope you enjoy them as much I did writing them."